Conflicting Spirits

Unseen Forces

CAROLYN MURPHY

Order this book online at www.trafford.com
or email orders@trafford.com

Most Trafford titles are also available at major online book retailers.

Printed in the United States of America.

ISBN: 978-1-4907-0741-9 (sc)
ISBN: 978-1-4907-0740-2 (e)

Trafford rev. 07/01/2013

 www.trafford.com

North America & international
toll-free: 1 888 232 4444 (USA & Canada)
fax: 812 355 4082

ACKNOWLEDGMENT

I want to thank the following people for their help in making this book a finish product:

Thank you Ralph for your input in editing this book, making the cover, and your timeless help with YouTube, website, print material, and so much more. I could not have done this without your help.

Thanks to all my friends who prayed for me while writing this book. Thank you to my wonderful children who stood by me when I was busy working and could not talk over the phone. I am grateful to each of you.

PROLOGUE

From deep within the abyss, they came crawling, slithering beneath the house anticipating her arrival. A legion of darkness hovered over this area, polluting the territory. Everywhere they landed their filthy stench penetrated, filling the air with fear, murder, and hate.

They waited unseen in the darkness for the young girl to arrive.

The head lieutenant snorted fire displeasure from his huge nostrils. He turned to his cohorts roaring with rage.

"HOW COULD YOU DIRTY ROTTEN, DESPICABLE, FOOLS ALLOW HER TO ESCAPE OUR CLUTCHES? GO AND TEAR DOWN HER DEFENSES, MAKE HER WEAK, AND VULNERABLE. I DON'T CARE HOW YOU DO IT BUT DON'T LET HER BECOME STRONG! NOW MOVE FROM MY FACE AND GET HER BACK NOW!"

INTRODUCTION

E vil destruction has invaded and set up camp in a small farming town in central California. These unholy forces have gained a deadly stronghold on some unsuspecting citizens through the family of a young girl named Rachel. From her ancient ancestors down, her family has been soul ties to witchcraft.

Now the gateway door is opened, and the demons are quickly spreading their poisonous influences throughout the sleepy little town of Queen City seeking human hosts.

Their leader, the prince of darkness has commanded his legions to reel them in through evil seductions, unholy lustful desires, and depraved immorality. His only existence is to drag them to hell along with him, and his fallen, angles!

A few of God's mighty Christians have become aware of the dark devious rock that's descended upon their small community, they are armed wearing the whole armor of God, fighting for the survival of their loved ones.

Young, newly born-again, Rachel, who has given up witchcraft, has become an earnest Christian, is also raging war against these soulless, decomposed slaves of darkness. She fights to save her occultist mother Nicky trying to persuade her to run away from the destroyer. Nicky believes in and uses white magic she is deceived into thinking her power is helping others. Rachel must use everything she learns from her Church family to convince her mother of the diabolic deception Satan has planted in her mother's mind.

Ward Rachel's father, better known as Wolf, is completely emerged in the viscous trap of Lucifer. Wolf uses black magic against these lost beings, looking for excitement. He snags them into the mouth of darkness by trickery and fear.

Agnes, Rachel's grandmother embraces the same power of death is using séance, crystal balls, tarot cards, and potions to get what she desires. Rachel's family is caught up in a tangle web of deception Satan uses against them, because they allow bitterness to control their lives.

Detesting Christians, Ward and Agnes inbreeds evil through scorn animosity, vicious vengeance, and brutal malice both has a growing thirst for power and blood. Young Rachel needs to keep her salvation hidden from them if she wants to exist under their roof and live.

God Omnipotent is totally aware of the plans and strategies of these filthy spirits. As the prayers of the righteous go up breaking through the black rock, God sends His mighty Warriors of light, to deliver His saints from complete destruction. Jesus commissions His Holy Angels to tear down and demolish these demonic strongholds. The battle rages between good and evil in the spirit and in the natural.

Although there are a few other Churches that claim to be strong, most of them are laid back in their comfort zone, unaware of the empowerment the darkness is using against them. They feel content, safe, secure, and chose to disengage themselves from the truth. They are unarmed, spiritually naked and cannot protect themselves from the devious strategic plans of Lucifer.

If you dare, take a peek and walk into the unspeakable horrors of life without Christ . . . Who will survive?

The coming of the lawless one is according to the working of Satan, With all power, signs and lying wonders, and with all unrighteous Deception among those whose perish, Because they did not receive the Love of the truth that they might Be saved. And For this reason God

Will send them strong delusion that they should believe the lie that they all may be condemned who did not believe the truth but had pleasure in unrighteousness.

2 Thessalonians 2:9-12

CHAPTER ONE

The cracked asphalt on Main Street was a bit bumpy that Sunday evening as she headed home. She wished she had taken another route, but now it was too late. She clunked along at a moderate speed in her old beat up Chevy. She wanted to get home quickly, but the inexpensive way the streets were repaired held her back.

Warmer weather earlier had now cooled down quite a bit, and she hadn't brought a jacket. She immediately touched the heater to turn it on, but realized it still wasn't working. Her parents were supposed to get it fixed and never gotten around to it.

Night quickly descended down and the streets were getting dark. She drove through some light traffic, turned on her headlights, lean back tuning into her favorite pop station K.P.P. 101 fm.

She enjoyed listening to this station hearing the love songs sent out over the airwaves. She hoped someday her boyfriend Phillip Jr. might decide to dedicate something special to her.

She turned down 4th Street and stopped at a red light. The smell of food caught her attention and her stomach began to growl. She realized that she hadn't eaten since earlier that afternoon at St. Marie's hospital while waiting for Phillip Jr.

Rachel couldn't wait to get home to one of her mother's large bowls of homemade soup and a warm fire by the hearth. She hoped her father had stoked the fireplace on this chilly night.

She sure did miss the old times when her family would gather around the fire after dinner drinking hot tea, or apple cider spiked with rum. Now those days had long past, a different time, a different season, a different life.

The temperature dropped drastically and the cold chilled her bones. Rachel wanted to put her foot to the pedal like she's done many times before, but something inside stopped her. She didn't understand why, she just knew it was wrong. Maybe it had to do with her new conversion. Rachel only knew she felt different.

Thinking of this brought her mind back to earlier in the day. A lot had transpired and she wasn't sure if she could share this wonderful experience with her family. How could she when it still was so new to her?

Rachel spoke audibly, "Lord, I sure wish my family would understand what I feel inside, I can't image trying to explain this to my father. Oh NO! How would I ever explain my new like without him freaking out? I can see it now; he would literally lock me up for the rest of my life and throw away the key if he didn't murder me first!

Besides my dad has been acting real strange lately not that he hasn't always been kind of strange, but now he is even more distant, moody, and even meaner, something has surely changed inside him; and I don't know why. I just know we aren't close like we were in the past.

Not to mention my mother and grandmother. How will I ever expound upon them how important Salvation is? I can just hear their reactions.

"What in the world is wrong with you girl? Have you lost your brain?" That would be my granny, Lord she really believes we witches are not suppose to mingle with Christian folks, as she would say. And surely, don't ever become one of them! My mother, well she has been a good witch all her life and that's all she knows. She believes the power she uses is sacred.

I guess I will have to keep this wonderful news to myself for a few days, at least until I can find a way to break it to them gently. I just don't know when and how to do that.

The Holy Spirit and Angel of Mercy understood what Rachel was up against even if she didn't. Knowing she needed strength and encouragement the Holy Spirit spoke to Rachel's heart encouraging her too pray feverishly now!

Rachel's heart responded, "Father God, I don't understand why, but I'm frightened. The very thought of going home scares me. I feel like a stranger in familiar surroundings. I look around and things seem the same, but somehow they are different. Please Lord, tell me what I should do, protect me from . . . Wait a minute who am I afraid of?"

At that very moment, a soothing love song came on the radio and distracted Rachel. It tore at her heartstrings and took her back to a special time when Phillip first kissed her. Her mind became dreamy as she listened to the sweet love tune. Her heart went sailing on a ride of lust and desire. All thoughts of prayers were lost, as she gave into the forbidden trap.

*　　*　　*

Shadows of repulsive images moaned and screamed, shattering the deadly silence. The feeling of defeat ripped at them and they were drunk with vicious vengeance. These disembodied slaves of darkness were delirious and irrational in their scheming. A, foul erosion exploded within the walls of this house, causing a decaying, sickening, deadly, smell to swarm over this God forsaken territory. In the demolished space of darkness, it reeked of infestation demonic activity. These evil images lurked around in the darkness waiting, waiting, waiting for her.

* * *

Just a few blocks from home Rachel almost missed the stop sign. She abruptly slammed on her brakes and came to a screeching halt. Her heart palpitated unsteadily while her breathing became labored. New fear took hold of her soul as cold sweat formed on her forehead.

"What is wrong with me for god's sake I'm going home. Why do I feel this horrible twisting in my gut? Lord, my stomach feels nuisance like I'm going to throw up."

Rachel moved her seat back bend over and put her head between her legs. The thought came to her mind; 'maybe I'm just too hungry'.

"Yes a full stomach is what I need." She whispered.

She put the seat back into its' customary position, and started the car suddenly it became very hot and stuffy inside like an oven was turned on high. She rolled her window down to grab some fresh air, when something grabbed at her instead. In an instant, abnormal fingers flew inside squeezing the last full breath from her unsuspecting lungs.

Rachel wheezed, choking, her body thrust forward so terrified with fear her foot unintentionally hit the accelerator hard, at high speed just as a large black cat came running across the street in front of her. The cat stopped for a brief moment staring at Rachel with glassy raging angry eyes. Something in those gruesome eyes alarmed her, she tried too late to swirl out of its' way hitting the animal with violent force. Its' body bounce into the air and flew into her windshield, blood spatters on her windows before the dead thing fell to the ground. The evil screams as it flew out from the dead cat's body melting within the street before her eyes.

"OH MY GOD WHAT WAS THAT? She screamed. Rachel rode over the dead animal trying to escape, completely losing control of her car.

Tearing down the street at a high reckless speed with some malice evil strapped around her neck, her car thrust into the opposite lane on the far side of the road. Rachel tried to catch her breath and dodge the on coming traffic. A blue utility truck coming straight at her caused her to swirl right just in the nick of time.

A young man in the utility truck shouted loud profanity. He stuck out his finger in a swear sign; balls his up fist in anger shaking it at her. Rachel shouted out the window, "I'm SORRY sir I didn't mean too . . . PLEASE CAN YOU HELP ME, I CANNOT STOP!"

His look told her 'go to hell.' Her car hastens past him racing down bumpy roads at a reckless speed. She hits the brakes as hard as she could as she tries to avoid more oncoming traffic. To no avail it was as if this automobile had a mind of its' own; nothing seem to work. She swipes an on coming gold Lexus with an older man inside, as she continues flying through the streets. The frighten man pulls over to the curb trimming.

Totally frightened, Rachel continues to bump over uneven pavement violently rocking back and forth down another steep street after another. She almost collides with a red new Chevy carrying a young mother with two small children. Rachel swirled sharp just before a deadly impact.

Rachel's heart was beating so fast she knew if this keep up she would surely die! At the top of her lungs she screamed, "PLEASE JESUS GIVE ME THE STRENGH TO STOP THIS CRAZY CAR!"

At the bottom of the hill with all her might, Rachel forces the car to the left hitting the curb with force. Her car bounced into a yard knocking down the mailbox as it continued to lunge forward hitting a vacant house smashing the left side of her Chevy. Her airbag inflated as her neck snaps back and her body thrusts forward savagely biting down on her tongue, almost chewing it in half. Black smoke rises up from the hot engine. More pain whipped through her aching body. Only by the grace of God she didn't break a bone or two.

The cats' blood was still covering part of her windshield and warm blood running out of her nose, mouth, and a cut on her head. She wipes her nose and mouth on the sleeve of her shirt. She rubs her neck still shaking trying to catch a full breath.

When she could finally breathe a bit better, she shut off the engine laying her head on the steering wheel and began to cry, brokenly.

Even in her fragile condition she is glad the neighbor on the left is not home. She didn't need old mean, George, as many call him, whom she knew hated loud noise to start fussing. He would have phoned the cops for sure claiming she was drunk or on drugs. This man always complained about her car being an old beat up bucket not fit to be on the road. Whenever she sees him at stores he yells at her, 'your car should be impounded off the streets to keep it from polluting the air!'

On the other side of this vacant house, lived a lonely timid senior citizen. Rachel remembered this woman who never gets involve with anybodies troubles. Always keeps to herself no matter what happens in their neighborhood. Rachel knew she could never count on this woman to help her in any situation.

As she sat in her car crying, she could sense that woman standing at her window, peeking out from behind her blinds. Not because she cared about Rachel, no only to see who was causing the racket on her street. She always stepped back behind her blinds hiding her face, if she thought someone was looking in her direction.

Now the neighbor directly across the street wasn't much different from the other two. That old man was always in a cranky rude mood. Rachel hated the fact that she couldn't get any help from either of these neighbors. The old cranky man never liked being around kids of any age. She knew he was married, but his wife died some years back, never had any children. He once screamed at her 'you kids are all hoodlum, and the world would be a much better place if people came out like Adam and Eve already fully grown!' No Rachel knew he wouldn't help her even if she died right where she sat. This man would only spit out his snuff, shake his head, mumbling under his breath 'serves you right' than go back to whatever he was doing without a backward glance.

Cold, yet relieved to be alive, Rachel shook uncontrollably. Her neck and back hurt, but she kept fighting to calm her breathing. At least the pressure of evil fingers squeezing her neck had ceased.

With trembling hands she reached for the large manila envelope that fell on the floor of the passenger seat slowly took deep breaths into that envelope.

Moment's later with new air into her lungs and hot tears still steaming down her face she thanks God for her safety, relieved that this house was empty. It had been up for sale for months. The damage was not too bad because the curb and her car took most of the impact.

Her real concern wasn't for her busted up old car, as long as it worked, got her home, or the house she hit. Her worry had to do with this vicious evil manifesting in her life. Why? How would she rid herself of it?

After fifteen minutes of sitting trying to stay calm, she started the car again, "YES" she shouted thank God beat up and all, it function enough to get her home.

Driving slowly she can't help but say, "Oh Lord, this is supposed to be the happiest day of my life, with you living in my heart and getting Baptism at Church today, so what went wrong?" Her shattered emotions screamed.

*   *   *

This large old house of ancient evil shook, expands, and swells. It pants deeply as it suppressed its unholy position, like an aggressive flutter that was unrestrained. The doors and windows open and shut rapidly, banging, clanging and slamming against it. The forlorn evil, angry anticipating the intrusion it knew would soon come!

*　*　*

Rachel looked in the rear view mirror and saw her familiar home just a few houses down on the other side of the street. She sighed with great relief until she notices there were no lights on inside or out. This causes her heart to flutter nervously again. Her parents always leave the lights on for her, when they weren't home.

Where were they? Sorely disappointed she made a U turn, drove the short distance, pulls into her driveway, and turns off the engine and phoned her mom, while still waiting in the car.

"Mom, where are you? I thought you would be home by now, I really need you."

"Honey I'm sorry we're still at the store. Your dad had a large crowd today we couldn't leave him alone you know that. Don't worry your grandma and I will be coming home soon enough okay?"

"But mom, I am . . . am, so . . . scared . . . starving, can you please come . . . any sooner? I need to tell you about . . . the accident . . ." Rachel's voice fades into the background from the noise in the store her mother did not hear her clearly.

"Look honey you can tell me all about it when I get home. Your granny made some soup and I started the bread. You can fix the salad and finish the bread. The dough is in the bowl on the counter covered with a towel. Just turn the oven at 425 degree, place the dough in okay? We will be home in about 30 to 45 minutes."

Rachel sighed heavily, "Okay mom, I guess it can wait . . . ."

They said their good-buys and she closed her cell slips it back inside her side pocket, got out of the car rubbing her painful neck. All she wanted was to get into a hot shower then eat some soup and go to bed.

She walked toward her front door, mind still in turmoil about what just happened. She wanted to put her mind at ease so she thought of the responsibilities her mom just gave her to help relieve the anxiety building up.

The wind kicked up quit a bit as it whistles howls and groans like a dog in pain, around this mystified house.

Rachel made her way hastily toward the door blocking her face with her arms as much as possible from the wind. The unearthly wind continues to blow stinging her eyes as it blew hard against her tender face whipping at her hair. Her skirt whirls around her thin legs violently, causing them to burn. Rachel rubs her arms trying to bring some warmth back to her aching cold body, nothing helps.

She covers her face again against the harsh wind, peeking out from under her left arm. Did she see something moving quick and fast through the air? It landed near the oak tree in her yard. This dark image moved so rapidly she wasn't sure if it was her imagination or if it was real. As hasty as it appeared, it disappears, blending into the coarse thickness of the bark on the old oak tree.

She jumps timidly and calls out. "Hell-o, hell-o, is somebody there?

Her voice echoes off dense space penetrating in the darkness. She stood staring behind her into the night too frighten to move.

All of a sudden a mighty violent spirit came swift and fast at Rachel hitting her on the side of her head with extreme force. She fell to the ground. From the corners of her anguishes eyes she sees this disfigured, distorted, horrifying pig face image move back under the shadows of the tree. Rachel screams jumping up running toward the door as fast as she can, while fumbling for her keys.

At the entrance of the door her trembling hands tried to unlock it in haste. She drops the keys on the ground. She bends quickly to retrieve them.

The sinister evil came at her again and raked her face with its' hard inhuman claws. She is beyond words, an instinct to run screams in her spirit. She obeyed running with panic beating at her heart, an insanity driving her on. She runs much slower than she wants, because the pain in her body holds her back.

She hobbled along deep within the darkness on unlit streets. The Neighbors has their curtains and blinds closed. Not a single soul out. Most in this sleepy little town turn in early.

Down street after street in rundown old areas Rachel continued her clumsy limp. Shear panic drives her on.

Seemingly, out of nowhere, huge drops of rain come pouring from the sky. Thunder follows, roaring from the mountains tops cracking across heaven. Lighting flashes through the open sky, but nothing could stop her from trying to escape this horrifying nightmare.

Completely soaked, cold, scared, also cramping badly, her walk slows to a crawl. The terror hovered over her head following her pace laughing. It swooped down in her face from time to time just to keep her in fear. She hears this hatful laugher bouncing off stale damp air. She continued screaming as she wobbled faster her voice blending into the storm. Rachel had no idea where she is headed, only that she needs to keep moving. Nobody came out of his or her warm homes to see what was happening. The evil silenced their ears from her screams.

Her legs feel like shaky rubber, her head pounds and her chest pains. One foot stumbled on a hard jagged rock causes her to trip over. Both of her wet tennis shoes flew off into the air. She goes tumbling down hard to the ground. More excruciating pain struck her in the side followed by fear smashing her on the head. Rachel struggles around in the mud, forces her body to move and get up.

Terrified, wet, hungry, and completely drain, not knowing where she was going, she steps onto something else hard and sharp. Her foot began to bleed, but she refused to stop. Her need to get away is stronger than the intense pain she feels. Rachel's heart continues to beat so fast it threatens to burst from her chest. She thought surely she would die from extreme exhaustion.

Miles under her feet, Rachel come to a house with no grass in the yard, she collapses falling face down onto the wet cold muddy dirt wheezing badly. She crawls near the corner of this deserted street before her weak body gives into the still blackness.

CHAPTER TWO

A plain looking middle-aged woman dressed in an oversize bohemian blue top with a gypsy skirt put the closed sign in the window and closes the blinds. She pushes her waist length graying hair out of her tired drain face. She turned to her mother.

"Mother, Rachel called a little while back, we better hurry, she came home and I told her to pop the rolls in the oven. You know how Ward likes his bread, fresh out the oven, hot not dry or hard, so lets get a move on."

Agnes, an older slow walking woman of seventy, with short white stiff hair sweeping the floor looks up. She is dressed modern and snappy for a woman her age wearing her make-up neat and clean. This very outspoken, dominating woman likes to have her way at all times.

In her course cracked heavy voice the old lady blurted, "You better not cross your husband Nicky! Ward is a hard-working man who takes good care of you and Rachel. The least you could do is, make sure his dinner is hot and ready when he gets home."

Nicky turns to her frowning; "Mother that is exactly what I'm saying, so could you please hurry so we can go home."

She turns and walks to the back of the store through the double doors down a long hall toward the ware-house knocking on the door of her husband's office. She passively spoke;

"Ward honey, are you finished with mother and me? Can we please leave now or do you want us to wait for you? Rachel just called she is waiting for us to come home." There was no answer, "Sweetheart I didn't mean to disturb you," she pushes the door open a crack. I just thought . . ."

In his cold detached tone he says, "Don't come in here woman, you know this room is off limits to you. If you're finished straightening the front of the store, go, don't let me stop you. I got other things to do before I leave . . . and don't wait up for me either."

The ice that drips from his voice stung her. She backs away somewhat from the door. But her need for him drives her on.

"I just thought since Rachel was eating at home tonight we could all eat together as a family like we use to . . . remember? Aren't you hungry? You haven't been home for dinner in quite a while . . . I made your favorite . . ."

She heard him bang his fist hard on the desk. Nicky jumped back away from the door hearting beating rapidly. She grabs her chest with the palm of her right hand. Her mouth opens numb with shock.

"Nicky are you deaf? I said get the HELL OUT OF HERE! Now leave me alone before you wish you had."

Fear gripped her mind. Nicky quickly backs against the wall, wiping the tears that forced their way down her face. Ward got up and slammed the door shut in her face. She could hear him cursing as he went back to his seat.

She hastens down the narrow hall through the doubled doors back into the open store area toward the display counter. Nicky rapidly retrieves her personal belongings all while her head bent low. No way could she allow her heartless mother see the hurt she felt or the tears that sting her eyes.

She wipes them away, took a deep breath and pasted on a fake smile like she's done countless times before.

In a light tone she said, "Mother let's go. I'll grab your shawl and purse okay?"

"Is Ward coming with us?"

"No mother, he said he'd be home later."

"Later? Isn't he going to eat supper? He has not been home for dinner all month."

"Well mother I'm sure he'll grab something later. Leave it along okay?

Agnes gave her daughter a knowing stare. She shook her head drawing her lips tight, but couldn't stop the words that spilled from her uncaring mouth. "Umm hmm yeah, I just bet he will, working late my foot. Ward's been working late for months now. Haven't you realized it yet silly woman, that man is seeing somebody, and I don't blame him one little bit. I blame you for not catering to his needs."

"Mother, STOP IT," Nicky covered her ears and squeezed her eyes shut against the burning reality she didn't want to face.

Angus snatched her purse from Nicky hand and took out her compact mirror held it up for Nicky to see her reflection. She pulled down Nicky hands from her ears forcing her to hear.

"No Nicky, you are going to hear me out once and for all. Have you stopped to look at yourself lately? Can you blame the man? Maybe he would come home if you fix yourself up more."

Nicky turned away against the gloomy image facing her. She knew what she had become, a used up dry middle age woman with no hope.

"It doesn't matter what I do, or look like mother, Ward is dead set on hurting me. Even when I look my best he turns his back on me. He stopped looking at me a long time ago . . . even in bed."

The last words choked from her throat. She bit her bottom lip, tried to square her shoulder forcing the words out from the depths of her being.

"I don't think he loves me anymore mother."

"Do you blame him? Any man would feel that way if his wife didn't do everything she could to keep him happy in every way. That means looking your best at all times. I know you don't want to hear this, but I'm going to say it anyway. You need to lose that stomach, dye that gray out of your hair, put on some make-up, and please buy some new clothes. I'm tired of seeing you in that old blue rag and I'm sure Ward is too. You act like it's the only thing you own."

"PLEASE mother, don't start that again. Everyone can't be slim like you. Let's just go home. Rachel is waiting for us. Aren't you tired, you should be?

"Do you hear what I just said Nicky? You know what girl? If Ward's not eating with us again tonight I am taking my supper to my room. I do not want to sit around and watch you destroy your self respect."

"Whatever makes you happy mother. I just don't care anymore."

Nicky walked over to the door, opened it sees it is still raining out turns back to her mother.

"Mother put your shawl over your head, it is raining out and you don't want to get wet or catch a cold. I didn't know it would rain today or I would have brought . . . ."

Agnes waves her hand for silence put her shawl over her head half covering her face, walks to the door ahead of Nicky still frowning.

Some young girl sixteen trying to look twenty-five, flippantly rushes past Agnes flinging water all over her from her umbrella.

"Old lady get out of my way." Katrina rudely spit out the words.

Agnes reaches out and grabs the girl by the arms. She holds her still staring her in the face.

"What is wrong with you, getting me all wet, and who do you think you are talking too, you disrespectful brat? Before you get near my age you will be all used up you snotty nose inferior slut! You don't impress me one tiny bit with your bleached out so-called blond hair and those cheap whorish clothes. Now get out of MY face before I knock you down and I will too!"

Katrina moves away, whispering under her breath, "whatever."

She sees Nicky who stands timidly behind her mother eyeballing her. Katrina stared back at Nicky before she rudely said. "So what are you looking at hag, move. I'm here to see MY Wolfie, the one you call Ward I believe."

Nicky is besides her self with angry how could this young girl speak to her in this manner? She looks at Katrina in disbelief for quite a while before she quietly moved aside and let Katrina walk pass saying.

"He is in his office. I'm quite sure he is waiting for you."

There was no way Nicky would allow this young kid, her daughter's age see the hurt and humiliation she feels inside. If she had nothing else, she would keep her pride.

Katrina skips through the door. Nicky quietly shut it behind her closing her eyes and shaking her head to clear it. She felt her mother grab her upper arm hard.

"What's gotten into your thick skull girl? You let that no good, slut of a child, walk all over you, and you do NOTHING! How can you have any respect for yourself?

"And what did you expect me to say to her mother? We both know what she is here for . . . She paused . . . at this moment I can care less what Ward does. The only thing on my mind right now is my daughter. The more I think about it the more I sense something is deadly wrong, and I can't shake it. Besides, Ward hasn't hugged me or kissed me in months, but I bet you knew that didn't you mother? So let's just drop the subject and go home alright?"

Agnes grabs and shakes Nicky until her teeth raddled. "What is your problem Nicky? You should be fighting for your husband not letting some young brat walk all over you and take your man. Handle your business Nicky like a real woman should."

"Oh like you handled daddy mother? Now that was a sight to see. I do not recall; neither you nor daddy, ever being happy together."

Before Nicky knew what happened, Agnes slapped her across the face hard.

"You keep your dirty mouth shut about me and mine. You don't know a thing about my relationship with my husband. He was mine long before you came and you better remember that! If it hadn't been for you we would have made it!"

Nicky jerks her arms away, rubbing her sore face, turns, walks over to her SUV climbed into the vehicle and starts it without another word. What could she say? Her father was gone now why speak ill of the dead.

She reached in the back seat and grabs a rag, wiping the rainwater off her arms and face, and stated the SUV. Nicky has been on shut down mode, for so long it was easy to hold her true emotions inside. It became easier to control her inner being if she just gave in, not fighting her mother, or Ward.

Agnes followed her over to the SUV and climbed in on the other side. For the moment no words were exchanged between them. Two mixed up women, both hurting for different reasons sat in total silent.

Nicky, deep in thought about her frail loveless marriage and the life of pain, she now accepted. As the hard rain poured down outside her windows, and thunder roar through the mountains nothing could match Nicky's gloomy emotions as she headed home.

Agnes coldly stares out the windowpane fury mixed with bitterness eating at her heart. Old negative memories of her deceased husband forced their way into the surface of her mind as cold unshed tears choked her throat. She allowed the bitterness to control her heart, but wouldn't allow the tears to fall.

*   *   *

She lazily lounges on the sofa talking on her cordless phone to her best friend from school. One long leg flung over the back of the sofa and the other dangles off the edge to the floor.

She is an attractive gangly fifteen-year-old with long golden hair that feathered over the cushions, still in her cheerleading outfit, eating out of a greasy bag of chips, smacking loudly she talked non stop about sex and boys.

"Did I tell you, my dad has another hot date tonight? That means I'll be here alone just the way I like it, maybe I'll call him tonight."

"Alone, don't you ever get scared?"

"Scared of what?"

"I don't know, late, alone, dark, you know."

Jenea laughs. "You're so silly. Anyway, like I was telling you about this boy, he is so cute. His name is Mad Dog and he like totally turns me on. I can't wait to see him again."

"When did you say you were leaving?"

"In a couple of weeks, than it will be Mad Dog and me."

"Isn't that the small town you were telling me about? Aren't you going to get bored? What did you say it was called?"

Jenea, giggled, "It's called Queen City. The smaller the better, the closer I can get to Mad Dog and he can't get away."

"So tell me, if he's so cute, why doesn't he have a girlfriend in that Queen City's little town?"

Flippantly she blurts, "Because, my demented friend, it's me he's waiting for that's why."

"Whatever."

* * *

Katrina knew exactly where she was headed. She sashayed down the cold dark hallway and saw the light illuminating from under the closed door. She didn't hesitate just recklessly threw it open. Blinded from the bright light, she cover her eyes blurting out, "Hey Wolfie!"

Sitting at his desk bent over a wooden crate started by the intrusion he yells, "What the HELL ARE YOU DOING I HERE LITTLE GIRL?"

His deep bark and the cold stare from his dark piercing eyes frights her. She backed up a few steps and her eyes filled with unwanted tears.

"I—I'm so so-r-r-y Wolfie I didn't mean too-too."

"Next time remember to knock before you barge into my office, do you hear me?"

"Katrina turned her head she couldn't stand to see the cold look Ward gave her.

Ward got up from his desk walks toward her, his tone softer, "Look my little pumpkin, I didn't mean to scare you. I thought you were my wife." His lie spoken smoothly with a touch of coolness was believable.

"But I saw her leave Wolfie." The tears continue down her cheeks. She forcefully wipes them away with the back of her hand.

Ward put his lean muscular arms around her narrow shoulders and gently kissed her damp lips. He than took her hand, "Come my sweet, I got something to show you."

She smiled bashfully and followed him over to the wooden crate that sat on the floor. When she saw it, she gasped out loud, both hands flew to her mouth with excitement, fear, and dread.

What in the WORLD IS IT? Is it real? Is it legal? Can it move? Where did you get it? What are you going to do with it?"

He laughed a hardly laugh. When he caught his breath he quietly spoke,

"So many question, what do you think my little dove?"

CHAPTER THREE

The heavy rain finally slacked up and most of the traffic had thinned out. Slippery streets caused many people to stay indoors. Only a few brave drivers headed home from work or some event graced the wet streets.

A red pick-up Ford coming to a stop sign drove up to the corner with two passengers inside. The married couple lived across the street from Rachel's family were just coming from a local gathering of friends. Still in a very good mood from drinking, old salt and pepper head Tom who is sixty-three glances out his window. He recognizes a limp body balled up on the walk near the curb, but couldn't see her face yet. As he came closer he could tell by the streetlight illuminating her face that she is bruised.

"Hey honey, isn't that the kid from down our way?" He turns to his wife pointing at Rachel.

She leaned across her husband and peeking more closely at the young girl doubled up on the walk.

"Oh my Lord, I believe that is! Honey pull over closer so we can get a better look. I wonder what happened to that poor child. She looks like she been beat up or maybe . . ."

"Or maybe drunk? That's what I think. Wouldn't surprise me none if she was, you know that's what them young folks do on weekends, get all tanked up and all. Boyfriend could have tossed her out after a fight. One way to find out if she is drunk or maybe dead, I'll see for myself if she is napping or what." He laughed.

"My goodness Tom, that's not funny! This girl could be seriously hurt. We got to help her get home, or call the police . . ."

"For what, they got better things to do than come out in the rain over a drunken youth! Let's just see for ourselves 'fore we go calling the po-lice."

Tom and his wife got out of the car; Tom, stared down at her awkward angled body. Rachel moved her head ever so slightly and moaned.

"She sure ain't died that's 'fore sure, cause she moved, must be mighty drunk. I know we sure did have ourselves some fun drinking tonight didn't we honey?" He laughed.

His wife shook her head, "Tom that's not the point, we got to help this unfortunate child get home. Drunk or not we can't leave her out on the streets like this, it's cold and she is wet."

"Whatever you say honey, but let's hurry before the rain kicks up again, cause it's been mighty stormy earlier on, that's why we waited till now."

Tom opened the door to his truck, got out, lifted Rachel's limp body and placed her carefully on the large seat of the cab. He droved her home while deep in thought. Never did it cross either of their minds that maybe she needed some medical attention.

After Tom and his wife reached Rachel's home they parked their truck, got Rachel out on wobbly legs half walked half carried her up to the door. Tom noticed some keys left on the walkway, told his wife to pick them up to see if they fit the lock. After she picked them up she brought them over and tried the lock.

Once inside, her husband laid a wet trembling Rachel on the sofa. His wife covered her with a blanket that was thrown across the back of the couch. They stood together looking at her for a minute making sure she was alright before they leave. Both noticed some bad bruises, and cuts, they assumed were from her fall, but nothing earthshaking her parents couldn't handle when they returned.

"She will probably sleep it off fore her folks return home. I for one don't want to be here when they get here. Them folks are mighty strange people specially that father of hers, never did like him much, looking down on us like we trash and all."

"Can't blame you Tom, I'm not too thrilled with her grandma either, something about her always bothered me. No one around these parts knows much about them. That mama of hers stayed to herself most times. I don't reckon she has any friends. They are not from around these parts no way. She looked around the room and jumped when some dark ugly shadow form moved down the hallway. Lets get out of this possessed crazy house it gives me the creeps."

"I'm right with you mama." Tom took one last look around the living room. It wasn't the decorations or the furniture that kept him staring, he never liked that style anyway, he has a cold feeling they were not alone. Something hid within these walls he could feel it, smell it almost taste it. Some unknown invasion you couldn't see, but deep in your bones you knew it was there. This morbid evil reeked everywhere in every corner, of every area, and it told them they were not welcome.

Rachel opened her aching swollen eyes slightly. Her whole body hurt badly. She tried to move too quickly and fell back against the cushions. She could hear their voices in the room of the neighbors or . . . Raw pain hit her body, causing her to scream out.

"My lord what is it child? The Misses went to her side bending low. "You are safe now, in your own home. We found you about four miles up laying on the sidewalk, out cold. Tom and I was on our way home when we seen you, so we brought you here.

She patted her hand. Now you rest some I'm sure your folks will be home soon."

From her dry lips Rachel managed to whisper, "Thank you." She wanted to say more, but the words were lost in her brain and wouldn't come forth. She closed her eyes against the pain for a few seconds, and when she opened them the couple had quietly left.

The room lights flicker, causing Rachel to become more frighten. She didn't want to be left alone in this house. Why she did not understand, it did not feel like home. All she knew was evil lurked in this place trapping her inside its' clutches.

Her heart skipped a beat, then beat louder and faster, until it became deafening. Frozen with paralyzing terror Rachel's brain tried to comprehend what was happening to her. It sounded like two hearts beating as one. For a few moments she laid still listening than pure instinct mixed with panic forced her to jump up from the sofa running toward the front door screaming at the top of her lungs. "HELP—HELP!"

Her screams so intense the noises deaden her eardrums. Rachel grabbed the doorknob shaking it violently the doorknob became loose in her hands spinning around and around as if it was broken.

The very foundation of the house began to shake savagely. It inhaled deeply. Viciously it blew her like leaves in fall, suspended in thin air. Her body slammed into the wall again and again. The wall opened up sucking her inside its roughness with brutal force. Her weaken frame became one with the structure of the walls.

Every door and window of the home savagely open and slammed repeatedly. The house screamed in a high tone echoing through the rooms. A rotten putrid smell oozed it way throughout the house. Tormenting decomposed demons of all shapes and sizes spilled from the corner and cracks of the home. Each room took on a different characteristic form of an animal howling, growling.

Petrified she stares from her prison position as the black shadow figures crawl over her immobilized body. She tries to move to no avail. She was trapped inside the wall melted within the structure of the house. Every part of her body except her eyes are completely emerged in plaster.

These disembodied slaves of darkness tore into the walls with unmasked rage, hissing, raking, biting and tearing at her helpless form. Their threshing sounded like rumbling thunder, hot blaze of sharp pain ripe through her body, savagely.

The filthy invasion suffocates her, chokes her as it torn down her throat in rage. She tasted the foul odor of blood and death as the evil saturated in the pit of her stomach. She felt warm blood oozing from her mouth, nose and uterus, but there is nothing her fog brain can do to stop the vicious attack.

Locked in her clogged mind is the single word 'help' before the blackness took full control and Rachel succumb to the power falling into a deep paralyzing fear of still sleep.

CHAPTER FOUR

Late that evening Danielle sat at her mahogany dressing table, bushing her short shining curls. She was tired, getting sleepy, but not quite ready for bed. The rain had finally stopped about an hour ago. Danielle couldn't help but be relieved, because she did not like to sleep during rainstorms. She always hated it, even when young.

She sat admiring herself in the mirror in while deciding if she should turn in.

Normally she only needed a few hours of sleep to feel refreshed so she decides to stay up a while longer.

What a hectic day it has been. With her brother Phillip Jr. laid up in the hospital close to death twice, her sister-in-law Cam coming back from the dead, not to mention her husband, Thomas, moving back home. It was almost too much for her brain too contain. She needed some relief from all this stress, anything to keep her mind off what happened.

"If I could run away from this mess I would fly away with Bob . . . My goodness what am I saying? I'm glad my brother and Cam are alive. She paused before saying, now Thomas is another story. I'm still not sure if I did the right thing allowing him to come back home. I guess I was too afraid to be alone tonight, I never thought about what would happen next."

As she sits brushing her hair the earlier conversation she had with Thomas enters her mind.

"Thomas you can sleep in the guest room until we can sort out our differences. The children I'm sure are glad you came home, but don't let that fool you into thinking all is well with us. You know this will take some time."

She remembered how happy he seemed just to be home laughing with the children. At least he was good for something helping her with the kids tonight, giving them their baths and reading them a bedtime story. This gave her the free time she needed for herself, to think about the one man who thrilled her every moment he was near.

"Bob must be worried the way I ran out of the office this afternoon. I wonder if it's too late to call him."

She looked at her clock on the wall next to her picture, only 7:53p.m. Yes plenty of time to give him a quick call before turning in. Danielle hurries over to her door peeking out, there was no sound coming from Thomas's room, but the lights were still on under his door.

"I better be quiet just in case."

She got her cell phone off the table dialed Bob's home number and waited impatiently for his deep voice to answer.

"Hello, Danielle what a surprise, I wasn't expecting this honor."

"I hope I'm not intruding on your time Bob. I never got a chance to explain my disappearance this afternoon and I wanted to . . ." Her heart skipped a beat and she couldn't continue.

"You did leave so fast, and you left your car in the parking lot. I wondered if you intend on coming back tonight to pick it up. I even hung around the office until around 7:20, just in case. I just got home a few minutes ago myself."

"It's a long and dreary story, and I don't want to get into it tonight, but I will tell you about it soon okay?"

"You seemed upset Danielle, is there anything I can do to relieve some of that tension?" His voice sounded strong and caring.

She shifted in her seat, "Just to hear your voice helps me tremendous, you have no idea how much."

"Thank you my dear. You got to know I'd do anything for you Danielle. I think about you often. Just today I was in Jackson's office going over a case and somehow you slipped right into my thoughts, after that it was all over. I couldn't think of anything else for the rest of the day. What are you doing to me woman?

She smiled . . . shyly blushing . . .

"I stay on your mind, Bob? That's the sweetest words anyone has ever said to me."

"You still never answered my question so I'll ask you again. What have you done to me?"

"It's what we done to each other." Her words were soft and sexy.

"I find myself thinking about you at odd times of the day, and I wonder what it would be like to be in your strong arms. Maybe I shouldn't have said . . . is it wrong?"

"No Danielle." His husky voice breath, I think we both knew this was coming. Look, why don't we get together tomorrow and find out some of the answers to these questions?"

Butterflies churns in the pit of her stomach, goose bumps run up her arms. She felt light headed, giddy all at the same time.

The words melts out her mouth, "I would love to see you Bob. You bring out my enter most emotions and I feel so very sexy, smart, wanted, and desirable when I'm around you."

"Babe I want to make you feel much more. I need you to love me like you never have any other man. I can hardly wait to take you in my arms, hold you and love you until you beg for me to stop."

"Stop it or you will find me at your door steps tonight . . ." She looked around her room than at the door making sure Thomas did not hear her. "I better say my goodnight now."

"Sweet dreams my love."

"Same to you Bob."

She held the phone to her chest for several moments allowing her body to react to the sweet memories he caused.

She took a deep breath, put the phone away, went into the bathroom and ran her bath. Her mind still on Bob, she undresses, stares at her reflection in the mirror over the vanity. She loved her body, her smooth tight curves, her high lifted breast, her sensuous lips and thick shiny hair.

Thomas came to the bedroom door to say goodnight to Danielle. He called her name three times. When she didn't answer he walked into the room looked around and headed for the bathroom, just as she was about to step into her bubble bath.

Danielle face turned beet red and she grabbed a towel covering her nakedness.

"Thomas what are you doing in here? Can't you knock before you come barging in here?"

Thomas stood perplex gazing at her half covered nudeness. He wanted to hold her, kiss her all over, his wife whom he loved with all his heart. Instead he turned around facing the door.

"I'm sorry sweetheart I just wanted to say goodnight before you turned in." With tension in his voice he adds. "I am still your husband you know."

"Than earn your way back, you owe that. Look Thomas I was about to take a bath. I'm tried It's been a long day, goodnight. I'll talk with you in the morning."

Her voice a bit too sharp caused anguish emotions in Thomas. It made him feel so lost, and rejected. He missed his wife so much. But he walked out of the room, closing the door behind him. He went into the kitchen for a cup of black coffee. He knew he wouldn't sleep much tonight. This was a lot to digest his wife's rejection, questions he needed to ask his God.

He sat with his black coffee talking to God from the depths of his being.

"How could I be so stupid believing one day would make a different to her Lord? She asked me to come home, but why? What was her real motive? I have so many unanswered questions I need to understand. I can't stand this wall she sat up between us. I got to find a way to tear down her shield. Lord I'll do anything to have my marriage back the way it used to be. Please tell me what to do."

*   *   *

Katrina is mesmerized by Ward. He can do no wrong in her eyes. This good-looking older man, whom she met through her Dad intrigued her.

She never did understand what the two men has in common, or how Ward got the nickname Wolf. All she knew he pulled her into his blazing dark blue black eyes with a force that both frighten and fascinated her at the same time. Willingly she gave him all he desired obediently she obliged his every whim.

She knows Ward likes the affect he had on young girls, women, and men. This man uses all his charms to captivate them and seduce them to his greatest achievements. Katrina knew Ward enjoyed having power over them, made her want him more. He told her once, 'people are gullible weaklings and makes me feel supreme and in total control.'

Her father warned her to stay away saying, 'Ward liked being master of his own destiny with a weak following Katrina. He loves gullible pones, who desire a leader of his status lonely blind sighted beings who thirst for something they never had in their dull uneventful life. You need to leave him along.'

Now looking at him strangely she could see the excitement yet hostility on his face. Ugly laughter echo down the hall out of Ward's mouth, she watches him sit staring at nothing.

The look from his hard, cold, distant eyes always caused her fear. Should she wait, run or touch him? He sat there lost in his own secret space for the longest of time.

It freaked her, but she still waited, trembling in awe. Finally she spook,

"Wolfie . . . are you alright? Please say something, anything . . . ."

She timidly moved closer called his name again and again in her mystified confused voice. "Wolfie . . ."

He focuses his smiled on her. "What is it my child?"

"I asked are you alright?" She whispered.

"Why, yes Katrina I'm quite alright what makes you think different? By the way, I was just thinking maybe the next trip I take for supplies I'll bring you alone, how about that my little dove?"

She was sitting on the edge of his desk, now she hops on his lap and throws her arms around him.

"I'll go wherever you want me to Wolfie, you know that. When can we go?"

He placed his hand on her thigh giving it a small squeeze. "First I want you to do something for me my child."

"What is it you desire of me?"

His smile became sinister and his eyes black as night. "If you really want to come with me, I want you to get on your knees and beg me and call me master."

Katrina obediently bounced off his lap on the floor half under the desk. She folded her hands in a prayer position.

In a soft tone, "Please master take me with you." She smiles thinly, her hands trembling.

Ward pulls her to her feet, kisses her hard so hard it hurt her thin lips.

"Take off your clothes Katrina and crawl on the floor toward me."

There was no passion or tenderness in his words, yet she obeys him completely.

CHAPTER FIVE

J enea had called Mad Dog earlier on his cell there was no answer. She tried again for the third time and on the second ring he answered. She heard his boyish devilish voice clear just the way she liked it.

"Hey girl, what's up?" Mad Dog sat on a bench in the park under a tree just chilling.

"Mad Dog where have you been, I've been calling you for some time."

"I'm here now; so speak."

In her young seductive tone, "Well I miss you. And I just wanted to see how things were going. I haven't talked to you for a while and . . ."

"Things are going, so what's up with you?"

She lay across her bed on her stomach with her legs crossed, "Looking forward to coming your way. Do you miss me?"

"Sure I do. Guess who I met the other day, your uncle, went by his shop last week. He's got some really cool things, like all that black gothic stuff."

"How did you know it was my uncle you met?"

"I didn't a first, than I remembered you said he had a out of the way back woods place. Not too many places like that around here. And remember you told me the name of the place "Stone and Feathers," I was in that area the other day, and there it was."

"He does have a great variety of unusual things, if you are fascinated with the under world."

"Yeah, I'm going back cause there are a few things I want to buy."

"That cool, my dad and uncle are expanding the business, that why we are moving there,"

"Great, your uncle is way cool, not like other grown-ups."

She laughed, "Well my dad is way cool too. We are more friends than father and daughter. When my mom died some years back, my dad needed me to console him. He depended on me for a lot of things, if you know what I mean."

"He never remarried only dates, but not any serious relationships. Mom was the one woman he loved and he said I look like her. Tell me about your parents."

Mad Dog sat up straight and frowned he didn't like to talk about his family.

"Dad was a drunk, beat up mom and me; left us with no money end of story."

"I'm so sorry, what about your mom what kind of person is she?"

"Nothing to tell, she works a lot, gone a lot, and she don't give me no trouble no love either." He whispered.

"What, I didn't hear you."

"Look, I don't feel like taking about them okay, I gotta run."

"No please Mad Dog, don't hang up. I promise I'll never ask you again about your parents. I want to know more about you okay?"

"Okay, we'll talk when you get here right now I got places to go and my peeps to see."

*　*　*

What a time to have a flat tire. It was way past 8:00 and Nicky had not gotten home. She stood outside her vehicle trembling. She cocked her head to one side looking at her tire on the right side of the SUV. A mist still drizzle down from the sky, cold and wet, it didn't brother her nor did she care. The rain was an excuse to cover her strain emotions cause by her concern for her daughter and uncaring parent.

She had called the toll truck, now waiting for them to arrive. It never occurred to her to phone her husband she already knew what he would say, "What did you call me for? That's why you have insurance."

"Nicky what's taking so long for darn truck to get here? I'm tried, hungry and cold."

She pacified her mother, "Mother they will be here as soon as they can. Now stop complaining okay I can't make them come any faster. Any way I'm worried about Rachel, I told her we would be home soon and now this."

She paced back and forth in front of the vehicle stretching her neck looking left and right, frantically searching in hopes of seeing the tow truck coming soon.

Agnes sat in the SUV arms folded lips thin, staring out the windowpane at Nicky. Demons of un-forgiveness lurked, leered and manifested in old Agnes's tired eyes. Her pupils dilated with bitterness and darts of pure hatred shot out toward her daughter. If looks could kill Nicky would drop dead on the spot. Her negative feelings force there way to the surface. She rolled down the window spitting out the words.

"Well if you ask me, you give that daughter of yours too much free time. Who knows what she does when she's not home. I bet them boys hang around her like bees to honey. Give her enough rope and she'll hang herself foe sure."

"Mother; that is a mean thing to say about your own granddaughter what has gotten into you? You know that Rachel is an obedient child."

The tow truck pulled up besides Nicky. "Lady did you call a tow?"

"Yes, my SUV has a flat and I don't have a spare tire. My husband took the one I has for some friend's vehicle and never replaced it."

"Don't worry lady, we might have a used tire you can buy."

He got out of the truck and before they knew it they were hook up unto his truck on their way to 'Towing and used Parts.'

Nothing satisfied Agnes foul move, in fact her disposition deepen. The vile taste in her mouth was her everyday companion. Evil had long ago invaded her body, she was most comfortable when it took full control, and tonight was no exception.

* * *

"Rachel honey, what in the world happened to you? My stars did you fall into the bushes outside? Speak to me!"

Nicky gently applied a cool cloth to her daughter face. The effort it took her and Agnes to get Rachel on the sofa was more than she expected, but with her mother's help they were successful.

Nicky's tired body drain from working all day, then coming home to find her daughter out cold was almost too much. When they first got home, they found Rachel balled up on the floor cover with dried and wet blood. There were huge ugly red, purple, and black bruises all over her body. First thought was to help her get on the sofa. All else would wait.

Nicky sat on the sofa holding her daughter's head in her lap. Agnes had gone to the kitchen to make some of her special healing potion. She believed it could cure anything from a common cold to deadly diseases.

"Mother, hurry up. I need your help. We got to get Rachel into her own bed before Ward gets home. I don't need him asking question I do not have answer to. Haven't you finished making your medicine? We need to get some down her throat now!"

"Hold your horses Missy, I'm coming, I'm coming. You know I can't walk as fast as I use too."

Agnes walked with stillness from the chill she got in the rain. Her bones cracked as she continued. She came down the hall carrying a hot cup of her home made special brew. She moved over to the sofa spilling the hot stuff on her hand.

She growled, "What the hell . . ."

"Be careful mother, before you spill some on Rachel. You should have brought a towel with you."

"Do you want to do this yourself?" She utter with a grunt. She bent over Rachel watching her closely.

"Mother, stop staring at her and help me please. Just hold her head back . . . yah like that."

Nicky carefully opened Rachel's mouth and fed her the potion slowly. Sip after sip she forced the liquid down her daughter's throat. Some of the hot fluid spilled down Nicky's chest as she continued feeding Rachel. She didn't notice or care, her only concern was to nurse Rachel back to health. Her body was so limp, frail and bruised it scared Nicky.

What could have happened to mark her body in such a horror way? And where did those huge bruise come from? Was it from the brushes out side the house? If so it had to be after she phoned home. 'Was she trying to tell me something than?' This question plagued her Nicky's mind.

"Mother what do you think happened to our Rachel? Do you see how busted up her face and body is? Just look at her! I said look at her mother! Nicky was beside herself with worry. Now you tell me what could have made these ugly abrasive . . ."

Nicky pulled the blanket she had placed over Rachel back. Agnes still standing over Rachel back began to hurt. Cold, hungry, and still angry, she reached over gabbing Nicky's forearm and held it tight.

Hate penetrated from her eyes. Nicky recognized that look. She's seen it far too many times. She meekly shut up and closed her eyes against the fear she always felt when her mother got in this killing mood.

"Shut your mouth up! I got eyes and can see plenty! Now you listen to me Missy." The words spit out from Agnes mouth. "I don't know what happened to the gal, and neither do you. So stop pestering me about it and wait until she comes around! You hear! Just keep feeding her more of my medicine while it's hot. It'll kill whatever is ailing her, and leave me alone!"

"Yes mother." Nicky meekly uttered.

Agnes took her time to sit down on the floor close to Rachel's head. She again held it up for Nicky to feed her the hot medicine. Rachel moved her body ever so slightly and groaned softly.

Nicky reach down and pulled her daughter up close. She squeezed her in her arms tightly almost spilling the rest of the brew held in her other hand.

"Honey can you hear me?" Nicky reach across her and sat the liquid down on the coffee table in front of her never taking her eyes off Rachel's face.

"Baby can you open your eyes for mommy?'

"Nicky hush up, she is not a baby, give the girl some air! You are suffocating her."

Nicky hadn't realized how close she was holding Rachel. She reluctantly released her some. Still with her eyes on Rachel's face, she thought she saw some dark shadow thing race across her closed eyelids, then sink inside her eyeballs beneath the skin. Nicky blinked fast and stared again, but it was gone.

"Mother did you see that, her eyelids moved or something moved them! I'm sure of it. I'm not clear on what it was I saw."

She bent even closer to Rachel's face, almost touching her. "Baby can you see me? Open your eyes, mama is here now, please, honey open your eyes for mama."

Rachel heard her from some deep place, tried to force on the voice of her mother. She fought to come back to reality. Just the comforting smell of her mother's body, help to slightly force her eyes open. Through the slants of her eyes, she could see her mother's concern face. She compelled her eyes to obey her brain and slowly her swollen eyes opened a little wider.

Nicky voice shook slightly with deep love and emotions. She held back her concern, and hid the terrified anxiousness she felt. With a comforting smile she spoke.

"We are here honey. Your granny and I were worried sick about you. What happened tonight? Did you . . ."

"Nicky get a hold on yourself." Old Agnes stressed, you're not giving her time to answer one thing, before you go asking her more questions. I think what this child needs is rest. My brew should be taking affect by now. Let her sleep some. There is plenty of time for questions."

Nicky wanted to shut her mother up. How can she be so nonchalant about her granddaughter? It was bad enough finding Rachel in such a way, her mother did not have to add to this with negative remarks.

With lips dried and cracked, Rachel managed to whisper. "Mama"

Nicky pulled her up rocking her back and forth.

"It's okay sweetheart I'm here now. I'll take good care of you."

Agnes frustrated got up slowly from the floor, holding onto the sofa for support. Her knees ached badly. Not only from the carpet burns, but old Arthur came to visit again. She rubbed them for a minute or two than sat on the chair angled from the sofa. She leaned in closer to watch her granddaughter for a few minutes, than decided to turn in for the night.

"Rachel I see you're alright for now, so I'm going to bed because I'm tired and sleepy and not getting any younger." She paused a moment longer, "It's been a long an dreary day working at your papa's store than coming home without supper. Nicky, you better do the same. Let the child rest. She's not dying."

She waited for some response from either of them, when none came she got up and walked slowly down the hall to her bedroom. You could hear her fussing to herself or too someone as she walked in anger.

"I hurt." Rachel mumbled weakly peeking at her mother.

"I know you do dear. Your granny's medicine will take full affect soon"

Nicky kissed her forehead and continued rocking her. I'll stay with you until you fall asleep. Tomorrow you can tell me how you fell down into those rose stubbles outside okay? I've been meaning to cut them back, never liked the huge thorns on them, it must have happened during that bad rain storm."

She gazed down at Rachel seeing her fast asleep, Nicky carefully moved out from under her body. She got up went into her daughter's room, grabbed a fresh nightgown from her dresser drawers. She walked back and carefully changed her daughter's wet clothes into the dry ones. All alone still wondering what really happened tonight. She knew in her heart those rose bushes couldn't have made all those nasty ugly gashes found on her daughter's body. They looked more like bites and deep scratches. There had to be some other explanation, but what?

*   *   *

Sometime during the wee hour of morning Ward carried Rachel into her room. He came in late; saw her sleeping on the sofa did not want to awaken her. Ward never noticed the gashes all over her body because he did not turn on any lights. He saw from the moonlight shining through the light curtains hanging at the windows her body lying on the sofa face half covered. To him there was nothing unusual about her sleeping on the sofa he assumed she was watching TV and fell asleep. Teens do that.

CHAPTER SIX

The rain had stopped last night leaving wet dew to rest on the grass, trees and plants. Fog rolled in off the horizon hiding the sun. The day began like many mornings deep in the valley, with dark clouds hovering over the sky before the sun burned away the haze.

Last night before turning in for bed, Nicky cleaned her daughter room with sage using it to get ride her room of any negative energy, praying to her goddess, the smell of the herbs still linger in her room, when she woke on this hazy morning.

The alarm clock howled at 6:45 a.m. in her room. Her mother Nicky hated the howling sound that despicable clock made. Before Ward gave the gift too Rachel, Nicky pleaded with him not to, but her words fell on death ears.

That ugly clock was in the shape of a wolf's head. Two of its' long sharp teeth were the buttons to set it. If this wasn't enough when it went off it sounded like real wolfs howling in the night. Nicky felt the whole neighborhood could hear it, but her daughter thought the clock was "way cool" so it remained in her room.

Nicky opened the door to Rachel's room just as the wolf clock howled again. She hurried over to the nightstand too turn it off. When she touched it, electricity surged from it through her fingers shocking her. She jerked her hand back, covered her mouth, and screamed into her hurting hand. She licked her wound, rubbed her sore hand with the other anger with Ward for buying the hideous clock.

"My god, I hate this thing. What possessed Ward to bring this mess home? I knew he bought strange things for the store, but to buy this and bring it home . . . she whispered."

She heard Rachel move and she hurried over to check her temperature. She laid her cool hand against Rachel's forehead. During the night she has a fever, but now her head felt cool to the touch. She looked closer at her daughter's face. Her body looked like it was raked from top to bottom by some inhuman claws. Her skin ripped in many places, tears streamed down her face as she watched in horror at the deep gashes on Rachel's face, neck, chest, arms, stomach and every place possible.

Rachel moved her head ever so slightly.

"Honey, are you awake? Can you hear me? Come on honey open your eyes for mama."

Nicky sat on the side of her bed. She leaned in and lovingly touched her daughter's face smiling.

Her instinct was to grab her and hold her tightly begging the god.

Rachel opened her swollen eyes, peeked out through the slight opening. She recognized her mom, from her thick swollen lips she forced out the word, "Mom."

Nicky put on a brave smile, brushed a small lock of Rachel's hair from her face. "Yes darling."

"Water," she managed.

Nicky jumped up too quickly from off the bed, causing Rachel to cry out in pain.

"Baby, I'm so sorry I didn't mean to hurt you. I'll get you a straw and some water okay? She kissed her on the cheek and hurried into the kitchen. Nicky opened the refrigerator filled a glass with water and lapis Agnes mixed last night for Rachel, and returned to the room with a straw in the glass. Nicky brought the glass over to Rachel and lifted her head so she could sip the cool fluid.

After a few drops went down, Nicky sat the glass on the nightstand next to the bed.

"That is enough for now honey you can drink more in a little while. Now please tell me what happened last night, I've been so worried.

Rachel looked at her mother bewildered. Nicky thought maybe she didn't understand the question, she asked again.

"Rachel did you fall, or did something else happen? Come on tell me sweet."

Rachel stared at her mother dazed a hint of a frown creased her forehead.

"Honey listen, do you understand what I'm asking you."

She blinked slightly shaking her head ever so slowly.

Nicky wanted to scream out, "what happened to you?" But her daughter still had that numb blank look on her face. Nicky bit her top lip until it hurt to keep from crying. She massaged her temple trying to stop the pain of a headache from coming. She whispered,

"Okay honey, do you remember anything that happened to you last night?"

"No mama." She muffled.

"Nothing! . . . Nothing at all!"

She whispered, "All I remember is, you and granny . . . giving me something to drink . . . She licked her dry lips. "Can I please have . . . more water?"

Nicky sigh, held her daughter's head up some and fed her more of the lapis mixture. All the while wondering if Rachel couldn't recall what happened, maybe her mind was too foggy from the accident. She might have a slight concussion. Yes maybe, that was the reason she didn't remember about last night. That had to be the answer. What else made sense?

"It's alright sweetheart, mama will take care of you. Now rest while I fix breakfast for your granny. I'll come back later to check on you."

Nicky bent down to kiss Rachel on her cheek. Fear in Rachel's eyes caught her attention.

"What is it Rachel? Don't worry I'm right here. I'm not going anywhere. You are safe now. I'll be right in the kitchen okay?"

She patted her on the shoulder turned to leave when she heard Rachel gasping for air she turned back to her and saw Rachel white as a ghost. The sockets of her eyes were as big as saucers. Rachel began to shake as if she was having convulsion reaction to something.

"What is happening," Nicky screamed, "one minute she's fine and the next this?"

Nicky quickly grabbed a blanket from the foot of the bed throw it over Rachel's quivering body. She sat on the bed and held Rachel down with one arm holding her head back and stuck her fingers in Rachel's mouth holding onto her tongue to keep Rachel from choking and swallowing it.

Nicky knew something was deadly wrong with her daughter. She hurriedly called upon her pagan goddess again, for help praying loudly. She wanted these negative spirits out of her home now! Her daughter's body cold and clammy soaked to the skin and white as a sheet continue to shake uncontrollable.

"MOTHER COME QUICKLY!" she shouted for several minutes in a hoarse voice still trying to hold Rachel still.

Agnes wearing her long dark green flock used as a nightgown walked her weary body down the hall into Rachel's room on stiff wooden legs. She never did get enough rest during the night. Her legs still hurting from old Art, she was not in a good mood. With no sympathy for anyone but herself old Agnes didn't care if the house was on fire. Her foul spirit cranky she pushed her white stiff hair out of her eyes took out her glasses put them on, opened the door wide. It hit the wall behind with a bang!

"What are you fussing about now Nicky, are you trying to wake the dead? I can hear your whining plum down the hall. This better be good, you pestering me this early in the morning. What do you want?" She spat.

Nicky had just about enough of her mother's negative attitude. She hadn't gotten much sleep waiting up for Ward, and worrying about Rachel. Her headache was now full blown. Bad enough she never heard Ward leaving this morning. The only way she knew he had been home was his clothes left on the chair in their bedroom. And the smell of his spice fragrances cologne lingered in the room.

"Mother, will you please stop your complaining for once!" She shouted and surprised herself how aggressive she sounded. Her concern for her child brought out the fire she never knew she had.

"Listen mother, Rachel is very ill and you better help me do something for her. Look at her will you, she is soak and wet. Her convulsion is subsiding now, but you should have seen her just a minute ago. Now we don't know what happened last night, but one thing I do know something or someone put these ugly gashes on my daughter's body and it wasn't the roses. If you don't use your power of prayer to help her, I'll find someone who will!"

*   *   *

Danielle almost overslept; she had never used alarm clocks, never like them. She, awaken to a radiant beautiful sunshine morning. The sun steamed through her windowpane, brightly on her face causing her to open her eyes.

The late morning sun had burned off that earlier haze leaving the dark clouds behind.

She could hardly believe it rained off and on through the entire night except she kept waking up. She never did sleep soundly when it rained. Funny, her mother had told her how most people loved hearing the raindrops falling on their rooftops, helping them too sleep better. Not Danielle, it was just the opposite. It disturbed and annoyed her. She hated the sound and was glad the rain had stopped. She had plans for the day that didn't include rain.

She got up excited and rushed into the day with enthusiastic energy. She hurriedly got her children ready off to daycare and pre-school using her husband's car. Then rushed back home so Thomas could take her to work on his way to the University. She even lightly kissed him on the lips before taking the children to school to thank him for taking care of them last night.

Now she was on pins and needles waiting for Thomas to drop her off at work. Just to see Bob filled her every thought. Her lustful imagination surged her on, carrying her alone on a dangerous ride of desire for beyond any she ever known. Her mind could not stop the unrestrained sexual cravings she felt.

What would it be like to have him kiss her hard, hold her and love her completely? Very soon she would know. Danielle thoughts so intense she almost didn't see her turn coming up. She quickly hollered for Thomas to turn left just as they came close to the turn.

Thomas glanced at her peculiar wondering why she was so tense, but said nothing just did as she commanded. He so starved for the little attention he received this morning he didn't want anything to come between him and her now.

"My goodness, she told herself, get a grip on your emotions girl. In two short minutes you'll be at work and you don't what Thomas wondering why you are so flustered. She took a deep breath, that's better, be cool calm and collect, it won't be long now."

"Thomas you can drop me off here. It's such a wonderful morning I think I'll walk the rest of the way, its' not that far."

"Babe I don't mind taking you all the way, and besides, I want to meet your new boss."

Danielle face flushed red. She hid it by turning her face looking out the window. She spoke in a cool stiff manner.

"Thomas, I said I wanted to walk okay? Besides my boss won't be in until later this morning and you got to get to your job on time. She looked at him with scorn in her eyes. You know you don't want to mess this job up."

Thomas could tell she was somewhat uncomfortable. He did not want her upset with him, not after that kiss she gave him earlier. So he let it go as usual, put a smile on his face, and lightly kissed her cheek.

"You are right dear. Do you want me to pick you up after work?"

Danielle gave him a 'what are you taking about' look like he was from another world. She closed her eyes and shook her head counting to ten. When she opened them again she felt better.

"Thomas use your mind . . . think . . . remember my car was left at work yesterday. I will be driving myself home tonight . . . and by the way did I forget to mention, I'll be late coming home. I have some typing I need to finish for my boss because of leaving him in a bind yesterday."

Now it was Thomas's turn to breathe fresh air into his lungs holding back anger. He took slow and easy breaths before he spoke. He bent his head and made a fist with his right hand, he bit his knuckles trying not to show his disappointment. He knew that wouldn't help matters. In a low voice he began looking out the window.

"I see . . . well I guess I'll have to heat up leftovers for the kids tonight. Do you want me to put a plate aside for you?"

"No, I'll grab something from the deli across the street. But thanks, I got to run."

She opened her door without waiting for him to open it, without a backwards glance got out, walked swiftly down the street toward her building.

*   *   *

Danielle's department was still empty. She had forgotten on Mondays the office didn't open until 11:00 a.m. and it was only 9:46 a.m. She opened the office door to her little space and noticed on her desk the most beautiful spring flower arrangement she has ever seen. She hurried over and smelled them reaching for the card and read.

"My Angel, last night you made me the happiest man alive. I can't wait to see you Bob."

Danielle held the card to her chest, closed her eyes and smiled.

"Oh Bob, she whispered as she reread the card. I can't be falling in love with you. I'm still a married woman. You make me so confused. I know I care about you, but I still love my husband too. What am I going to do?"

She sat down behind her desk with thoughts of both men rushing through her mind.

"I believe I could fall in love with you Bob if I let myself. You bring out things inside my heart I've never known, things that burn and awaken a hunger deep within me, you leave me weak begging for more. I can't stop thinking of you even if I tried.

My husband Thomas, well, he is faithful, steady, father of my children. He is down too earth and I can depend on him, well most times. Boy does that sound boring. I know he loves me, but something is missing from our relationship."

Her thoughts continue comparing the two men when the phone on her desk rang startling her. She quickly reached for it and breathlessly answered.

"Hello" . . .

"Well I see you make it in my love."

His deep voice brought butterflies fluttering in the pit of her stomach.

"Did you sleep well?'

"No, yes, I mean," she laughed. "What I'm trying to say is I had a wonderful sleep dreaming about you."

"So did I, did you get the flowers?"

"They are the most beautiful flowers I seen in a long while. Thank you, Bob."

"Not as beautiful as you are. Danielle, I can't wait to see you."

"Me either, I need to see you too, when will you be in?"

"How about right now, is that soon enough?"

She looked up and there stood Bob in her office with his cell phone still at his ear. A few long strives he was around her desk. She dropped the phone on the carpet stood up and neither knew who grabbed whom first. For about 15 minutes, they were deeply engrossed locked in each other's arms, kissing, hugging, and touching each other everywhere. Neither came up for air nor did they want to. Danielle felt breathless her knees weaken her body limp. She moaned for more.

When Bob could finally catch his breath he held her at arms length, smiled down at her with something close to love in his eyes.

"Come with me now Danielle. I need you."

"How can I say no?"

She reached for him and pulled him close again.

*   *   *

"Honey, I'm so sorry mommy took so long, but your granny wanted me to fix breakfast and it took longer than I expected. Are you feeling better?"

Rachel eyes filled with tears, her voice trembled.

"I'm so afraid mom. I'm afraid to stay alone in this house, and you know I've never been afraid before."

Nicky went to her daughter, rocked her slowly in her arms. She tried to make her voice sound soothing even though she did not feel confident.

"It's okay to be afraid sometimes. But sweetheart whatever happened it's over now. You are safe, home in your own bed, with your family around you. Do you remember anything about last night?"

Her face almost buried in her mother's bosom made her voice sound muffled.

"I see scary shadow images everywhere, I can't figure out what they are. I only know they mean me harm."

Nicky held Rachel's face between the palms of her hands looking deep into her eyes. She saw the fear dripping from her daughter's sockets and there was nothing she could do about it. All she could do was try to reassure Rachel that she was safe with her.

"It's okay you don't have to worry, or think about it right now, just lay here in my arms and relax I'll protect you I promise. She pulsed cleared her throat. You know what I think; my goddess answered my plea and sent you your spirit guild. They are here to help you. I did pray to the goddess for your protection. I thank that they have come to watch over you Rachel. Just listen to them and you will be alright."

Nicky believing what she said felt better. She rocked Rachel for an hour singing until her daughter was sleeping soundly. She quietly moved from under her and laid Rachel's head back onto the pillow gentle stood up ready to leave. When she was just about at the door she heard Rachel's stain voice saying.

"No mama! Please don't leave me alone!"

Startled, Nicky turned back to see her daughter's eyes wild and her arms reaching out toward her. She rushed back to her and kneeled beside her bed.

"Honey I thought you were sleeping. I'll stay awhile longer, but I got to buy some food for dinner okay? Maybe your granny can sit with you while I do some shopping. I would send her, but you know she can't drive anymore. Don't worry about it right now. I'll stay until you feel better."

She sat on Rachel's bed, stroked her hair, song to her again until she was sure Rachel was at last hopefully asleep.

CHAPTER SEVEN

L ocked within a tightly concealed glass jar, the creature with huge yellow repulsive eyes, and gruesome face, searched about the room looking for some sort of earthlings. It had a thirst to devour all mankind. Emptiness irritated this decomposing thing causing it to swell within its' enclosed confinement.

Full of hate angry blades of fire shot out from the place where a nose should be. Thick dark clouds of smoke saturated the room along with filthy smells that penetrated the air.

Abomination of evil restricted within its' prison walls, stank down. A crude smile appeared from the blood dripping mouth.

Nobody was around to witness or feel its' violent hostility. This creature only came alive when time stood still, at least for now. Things were just about to change.

*   *   *

Sharron, nibbled on her chicken salad thinking, "where in the world is Danielle? Why didn't she answer her cell? I know she should still be at work."

She dropped the fork on her plate grabbing the cell again, dialing Danielle's number waiting for either her voicemail or Danielle to pick up. After the third ring she heard her friend say soft and sexy.

"Hi Sharron,"

"Where have you been Danielle? I've been calling you for the past two hours. Why didn't you answer my calls, are you that busy?"

Danielle giggled. "I'm so sorry my boss had me all tied up for some time."

"Even on your lunch break, what did he have you to do, sit in court all day?"

"No, we were both out of the office most of the day. This business had to be very private," she laughed.

"Private, come on now what is going on? If that hunk of a boss needed some privacy with you, something has to be up. Spill the beans girl and I want details."

Danielle flushed red. She was glad her girlfriend couldn't see her face. How could she say, "Our business took place in a motel right outside of town, we just got back to the office after five and a half hours of hot sex."

"I'm waiting Danielle, and don't give me that, "what are you taking about speech." This is Sharron you are talking too and I know the ropes. That man has had the hots for you every since he met you."

Still a bit unsure if she should share this with Sharron, Danielle hesitated. She chewed on her lower lip, brushed her skit off and waited.

"Danielle I'm not letting you get by without sharing with me. Come on girl, I tell you everything, now what happened between you and Mr. Hunk?"

"Alright, but this is just between us okay?"

"Have I ever told anyone what we share?"

"How do I begin to explain how wonderful a lover Bob is?"

"Start from the beginning and don't leave nothing out."

"It started with our talk last night, and then this morning he sent me flowers. He came to work early and so did I. We kissed, then left and the rest is history."

"Danielle girl, if you don't spill the beans in every detail to me now, I'm coming over to your office and asking Bob myself."

Danielle covered the phone with her hand and said softly.

"You wouldn't."

"You know me long enough to know I will. So tell me what was said over the phone last night, start from that."

Danielle had no choice but to tell Sharron all that had taken place. She laughed and giggled through the details until Sharron knew the whole sorted story.

"Wow girlfriend, I didn't know you had it in you. You and Bob have to come with David and me. We are going away this weekend to Mexico. It is just a little bed and breakfast, but I'm looking forward to spending some quality time with my man and I am willing to share our little get-a-way with my best friend. So do you think Bob would join you?"

"I would love to, but I have a husband and children to think about remember?"

"Yeah girl right, well you can tell Thomas to watch the children and we can tell him, its' girls night out or girls weekend or something. You know how to lie."

"I don't know, what if, I mean what if . . ."

"Stop it Danielle, you didn't worry about "what if" this morning when you two lay naked in bed together tearing up the sheets. All you have to do is tell him I got a buyers' trip for the weekend and invited you to come alone for company."

"That might work, or maybe I can say, you and I are going to San Diego for two days of shopping for your boutique business that won't seem so far away."

"Does not matter what city you tell me we are going as long as he takes the kids. We can leave after 8:00 p.m. this Friday. You can come over to my place after work, okay."

"Wait Sharron let me think, this is all happening so fast. I feel sort of guilty. I really do love my husband, and I'm not sure what I feel for Bob yet. Why I'm so addicted to him I don't know, all I know is its' scary."

"Lust my dear, it's called pure lust. He brings the tiger out of you and Thomas well you know . . ."

"No it's so much more than that. He makes me feel like a special woman. Like only I exist. He is kind, sweet, thoughtful, and very much a gentleman."

"Look I'm not saying you don't have feelings for him, I'm sure you do, but face it, Thomas is fat, old, and not too romantic. Need I say more."

Danielle had been sitting at her desk, now she pasted the floor. Part of her wanted to run and just move with the flow, and the other part felt guilty. Her children loved having their daddy home spending time with him, but was she being fair to Thomas?

"Listen Sharron, I really do care for my husband deeply. I know at times I don't always show it, but . . . I got these feelings for Bob also. When I'm with him, well I just melt inside. Call it whatever you want, it's confusing I know. I just know I can't stop seeing him, not yet."

Sharron laughed until tears formed in her eyes. Danielle flushed with anger. How could her best friend take this so lightly?

"That man must have had you swinging from the chandelier naked, hollering "I'm Jane you Tarzan!"

"Stop it Sharron! I should have known better than to share this with you, because you don't understand anything about love or real emotions. This is no laughing matter!"

Danielle was close to crying. Sharron did understand her pain. She calmed down and in a sober tone said;

"Yes I do understand what you are felling. Believe it or not, I feel that way about David. This man brings out a part of me that I didn't know existed. These erotic emotions inside me . . . well, lets just say, I understand."

The phone rang on Danielle's desk business as usual took full prestige. The two women got off the phone with Danielle promising to ask Thomas could he watch the children while she went with Bob, Sharron and David to Mexico.

CHAPTER EIGHT

Mad Dog drove the distance he had driven a few days earlier coming down the same bumpy dirt road headed toward Wolf's business. He recognized the identical twisted lined oak trees and the similar old boney branches that reached out like ugly giant arthritic fingers.

Today somewhat different than the last, he felt on top of the world, in total control over his destiny. The trip down the bumpy road didn't bother him as it had the first time. High as the sky in his own twisted world, he looked at the trees thinking.

"You are my subjects. You are reaching out for your king, me. I am in control of the universal around me. I am invincible."

Vile evil couched down from across the rugged crooked road. The haunt knew it wouldn't be long now as they were ready, in place, waiting for the right opportunity to pounce on this gullible youth.

The demeaning atrocious lieutenant in charge called his little disfigured imp drooling out his commands with a drub.

"What is it master?" His foul breath clang in the air; fumigating it so badly birds took fight, and flew away as quickly as possible.

"What have you done to get that girl Rachel to denounce her God?"

"Everything, we sent deceiver and deception to her, we are in the process of sending Mad Dog back. 'Deception' controls him and being her boyfriend's best friend, I believe she will listen now. We are trying to get both of then to listen. I'm sure they will take the bait master. Mad Dog is on his way here right now to see her father we got plans to trap him.

Don't worry, that Rachel girl is in the palm of our hands. I brought fear upon her and she can't sleep alone without tormenter entering at her rest. Her mama or grandma can't help. He is constant vaccine for her spirit even in the day. We even brought her sickness, and pain after tiring into her body. She will not run to that James' family, her body is much too weak. Master we got all her family right where we want them, believing their power is supreme; they have no reason to doubt us. They have been deceived for a long and will continue being deceived. What else is there to do?"

Destroyer sailed through skies on broken wings and complete hatred. He wasn't satisfied he had to get Rachel back into witchcraft, but how? His plan was to make Phillip Jr. embrace the power of evil again, keep Danielle thinking she was in love with Bob, fighting her husband. Nothing else would do!

In a cold squeaky evil voice his imp said, "look master, see here comes that boy Mad Dog, I told you, I told you he desires our power just the way we intended." He jumped up and down on his short frog legs.

"Listen to him brag as the drugs use him."

"Than follow and bring him to his knees!" The destroyer screamed.

Some dark sinister demons crawled from beneath the floor of Mad Dog's mustang. They made their way up his leg and slider like snakes hissing out foul fumes that fumigated the whole car. This caused Mad Dog to choke, rolling down his window for fresh air that wasn't there. The outside air being worse than the inside surprised him.

Three more huge black creatures appeared from the abyss, sat on Mad Dog's hood facing him with malice hate saturated throughout. They waited for this moment to hurl slimy green putrid vomit on Mad Dogs clean windshield.

"Oh no, not again, what is up with this area, that every time I come through here this happens? I got to find that huge bird and kill it, crapping on my car like this isn't funny."

He stopped the car got out holding his nose; he walked in front of his car looking for that bird who crapped on his clean ride.

"I'll find you, you nasty pest and than it's me and you. I'll shot you when I come back through here!"

He looked toward the trees, road ahead, sky above, but not a bird in sight. He pressed his nose between his fingers hating the bile smell.

"Must be some dead animals around here, this smell is killing my high, where is that dam bird?"

Mad Dog quickly wiped off his car using a roll of towel paper found in his trunk. He hoped back inside to continue his short ride to Ward's place.

Mad Dog started the car and before he could put it into drive the car sped off fast going backwards down and around the bumpy dirt road headed off into the wilderness.

"What the hell is happening?" He shouted to the air.

He stomped on the brakes several times. He kicked the brakes put the car in reverse then back in drive, but nothing helped. Mad Dog tried everything he knew how to do to stop his run-a-way car to no avail. The car kept bumping and clumping alone backwards through the slight openings of the trees out of control. He tried pulling his brakes to stop that way, nothing helped. For ten long agony minutes his car took him on a roller coaster ride deep into the woods at a frightening speed. He though about jumping out of the car; being somewhat reluctant he stayed glued to his seat part of him enjoying the ride.

The drugs he took earlier kept him from panicking. His mind told him he controlled the car. He assumed it had to be the drugs that made him feel the car was moving out of control.

"This would be so cool if I knew for sure, I controlled the ride. I wonder what is making my car move like this? Okay high or no high I'm game, you drive me around."

Mad Dog was so full of pills believing in his own power, he gave in.

The vehicle suddenly slammed into a huge oak tree and stopped. It threw him viciously forward, his head almost hitting the windshield because he wasn't wearing a seat belt. His neck and body snapped back against the seat. Pain shot through him. All he could think was what a blast!

He sat for a moment, until his thoughts caught up with his mind.

Than, irritation set in his heart and his breathing became hard. Mad Dog sat back in his seat for a long moment cursing his high almost gone. He rubbed his neck and arms. He thought a fun bumpy ride was one thing but this was something else. Where in the hack was he? In his dazed brain he tries to put pieces together. What was really happening here? Why the woods?

He looked out the window trying to collect his thoughts. With his high leaving replaced by tangled thoughts, he seemed to see strange images dancing in his brain. He shook his head to clear it, but the pain he received told him this was no joke something brought him out here for its' evil pleasure.

He opened the door, got out of the car, slowly looking at the damage his car undertook during the backwards speed. He walked to the back what he saw had him in an uproar. The left backend of the car was badly bent and twisted with his taillight hanging off.

He hit the back hood of the car with his fist in anger, swore loud for several minutes and kicked the tree behind his car. He knew it didn't do any good but it made him feel somewhat better. Who else could he blame?

Mad Dog turned around staring at his surrounding, but all he could see was a bunch of old half dead trees, brushes, weeds and thistles. Something or someone else had to be out here besides him. He could feel their breath on his neck. He understood this was supernatural, something beyond his control.

He sensed an evil presents around him. Chills ran up his spine. His clogged brain yelled at the trees to stop scaring him!

"Who are you and what do you want with me?"

One gnarl demented demon twisted its' revolting mouth and sneered. It watched from the hood of Mad

Dog car with hate dripping from those deformed eyes. Even though they pushed Mad Dog to take drugs, have unprotected sex, to read and learn about witchcraft, they still wanted so much more evil out of him. They wanted to completely be in control over every move he made, not giving him room for repentant.

Another revolting vicious demon sat in the tree crashed Mad Dog's car just moments ago. It stared at Mad Dog with such force that Mad Dog closed his eyes against the fear creeping up and down his body. He felt the call of the demons calling for his soul. He obeyed their wishes giving into their desires.

"How about if we use this dense boy to bring us more youth some young ignorant fools who thirst for power from our master?"

The demon on his car spat out.

"That's why we brought him here you rotten piece of . . . Just do it now!"

They forced their evil into Mad Dog's spirit. Mad Dog embraced it deep within. He obeyed their call and allowed them in. The evil over took him completely and he became one with them. He knew just the youth he would bring to Wolf's place of business. Still fear gripped him. They had to control him using fear so intense he thought he was going to die. He fell down worshiping the devil too afraid not to. When he opened His eyes he saw demons in the trees all around his car. He trimmed staring back at the things listening to them telling him what he must do. Quickly he got into his car locking the doors. He did not like weakness, nor was he going to give in to his fright. Just do as they command he kept saying over and over.

His heart beat fast all he wanted to do was get out of this god forsaken place. He started the car roaring it to life.

The demons laughed. "Let's have some fun with him. Call more of our mighty forces and follow him. Let him see us everywhere."

Out from under the abyss into the atmosphere crawled hundreds of huge, repulsive, creepy, devilish demons. They move with force toward Mad Dogs car, flying overhead, flying beside him, and under his car.

"I hate these human beings, one of the lesser imp shouted. I hate them thinking we are under their authority, we rule them! Satan has the power they use and we use that power to control, tear down and destroy!"

The head destroyer shouted.

"All of these gullible human that call on Lucifer will be used to the fullest of our use. Now get him to call on our master with all his heart. You know what the written word says Christ will soon return. We can't have Him return without as many humans as we can give too our master."

"Let's keep their minds in bondage and fear. Torment them with pain and suffering. Take away their substance to live on, and they will surely curse Him who created them. Now go into every part of Queen City, bring me back souls!"

A low groan started among the demons. It sounded like the wind in pain. The moan became louder and louder. It moved through the trees whipping and trashing as it passed.

The sound raddled windows in Mad Dog's Mustang. He press down hard and shot out so quickly he hit another tree in front. He backed up seeing a clear path to pass. The demons grabbed hold of his arm with mighty force. He let go of the wheel, but grabbed the wheel again. Hounding fear drove him on as he held the wheel with all his might. Mad Dog willed the car to obey him. The demons laughed continuing to hover over him hissing. Mad Dog saw the creatures of night all around him and he knew within his spirit they were in control over him. His spirit gave up letting them take full control.

"Whatever you want I'll do it, just leave me alone. Please just go away 'I'm yours okay. I said I'll go where ever you want, let me go!"

The forces let loose laughing so loud Mad Dog ears hurt. They knew this subject was theirs for using for Satan. They were satisfied for now. Mad Dog speed to Ward's place of business quickly, not looking back. Whatever had him controlled his movements and there was nothing he could do.

*   *   *

"Hey son what's your rush? Slow down, you came in like a bat out of hell. Catch your breath and tell me who or what is after you. You are Mad Dog aren't you?" Ward smiled.

Mad Dog took a deep breath, shrugging his shoulders stuffing his hands in his pocket. He wasn't about to let on to anyone about what just happened to him, certainly not this man whom Mad Dog wanted to know. Whatever reason this evil came on him, he wouldn't allow anyone to know. He told himself to stay cool.

"No sweat just passing this way and thought I would stop for a moment. You remember my name?"

"Why yes son. It is my business to remember people who come into my store."

"You busy?"

"No not at all, this is my lunch break, and most of my customers know I close for lunch for about an hour or two. I was just about to put the 'close sign' out when you came busting in here."

He looked at Mad Dog grinning. Ward wanted to knock that smile off his face. He hated kids who thought they were somebody special. 'Who did this punk think he is coming in my place without calling.'

Mad Dog tried to grab his composer still smiling. He felt a bit uncomfortable around Ward, at the same time kinship to him.

"Yell that's me fast and witty it what they call me. I hope I'm not in your way, cause I can leave."

Mad Dog started toward the door when Ward put his hand on his shoulder.

"My boy what is your hurry and what is that smell you brought in here? Did you run into a skunk? It is a lot of them running around these parts."

Mad Dog lifted his arms and sniffed under them. He smelled bad but what could he say, a demon sprayed me?

"Don't know."

Mad Dog walked over to a wooden chair with large boxes stacked high next to it and sat down. He didn't have an answer to the question and didn't want Ward to press for one, so he asked instead about the boxes.

"What is with the boxes, you moving or something?"

"It's okay kid, nothing to be a shame of. I gotten spayed a time or two. Those frisky creatures don't play, do they? Tell you what you can go into my office find a pair of my old work jeans, and shirt, get yourself clean up and please throw away your things. Don't what my customers to get a whiff of this. Come I'll show you where you can change."

Mad Dog was grateful to get out of his smelly clothes. He jumped up following Ward into the back of the store. He saw many more boxes stacked against the walls.

"What with all these boxes you moving or something?" He repeated.

"No I'm just adding. I'll show you after you shower what is in a couple of them. You better be glad it is lunchtime or you would run my costumiers right out of here, than I would have to run you out. Boy, you smell bad. Would have been mighty embarrassing for you to run into my friend old Mack. You see he doesn't like kids, especially ones that stink, can't blame him either. We both know why you smell now don't we?" Ward laughed

Mad Dog was already embarrassed, he wanted to run and hide. There was nothing he could do but follow Ward hurrying out of his clothes. He knew it had to do with those demons he encountered.

"Okay you had your laugh now where is your bathroom?"

While Mad Dog showered, Ward pulled out his secret box from his office hidden in the back of his closet. He still didn't know how he wanted to use the horror thing, but ideals were forming rapidly.

*　　*　　*

Snake was glad school was out for the day. It was strange not seeing Worm, Rachel or Mad Dog in class for three days. He heard what happened to Worm and he was on his way to see him at the hospital. Maybe that's where the other two were.

He called his mom so she wouldn't worry. Every since his dad died, his mother clang to him like a wounded child. He knew she was lonely but enough was enough. He needed some space, some peace and quiet. At the same time he didn't want to see her so sad.

"Hey mom, a friend of mine is in the hospital and I'm on my way to see him. I'll be home in a couple of hours okay?"

Just the mentioning of hospital brought tears to Snake's mom eyes. He felt the negative emotion from the other end of the line; and the last thing he needed was more tears.

"Mom, don't cry, I'm sorry, it's going to be okay. Look how about you and I going out for dinner tonight? Just you and I, would you like that?"

She dabbed at her eyes, "Steve that would be so wonderful, I would love too. Where would you like to go?"

"Anywhere mom, anywhere that you like, but first I gotta see my boy, I won't be too long okay?"

Before she could say another word Snake hung up. He saw his stop and pulled the line, hopped off the bus and walked the two blocks down to Saint Marie's hospital.

The door was slightly ajar he quietly opened it and listened before he entered.

"Worm man, are you awake?" he whispered.

Junior sat up in bed reading the Bible. When he heard his friend's voice he smile and said,

"Come in Steve, man am I glad to see you."

Both boys hugged each other and Snake sat down next to the bed.

"How is it going? Man I was so freaked out. You left this world and went . . . boy that sounds so spooky. What was it like?" He pulled his chair up closer to the bed.

"Oh man oh man, I never in my life want experience anything like that to again. I wouldn't wish it on my most hated enemy."

"So you did die Worm. Why didn't my dad come back like you did?" Unwanted tears formed in Steve eyes.

"That I don't know. All I can tell you is; I hope he didn't go where I went."

The thought of being in hell made chills run up Junior's spine. He closed his eyes willing the images to leave.

Steve got up and walked over to the window and stared out in space. After a moment he said.

"Steve? This is the first time I heard you call me Steve. What's up with that?"

Junior thought for a moment. "I don't know, it just sounded natural. He paused, you know my sister-in-law died too, but she had a different experience than I had."

Steve turned back to Junior. "Why was it different for her?"

"I guess it depends on your faith walk with God. I'll tell you one thing, after what happened to me I know God is real. He loves us and He desires us to follow Him. I don't understand all about the Bible and what it says, but I do know now there is a Heaven and hell!"

"Where did my dad go to Heaven?"

"Maybe he did, I don't believe he was where I was. You told me he believed in Christ."

"Tell me what happened." Steve walked back to the chair sat facing Junior.

"It is called outer darkness, Hell, the abyss, I know people will not believe this but I saw many demons, heard about their plot against mankind. I was so freaked, no high could have prepared me for the horrifying things I saw and heard. I felt total fear like you couldn't believe."

Junior stopped to catch his breath. Every time he allowed the thoughts fear would take over, but he knew he had to share this with Steve.

"Those demons took pleasure in tormenting me. Steve it is so hot you can't breath. Worms and every kind of terror is everywhere, all around you. You are so thirsty but there is no water to be had. All your inner fears come to life one hundred times over."

"Man, stop it, you are freaking me out, how did you get out of that mad house?"

"Only by the grace of God, Steve I screamed Jesus' name over and over again. My mom and dad told me when I was little, if I ever needed help and they couldn't be there, to always call on the name of Jesus, and I did. That is the only way I got out.

"I was a fool not to trust in the way I was brought up by my parents. The Ouija board is bad news man it has devil power that can kill you and send you to hell!"

"I do believe my dad is in Heaven because he believed in the Bible and was always reading it. My mom and I never did understand the Bible even when dad tried to teach us. He went to Church a lot but mom said that was his way. We went with him only once when I was about six. I remember because of the music it was so nice, the large organ playing . . ."

"Steve it's not too late for either of us to learn. Mom said Jesus has grace for people like us who go down the wrong track."

The two boys talked nonstop for over two hours before Steve realized he needed to call his mom about dinner plans. He said his good-by and hurried home promising to go to Church Sunday.

*   *   *

CHAPTER NINE

C am has dinner on the table and was at the stove when her husband came home. Bernard walked into the kitchen with the smell of corn beef and cabbage tingling, his senses. He loved corn beef and cabbage, together with chef salad, hot rolls, large glass of lemon aid, nothing could be better.

"Hey honey that smells so good." He walks over and kissed her cheek.

"I'm fixing enough for Junior also. That food in the hospital is not the best and I'm sure he could use a home cooked meal." She smiled at her handsome husband.

"Need any help?"

"You can get the salad and lemon aid out of the frig. The dinner rolls also need buttering. It is such a nice warm day after the rain I thought later we could have a bowl of ice cream on the patio when we get back home from the hospital."

"Sounds great."

Cam put the hot rolls in a wooden bowl, covered them with a towel brought them over sitting them down on the table. She sat across from her grinning husband.

"You look absolutely radiant Cam. I have the most beautiful wife in Queen City."

"That's because you my love are prejudice.

"Maybe I am, but for me there is not another woman like you, and that's saying something since my dad thinks mom is the most beautiful woman." He reached across the table and held her hand with all the love in his heart visible on his face.

"Oh honey that is the sweetest, most nicest complement you could give me. You know how I feel about you, and your entire family. Your mom is the best friend a daughter-in-law could have, and your dad is like a dad to me."

She moved in closer kissing him on the cheek.

"You my love, life could never mean the same without having you in it. I am so blessed to have a family like yours. When I lost my dad and mom in a car accident some years ago I thought life had stopped for me. Then I met Jesus, He showed me life had only begun it was all about trusting in Him. Then you walked into my life three years ago and . . . well . . ."

The phone rang on the wall Bernard got up to get it. "You sit and eat my love I'll see who it is. I'll tell whom ever it is to call back later."

After Bernard hung up he came back to the table sitting back down.

"That was as you already heard mom, she wanted to see if we were free this Saturday to do a workshop on relationships at her Church. She was going to do it but she has to watch the grandkids this Saturday. I told her we will call later and let her know."

"Yes honey you know that will be fine with me. I remember pastor talking about it when we visited her church last week. But I thought Sister Franklin, and her husband, were doing it?"

"She can't, that's why she asked mom, now she can't either so it's up to us."

"I think that would be a wonderful way to share what God has done in our marriage. We need to tell the young and older couples that they can be successful in their relationship with the help of Almighty God."

"Sweetheart, are you sure you will be up to it? I wouldn't want you to say yes, just because mom asked. There are others couples at the church you know."

She got up put her arms around his neck from behind, kissed him on the top of his head, turning his face to hers and kissing his lips. Food and time was forgotten, just her smell sent him in a lovemaking mood. They went into the bedroom, and he loved her ever so gently, so completely.

*   *   *

Junior dialed Rachel's cell number again for the fourth time. He tried most of last night with no response getting worried. It was unlike her not to call him for days. He kept getting 'the caller is not accepting calls at this time.' Where is she and why didn't she go to her classes? Steve had said she wasn't at school yesterday but today is another day. Yesterday he left messages for her to call him, not a single call.

The phone rang in his hand four times before he heard a woman say,

"Hello"

"Is this 555-7070?"

Yes it is. Who are you? If you want to speak to Rachel I'm afraid she is too ill to accept calls. Whom may I say is calling?"

"I'm a friend from school are you her mother?"

"Yes, I'm Nicky, I'll tell her you asked about her."

"Wait, tell her it's Junior, and tell her my family and I will pray for her. I hope she feels better soon please ask her to call . . ."

Before he could finish talking the line went dead.

"Man so cool and blunt, I hope she remembers to tell Rachel to call me."

He put the phone on the night table and lay perplexed on his bed wondering what made her so sick that she couldn't answer the phone. While these thoughts ran through his mind Cam and Bernard came into the room.

Cam had flowers, blooms, and a very large card. Bernard carried a hot plate of food, Cam's bag and his pouch.

"Hey little brother what's up why the long face?"

"Hi guys, I just tried to call Rachel and her mother answered her line, said she was ill, and practically hung up in my face."

Cam put the flowers in water, let the blooms float to the ceiling next to Junior's bed and sat the card on his nightstand. Bernard sat the food down on the tray and grabbed another chair from the other side of the bed brought it around next to the other chair for Cam. They both sat down before either of them said another word.

Cam spoke first. "Oh I wouldn't be so worried if I was you, the flu bug is going around, I'm sure her mother just wants her to rest and get back on her feet."

"Yeah Junior that's probable, right he paused, look Cam and I brought you dinner and some goodies."

"I'm sorry guys, thank you I didn't mean to be rude. M-m-m that smells good."

"It's steak, bake potatoes, there is salad, rolls, and a cake."

"Wow sis you really know how to spoil a guy, my brother is a lucky man."

"No luck man, just blessed by God. Now eat before I eat it myself."

"We would have brought you dinner yesterday, but a certain man, need I say who kept me pretty busy and when I looked at the time it was way pass your dinner." She giggled.

"Cam I can't believe you said that," Bernard join her in laugher.

Junior was lost on the joke but he ate the food with great enjoyment.

After reading the card, thanking them again for the flowers and blooms, Junior had some questions he needed to get off his chest. First he gave Cam an apology for his negative behavior when she tried to tell him about her experience. Now more than anything he wanted to understand what happened to her when she died and was she in the very presents of the Almighty God?

He waited for her to finish telling him about the relationship class at Church she and Bernard were going to teach. Next came how the Church was doing, when there was a quiet moment, he hurriedly asked.

"Cam, please tell me what happened when you saw God in Heaven."

Cam sat for a moment with the most radiant smile and peace on her face.

"Junior, how can I explain to you or anyone what I experienced when I came face to face with our Savior. I cannot comprehend the intensity of love I felt for Him, and His love for me. It was pure joy, love and goodness all wrapped up in one wonderful packet. His love saturated my soul, I dropped like a wet noodle and lay quibbling on my face before His Great presences. The very thought of being before the King of Kings overwhelmed me."

She closed her eyes and continued.

"His radiance was so bright, as His great glorious presence came nearer. He stood me on my feet. I beheld the very essence of His glory, the living God. His Holy power move on the breath of the Universe, it was like standing in the mist of still air yet on firm ground. His brilliant light so intensified it almost blinded me, coming from the fire in His eyes that penetrated my very soul.

I saw radiant colors like none I've ever seen before, colors bright, so clear and brilliant. I hear wonderful music, coming from everywhere, voices singing and worshiping from every area of Heaven, yet I could hear each note, each word individually. My every sensation, every thought, came alive within me. He knew and I somehow knew also what He related to me without words."

"The Thunder roar with gladness and His Splendor pour out over me like pure oil. I felt Him within and without and all around me at the same time."

"I saw flowers of every color of the rainbow and some colors I never seen before. They were everywhere. Their fragrant was beyond any on earth."

"I looked and beheld His love it was like fire that flooded my being. The very thought of standing before the Shekinah Glory of God was so overwhelming I wanted to melt in His love forever."

When she opened her eyes Junior was crying. First softly, then the dam broke within and he pour out his heart to God. Every sin he could think of he let it go asking Jesus to forgive him. He realized he was a sinner and only Jesus could save him. He wanted what Cam had the peace and joy of knowing where she was going when she left this world.

Cam held him close and let him release his soul to God. When he smiled at last Cam knew Junior had met the one and only Savior. After many hugs, Cam Bernard and Junior got on their knees in pure worship unto the Lord. Thanking Him for His goodness and mercy.

*   *   *

Mad Dog felt elated to have the privilege of seeing something so drastic and unusual as the object in Wolf's box. They talked for an hour about it and what it could be used for. Mad Dog wanted to handle it, but even in his 'I dare you mind', that was out of the question for fear caught hold, so he kept quiet about his desire.

"So what are you going to do with it?"

"Oh, I got some real plans for this one my boy, believe me." He petted the top of the glass jar.

I see you like excitement. Well stick with me and I'll show you more excitement than you can handle."

Mad Dog laughed, "Old man I don't think even you can show me something new, but I'll be willing to see what you got."

"Are you? Wolf cunning smiled. Let's see how brave you really are. I'm getting together some very, how shall I put it, let just say, unusual individuals for a gathering, in about two weeks. My brother and his daughter as you know will be moving to our fare city helping me with the store. This is a welcome of sorts. I think you will find my friends interesting. Yes my boy I think you'll fit in quite well, very well indeed."

He patted Mad Dog on the shoulder with a smirk. The look on his face was so sinister that Mad Dog fought the urge to swallow hard. He turned away so Wolf could not see the fear that ran in his eyes. He got up enough courage to say.

"Hey will you cut the boy crap, I'm not your boy."

"Oh-h-h touchy, touchy don't be on the defense Mad Dog, it's just my way of, how do you say, endearment . . . What if I called you 'Sir Mad Dog,' would that meet with your youthful taste?

Wolf bowed before him, mischievousness dancing in his eyes, pulling Mad Dog into his evil clutches by the power of his mind. Mad Dog couldn't help but grin. He was flying high from some drugs he and Wolf had taken. In his confused mind, Wolf became his friend. His eyes were blinded from the deceit, pregnant in his skull.

"Okay, I see you at your party my man. Can I bring some friends of mine?"

"The more the merrier."

Mad Dog dug in his pocket and pulled out a hundred dollar bill.

"Can I get change for this? I want to get a soda from the coke machine outside."

Wolf removed the 'out for lunch' sign and walked to his cash box pulled out four twenties, a ten, five, four ones and four quarters.

"Here my boy, I mean Sir Mad Dog."

From the moment they exchanged the monies some unearthly power grabbed Mad Dog's hand curling around his fingers tightly. White-hot fire bit into his hand burning from inside out. He dropped the money hastily jumping back screaming.

"WHAT THE HELL IS THAT? WHY DID IT THAT MONEY BURN ME? ARE YOU A WIZARD OR WHAT?"

Ward laughed hard and mean. His voice vibrated through the room sounding like many wolves from one vicious channel. The eerie sound stopped. Ward started at Mad Dog before he answered.

"What was what sir Mad Dog?"

Mad Dog looked back at him like he was crazy thinking this has got to be the drugs. He stuck his fingers in his mouth trying to stop the burning pain sensation.

"What kind of game is this? Are you trying to get a ROUSE out of me old man?" Cause I'm not stupid, you know something stung me from that money and it's not funny."

Wolf grinned reaching out and touching Mad Dog's hand. The pain disappeared as rapidly as it came. He picked the money off the floor, grabbed Mad Dog's hand breathing in the boy's fear while placing the money in Mad Dog's trembling hand.

"Take it my boy, have some fun with it. You can handle that can't you? It's my gift to you. Use your imagination, but use it wisely my friend. Don't let it kick you in the butt." He winked at Mad Dog.

Mad Dog stood there not knowing what to do next. Should he leave or stay? His mind wanted to get out of there as fast as he could for he knew this was beyond him. Finally a small grin came to his face, as he took hold of the tainted bills firmly.

"This is more like it. Thank you Wolf, I will and whatever I can do for you just name it. I'm at your service."

He turned heading toward the door. Wolf watched as Mad Dog left the store with the money stuffed safely in his jean pocket. His smile turned icy cold his eyes razor sharp, his mind focus on how he would use Mad Dog as his useful tool to bring in more souls to the kingdom of doom. Although he wanted to use this kid he didn't like him. What he didn't like was the boy's cockiness and self-made bad attitude. He had to knock him down, show him who really was in control.

Mad Dog made a dash toward the door he heard the crude terrifying laughter following him out on a beam of darkness. It frighten him, sucked him in like a giant vacuum until his mind succumb to its' will.

CHAPTER TEN

Carol sat at her neat kitchen table reading the newspaper and drinking a glass of ice coffee. Phillip Sr. walks in, sat down across from her and grabbed the other half of the evening paper.

"Anything interesting in our fair Queen's City daily?'

She smiles at him over the top of the paper.

"I guess some things never change. Mr. Hall is having a sale on asparagus again this week I will buy some tomorrow for Sunday's dinner. I cut out some of the hardware store coupons for you. You can check and see which ones' you want. She turned back to reading the paper. Let's see, oh yeah the town's picnic is coming up in two weeks and our Mayor is still pouting about the baseball game we didn't win last year."

They laughed.

"I tell you Carol, you are right, this town hasn't change since we were kids growing up. Maybe a few new neighbors, a couple recent stores here and there, like that one near the baseball field. I wonder what the owner sales there? Have you ever been inside that store Carol?"

"Can't say I have honey, it's too out of the way and not the kind of place I would shop. That is the place Rachel's dad brought, a few years ago remember. You know what she said about her family, all of them are generational witches. Even through I like Rachel, and I'm glad she gave her heart to Jesus, I'm not so sure if I want to meet her family. White witches or not, evil is evil in any form."

"Well Honey, at least Rachel understands the evil and has turned away from it. Maybe one day her family will have ears to hear and really listen as she witness to them about Christ."

Carol shook her head in agreement and continued to read the newspaper. Phillip Sr. went to the refrigerator filled a glass full of lemonade sat down at the table and resumed their conversation.

"By the way speaking of witnessing, have you heard from our beloved daughter? Someone needs to set her straight on a few things too."

Carol put the newspaper down and drank some of her ice coffee before she spoke.

"No, and I'm not sure how things are going between Thomas and her. She hasn't called me in a day or two. I want to know how our grandchildren are doing, I think this is as good excuse as any to call her."

Carol reached over picked up the cordless kitchen phone on the counter, dialed her daughter's home number waiting for someone to answer. Phillip smiled shook his head still engulfed in the newspaper.

"Hello Thomas, how are you . . . , your father-in-law and I wanted to talk to the children. Has Danielle put them down yet?"

"No, as a matter of fact Danielle came home late and the kids are telling her stories about their day at school. Say hello to dad for me . . . Wait a moment, I'll get the kids."

Moments later Carol heard her three-year-old grandson, Tommy.

"Hello grandma, guess what mommy brought home? Cake and ice cream and I got a big piece. It was this big."

He held out his chubby arms, almost dropping the phone.

"Hold on honey, grandmother can't see you, but I bet it was a large piece." Carol laughed, wiping her eyes.

"Yes and guess what, my teacher said I paint real good and we done ABC, and . . ."

She heard Sherrie's voice in the background.

"It's my turn, let me talk to her, let me talk now Tommy."

Sherrie grabbed the phone from Tommy. In her I'm smarter than you voice.

"Hi granny, I had a bigger piece than Tommy, and my teacher said I was the best writer in my who-o-l-e-e-e class. What to see my paper?"

"I would love too sweetheart, when you come over you can show me how well you print okay. Honey is your mother busy?"

"She and daddy are talking but I can't hear them much."

"It's okay, when she is finish taking too your dad tell her I want to speak to her okay?"

"Mommy looks mad about something, wait, here she comes."

Danielle took the phone from Sherrie, shooed her off with a pet on the behind.

"Hello Mom, I need to ask you for a favor. Can the kids' stay overnight this weekend with you and dad? Sharron and I will be going to LA on a buying trip for Sharron's business. Thomas can't watch them because he will be working on a class paper at the library all day Saturday, so can you and dad take them?"

"Danielle I thought you and Thomas were working on your marriage. Why are you going off with Sharron?"

"Mother, Danielle said in a defensive tone, I need some time to myself for a change. There is nothing wrong with Thomas and I. We just need some space.

He can pick them up from you after he comes back from the library okay?"

"Danielle it looks to me like you are running away from your problems instead of facing them together with faith. You are not a single woman anymore so why are you acting like Sharron? You know how I feel about her overly sexual ways; she acts just like a slut."

"MOTHER, if you are going to insult my best friend then I'm hanging up!"

"Danielle wait, I'm sorry, I was out of line. You're right I had no right to say that about her. It's just that, honey she is single and living a single life. You on the other hand have a family. She hesitated before suggesting. Honey why don't you and Thomas do something special this weekend? It would do you both some good. Your father and I would love to watch the children while you two get away."

Danielle could hardly contain her anger. She bit down on her lower lip hard to keep from screaming at her mother. She closed her eyes against the negative hostility building inside her mind. When she could speak somewhat without the anger controlling her, she spoke each word slowly and evenly.

"Thank you mother, that's very sweet of you, as I said Thomas, is busy working this weekend, and I need to have a little time all to myself, you understand what I mean?"

Danielle waited for her mother's response, before she began whimpering in a child's voice. "I'm with the kids most of the time, it's not fair, it's like I'm . . . I'm . . . I'm drowning in housework, kids, their homework, and . . ."

Carol knew her daughter all too well. She understood the acting game of fake emotions. Danielle was use to having her own way her stubborn personality came to full circle. It worked better on her father. The two went around and around on this subject for over five minutes before Carol gave in. Although she did not like it, her very determined daughter was going to LA, with or without her help so she gave into her daughter's wishes just to keep the peace.

"Okay Danielle, you don't have to start bawling, I get it. We will watch the children for you this time, but you had better get your priorities straight cause this has got to stop. When do you want to bring them over?"

Danielle smiled to herself she didn't care what her mother thought as long as she took the children. "I think around 7:00 Friday night. That will give me time to fed and get them in their pajamas.

"Then I'll see you in a couple of days Danielle, tell Thomas we will see him this weekend, love you."

Carol hung up reluctantly. A knot formed in the pit of her stomach. Call it mother's intuition; all she knew was something smelled in Queen City and it wasn't the skunks.

Phillip lower the newspaper, he gave Carol a quizzical look.

"Honey you sounded a bit upset with Danielle, is everything alright?"

Carol looked up with scorn on her face. She folded her arms saying,

"Phillip your daughter has a way of getting under my skin! I don't know what she is about to do, but I do know it's not good. Danielle is up to something with that girl Sharron I can feel it, running off like a, like a two bit tramp, there I said it!"

Phillip laid the paper on the table reached across the table for his wife's hand.

"Honey calm down, don't let her upset you like this. Sweetheart, I need to understand what is going on, so tell me what was said before you to make that cruel statement."

Carol smile thinly. She rubbed her husband's large hand looking at the way the huge veins stood out. She brought his hand to her lips, kissed it with tenderness. Her blue eyes looked into his with a hint of tears.

"I have a strange feeling about this trip Danielle is taking with Sharron. I can't quite put my finger on it; I just feel it is a trap of the enemy against Danielle's marriage. Maybe I'm wrong, but this knot in my stomach tells me I'm right and I don't know what to do about it."

"Honey when you don't know what to do, prayer is always the answer. Let's take this to God, and pray for her direction, protection, safety, and common sense. We will leave it in the mighty hands of God. He knows just what to do. Whatever she has plan, God can counteract."

They bowed their heads in total submission letting the power of the Holy Spirit lead them in a prayer of faith, hope, and reassurance.

CHAPTER ELEVEN

F riday morning promised to be a crisp clear day. Yesterday had been overcastted gloomy and misty most of the day. The bad whether had Rachel sleeping the entire day.

The early morning sun shone brightly on her face through the slight opening of the light drapes. She opened her sore pupils for the first time in days and peeked out blinking before her eyes adjusted to the newness of day. Her body felt stiff yet, her need to get out of bed and get some fresh air overwhelmed her. Although she still hurt, she had to try to get up.

The thought of seeing her Christian Church friends, and being together with them at the Church, and seeing the James family, gave her the strength she needed to continue. Granny's healing brew helped to some degree; but it wasn't enough to completely heal her hurting body. She needed to go to the Church where Jesus lives to get her healing.

She slowly pushed back the light blanket eased herself out of bed. She stepped onto the carpet, found her house shoes near the bed. She slipped them on feeling somewhat wobbly standing on her weak legs for the first time in days. Rachel held onto the wall as she continued taking one step at a time. When she reached the bedroom door, she stopped holding onto the doorknob and listened; intensely, no sound from the other rooms was heard.

The thought of seeing her dad was beyond frightening. It terrified her. What she remembered, was his cold icy eyes looking down on her. Ice blazed through the pits of those eyes like chilled bits of steel. That look was more vicious and cruel than anything she had ever encountered. This was a new feeling she wasn't use too. She always enjoyed her family even when her father is so out spoken. Yes he was rude and even cruel to her mother, yet she never felt this afraid before. This feeling was so totally difference, like he is . . . her spirit voiced it before her mind comprehend the answers; 'he is demonic.'

Standing here this strange and very uncomfortable feeling washed over her again drowning her in fear. She stood at the door of the bedroom waiting for her nerves to calm. She listened more intensely. No, there wasn't a sound of her father, mother, or granny. She opened the door quietly and peeked out cautious. Nothing out of the ordinary, she tipped toed out the bedroom and closed the door behind her. When she didn't see anyone around, she hurried into the bathroom down the hall and ran a quick hot shower. The hot sprays felt good on her aching body.

After her shower, she tipped toed back into her bedroom and hurriedly dressed in jeans and a dark blue pullover sweatshirt. She assumed her mom must be at the store helping her dad or maybe she went shopping, granny probably was with her. Knowing her mom was gone and she in the house alone made her feel somewhat uneasy. Rachel hurried herself she knew she should inform her mom of her whereabouts before she left the house. She did not want to worry her.

Rachel dialed Nicky's cell phone, "Mom, you alone?" She whispered.

"Oh Rachel you awake? I'm sorry I stepped out for a moment to buy food I thought I would be back before you woke . . . Are you feeling better?"

"It's okay mom I'm fine. Is granny with you?"

"No she had me drop her off for an early hair appointment at 8:00 this morning. I will pick her up in an hour. Are you hurting, hungry, do you need anything? Do you want me to pick up something special for you?" I can make it home in half an hour if . . ."

"No, no don't worry about me, I'm feeling . . . better. I can pick up something later."

"What are you talking about? You are not leaving the house are you?"

"Yes mom, I need to find out what I've missed in my classes and get some fresh air. I'll go crazy lying around here waiting to get completely better. I'll be back before dinner okay?"

For some reason, Nicky felt panic rise inside for her daughter. She had to try and keep Rachel home and safe.

"Look Rachel, you'll still much too weak to be up and about, specially going out, it's much too early, you are not fully well. What if something goes wrong and I'm not there to protect you? No I think you should stay at home until you are completely healed do you hear me?"

"Mom you are a worrier. I'll be back before you know it, and if for some reason I feel too weak, I'll call you to pick me up, got to run, love you."

Rachel hung up quickly. Her cell began ringing again but she didn't answer it. She didn't want her mom to talk her out of going out. She needed to see Junior and his family. She wanted to tell them what happened to her, why the horrible gashes cover her body, and the thing haunting her spirit.

She grabbed her keys, sunglasses, and rushed out to the bus stop headed for Carol's home. She needed that peace she always felt with the James'. For the past few days it had been pure hell.

* * *

Hurry Junior I thought you would be ready when we got here, not in the bathroom combing your hair. You must think we had Rachel with us or something."

Junior shouted from behind the closed door.

"I'm brushing my teeth not combing my hair. No mom I knew Rachel wasn't with you. I tried calling her for days, but her mom want let me speak to her."

He opened the door. I'm worried about her mom. It's not like her not to call me. How can a cold be that bad she can't come to the phone?"

"Honey I'm sure it's okay. Her mother is just protecting her I'm sure. When you get home you can try again. Now get a move on."

She kidded him out of his negative mood. Junior laughed and as he finished getting his things together.

"Mom you are something. Thanks, I needed that reminder that life is too short and we need to make the best out of all situations we face."

He kissed her cheek.

"Where is dad?"

"He is checking you out and should be here any moment."

Carol hugged her son, smiling.

"You don't know how many prayers your dad and I prayed waiting for you to accept Christ into your life. To see you so sold out for the Kingdom is better than any gift a mother could receive. I'm so proud of you Junior."

Tears of joy in her eyes she hugged him again so tightly he playfully shouted stop you suffocating me.

Phillip Sr. came into the room pushing the wheel chair. Phillip Jr. looked at the chair frowning.

"Hey wait, dad I know you don't expect me to leave in that thing."

"Sorry son, it's the rules. You have to ride in it at least until you get to the car. Come on it's not that bad

"Dad you have to promise you will never tell anyone I sat in that okay?"

Phillip couldn't help but laugh seeing the look on his son's face. Phillip Jr. sat down and Carol put a light blanket over his legs.

"Mom what's with the blanket? I'm not some invalid, or an old man, I don't need a blanket."

He took it off and handed it back to his mother. He looked around the room for the last time. A lot of memory flashed through his mind, regrets, relief, reformed, refresh, that's how he summed it all up. Now he wanted to get home and warn other youth about the so-called fun games of Satan. He understood the vicious, crude, terrifying reality of traps the devil sat up to entice youths and he couldn't wait to share this experience and to warn the others about the devils' lies.

"Come on you guys lets blow this joint."

Phillip Sr. laughed, "nothing but a word, nothing but a word.

Carol lovingly swapped her husband on his behind.

"Why Deacon James where do you get such language?"

All three busted out in laugher, it felt so good Phillip Sr. thought to see his family laugh together.

* * *

Danielle sat at her desk typing legal papers deep in thought. She couldn't keep her mind completely on her work and made many mistakes. The excitement over whammed her, she wanted this day to end so she could be on her way to Mexico with Bob. Two whole days with the man of her dreams, what could be better?

'Thomas will take the children to my parents tonight after dinner; I will spend the night at Sharron's house. Tomorrow morning we would meet the guys and on to Mexico we will go. This time tomorrow night I will be sipping on a daiquiri on the beach with Bob at my side. On Sunday night we must return home, or maybe . . .'

She continued thinking "what if we stayed another night and came home Monday evening instead? Thomas could take the children to school and daycare and then pick them up. He can take them to the 'Kiddy Fun Center' for dinner on Monday; yes, the kids would love that. Oh my god what am I thinking? What is wrong with me? Am, I wanting this man Bob so badly that I'm willing to sacrifice my children for another day?"

Danielle put away her workload, grabbed her things and left the office. She felt guilty for just a moment, then the thought of Bob rushed full force in her heart and nothing could stand in her way of being with him, as the filthy lust troll invaded Danielle's opened heart wrapping it's self around her mind, suffocating reasoning. The thing invited scorn, illusion and cold restlessness they echoed her words back to her of deep desire for this man Bob. These stronghold brought blindness, deception and a hungry for relief from her old marriage to Thomas.

Somewhere in the corner of her mind she realized these thoughts were wrong but the lustful imaginations of Bob held her in chains.

Stormy feelings of her marriage continued to surface bringing ugly thoughts. Delusional love for Bob breath deceit deep within her mind, swelling tides caught her and pulled her into its web. A horror looking pitch-black demon sat on Danielle's lap, licking her face with putrid brown slime running out of its mouth. It wrapped its scaly formed around her and squeeze her hard. She felt the pain and screamed, thinking it was something she eaten earlier. She rubbed her middle with tears forming in the corner of her eyes. She never thought to pray or claim the word over the pain, she gave in and suffered until it subsided still locked in her dirty thoughts of Bob.

"How well these stupid, gullible humans obey when they think love moves them, he laughed. She is ripe for whatever we want to do. Let's rip away all her covering, no more of her mommy's prayers, or her daddy's hope. Take her on a trip she will never forget. She belongs to our master now, use her!"

One rotten deformed demon shouted, "Choke out all honor, goodness and truth. Lead her in the path blackness and death; yes murder her upbringing in the mist of her filthy thoughts."

Their laughter rang out loud and evil penetrating the thick air.

*   *   *

Rachel sat on Carol's old rocking chair waiting for any of the James family to come home. She didn't think to call before she showed up she just needed to escape her own horror surroundings. The need was so strong she rushed out, not thinking that maybe no one would be at home.

She's been sitting for over an hour watching the cars pass by not darning to leave. She wanted to find peace again in her heart, the joy and understanding she almost forgotten. Only with the help of this family could she find the hope she needed so desperately. She had it once and she would do whatever it took to get it back.

Rachel so deep in though, she didn't hear the car pull into the drive. The two large trees shield her from the view and they didn't see her either.

The excitement of Phillip Jr. coming home cause their voices to rise and Rachel finally hear them. She jumps up waiting for the car to stop. Pure excitement took control of her heart and she ran toward their car shouting before the engine shut off.

"Ms. Carol, Mr. James, I'm so glad to see you, I've missed you guys so very much! And Phillip Oh my God, how I missed you too . . ."

Phillip Jr. jumps out the car and ran around the side toward Rachel. He picked her up swinging her around in the air laughing and crying at the same time. Rachel held onto her dark large sunglasses so they wouldn't fall off her small face. She did not want them to see her scars until they were inside the house where she could explain.

"Rachel, Rachel I'm so glad to see you too. Where have you been? It's been days without a word. Did your mother tell you I called? Hot pain shot through him in his excitement. Oh my God . . . dad I hurt . . . please take her quickly!"

Phillip Sr. gently took Rachel out of his son's arms and sat her on her feet. He placed his arms around his son shoulders and helped him to walk to the door.

"Son you just got out the hospital from a car accident, take it easy, too much excitement can go both ways. You don't want to land back in the hospital do you?"

He turned to Rachel who was already hugging Carol tightly.

"Rachel we were all worried about you, so glad you came by. Let's go inside the house before our neighbors think we are hurting you or something swinging you around; like some rag doll." All laughed at the raw humor while Phillip Sr. unlocked the door. Pure joy rested on them as they enter the house hugging each other.

After cold drinks and snacks were made, the couples sat down at the kitchen table.

"Honey what was wrong with you? Did you have the flu?"

A dark cloud covers Rachel's half hidden face and unwanted tears rushes down. She started too wipe them away when Phillip Jr. took her hand and held it.

"Rachel it's okay. You are safe now. Nothing can hurt you. What happened to you? Did your mother give you my message?"

She stared at them through the lens of her dark sunglasses feeling safe for the first time in days. She saw compassion on each face and something else, love, real love, stood in their eyes. She smiled and closed her eyes. She too felt love for this dear family.

Carol spoke again, "Rachel whatever it is you know you can talk with us, we are here for you. You can depend on that. Now tell me sweetheart why the tears?"

Rachel took off the sunglasses holding her head down, while looking at her left hand lying in her lap. They still could not see all of her face.

"You might think I am crazy or something but I don't know what was wrong with me . . . I think I fell in our bushes out front of my home, or maybe something stung me. All I know is when I woke up these . . ." She looks up pulling her top exposing the ugly red black and blue marks on her entire stomach.

"Oh my goodness Rachel, what is happening to you?" Carol started to touch the hideous marks too.

"Please No! Mrs. James, do not touch them. They hurt me when touched."

"How did this happen? Phillip Jr. questioned his voice raising high.

"Remember the last night I saw you? I was on my way home . . . I do not remember everything. Anyway some evil followed me and the next thing I remembered was this. {She points to her body.} My face was worse, but my grandmother's medicine helped. These nasty bruises are not only on my stomach, but my arms, hips, legs and even on my back. They came out of nowhere. I don't understand where they came from or why they are all over me. They feel like my skin is on fire when I, or anyone tries to touch them. But that's not the worse, they . . . how can I put it? They somehow talk to me or maybe I hear voices coming from them."

"What are you saying Rachel? Who talks to you? How can open sores talk to you?"

Phillip Sr. stood up and walked near Rachel. He bent down and took a closer look at the huge weird ugly wounds that cover her arms. Some were in the shape of snakes with yellow puss oozing out.

"You say you don't know how they got there and they talk to you? I say this is demonic. Look; that was the day you got baptized, then on your way home that same day you received these opened bruises on your body. What else could it be? Not only that, but your family is into heavy witchcraft. I say the voices are demons, trying to scare you back into witchcraft. The devil is angry because you defied his rule and became a Christian. We need to pray and pray now to bind these evil forces!"

"Wait Mister James there is more I need to tell you. These things or whatever they are, move inside me like snakes. I can feel them moving around in my stomach at night. I think they want to kill me. Not only that but, I see these hideous dark images every night standing by my bed. What scares me the most is the same evil is on my father's face, in his eyes. I watch them bleed through his skin whenever he comes near me. What is happening to me?"

Rachel cried out and laid her head on the table covering her face with her arms crying brokenly.

Carol came over bend down and pulled her in her mothering arms, rocking her and quoting 'Psalm 91' . . . Surely He shall deliver thee from the snare of the fowler, and from the noisome pestilence. She quoted the entire Psalm before either Phillip Sr. or Junior said a word.

The reading of Psalm quieted Rachel's spirit and peace flowed through her as she rested in Carol's loving arms.

Phillip Jr. pushed Rachel's sleeve up and lightly touched the red marks. It burned his hand and he jumped back with a howl.

"Hey son, what happened?"

"Dad those marks or whatever it is on Rachel's body burned me too."

He pointed to her arms before rushing over to the sink and running cold water over his burning hand. Phillip Sr. cautiously touched the bruises on Rachel's arms to see for himself. He felt the burning sensation he too snatched his hand back quickly rubbing the pain in his hand.

"My God what in the world are these bruises? I have never seen or felt anything close to this."

Carol looked down at Rachel's face. The tears returned in her eyes.

"Honey it's going to be alright. No weapon formed against you shall prosper. You are a child of the living King and Jesus paid the price for your healing, inside and out. All you need to do is trust in Him with all your heart. You know Rachel, the enemy is out to steal, kill and destroy, but honey greater is He that is in you than he that is in the world. Do you understand?"

She lightly held Rachel's chin up and looked intently in her eyes, paused for a moment and continued speaking.

"Rachel where is that smile we all have come to know and love?"

Rachel stared into Carol's face smiling thinly. The peace returned and rested once again in her spirit. Deep within her, she knew no matter what she faced Jesus would be there and keep her in perfect peace.

"Rachel we need to pray now. This is spiritual warfare coming against you."

"I'm ready mister James, I knew the voices were not good, but my mother told me they were my guarding angles. She said to listen to them they would help me be safe. Now I know she is wrong, they want my life."

"That's because you parents are witches and into witchcraft!" Phillip Jr. shouted above the running water.

"The devil is anger because you brought salvation into a home full of demonic deeds and deceit. He out to destroy you but Jesus came to set you free. You are not alone. Where there is two touching and agreeing God is in the mist. One can put 1000 demons to fleet and two can put 10,000 demons to fleet. We are four guests how many we will put to fleet. I'm going to get our Bibles."

Phillip Sr. went upstairs and brought back Carol's and his study Bibles. Phillip Jr. pulled his out of his suitcase still in the living room sitting on the floor.

"Dad why does Rachel have to go home later, can she stay with us until she is stronger to fight this thing?"

"Son, we have no say in this, but we can ask her parents."

"Ask them Rachel can you spend the night here. I don't want you going back there until it's safe, and that might never be."

Rachel sat up ready for prayer. She wanted so badly to stay over but deep inside she already knew that would be impossible. How can she get them to agree? What would she say without lying?

CHAPTER TWELVE

S harron sat on her bed packing her lacy hot pink and black underwear. She added her sexy red baby doll set. She hummed to herself as she chose short low cut dresses from her large closet.

"Let see, what else would I need, oh yes shoes to match, maybe a light coat in case it is chilly."

Her mind went back to the first time she met David. It's been over a month now, wow how times flies. She wished every one of those days could have been spent with David but this man wanted to date other as well. That will soon change, she thought.

"David is going to be mine and only mine, I'll see to that. I'll wear the right perfume tonight, 'mid-night madness from Paris' yes, the smell is supposed to drive men wild and wild is exactly what I have in mind."

Her cell phone rang three times before she realized and reached for it laying on her nightstand, saw it was David number and answered in her seductive tone.

"Why hello lover boy, I was just thinking about you, some arousing thoughts I might add."

"Arousing you say don't be shame of thoughts like that. I like a women who knows how to please, but sweetheart I'm afraid I have bad news for this weekend."

"Bad news, what is it Davie?"

"A case I've been working on I thought wasn't needed until next Friday, I was told is going to trial the middle of the week. I got to finish my research this weekend. Sorry love maybe we can go next weekend."

"Oh no David, I was so looking forward to seeing you. Can you do half of it and finish before it's due in court?"

"Half won't do. He laughed; I need the time to go over every possible angle. This is a very important case and we got to be ready, no slip-ups. The judge moved the case up a week earlier and there are last minute details I need to finish. Look I'll make it up to you later okay?"

"What are we going to tell Danielle? She is totally looking forward to seeing Bob."

"I talked with Bob earlier and he wants to still go with Danielle. You can go to if you like. Have some fun in Mexico."

The very thought of seeing Danielle wrapped in Bob's arms all weekend and no man for herself angered her. She twisted her lips into a frown and closed her eyes against the thoughts coming in her mind. "Not that I am jealous of her. Oh let's face it, she realized, I am very jealous of her so-called sweet innocents. She gets whatever she wants starting from her dear daddy and then there is her loving husband. That man even steals money just to give her heart's desire."

Lost in her negative thoughts, she almost forgot David was on the line. She heard him clear his throat waiting for her to answer.

"I will not be a third wheel David! I'll find something else to occupy my time thank you, but no. Maybe I'll go out tonight there are many men who finds me attractive."

"Woman, I'm sure you are right. Look, go out have some fun, because I got to get back to this case. I'll call you maybe Sunday night okay?"

"Davie, I'll be bored without you, it's not the same and it's not fair Danielle gets to see Bobby and I can't see you." She pouted.

"Calm down Sharron. You know I would go if I could. Now be a good girl and find something else to do while I'm busy. I told you if I get a free moment I'll call you Sunday."

This wasn't the response she hoped for, knowing fretting was not going to help she said.

"Okay lover, you know me I'll find something to occupy my time, be sweet and do call."

"That's my girl." He laughed and hung up.

David went back to working on his case hoping that he could find a moment or two with Sharron.

She sat on the bed with the phone still in her hand then flung it against the wall in anger. She had wanted to see David for days and now all she saw was an empty lonely room, Sharron hated being lonely. In a rage she threw the suitcase on the floor, kicked the side of her cherry wood dresser, nothing helped. He would surely pay for standing her up.

*   *   *

Mad Dog only went to school Friday to meet up with his friends. He aced his test in math yesterday always getting good grades. He knew he had a very good memory. When he was much younger his teachers informed his mother he had a very high IQ. Good thing, most of the time he was high on drugs and sleepy in class. His poor teachers did not know what to do with him, besides that they thought he was a strange kid. As long as he passed their classes, didn't cause them problems, they never cared what he did or didn't do.

Without his old friends Worm and Snake, Mad Dog felt kind of lost. He would never admit this even to himself and it bothered him. He knew he needed new friends, new followers. Someone he could control. That is why he allowed someone like needy Sandy to tag alone with him. Raymond was a different kind of specie who followed no one. Mad Dog felt he could get him to obey if he stayed around long enough. He knew this was a real challenge. Who knows maybe Raymond would be useful sometime in the future. Anyway he couldn't wait to show them around and introduce them to his new grown friend Wolf. See if Raymond could top that, Mad Dog thought.

These two new friends were different as night and day. One was a loner and the other a football jock. They had different backgrounds too. The jock was rich and the loner poor. He had met Raymond the jock after a football game last year, never said much to him until now, even though he was in two of his classes this semester. Sandy, Raymond sidekick came with the package.

Sandy, a tall skinny, sad soul, who for craved attention, he had no siblings or close family beside his parents. Both of his parents worked as a team driving long haul trucking across County. They owned their own business but still struggled to keep a roof over their family's heads. They came home every few days tried and drain, was back on the road as quickly as possible to make all the money they could.

Sandy missed them greatly, but had to finish high school before he could accompany them. Those were the times he loved most. Being with his family meant the world to him. He hungered for a brother, sister, or anyone who could understand him and his needs.

His next-door neighbor Ms. Butler helped out all she could by cooking him a hot meal once or twice a week. She saw the young kid with his head hung every morning going off to school. She felt sorry for him but what more could she do? The arrangement help but never could fill the longing for love he had in his heart.

He is a sixteen-year-old youth, needy kid wanted people around to make him to feel loved. That is why he saw Raymond as a good friend. Even if Raymond used him, at least he could hang around with him. Most of the kids he knew saw him as a gopher, but he didn't care as long as he had friends that did matter.

Raymond a leader has most kids eating out of his hand, handsome, smart, tough, and strong kid he knew how to charm them. That's why he liked needy Sandy, a naive follower someone who could do his biding. Everything Raymond did or said Sandy thought was so terrific.

Raymond's rich parents were the pillow of society, Show off, always having fun raiser and trying to out due others. His dad had a large stock market corporation based in San Jose', and many times he had to stay overnight to complete his business. Raymond's mother was always close at hand. She didn't want some young woman hoarding in on her husband's wealth.

They drank champagne, held business parties and even when they were in town stayed out late many nights. Nothing stopped their social life not even their son as long as he brought in good grades and didn't embarrass them. They had high hopes for him the day he would run his father's company, when he finished college that is.

His family embraced the new age movement it was a way for them too expressed themselves. All their friends felt the same even their son Raymond. He never did attend any Churches, his upbringing never allowed the Bible into his home, so it was easy for him to fall into demonic temptations of all kinds.

Raymond had one sister who attended the 'University of Purdue.' She had two more years to go before graduation. She majored in Science, had no intentions of working for their dad. This left a lot of pressure on Raymond, because he wanted to play professional football not work in his old man's business.

Always left to his own devices, Raymond did whatever he please just the way he liked it. Unlike Sandy he loved his freedom. He came and went at his pleasure. No one told him what to do.

Raymond was in two of Mad Dog's classes. Only lately did he become friends with this weird kid called Mad Dog. Yes he thought Mad Dog was strange, like the others students but most intriguing too, a person with his own ideas who didn't take crap from anybody, just like him.

"Hey wait up Mad Dog."

"Say what took you so long class was over ten minutes ago."

"Raymond my man, you know me always got something else to do. Hey Sandy, what's up?"

The guys greeted each other in their usually teen way and left the school building headed to the parking lot.

"Got some place I want you guys to go. Are you game?"

"Hell yeah, where ever you go I'll go." Sandy said without shame.

"Cool, let's blow, your car or mine, Raymond offered."

"Let's take your ride Mad Dog said."

He remembered his last two trips to Wolf's places and that large bird he never could find or whatever it was, he wanted none of that slime on his clean windshield this time.

"No sweat, I'm staved let's stop by and grab some chicken from 'Mama's chicken' place, better yet burgers form the Bistro."

"No chicken? He grinned. First follow me home to drop off my ride. I don't live far from the Hamburger Bistro. We can eat there then head over to my friend's place okay."

Sandy jumped in the back of Raymond black SUV. He sat in the back where he could lay down in the seat while listening to Raymond's I-pod.

After Raymond followed Mad Dog home, the three headed for the Hamburger Bistro. Raymond asked him about the place they were headed.

"What's so special about this store, that you want us to go on a Friday when we could be seeing some hot chicks; dude?"

Mad Dog leaned closer in his seat toward Raymond grinning.

"This is a trip you guys wouldn't want to miss. He is way cool, got some strange ways and stranger ideas but the dude is something man. Like he can look at you and you know he's seeing into your soul. Creepy, I can't explain it, you got to see this for yourselves; plus he got this ugly thing . . . look when you get there you'll see."

It didn't take long for the boys to get to the burger joint. The place was almost empty, just a couple in a booth with eyes only for each other, an old man, and a mother with two screaming kids. The couple was seated in a booth behind them kissing and they never looked up.

Sandy spoke . . .

"Hey guys check them out kissing. By the way could someone shoot me a five, I don't have cash."

"You never have cash. Raymond joked. Hey, it's okay dude I got you, don't I always? Look here comes' the waitress. I'm buying Mad Dog, so put your money away and say what you want before I change my mind."

Sandy smelled the fresh burgers and fries, his stomach growled as he realized he hadn't eaten this morning before class. He was grateful to have a friend like Raymond who always had money to spend and was very generous with it.

He wished his parents made more money. There was never enough for things like fast food.

"Bring three double cheese burgers, three large fries, and three strawberry milkshakes."

"Can I get two double burgers Raymond? I didn't eat breakfast this morning you know cash flow low."

"Sure Sandy, two it is my man, anything else?"

"No that will be enough for now thanks."

Later that day, everyone had left but the young couple. The boys finished eating sat back chatting about this and that, when the couple holding hands finally walked out into the bright sun light. The waitress came with the bill. Mad Dog looked around saw no other customers pulled out one of the twenty he gotten from Wolf. He wanted to see what would happen if the waitress took the money. He laid it on the table, looked at the middle age, graying, over weight limping waitress daring her with his eyes to take it with a slick smile on his face.

"Hey man let me pay. You can buy another time."

Raymond pulled out his credit card and placed it on the waitress' tray. He reached for the twenty. Before his hand could touch it, Mad Dog grabbed it.

"I told you I'll pay. Put your plastic card away. I'll even pay for the tip."

He smiled, his eyes never leaving the waitress's face.

She gave him a cold frown. Her patience was wearing thin, on her feet all day she was not in a joking mood. She thought, "Everyday these young punks come in here like they own the place. They don't tip much and expect you to wait on them hand and foot I'm sick of it. There is something about this one, his eyes I don't trust they looks evil. I just want them to hurry and get out of here."

"I don't care a hoot who pays as long as someone does."

She rolled her eyes reached out grabbed the twenty. A feeling like red-hot poker raced up her hand. It torched its way into a huge red blister, swelled in seconds. She quickly dropped the money, as the pain took hold. She shouted at them, holding onto the lower part of her arm, trying not to panic.

"What kind of game are you sick puppies' playing! I'm calling the owner and have you boys thrown out of here now! No the cops they will get to the bottom of this!"

Sandy jumped up from the booth rushed toward her. She took a few steps backwards.

"Get away from me you sicko, Bill come over here quickly!"

"We're sorry lady. Look I'll get it for you."

He stooped down and picked up the twenty. Never had he experienced more excruciating pain. Hot lighting pain shoot up his arm, ran down though each of his fingers. He yelled, and fell down on his knees holding his arm at the elbow.

"Oh my god, oh my god, oh my god," he kept saying over and over, tears in his eyes.

The waitress was in shock seeing Sandy on the floor crying out in pain. Her own pain kept her immobilized. This was no joke, something was surely wrong with the money, and that boy had something to do with it. She waited for Bill the manger to come while keeping an eye on a Mad Dog.

Mad Dog picked up the cash quickly without a hint of pain. He turned hiding his sinister smile. He turned back around again.

"Get up you cry baby, we should have left you at home with your mama."

He shook his head, pulled up Sandy from the floor and lightly backed into the waitress at the same time. She didn't have time to move out the way. When his body meet hers all pain suddenly stopped, both the waitress and Sandy felt as if they awaken from a bad nightmare. It was as if they never felt any pain, like a trick of the mind.

Reasoning with herself she thought, "Sometime your mind can plays tricks on you. No this was no trick maybe he put some sort of hex spell on me. If he did, why did his friend experience what I experience? Whatever is happening, I'm staying as far away from that voodoo person as I possibly can." Fear rested in herm eyes.

"Will you just pay your bill and leave! An don't give me anymore that money the credit card will do."

Mad Dog sat back in his booth, took a cold fry from Raymond's plate popped it in his mouth.

"I don't know what all the fuss is about. You guys are tripping. Raymond, man, go ahead and pay the waitress and let blow this joint."

Raymond who been sitting and watching in total amazement with his credit card still on the waitress tray, he walked with her while she limped over to the cashier signed for the bill and gave her a large tip thanking her for her service.

The owner had been busy in the back stuffing frozen goods in the refrigerator from the freezer.

Noise level is low from the back of the store he could only heard some of the commotion. He walked over questioning the youth.

"Is there some problem I can help you boys with?"

"No sir we were just leaving Mad Dog said."

"I think you have better stay out of this place until you can keep down the noise. I could hear you all the way in the back. I don't know what happened out here but from the loud commotion it is better you don't come back. Do I make myself clear?"

"Hey, you don't have to repeat a word mister we are leaving. This place sucks anyway."

The owner stood tall folded his arms waiting for the boys to exit his place. Whatever the problem was he would get to the bottom of it.

Mad Dog grinned at him and winked at the waitress standing behind the counter. She turned away pretending to be busy, frighten of the boys. The young men gathered there things, and left the burger place without a backward glance.

CHAPTER THIRTEEN

Agnes looked nice with her fresh short cut perm sitting on the sofa, dressed in her good navy and white top with her white slacks. All dressed up with nowhere to go. She had intended to visit some friends after getting her hair done, but Nicky wanted to go straight home said something about getting dinner on the table for Ward.

She turned off the TV when her favorite soap opera ended, walked into the kitchen sat down restless on the gray bar stool at the counter. There was a pitcher of ice tea waiting and she poured a glass for herself. In her rude normal voice asked.

"Nicky, where in the world is Rachel? When a commercial came on I went in her room looking to see if she was okay; found her bed empty. First I thought maybe the bathroom, so I returned to my show, when another commercial came on, I looked in the bathroom to see if she was there; no Rachel. Assuming she was with you I came in here. So where is she?"

Nicky busy chopping carrots and potatoes put them in the stew. She really didn't want to get started with her mother. She already knew what Agnes would say and arguing about it would not help. She frowned kept her head bent over her task. Maybe if she said nothing her mom would shut up. That would be the day.

"She was feeling much better so I allowed her to check on her classes she missed, she should be home any minute now mother."

Agnes stood up pounded her old arthritis fist on the counter splashing the tea in her glass.

"You let her leave knowing she wasn't completely well? Nicky where is your head? That girl needs more rest and my healing medicine, she should not be out of bed and certainly not out and about doing who knows what."

"It's okay mother calm down, she has her cell with her and I'm sure if she feels ill she will call us, or come home."

"Nicky we don't know what all happened to that gal fore we got home. She might have fallen in those rose bushes, hit her head hard you know she can't remember how she got those ugly bruises all over her body. Have you thought of what her teachers might think when they see it? Of course not, cause you didn't think!"

Nicky didn't stop what she was doing, nor did she look at her mother. She allowed her mind to go on melt down to keep from screaming. If she pretended not to hear maybe Agnes would just shut up.

"Nicky yesterday the girl stayed in bed all day and we had to help her to the toilet, how can you think she is better now?"

Agnes grabbed an apple from the bowl on the left side of counter and threw it across the room at her daughter. It hit the wall and splattered in pieces. Nicky took a deep breath hurried to clean it up before Ward came home. On her knees, her face flushed tired and getting angry she tried to calm herself. She spoke softly when the anger subsided.

"Mother will you stop it, Rachel is not a little child, she knows when she feels better, calm down she is coming home for dinner and will be here any moment. If you want to handle food you can help me finish dinner before Rachel and Ward comes home, I could sure use the help."

Ring, ring, ring, the phone chimed. Agnes picked it up speaking in her dry hard voice said,

"Hello, oh it you Ward. We were just mentioning you. Yes, Nicky is here, what? . . . Okay."

Nicky got off her knees, wiped her hands with the towel hanging on the stove door handle, fluffed her hair before realizing Ward couldn't see her. She hurried over to the phone, just before she grabbed it Agnes boasted,

"He hung up, just wanted you to know he's not coming home for dinner again tonight. Said something about people coming over, late night, you know the story he is always coming up. You ask me, he's up to no good. Probably with that young trash we saw him with, you remember her I'm sure." She grinned slyly.

Outrages despair churned in the pit of Nicky stomach. She nested in her self-pity, the miserable unreturned love from her husband and her mother was more than she could handle. Licking her pride, the swelling tides of misery took over her mind, body and wretched heart. Her grief was her everyday existence. Her heart wanted to scream out her pain. Instead she pushed it down inside. There was no one she could release this too. She stopped believing in a loving caring mother whom she could talk too. Someone sweet not this heartless cold fish who sat before her grinning with pity. She felt trapped in an isolated relationship with a man whom she knew was seeing that young child, so she hid her true emotions. Calmly she said.

"I didn't ask you mother. Whatever Ward is doing it's between him and me. It's none of your business, so stay out of our private life okay?"

"Private my foot! I see what's going on around here. That man is cheating on you and you know it . . ."

The phone rang again, Nicky hoping it was Ward race to grab it before her harden mother could.

"Hello . . . oh hi honey, are you alright? Umm, when will you be home? Rachel I don't think that's a good idea, I've already stated dinner and . . . Rachel who are these people and what do they want with you?"

She reluctantly listened to her daughter explanation before she sternly said,

"No I forbid it, now you come straight home before your dad finds out about this."

She listened as Rachel tried to reason with her but her mind was made up. She needed someone to dump her frustration on. Rachel just happened to call at the right moment.

Nicky hung up the phone dreading to face her mother knowing what she would say. Agnes she knew listened to every word that was said with contempt. Well Nicky figured she might as well get it over with. Before she could utter a sound Agnes spoke up.

"Nicky where in hell is Rachel? Don't give me that, you don't know crap, and why does she want to stay away from our home? Who are these folks; that's telling my granddaughter lies about us?"

"Hold on mother, you are getting upset over nothing, nobody said anything about lies. Where do you get such nonsense?"

Nicky sat down at the counter next to Agnes. She tried to take her mother's hand, but Agnes drew back quickly. She thinly smiled at her mother and explained to her.

"A few months ago Rachel confided in me about some boy she liked at school. From time to time she met him for dates. She never mentioned his name or brought him home to meet me, but I think it's the same boy who called the other day when she was so ill. Anyway, I think he has something to do with her wanting to stay over night."

"What! You mean to tell me some no good boy wants our Rachel to hop in the sack with him, and all you can say is; I forbid it? If your head was screwed on right you would tell her to get her behind home right now! You know how these young punks think all they want is that girl's body. Then have some unwanted child . . ."

"Mother, Rachel is not like that and you know it. One thing I know is my daughter she has good sense. That is not why she wanted to stay over. His family invited her to stay for dinner and study her missed school lessons I guess. Anyway I know Rachel is smart, so she will pick up whatever she missed without spending the night away from home with strangers."

Agnes pointed her boney finger in Nicky's face, twisted her nose and curled her lips in a snarl. She stared mean and hateful at Nicky with scorn in her dark eyes.

"Now you listen to me missy, you let that girl run all over the place without knowing where she goes or with whom. You don't know a thing about her where-a-bouts, and what kind of parents would ask a young girl to spend the night at their home without knowing her folks? These young hoodlum these days, are all up too no good!"

Agnes abruptly stopped talking she massaged her aching temple, and felt the strain and pain forming in her back area. For several moments she didn't move or speak.

"Dog-gone-it, now look what you gone and done."

What did I do mother? Are you alright, can I help you?"

Nicky stood up quickly reaching for Agnes' arm to help support her. Agnes pushed her advances away forcefully. The last thing she needed from Nicky was her sympathy or pity.

"Leave me alone you good for nothing fool just get out of my way, will you."

Agnes was determined to do this herself. She took her time and got up from her seat, without another word she made her way slowly around the counter out the kitchen, into her bedroom. Agnes fist hurt from the pounding she gave it on the counter top. Her back hurt from sitting on the backless bar stool too long and her legs ached from not enough blood circulation. She was in no mood to discuss Rachel or

Ward any further. Her need to rest overwhelmed her and her bed seemed the best idea.

A harsh bitterness crept inside Nicky heart. It twisted around her and sat beside the grief that saturated her spirit. She sank between the folds swallowing the lump that formed in her throat. Hopelessness joined them and oppression followed. She sat back down begin to moan rocking her weary body back and forth. The pain in her heart was unbearable. The spirit of depression laughed making room within her soul.

*   *   *

Rachel stood rigid biting her top lip. She closed her eyes to keep from crying and said in a low tone.

"Okay mom, I'll see you in about an hour."

She turned back to face her beloved friends. With a bit of sadness in her voice she told them what her mom said.

"Rachel, your mom won't even let you stay for dinner?" Junior sounded disappointed.

"That's about the size of it. She took Junior's hand. Can we pray before I leave again?"

Junior put his arms around Rachel. "You bet sweetheart."

"Anytime, honey, Carol said, I am so sorry your mother will not let you stay over. You have too realize, she never met us or have a clue about Christians. I'm sure she has her concerns. Maybe once she gets a chance to know us her feelings will change."

Rachel looked up with shock, and shook her head no.

"Even if she said it was okay Mrs. James, my dad and granny will never agree to it. Junior, that's why I never allowed you to come over or call my home, because I know what they would say. I did once mention you to my mother some month's back, I never told her who you were just that you were a boy from school I liked. I hope she doesn't put two and two together. She would have a fit if she knew I was seeing a Christian boy. You know, when I'm around you guys I feel safe. Isn't that strange? Don't get me wrong, my family always been there for me, but lately I feel afraid of them, and I don't understand why. I never had this feeling before. It's like I don't know them anymore. Especially my father, he . . . he . . . . what am I trying to say, I guess I want to say he is very wicked. I never realized that before."

Carol took Rachel by the hand and led her to the sofa. She sat down next to her with Junior on the other side. Phillip Sr. returned from the bathroom and sat in his favor brown recliner across from them.

"That is because you were different then. Now you are set apart, free from witchcraft. You are a new creation in Christ. Evil can never hold hand with good. We understand these conflicting spirits, they are truth and lies twisted in your brain. All your life you believed your family had a gift to use to help others. Now you know that so-called-gift is from the enemy. Honey what you feel is normal because you have the light of God living in your spirit, and your eyes are opened. Your family is into darkness, even if they don't see it that way. The two will never mix. The devil is angry because you came out of the darkness into God's marvelous light! You have been set free from sin and shame. Now greater is He that is in you than he that is in the world, remember that."

"That's right Rachel, Phillip Sr. injected. The devil knows you have the power to defeat him. He is more determined to cause trouble, because he wants you back into slavery. That is why you put on the whole armor of God, so you can fight and conquer the enemy with faith!"

"Tell me how Mr. James, I need to know how."

"When you got saved you received power from God. But if you don't use that power, or understand it Satan will use fear to control and torment your mind. This is his way to scare you so you won't cast him out. That's why you need to rebuke the devil whenever he tries to come at you with fear. Beloved, putting on the whole armor of God is the only way to stay strong. I want you to read over and over Ephesians chapter 6 starting at verse 10 and apply it to your life. You are in a great spiritual warfare fight, and need all your weapons at all times."

The Bible says, "For we wrestle not against flesh and blood, but against principalities against spiritual rulers of darkness of this word, against spiritual host of wickedness in the heavenly places." Carol added.

"That is found in verse 12. Always, remember our God is so much more; stronger than the enemy, He gave you His strength to overcome. You just need to use it.

Carol continued, "No weapon formed against you shall prosper as long as you keep your faith strong. That is the biggest weapon, faith in God!"

For over two hours the four sat and discussed the verses on faith, power and strength from the book of Ephesians and 2cd. Timothy 1:7.

Time passed quickly, before anyone realized it, Danielle came walking up the walkway with her children in toll. She rang the bell several times waiting for one of her parents to open the door.

"My, what is taking them so long? I remember telling mom I'll be here at 6:30."

"Maybe grandma had to go someplace," little Tommy said looking up at his mother with concern written on his young face.

"She does later Tommy to some Church function, but see, she pointed, there is grandma car parked in the driveway. I'm sure she is home. She may be in the back yard or the bathroom and doesn't hear the door bell."

The door opened and a surprise Carol gushed, "My goodness, I almost forgot you were bringing the kids over tonight. Come in we got pizza left over from dinner there is more than enough."

Danielle hurriedly rushed the children inside. "Don't worry mother the kids ate before we came."

"But we want pizza, Sharee and Tommy squabbled."

Danielle didn't want to argue the point she just wanted to get out of there.

"If grandma has enough for you guys it is okay, but only one slice, you had your dinner and I don't want stomach aches later."

The children bounce in the door hugging their grandmother legs, each on one side. Carol stooped kissed and hugged them tightly.

Danielle stood in the doorway watching, she waved to her children and blew them kisses.

"Good-by mommy loves you. I will see you guys in two days okay?

Carol waved to her daughter shaking her head with a slight frown on her face. At that moment Junior walked in, "Hi sis, come on in. I haven't seen you in days. He stooped down to Tommy, Hey sport, he ruffed his hair; we are going to have some fun tonight."

Sharee, put her hand on her hips, what about me Uncle Phillip?

Junior grinned at the sight of her grown-up stance, Yes you too Sharee, come into the living room, Rachel is here. You too sis, I am sure she would love to see you."

Danielle backed away quickly letting the screen door close. "I'll have to see her another time little brother. Sorry I did not go to see you but, you know how I feel about hospitals. Glad you are home and feeling better." She gave him a half smile, then turned and hurried to her car before Junior could utter another word.

"Junior, can you take the children to the bathroom to wash their hands before you bring them to eat? Also watch them for a couple of hours while your father and I meet Bernard and Cam at Church for the Marriage class?"

Phillip smiled his answer to his mother.

"Well, you guys it's just us tonight. Is that okay?"

Junior bent low and tickles the kids fondly. They tumbled to the floor in laughter, rolling and kicking covering there ticklish areas. Carol laughed until her eye tear. This was the times she loved most, her family getting together having pure fun. She wished her relationship with her daughter were like this.

They use to have such fun when she was younger. Where did the time go? She thought.

Grandpa and Rachel came in and joined the fun. Everyone took turns tickling and swinging the kids around, and around, laughing and joking.

Rachel could not help but wish her family were half this carefree and loving. The dread of going home pressed down on her spirit even deeper, she forced the negative feeling away. She needed to bask in this joy and happiness for as long as she could, home would have to wait.

*   *   *

Danielle smiled and felt no guilt on her way to rendezvous with her lover. Not even her best friend Sharron, whom she knew wasn't going could bring her emotions down. Secretly she was glad the events happened the way they did, having Bob all too herself was pure magic. His lips on hers, his strong arms holding her tightly, this was no accident, this was her dream come to life. She slammed on the brakes hard when the light turned red.

"My goodness, I got to keep my mind on my driving before I have an accident."

She drove more carefully about 15 more minutes before turning into his parking space. She quietly called his cell. "I'm here."

*　　*　　*

The youth talked nonstop on their ride to Ward's shop. They joked, poked, laughed, and kidded until they reached the bewitched, thick, grove where the road twisted and large trees stretched out toward the road on both sides.

Raymond asked,

"How much longer Mad Dog, I don't like these trees. They look weird and creepy."

"We will arrive soon Sandy. It is up this road about 10 more minutes, keep cool."

Something big and heavy hit into the back of the SUV with a hard thump.

"Hey dude what bump into my SUV did you guys feel that?"

Sandy sat up straight, looked out the back window, saw nothing out of the ordinary. "I sure felt something pushing into us, but I don't see anything."

"Hey guys don't freak, it was probably some dumb, now dead animal, you didn't see, cause it's getting dark Mad Dog said."

Sandy frowned, "I like animals, what kind do you think it was a deer? It must have been huge don't you think?"

"I don't know, but I'm going to find out, cause it hit into my ride."

Raymond pulled over to the side of the road, grabbed a flash lighter from his glove compartment for no lights were in this area.

"You guys can stay put, it won't take long. We could have hit against one of those long braches sticking out, be right back."

He got out shining his flashlight in front of him backing toward the rear of his SUV. He stood for a few moments staring into the darkness all around him, and saw nothing. Some distance noise came in his ears, a strange sound coming from the woods beyond. He listened more intensely, shining his light across the road then quickly back again on the other side. All at once he noticed on both sides, through the tall trees movements of some kind. It looked like some type of hidden infestation of weird animals. They appeared like see through mirrors reflecting images of another kind. As he looked more, closer, he saw giant black fingers, twisting in all shapes and sizes moving fast toward him. Was it the trees playing tricks on his eyes, his imagination getting the better of him? The trees did remind him of large boney arms with arthritic fingers reaching out to grab him. Still he was spooked by some terror larking about. Raymond ducked quickly behind his SUV turning off the light and couching down low, heart in his throat.

The foul air, stale and nauseating made him want to throw up. "What is that smell, he wondered?" Suddenly something huge and hairy rushed at Raymond with brunt force from the opposite side, knocking him back hard against one of the large trees. His body went sailing in the stale air before he hit face first against the oak. With the wind knocked out of him he laid shaking and bleeding. The evil licked the air from his lungs and squeezed his heart tightly. Wheezing hard, Raymond tried to catch his breath and fight this unseen horror, to no avail. Too weak to stand Raymond lay on the ground thrashing around. His arms fling about trying to knock off the evil that sat on his chest.

Surrounding him deep in the unseen world the demons lurked, slithered and moved about him and his SUV laughing. They infested this area of ownership. Their shadowy demented images snort their outrageous displeasure at the youth who dared to come into their territory. Their offensive smelly revulsion choked out any fresh air long ago within this part of the woods. In their dimension the lesser demon spoke in his cruel threatening voice.

"We will show him not to invade our area!"

A huge flaming red eyed, hairy ape, looking creature stood next to Raymond, staring with sharp blades of iron in his eyes.

"Don't worry he is one of ours now. We will use him to bring in more stupid fools for our master. But let's torment his mind first this will keep him under our control forever."

"O-o-o-oh let me have that coward friend of his, the one name Sandy, wouldn't he be a better choice don't you agree?"

"We will use them all!"

They roared with hideous laughter. The sound penetrated the darkness causing each of the boys to hear the echoing evil loud noise in the air.

Raymond's flashlight flew from his hand and hit a rock smashing into pieces. The blood oozed freely from his jagged cut he received on the side of his face that hurt badly. Very carefully his trembling hand reached out to touch it before rugged hands grabbed his legs dragging him into the woods with savage force. He cried out in pain and fear as his body raked over rocks and needle brush. His screams blended with their cruel laughter. They continue to rake his body over rocky ground through thick thorny backwoods briery. For several minutes they dragged his limp body through the dark damp woods. Then savagely picked him up and threw him over a deep clip. Raymond now almost incoherent, in a state of numb shock, fainted before his weak being hit the bottom about fourteen feet down.

Just before the demons were about to toss him farther down, the Prince of darkness who stood looking over his domain from his observation post stopped them. He needed more gullible people like Raymond, people full of self-righteousness who engaged in the unknown with a thirst for power. He swarm over on his broken wings too the area where part of his army held Raymond. His hostility rang out angrily.

"Let the boy continue on to his destructed destination, we got better use for him later. What I want is those mighty self righteous Christians, what are you doing to bring them down?"

The demonic sergeant dropped Raymond on the damp ground, speaking in a timid tone. "We are busy scheming laying snares as fast as we can to entangle them into your web master."

"I want you to do much more! Now go get me those SOULS from every area of this town! I want them from the NORTH, SOUTH, EAST and WEST. All who think they are strong in HIM I want them NOW!"

Many rushed off flying toward prayer meetings, and homes. A few flew back to the SUV for more cunning adventure. While some other demons crouched down in front of the 'Shepherds Way in Church,' waiting for service to end. Still other flew to other Churches, restaurants, hospitals, and anywhere they could find people believing in the word of God. Still more flew to clubs, bars, street corners where drunks hung, crack houses, jails anywhere there were empty souls lived so they could pour out their vengeance and keep the lost, lost.

"Did you hear that strange sound? It sounded like many animals laughing or something. Sandy looked out the window trying to see into the blackness of night, for no stars shown in the sky.

"Nah, maybe it's your over active brain playing tricks on you again. Here take another hit from this little baby it will make you see into another world man. This stuff is real cool.

Mad Dog passed the toxic drug to Sandy. He quickly indulged himself getting the high he needed trying to cast out the fear from his heart.

"Hey Mad Dog what's taking Raymond so long, do you think we need to go outside and look for him?"

"Cool it Sandy, it's a probability he had to piss, sit tight man he'll be back when he's done."

Sandy could not contain the high he needed but became more and more restless and nervous as he twisted in his seat on a full bladder. He was paranoid because he couldn't see outside the SUV it was much too dark and he need to relieve himself now.

"Man, I gotta piss, I'll just step out next to those trees for a moment, if you keep the door open, I can see from the dome light, be back in a jip."

Mad Dog had his I-pod listening to trashy rap laid back with his eyes closed. "Do your business man, just do your business."

Sandy grabbed the handle of the door and tried to open it. He tried several times before he asked for assistance.

"Hey Mad Dog, what's with the door? I can't get it to open."

Mad Dog opened his eyes, shook his head. "Are you trying to kill my high man? He pulled on the door handle and true it was locked from the outside. How?

"Sandy I bet Raymond is controlling the locks from his key. Man what a joker he turned out to be."

Mad Dog knocked on the glass window. "Okay, you got us now open this freaking door, Sandy's got to take a leak."

"I told you the door want open and I need to pee, bad." Sandy shook the handle more violently, but the door remained locked.

"This is tripping me out man, what kind of game . . ."

A loud prolonged groan came from the outside of the SUV. The sound raddled the windows and knocked against the door. Sandy jumped back and coward down in his seat covering his head. He wet his pants from fight. His body shook so badly he thought the van must be in action.

Mad Dog also freaked but he didn't intend for Sandy to know it. He sat back in the front seat closed his eyes and turned up the volume on his head set the rap tune cursed life and blessed death.

The sound outside turned to an eerie echo that got louder and louder carried through the wind racing across space. It sounded like haunting horrifying ill meaning wolves out for blood.

Sandy covered his ears whimpering and choking on his own saliva. The air cracked like thunder causing Sandy to scream.

"STOP IT STOP IT I can't stand it anymore. MAMA, DAD, HELP ME PLEASE."

He hid on the floor beneath the back seat in a tight ball white as a ghost, far beyond frighten. His heartbeat so fast he knew he could die out in this no mans land, with a cold fish like Mad Dog sitting in the front. How would his family ever find his remains if those wolves eat him?

"Mad Dog shouted. Shut up your freaking mouth Sandy! If I knew you were such a baby needing your mommy and daddy, I would never have invited you. Raymond is behind all this I tell you! You know he's rich! Probably got this whole thing rigged up to some loud speakers, controlling it from the outside. Sit tight Sandy He'll stop in a moment okay?"

Suddenly the noise stopped, everything became silent.

"See I told you now watch what I say, he'll come back as if nothing happened and laugh at us for being scared, so chill will ya."

"Were you scared too Mad Dog?"

"Shut your freaking mouth, no I was not scared!"

Sandy lay very still for a moment listening peeking through his fingers. When no sound was heard he slowly rose from the floor and sat on the seat in the wet puddle he just made.

"Hey dude can I have a beer?"

"Want some rum instead? I stole it from my mom's stash this afternoon."

Mad Dog took out the Rum from his backpack and passed it back to Sandy. Sandy torn off the cap and took a long swig. The warm liquid burned going down but Sandy needed that to remind him he was alive and well.

Suddenly the door opened and both boys jumped clear on the opposite side of their seats. Sandy choked on the rum going down the wrong pipe. He sputtered gasping for fresh air as the liquor splashed out his mouth, while falling against the door.

"Wait you guys, look it me! Raymond got in front breathing hard. I must have fallen down some steep hill or something, cause I hit the side of my face and I'm bleeding pretty badly. My backside hurts also."

"MAN, WHERE IN THE HELL WERE YOU? Mad Dog shouted.

"That's a good question. When I went outside to see what hit my vehicle, I saw something weird moving through those trees from both sides. I couldn't see what or who it was. All know is I must have hit my head backing away and fell down that steep embankment. He pointed in the direction he had been. I can't remember exactly what happened next. When I opened my eyes it was so dark so very dark, I couldn't see my way back. It hurt to walk so I crawled. I had to feel for the trees and listen for your sound. Mad Dog, I tell you we got to leave this crazy area now! Something or someone does not want us here!

"You mean to tell me you didn't hear that horrible noise earlier? That noise almost busted my eardrums, we thought it was you."

"I heard Sandy screaming if that's what you mean. I follow his voice and here I am. Look you guys let's just get out of this god-forsaken place. Hey grab me that rag from my grove compartment. The sooner we get started the better I'll feel. I need an aspirin badly my head is killing me."

Mad Dog sat up straighter, shook his head trying to figure this out, 'nothing else could possibly happen, they should continue on to Ward's. At least he could give Raymond some aspirins.'

"Say why don't we go on to Ward's place, I'm sure he can give you some aspirins. Besides he is expecting us, it's only about a couple of miles up this winding road. It would be much faster than going back."

"I'm not a person who scares easy, but man something is not right around here. Are you sure you want to continue on this road? Is there some other way we can get there?"

"This is the only way I know to his place. Are you a pussycat Raymond, afraid of a little darkness?"

He teased Raymond so unmercifully that he gave in, and decided to continue on toward Ward establishment. Sandy kept quiet, hidden in the backseat with chills running up his spine. He was freaked about the whole ordeal, but didn't want to seem like a frighten child.

The demon Sergeant roared, "These stupid fools see they are puppets in our hands. They are delusional being full of drugs and alcohol just the way we want them. Stay with the naïve boys. I got bigger problems to face with that girl Rachel. She thinks she can get a way from us, but she will soon find out she can't."

The large deformed demon flew low along side the SUV, watching the youth as they drove. He spat on the top of the van some dark green slime. His hate for the boys compelled him to defecate on the hood of the SUV also. He belched as he spoke . . .

"Why don't you follow those other Christian families? Some are not as strong as they supposed to be. We can use the weaker ones to confuse the stronger ones by deception, anger, need, and weakness. Let's destroy all their hope through their finances, jobs, and healings. Then we will see if they believe in the goodness of their God!

Chapter Fourteen

D avid worked endlessly on the case he had to prepare for court. His back and neck ached from bending over his PC for hours. He rubbed his neck and turned his head from side to side trying to get the kinks out. He stood up and stretched his arms over his head. It was time for a break, because his poor body could not take anymore. Besides his words were beginning to run together, he wasn't going to get any more work done tonight.

He needed a cold beer and his cushion recliner. David turned off the PC and went into his neat black, gray and white kitchen. He opened the refrigerator, found it empty of beer. It dawn on him, he drank the last one last night. Disappointed, he closed the refrigerator said out loud.

"Well I could pick up another six pack or head down to the bar and grill for a couple of hours, yes, I think some food, music and relaxation that should do the trick."

He rubbed his head and headed to the bedroom grabbed a clean shirt, brushed his hair, and teeth, got his keys and headed for his BMW. He drove the few miles to the local bar and grill, parked and went inside.

David found just the table he wanted, in a dark corner where he could chill, see people and not be disturbed. He though about calling Sharron and asking her to join him, but the thought pasted. Tonight he didn't feel like her kind of company. He liked her, but at times she was a bit more than he wanted to handle, tonight was one of those times. The case he worked on was a high profile that demanded his full attention and Sharron would demand that too.

Thinking of work he thought, "I better have only a couple of beers then head back home got to keep my mind clear."

The young blond waitress of twenty-three sashayed over, "What's your poison Mr.?" She gave David a flirtatious smile.

David eyed her clothes and returned her smile. "Just, a lite-beer will do; wait please add a grill ham and cheese."

"Got it." She walked back to her station with David's eyes following her every move.

When she was completely out of sight he leaned back in his booth, closed his eyes thinking. "Not bad, not bad at all. She must be new, cause I haven't seen her before and I thought I knew all the local babes."

Marlena, wearing tight dark green jeans, and a cream sexy low cut top, came in and stood at the far end of the bar. She tossed her long dark hair back, and looked around for an empty table, when her eyes caught sight of David. She moved smoothly like the dancer she was over to his table. David still sitting back with eyes closed did not see her approach.

"Hey lover, I thought that was you, sitting all along in the corner. No girl tonight?"

David jumped at the sound of her melting sexy voice. He stood up and gave her a big tight squeeze.

"Marlena, you look beautiful, where have you been, sit down. What are you doing on this side of town?"

She laughed, "One question at a time. I'm visiting a friend who wasn't feeling well. She is one of the dancers who work with me at the 'Pink feathers.' She lives just up the road, in those new cute duplex apartments, you know where they are I'm sure. I brought her some chicken soup, even though I have not eaten myself. That's why I'm here to get a bite. What about you?"

Her incredible deep blue green eyes seemed to look right into his soul. He couldn't get enough of her stunning beauty nor did he want too. Looking into her eyes he spoke.

"That's very endearing of you cooking soup for a friend in need. You my lady are so thoughtful. He drew her close and kissed her lips before she said a word. David continued; as for me being here, I am working on a demanding case I need next week, got thirsty, and hungry so here I am."

She cross her long shapely legs, and purred in his ear, "I didn't say cook sweetheart, I said, I brought soup over for her. It came from a can, but thanks for the sweet remarks."

His body responded to her closeness. He wanted to tear off her clothes, and take her right then and there. With all the noise, music, and people, he didn't care. He chewed on his upper lip while rubbing her thigh upward trying to control his emotions. Food was the farthest thing from his mind now. After a moment he remembered her saying she came to eat.

"You said you wanted to eat? I can have the waitress bring you over your hearts desire, well maybe not in this place."

"What ever you are having is fine with me David."

"Okay a grill ham and cheese it is."

"Sweet, make mine on rye and hold the cheese."

He motion for the waitress to come over, added some red wine to their order. After the waitress took the order, David asked.

"So what are you doing when you leave here?"

He hoped she would say go home with him. His manhood jumped at the thought. He couldn't keep his hands off her. Marlena laughed.

"Slow, down boy don't be too pushy. Let's see how the night flows."

After a few drinks, food and more laughs David asked Marlena to dance to an R & B old slow jams, she agreed. They were so enthused with each other nothing could have disturbed their sexual intimacy.

*   *   *

Sharron sat in her modern blue, white and rose-colored living room watching an old forties love story on TV trying not to be weary. But her loneliness along with boredom crape in and she soon got up turning off the set. She walked over and peeked out her condo window hoping somehow David would magically show up. She stared out into the night in deep thought. She sigh, "Oh how I miss him. I wish he would put aside his work for tonight and, come on over. It doesn't matter if just for a few hours I just want to see him. I can't seem to focus on anything but him. Why do I miss this man so much? His laughter, his arms and his, oh my where is my mind heading. I got to get out of here before I die of need. I can't stand it any longer. I know what I'll do head down to that bar and grill and grab a salad. I didn't eat earlier. I can dance with the local boys at least I want be lonely."

She hurried into the bedroom to change her clothes, comb her hair, and freshen, her makeup. She grabbed her jacket, keys and locked her door ready for some food, fun and laughter.

Fifteen minutes later she drove into the parking lot of Sam's bar and gill. She didn't notice David's car parked just two rows down. She got out, set her alarm, headed for the door and met two attractive men going inside.

"Hey beautiful, one of them said, you alone?"

Sharron gave them one of her sweetest smiles, and batted her long lashes. The two men stared with their mouths opened; at how really stunning she was.

"For now I am. I got a man waiting alone for me, but he is working tonight. So, I thought a bite and some innocent laughter might do me some good. You know what I mean?" She purred.

When the taller one could find his voice he said, "Is there any other kind?"

All three laughed.

The other guy asked; can we have some innocent fun with you? My wife is six mounts pregnant and visiting her sister in San Diego for a couple of weeks. My friend here, his wife left two months ago and we decided a few beers and as you said innocent fun was the way to go."

Sharron thought they were sweet enough for distraction from her loneliness. Two good old boys from Queen City out for fun just like her. What is the harm?

"By the way what do they call you boys? Mine name is Sharron, not Sharon like most people want to say."

"Sam, and this here is Nathan." He pointed to his friend.

"Glad to meet you." Sharron held out her delicate hand both men took turns kissing it.

"Oh my, what sweet gents you are. I'm glad we met tonight."

Sam, the married man made a joke about the place having the same name as his. "Come into my greasy spoon, you lovely lady, and I'll give you, your heart's desires, after all it not my name is on the door?"

The three laughed and both men held their arms out for her to take. Sharron linked her arms with each man on her sides, and they walked into the dim lit crowded bar, while Nathan held the door for them.

The loud noise hit their ears even before the door was completely opened. Inside after a few moments Nathan, lead them over to a half circle booth in the back that just became available. Most of the people wanted to get a table near the dance floor.

"We are the two luckiest men here, with the most beautiful woman. I see other men wondering how we scored. All of them will be jealous with envy.

Sharron gave her most alluring smile, Why thank you kind sir, flattery will get you anything." She winked playfully.

When she was seated, the men sat down with Sharron in the middle. She was wearing tight jeans and a hot pink pull over with no bra, with bare back hot pink sandals. Her clothes showed off her curves and full high breast. Never having children pay off in a huge way she knew.

The waitress came and took their order. This was not a place Sharron would have chosen or favored but for a night not planned it would have to do. The place was old, had a small dance floor in the middle of the room. In the front off to the side was the bar area, and there were four rolls of tables around a square and several booths scatter next to the walls. You could easily hide in a corner booth because of the lighting. Only low lit jar candles, and some color lights in the floor, where you danced, was for the most part all the lights this bar had, except for a few color lights strung above the bar.

Still the place was packed with people of all ages. There weren't much else to do in Queen City after dark on a Friday night, unless you went to Church for Friday night services, stay home watching a movie, or had company over for games like checkers.

Sam's bar and grill was the only night spot for 20 miles. Well you did have your local liquor stores and you could have a party at your home. But most of these people looked for fun and excitement through other lonely people like themselves lost in a web of deception.

A few drinks and nonsense foolish chatter, Sharron was ready to hit the dance floor and dance the night away.

"Which one of you smooth talking gents want to twirl me around on the dance floor."

Both men jumped to their feet at the same time. Nathan almost knocked his drink over rushing to beat Sam. Sharron laughed and said.

"Okay, I'll dance with both of you it is a fast tune anyway."

The three got up and headed for the dance floor squeezing through the crowd. When they found a small opening Sharron began to sway her hips to the fast tune and with her eyes closed she did not see David dancing just a few feet over from them.

They were tightly rapped in each other's arms, oblivious to the crowd and sounds around them. Their eyes were closed as they slow danced to their own private music. This woman fascinated David. She charmed him like no other ever had. He snuggled close smelling her hair, and drinking in your lovely body. Sharron was the last person on his mind and the last person he hope to see.

The music was loud and the crowd noisy, but Sharron was having the time of her life. Two attractive men begging for her attention, what could any girl ask for better? The music seemed to go on forever as the DJ mixed several numbers together. After dancing for 20 minutes straight Sharron said to her guys, "Let sit this one out until I catch my breath, you guys are too much she laughed."

They made their way through the crowed and back to their table.

"Wow woman you are a wonder on that dance floor. I bet your man would have fits if he knew you were out with us. Sam said."

"He was the one who told me to go out have some fun, so he can't be mad. Besides he is the one working tonight after we made plans to go away this week end."

Sharron picked up her watered down drank and swallowed the last bit. Nathan quickly ordered more rounds. The floor still full of dancers, and more had arrived just standing waiting for seats, she did not see David kiss Marlenea.

David whispered in her ear, "Come home with me to my place, or I could go to yours tonight."

"Babe, I would love too, but I got an early appointment and need to be on the road at four if I want to make it to Palms Springs on time."

David really disappointedly said; let's leave now so we can have an hour or two."

Marlenea knew how much David wanted her and she felt the same way, but sleep was calling her name. She needed at least four hours to drive to Palm Springs without falling asleep on the road.

"Tell you what, how about tomorrow when I get back, I can call you and meet you somewhere."

That wasn't the answer he hoped for, but it would have to do. He stopped dancing and gazed into her lovely eyes. Her heart skipped a beat and he gave her a tight squeeze. How anybody could look this gorgeous and not be taken, was beyond him.

"Okay one last dance for the road, and I'll let you go. Is that alright pretty lady?"

"That would be fine, think of this as a reminder of what will be waiting for you when I return."

She leaned in and kissed him hard. His breath cough in his throat and he returned her kiss with all his soul. They stood embracing for quite a while unaware that the music had stopped when the DJ took his break.

The dance floor became empty as all the people took their seats. Some stood around talking and drinking waiting for the DJ's ten minute break to be over.

Full of rum and coke, wine and beer Sharron was drunk, and feeling kind of sick. Her eyes were blurry, but she could hardly focus on what was seen or said. She knew she over did the drinking and she should be going home, because she never did eat dinner, but her body wouldn't obey her brain. Weak, she closed her eyes and leaned back against the booth.

Both men also full of liquor now slurring their words leaned over her talking about football. Neither one had noticed her quietness. Thought she was just resting.

When the music had ended, Sharron opened her tired burning eyes a bit, and peeked through the slight slants. The reality that faced her she would never forget, right in front like an old bad movie come to life was David. She must be dreaming, for this can't be happening, no not her David standing in the middle of the dance floor kissing a very attractive woman. Who was she? She rubbed her eyes with the back of her hand, and looked more closely trying to see if her eyes truly were playing tricks on her.

Her heart beat faster and faster and the rhythm of her breathing became short and quick. She sat straight up and stared at the couple until she knew whom it was kissing her David. How dare he do this to her? Why did he do this? Her brain screamed over and over. Her body would not move she felt like someone had sucked all the life out of her being. Here was the only man she felt she loved, kissing another woman when he was supposed to be working all weekend. What a liar.

She was frozen in time and space. Twisted in a fog of her mind were the shadows of love cover by lies. Her eyes locked on their flirtatious forms, their sexual encounter blew her away into some other reality, she just couldn't take the hurting sight any longer, and her mind completely shut down. Everything stood still. She no longer focused on anything or heard anyone. She sat in an immobile state, far away in some distant morbid world, lost where nothing could touch or hurt her. Her time stopped, and her sanity threatened to leave.

Sam laughed at some joke his friend told. He looked at Sharron. He felt bad leaving her out of their conversation even if for a short moment.

"Hey Sharron, We are sorry honey, we were just catching up on . . . Sharron? Look at me sweetheart. Are you alright?"

He turned to Nathan perplexed.

"Nathan, what is wrong with her?"

"Beats me man, she is probably playing a game I guess. Nathan stared at her a moment looking at her face closely.

"Sam, look at her eyes, how red and glazed they are, and she still looks good. Is she asleep?"

Sam shook Sharron, and still no response. He put his hand in front of her face hoping she would laugh, and push it away. Nathan grabbed her other hand in his drunken voice called her name softly over and over. The music started up again, and dancers were once more on the floor. No one heard or seemed to care about the three drunken people sitting in the booth.

David never saw Sharron at Sam's. He soon walked Marlenea out to her car, kissed her again and left for his place.

The guys knew by now something must have happened to Sharron. What they did not know or understand. They only knew she seemed to be on some shut down mode, maybe too drunk to answer, or she could be on drugs.

"Sam, we got to get her home. Did she say where she lives?"

"No, man and you know she can't come to my house. I can't have my wife finding out I was out with a young pretty single woman, in a night club while she pregnant visit her sister out of town, man she would kill me. What are you going to do with her?"

"Me!"

Both men sat for some time thinking, trying to come up with ideas. Sam said, they could just leave her here, or maybe put her in her car, after all they just met her. She could sleep it off and drive herself home in the morning. But Nathan thought that was heartless, besides he was really taken by her beauty, and he didn't want to do what his ex-wife had done to him, just leave. No that was unthinkable. He was still very hurt about how his wife walked out on him one morning without any known reason, just leaving a cold torn piece of paper, with the words she met another man, fell in love, and would not be coming back. How cold and inhuman is that. No, there had to be another way to help Sharron.

"Look I'll be responsible and take her to my place, she can sleep it off and in the morning when she is herself again, she can tell me where she lives and I'll take her home."

"Man, are you out of your mind? I was only kidding, you know nothing about this woman she could be some . . . some . . ."

"Some what Sam some lonely soul, who drank too much like we did, my mind is made up I'm not leaving her. I don't think she would leave us sitting in a cold car all night. Look at her she's like a fallen angel. I'll order some coffee because neither you nor I can drive in our condition either."

Sam soon agreed. After three cups of hot black coffee the men gently helped Sharron's limp body into Nathan's old blue 95 Chevy. He drove Sam home first who stated he was going to call his wife when he got inside no matter how late. Sam leaned inside the open window of Nathan's car and said.

"Man thanks for getting me out of the house for a while. This single life is for the birds, it made me miss my wife even more. Gail is a good woman and I don't deserve her."

"That's just the drinks talking Sam. You know you treat Gail right. And she is lucky to have you too. Women come on to you, but you always let them know you are married. Then you brag about your wife to them until they leave you alone. I just wish I had a . . . No I'm not going there, it's late and I'm going home."

Sam put his hand one Nathan's shoulder in a brotherly affection.

"Hey man, don't let the old negative memories get to you. She was no good from the start if she could leave like that. You gave her everything any woman could want, a home, car, nice furniture, and love."

"Yeah and she took me to the cleaners for it. Her new man got over like a fat rat. I paid a lot of the mortgage on that house they now live in. He is sitting on my furniture from my hard earn money, and driving the car I bought her last year, not to mention I still have to make spousal payments. How is that for ten years of marriage?"

Nathan was getting upset and Sam knew he shouldn't be driving home in that state of mind. This was his best friend who worked with him for the last sixteen years He had been with him through some difficult times. He had to find a way to calm him down, so he said jokingly.

"Look buddy, don't give me your sad story, you are the one who got a good looking babe to warm your bed tonight. I'm going home alone with only cold sheets, is that fair or what?"

Nathan stared at Sam like he was out of his mind, and then at Sharron's limp form slumping in the back seat with her eyes closed. When he could at last see the humor in it, he burst out laughing.

"Yeah right, I got a zombie who doesn't even know I'm there. I can see myself having real fun with this limp noodle. You crack me up man."

Both men laughed and the tension was eased from Nathan. After they joked, Sam went inside his house and Nathan drove to his one bedroom flat.

When he got there, he walked up the two fights of stairs carrying dead weight. He didn't care, like Sam said a warm body to hold during the night was better than nothing. It was now past two a.m. when he laid her across his unmade bed and he was tired. Sharron never moved nor opened her eyes she laid stiff as a stillborn.

He quickly undressed himself, and then removed her shoes. He wondered if he should undress her, decided he would. Nathan carefully took off her jeans. That was no small task they felt like they were glued to her skin. Nathan couldn't help but noticed her perfectly shape long legs extending from the black lace panty she wore. He was so tempted to rub her soft legs, but stopped himself short out of some unknown respect for this poor girl, who could not defend herself. When he removed her top, his eyes bulged, her twin firm breast stood at attention staring him down daring him to feel them. And her flat smooth stomach was more than he could handle, he quickly threw the blanket over her nudeness.

Nathan stood there for a moment staring at her face, willing her to open her eyes or do something. He had to shake off the temptation that was forming in his brain. When he was a bit more calmed, he went over to some boxes he had stacked against the wall, and pulled out the first shirt he saw a football jersey.

With his hands trembling he removed the blanket and gently lifted her head and slipped the jersey over her full breasts trying not to look. He would not allow his manhood to take control of him not tonight. This woman needed his help and he considered himself a gentleman. Nathan carefully covered her with the blanket again, turned off the lights and got in bed beside her warmth. He moved close to her body putting his arms around her slim waist, and immediately fell asleep.

CHAPTER FIFTEEN

An overcast swept across the horizon sphere, spreading dark clouds of dampness that threaten the possibility of rain, but watered the Queen City's vegetation. Most of the people didn't complain, because rain was needed for farmers. Although there were a few that hated it, because it kept them indoor, especially Rachel who wanted to visit Phillip Jr. and his family again today.

Lately she feared driving in the rain, why she could not understand. Her car had been repaired from the last time she drove it, but some distant bad memory of driving showed her racing down the street crazed out of her mind was absorbed deeply in her self-consciousness. Only fear made it through embedded in her brain told her not to drive.

All she knew was, every time she thought about driving unknown terror would creep up and down her spine, her heart would pulsate, and her stomach squeezed into tight knots.

Rachel lay huddled under the covers, staring through the open blinds praying for the sun to come out and the rain not to come.

"Dear Jesus, what is wrong with me? I never fear driving in the rain before, why now? Please Lord, not today, let the sun come out. I need to see Phillip Jr. Please don't let it rain, at least not this day, in Jesus name Amen."

The door to her bedroom quietly opened and her mother stepped inside.

"Honey, are you awake?

Nicky closed the door behind her. She noticed her daughter still in bed wrapped tightly in the folds of her blankets.

"Yes mom, I have been awake for hours. I couldn't sleep."

Nicky walked over and sat on the side of the bed. She gave Rachel a kiss on her cheek.

"What's wrong honey?" concerning written on her face. "Are you hurting again? You went to bed so early last night I did not get a chance to say good night. I just assumed you were tired so I left you alone."

Rachel sat up and gave her mother a much needed hug.

"I'm fine mom, it's just the rain, and these bruises on my body are so weird. The strange thing is, these things only hurt at night or when I'm feeling confident in myself, which is not a lot lately. But when I'm scared or unsure they don't bother me at all. How is that possible?"

"I don't know Rachel. That is very unusual. Look, honey you had a terrible fall, you could have hit your head and had a small concussion that's why things seem so mixed up. Your granny's medicine should have done the trick by now. I can bring you some more alone with breakfast if you like."

Rachel leaned back against the pillows frowning and said.

"Mom, I'm not hungry and I feel fine right now, I just got a lot on my mind that's all. Do you think it will continue raining?"

"Raining, I don't know Rachel, we certainty could use more rain around here. Is that what's kept you up half the night? Rachel, we need the rain, you never complained about that before, in fact you said you loved rain. Honey what's come over you?"

Rachel moved the blanket back and stepped into her slippers from the other side of the bed. Her back was turn from her mother.

"I want to visit some friends and I need to take the bus, if it continues I'll get wet."

Nicky recognized the fear on her daughter's face. Rachel looked down at the floor, bit her lower lip glanced toward the window and back. Her eyes darted back and forth to the floor to the window, as if she was seeing something her mother couldn't see. Nicky felt perplexed. This was certainly new for her brave dare devil daughter. Fear was not part of her makeup. So what was going on in Rachel's mind? Nicky tried to find the answers nothing came close.

"Why can't you drive yourself? That is why we brought you the car. Look honey, whatever is bothering you please tell me. Maybe together we can figure it out."

"I just thought it would be fun riding the bus for a change, but with rain that would be impossible that's all."

Nicky got up and walked around the other side of the bed she reached for her daughter, and pulled her close. After a moment she lifted Rachel's chin and looked deep into her eyes.

"What is really going on in that head of your young lady? Don't give me that rain excuse or riding the bus either, now you look at me and tell me the truth."

Rachel took a deep breath searching for the words to say. She never lied to her mother before and did not want to start now. What could she tell her, she feared driving? Or could she share her news of her conversion. She stood back for a moment pondering, and decided to tell her mom about her recant salvation.

"Mom, I got something to tell you and I'm not sure how you are going to take it. You are the main one I really want to share this wonderful news with. I became a Christian and got baptized last Sunday!

There, I said it and mom it has been the most wonderful experience I could have ever thought possible!"

The words tumble out of her mouth and her face lit up like a bright radiant beacon. Her whole body was alive with joy. She twirled around and around dancing to some glorious music radiating in her heart, laughing with joy.

Nicky quickly moved away in alarm. It wasn't that she didn't understand the gods. There were many she believed in. The universe, sun, trees, but serving one was not the answer, and this Christian stuff was surely not meant for her daughter! What had her frighten the most was her husband's reaction when he heard. What would Ward say or do if he found out, his daughter became a Christian? What about her mother Agnes? The thought terrified Nicky, she feared for her daughter's life. Despair moved in and panic gripped her heart. She could not swallow the saliva that formed in her throat. It drooled down her mouth and chin. A large lump caught in the center of her esophagus. Misery followed as anguish and sorrow tore at her soul. 'No, no not my daughter, how did this happen? Her mind kept screaming over and over, how did I miss this?'

While she danced, Rachel grabbed her mother's hand to continue dancing with her. Nicky, torn her hand out of Rachel's grip as if it was fire, almost falling to the floor in her haste to get away. When Rachel felt and recognized the withdrawal, she stopped moving and stared at her mom puzzled.

"Mom, what is it? What are you afraid of, dad or granny? Or is it because you don't understand who Jesus is? I can tell you now mom He is real so real! He is awesome, loving and kind. He is all I ever could desire. When you come to know Him, I believe you will feel the save way too."

She moved slowly toward her mom who kept moving backwards. Her eyes wide held fear. The closer she got, the more Nicky backed away. She backed close to the door ready to take flight. Rachel did not want her to leave yet. She silently prayed to Jesus for help while trying to calm her mother's fears.

"Mom, say something. I love you mom and I don't want you to be lost."

Hearing the word lost, somehow shook some deep-rooted emotions and anger gave her the strength she needed to speak.

"Lost? You are the one who is lost in some Mithraism. What has gotten into you Rachel? Don't you know who you are? You are a practicing witch, a good one at that. Your whole life has been doing this as you learned from a child, like me your mother, and grandmother, and all your great, great grandmothers before that. We are a proud people who do good deeds for mankind, not like those Christian who are fake wonders. Rachel, you will denounce this foolish religious garbage now do you hear me!"

Rachel was shocked, she knew her family did not practice, live or understand Christianity, but to say it was foolish garbage was way too much. All her life she felt something was missing, she never questioned it because she did not understand what it meant or what it was until now. She just knew there was more to life than what she had. Every since she met the James family, something in her spirit stirred. After meeting Jesus as Savior, she knew what had been missing. It was the first time in her life, she felt complete. Loving warmth took a hold on her, and something much bigger than herself moved in. It was the pure liquid love of Jesus as her Lord and Savior. That had been the best moment of her life, and she was not giving it up ever, not even for her mother!

"I'm sorry mother I can't denounce my Savior Jesus, I just can't! I wish you could understand how . . ."

"Shut up Rachel I don't want to hear it, and I will not take no for an answer! You are my daughter. You will listen and obey. You know if your father or granny finds out about this you will . . ."

Rachel rushed toward her mother and fell on her knees crying.

"No Mom, please don't tell them. Please . . . I trusted you with this because you are my mother someone I thought I could always rely on. Please don't disappoint me. I need your silence, please for me your only daughter don't tell dad or granny about this!"

Rachel somehow knew if her dad or grandmother found out about her conversion she would be dead, they would literally kill her. They hated Christians. She would never have come to that conclusion in the past. Up until the Holy Spirit dropped this revelation into her spirit, she believed nothing could come between her and her family. Now only Nicky would know the truth. Rachel felt her mother would never really hurt her, because she loved her completely. If only she could keep Nicky from telling her dad and granny, but how? Rachel continued crying and begging for mercy.

Nicky shook her head to clear it. She stood there watching her daughter pleading, part of her wanted to comfort her and the other part was irritated. A negative spirit held her back. So she watched her daughter cry out in anguish until her love for Rachel melted her heart, and in a soft voice she said.

"Only if you never bring up the subject again, and I want you to promise me something young lady. You will stay away from that Church and those people. Do you hear me Rachel?"

This was the hardest pill Rachel had to swallow in all her life, not to see Phillip, his family, or attend Church? That was not an easy thing to do. But the Holy Spirit spoke too her heart, and she knew what she had to say. With tears running down her face she whispered.

"I promise you mom, I will not go over to their home or to the Church where I got baptized."

She answered from the floor keeping her eyes glued shut. Her mother was satisfied with her answered and quietly walked out closing the door. Rachel got up and ran to her bed crying in her pillow, both for relief, sadness and pain. She would never be able to tell her mom about her love for Christ or share with her how Jesus forgives all sin. Her mother had always been there for her, now that relationship was gone finished. Knowing she wasn't alone helped calm her, she knew Jesus would never leave her nor forsake her.

Rachel thanked God for His love and great wisdom. She never promised her mother she wouldn't see the James again, or go to another Church of believers. At school or in parks, maybe out of Queen City, she would find a way to stay close to Jesus and the James' family no matter what.

* * *

The rhythm of rain dripped softly on the roof like a love song, causing her to curl up closer to the warm body lying next to her. She moaned half asleep and half awake. If this was a dream she didn't want to awaken. He held her close kissing her face, neck and lips, whispering his love for her in his deep voice. She echoed her love for him and retuned his affection.

"You are the best thing that ever happened to me babe."

"Oh love how I waited to hear those words."

She reached up wanting to pull him even closer. Her hand hit the back of his shoulder just as her ears heard snoring. Snoring? Her mind tried to coherence what was happening. He could not be sleeping. Awareness that she might have been dreaming sunk into her brain and she opened her eyes too quickly. The pounding in her head cause her to close them for a minute or two. When she did open them again, she knew the bed felt strange, it couldn't be her bed it was too lumpy, and the room felt even stranger, not her warm comfortable atmosphere. Where in the world was she, and who lay next to her, could it be David? His back turned against her view did not allow her to see his face and nothing about him felt familiar.

Sharron's heart moved to her throat as sickness churn in the pit of her stomach. Her foul, dry, stale breath caused her to gag, and her tongue tasted of stale liquor.

She rolled over quietly closing her eyes again. 'How and when did I get here, and who lay next to me?' Her mind screamed. She tried to remember but her mind drew blanks. Pressure pressed against her bladder, now she needed to get out of bed without waking this sleeping giant. She turned back bending over him, and peeking at his face with no recognition. Could it be she met him sometime last night and he brought her to his home? Boy she must have really laid one on when she could not remember her suitors. No more drinking for her she thought.

In the dimness of the glum room she tried to make out the walls around the stack of boxes. She needed to go to the bathroom she carefully moved the blanket back, stepped onto the cool carpet. It felt flat and coarse under her feet, nothing like her deep plush carpet in her condo.

The room was mostly bare, it contained a bed, a nightstand with a small lamp, and some old beat up chest drawers this completed the furniture.

She saw boxes stacked high against the wall on the left and a few on the right. She noticed her clothes on one of those boxes, and tipped toed over to retrieve them.

Her head hurt badly, her stomach ached and her mouth felt like it was stuffed with cotton.

She found the bathroom on the right side of the bedroom. She walked inside closed the door behind her standing there a moment before she switched on the light. It was so bright she closed her eyes against the brightness. She felt her way to the sink and turned on the cool water. First she rinsed out her month swallowing the water trying to freshen up her breath. Her head still pounding, she needed to find something to stop the pain. She looked into the medicine cabinet finding nothing she could take for the headache. Maybe, she thought a hot shower might relax her.

While looking in the bathroom medicine cabinet she saw some tooth paste half gone, but more than enough for her to put on her fingertip leaving plenty for the male stranger still sleeping. She rubbed her teeth vigorously letting the paste freshen her breath and clean her teeth, then she rinsed her mouth again with cool water.

After her breath was fresh she ran the hot tap in the shower to warm while she used the toilet. When the water was good and hot Sharron stepped inside the tub and allowed the hot spray to run down her body. She closed the glass door of the shower and fell back against the tile.

The hot water soothed her aching muscles. It felt relaxing and some of the tension left her body. She closed her eyes still wondering who was the stranger in the other room, and how did she get to his apartment?

Fifteen minutes went by before she opened the glass door ready to step out of the shower. Suddenly the bathroom door flew wide opened and cold air hit her nude body. She saw a tall attractive man carrying a towel in his left hand who hurried over to the toilet. He laid the towel on the sink, and began to urinate.

Sharron shouted, "Get out of here, can't you see I'm taking a shower?"

The tall man laughed and said, "Hello to you too. Look woman when a man got to go, he has to go now. I brought you a clean towel. I'll see you when you are finished."

When he was through using the toilet, he walked out closing the door behind him. Her heart beat fast as she hurriedly dressed and went back into the bedroom, grabbing her shoes and followed the smell of black coffee and toast.

"Good morning Sharron, how was your shower?"

She gave him a dirty look before sitting down at the counter.

"Who are you, and where did we meet?"

He wiped his hands with a paper towel, got two mugs out from the cabinet and poured hot coffee in both cups, before he said a word. He turned around smiling at the surprise look on her face.

"Nathan is my name and you met me last night at Sam's place. Don't you recall?"

"If I did recall, I would not have asked Mr. Nathan."

He laughed at her gruffness.

"Not a morning person I assume. That's okay, neither am I most mornings, but this morning was kind of different. Having a beautiful woman in my shower was very intriguing indeed. Want some toast with your coffee?"

Sharron shook her head still trying to clear it. Nathan placed two pieces of toast on a paper plate and sat down next to her.

"You could help me if you have something for this terrible headache. I will be grateful."

"Got something that will help, they say the hair of the dog that bit you will do the trick."

Nathan took out a bottle of scotch from the kitchen cabinet added the warm liquid into her coffee after pouring half her coffee out. He handed her the hot mug and she drank thirsty. After the cup was empty she sat back and smiled.

"Nathan I think you got something here, give me another one and I'll tell you if it works."

Nathan laughed, "I see it already has, but don't drink too much you might relapse. Just one more for the road."

"Who's counting," she laughed. At the moment she didn't care how they met, only that a good-looking man help cure her headache. She drank two more cups while they laughed about nothing as the rain came down steady. Later Sharron was in a much better move that led them into the bedroom, where some sexual fever was released from the both of them, for Nathan loneliness, for Sharron excitement.

Later as she lay wrapped in his strong arms she asked. "Nathan, tell me again in details how did we meet. I know this might sound strange, but I can't recall meeting you at Sam's. I would love to know how I met such a good looking, sweet man like you."

Nathan gently rubbed the firm breast he so wanted to rub the night before, and told her about their introduction, his friend Sam, dancing, drinking and her shut down.

"That's when I brought you here, I did not know where you lived and I could not just leave you stranded."

Sharron closed her eyes trying to remember the details Nathan told her. Way in the back of her brain from some distant place, like a frigate war vessel the memory came rushing back to the forefront of her mind. She screamed jumping up from the bed and crumbing to the floor in a naked heap, crying brokenly.

Nathan ran around the other side of the bed, sat on the floor gathered her close in his arms. He did not know or understand why she broke down only that she needed him, emotional pain that he did understand.

When her tears mingled with snot subsided, Sharron lay shaking in Nathan's arms smearing her tears all over his arm. Nathan reached over and grabbed his white tee shirt off one of the boxes wiping the mess from her face gently. He did not care about his arm as long as she stopped crying.

Anger took the place of grief as it twisted in the pit of her stomach and formed a hard knot around her heart. Then anger manifest, whirling like a tornado until it reached her soul. Bitterness spread its poison throughout her mind. She knew she would make him pay for the pain he caused her. She made her mind up to never allow love to enter her heart again, not for man, woman, boy or girl. She would always be in complete control over her emotions. Men were made to dominate at all cost. Marlena used her beauty to take David from her and she would use hers to destroy any man who got in her way!

The coldness dripped like melting ice from her heart and she coolly smiled at Nathan. He gazed at her with concerned and asked,

"Are you all right?"

"Yes Nathan, I'm fine. I just had some negative memories cross my mind, but I'm over it.

She moved out of his arms and got up from the floor.

Why don't you take me back to get my car, I need to get home, and change clothes. I got some errands to run."

Nathan wanted to continue holding her in his arms, she had felt so good, and it helped him to forget about his own negative memories. He stood up next to her and asked.

"How about if I fix you some breakfast then take you? You did not eat last night or your toast this morning. I'm sure your body will feel it later. You need your energy. I will not take no for an answer."

The last thing Sharron wanted was breakfast, on second thought more of that spiced coffee sounded good.

"Okay, just some dry toast, and if you promise to make me more of your special coffee I'll stay. Then you have to take me to get my car. Don't disappoint me Nathan cause I will call a cab," she added in a not so playful tone.

"Whatever you say my lady, I'm at your service."

The two went back into the kitchen while Nathan reheated the coffee. Over; coffee and toast, Nathan confined in Sharron about his failed marriage. How his ex-wife hurt him by walking out leaving only a note saying she found someone else and would not return.

Sharron felt only pity for this lonely sucker. She hated weakness in herself and in others. For his wife to use him and toss him away like stale leftovers, was not her concern. He was the perfect kind of man she needed to use against David, and use him she would.

*   *   *

Danielle smiled across the breakfast table at Bob, from their cozy five-star hotel. It had been a most incredible night of passion and lovemaking. This man knew how to satisfy all her intimate secrets parts. She did not want this feeling to ever end.

"Hey, she said in a sexy tone, want to make love again?"

Bob laughed, "Oh woman you are out for the kill, but I can handle it. You are so amazing. I never knew I could feel this happy with anyone. You have turned my world upside down in a good way."

Bob came around the table, took her hand, and stood her to her feet. He took her in his arms.

"I am falling in love with you Danielle and I have never told another woman this before. You make me feel alive, like I can conquer the world."

She melted in his arms and returned the passion long kiss he gave her.

"Oh Bob, I feel the same way, I really believe I'm in love with you too."

The kiss tuned into hot lovemaking right on the floor where they were. Several minutes later Bob said,

"If we keep this up, I will be flat on my back for a week in contractions," he chuckled. "I rented a boat for the afternoon to take you across the ocean for a late lunch, some shopping, and later some dancing. We can have dinner later tonight on the terrace if that's okay with you."

"Bob, you think of everything." She pulled his face down again close to hers. Her sweet fragrance melted into his soul. This woman belonged to him and he would never let her go. She had to be his wife for life, he would see to that.

*   *   *

CHAPTER SIXTEEN

"Sharee, honey, wash your hands and Tommy's too before you come down for breakfast."

Sharee, yelled, "Tommy, get in here so I can wash your face and hands. Grandma wants us to come eat."

Tommy came bouncing into the bathroom all smiles. This little guy never seemed to run out of energy.

"I can wash my own hand, cause I'm bigger now almost free."

"You mean three. You are not big enough to reach the faucet, your legs are two small."

"Oh yes I can reach too, I'll show you . . . see?"

Tommy tipped toes in front of the sink reaching up as high as his little arms could reach. He frowned still trying to reach it, but only his fingertips touched the edge. His face turned red and his bottom lip poked out, when his sister laughed at him.

"Here let me do it for you Tommy. I told you, you were too small."

Stubborn and determined Tommy kept trying until he saw he couldn't turn it on.

"When I get bigger like daddy, I will be bigger than you!" He said loudly.

"You can't be bigger, because I'm older."

"Daddy, said boys get bigger than girls when they are older."

"Not all boys do. Tommy when you get big you can turn on the water for me okay? We going to have pancakes for breakfast and I'm hungry."

"Me too," Tommy said in his childish voice, Sharee, when is mommy coming home?"

"I don't know, maybe today. We can ask daddy when he picks us up."

"I miss mommy."

"Me too Tommy, come on lets finish up so we can eat."

She washed their hands, turned off the water, grabbed a clean towel to dry them, she dropped the used towel into the dirty hamper between the sink and tub. She ran downstairs with Tommy's short legs lagging behind.

Sharee was at the table before Tommy come racing in. He almost ran into Carol bring a hot platter of pancakes with bacon to the table.

"Tommy slow down and watch where you are going. You could have run me over."

"Sorry grandma, I tried to beat Sharee, but she runs to fast and my legs are little."

Carol sat the hot place of cakes on the table and helped Tommy get into his high chair.

"Tommy it is not how fast you run, but how careful you are. You might have hurt yourself. Now eat your breakfast before your dad comes to pick you guys up."

Phillip Sr. walked into the warm inviting kitchen, sniffing one of his favorite morning meals. He kissed his granddaughter on the cheek, and gave Tommy a kiss on top of his head.

"Good morning sweetheart, hey sport how are my two favorite grandchildren doing today?"

Both kids laughed.

"We are your only grandchildren." Sharee smiled.

"Right you are." Phillip Sr. sat down and took four pancakes from the platter, four strips of bacon and poured himself a glass of orange juice and some coffee. Said grace before Tommy asked.

"Granddad can you take us the park today."

With a mouth full of food Phillip shook his head. When he swallowed the food he answered.

"Sorry Tommy, but your dad is coming before lunch and he is taking you to the 'Kiddy Fun Center.'

Both children squalled in delight.

"Awesome, Sharee said, I just wish mommy could go with us. Is she coming home soon granddad?"

"Honey, she should be home tomorrow. I know you miss her Sharee and I'm sure she misses you too."

With his mouth full of pancakes Tommy said, I want mommy to come now."

"Tommy, don't talk with your mouth full. Carol grabbed a paper napkin and wiped his mouth. Don't worry your mother should be home before you go to sleep tomorrow. Tell you what, how about we play hide-en-seek after breakfast."

"Yes, that will be fun!" Sharee shouted.

"Yippy, I love hide-en-seek, me go first."

Tommy tried to get down from his highchair, but the chair confined him. He wigged as hard as he could until his grandmother said.

"Thomas Jr. you better sit there and finish your breakfast or else you won't be playing any games, do I make myself clear?"

She hid her smile and looked over at her husband and winked.

Tommy sat up straight ate his food quickly without another word.

"Young man, I didn't mean to stuff your self." She removed him from his seat just as the phone rang. Phillip gathered him in his arms for tickles.

"Carol hurried to pick up the phone, before the answer machine clicked in.

"Hello, Danielle, she whispered, how is the trip going? Your children miss you and need you to hurry home. Yes, they are fine . . . yes . . . wait a minute I'll get her. Sharee your mom wants to talk to you."

Sharee had been joking with her granddad and didn't know her mom was on the phone. She ran over took the phone and breathlessly asked,

"Mommy, mommy where are you, when will you be coming home? Oh . . . well Tommy and I are going to the 'Kiddy Fun Center' with daddy we want you to go with us, but why? Okay, Tommy mommy wants to say hello."

She turned to her brother and held out the cordless phone. Tommy ran to her excited when he heard his mom was on the other line.

"Hi mommy, I love you. You gonna bring me a present? What kind of present? Okay . . ."

He turned to his grandmother who sat waiting to take the phone. Tommy handed the receiver to her and went back to playing with his granddad.

"Danielle, I hope you won't make a habit of leaving your family while you go running off like a single woman doing God knows what. Your husband and children need you."

From the beautiful hotel room where Danielle stayed, she listened to her mother's disappointed tone while looking out on the blue green ocean. She had felt some guilt earlier, and thought if she called her children the guilt would pass. But now her children, and mom made her feel even worse. She tried to reason with her mother her need to have some fun the words were empty even to her ears. She had to push past this guilt, and remember why she came here with Bob. She said good-buy and quickly hung up the phone before she changed her mind.

Yes the more she thought about it the more she felt she deserved to be happy. If Bob was the one to bring that happiness so be it. She was not going to let anyone tear away her pleasure, not her mother or children.

Carol stood holding the phone for a moment wondering why she felt something wasn't right. The kids had left to watch cartoons on the TV while Phillip Sr. cleaned the table. He notice how quiet his wife was and asked,

"Carol, are you alright? Here come sit down for a while. What did our daughter say to cause you to frown?"

Carol sat down at the table next to her husband. He poured her a cup of coffee.

"Honey, I can't put my finger on it, but I believe Danielle is doing something much more than helping Sharron. Something in my spirit is telling me she is being deceitful. Why do you think she's so interested in going out of town with a single woman to buy clothes, when she has a family who needs her? I just can't believe she wants to spend that much time with Sharron. They bump heads all the time. No something is up and we need to find out what it is."

"Honey calm down, I trust your insight, whatever she is doing it will come out in the light, give it time. We need to keep praying for her salvation and allow God to do the rest. She can't hide from God forever. Let's pray Carol."

The two held hands and prayed against any distraction that might come into Danielle's life. They asked for strength and a covering to be upon her life. They decreed and declared for the enemy to loose his hold on her life, for the mighty power, and blood of Jesus to cover her!

When the prayer ended, Tommy came running in the kitchen with Sharee behind.

"Granddad I thought we were going to play hide-en-seek, can we play now?"

The rain had stopped and the sun peeked out over the horizon lighting up Carol's kitchen. Both grownups laughed and each took a child swinging them around. Their laughter was contagious as Carol swung Tommy while Phillip swung Sharee. The children laughed, teased, and shouted they all fell on the floor tickling the kids. These were the times Carol loved most, having clean pure fun with her family. At this moment nothing else mattered, she new God would take care of her daughter.

Chapter Seventeen

Sunday morning service at the 'Shepherd's Way In' was everything Phillip Jr. hoped it would be, inspirational, and filled with excitement. Everything seemed wonderful except for the phone call he received Saturday afternoon from Rachel's mom. That call had his mind in a tailspin. Today those thoughts still plagued him.

Nicky had gotten Phillip's cell number from her daughter's caller ID, and informed him in no uncertain words that her daughter Rachel would not be coming back to the church nor was she to see him. He was not to contact her ever again. She told him if he did she would have him arrested for harassment.

Phillip Jr. deeply disappointed knew this wasn't Rachel's idea he had to see her and find out why, no matter how her mother felt. That Saturday he waited a couple more hours before he tried to call her cell hoping Rachel would pick up. There was no answer. He wanted to leave a message for her to call him back, then thought better of it. Her mom may do as she threatened.

*   *   *

That same afternoon, Rachel had seen her mother tiptoe into her bedroom, and quietly removed her cell phone from her jeans. She put it in the garage on top of a shelf behind some dusky old rags. Nicky had assumed Rachel was napping when she took the phone. Without Nicky's knowledge Rachel followed her quietly down the hall, watching where she hid her phone.

The next day Sunday when everyone was at the breakfast table, Rachel tiptoed into the garage over where the phone was and quickly retrieved it again. She slipped it into her pocket and waited for the right time to call Phillip Jr.

All day long she moped around the house picking at her food, and swallowing back tears. Her family assumed she still wasn't feeling well and left her alone. Granny did offer her some hot soup, which Rachel declined. She was glad her father left right after breakfast for his shop, and didn't return until way past dark. Rachel had so many mixed emotions about her family. She loved them, but so many uncertain memories clogged her brain that she now questioned. An oppressive sadness weighted down her spirit. Rachel did not know what to think, except she knew she had to talk to Phillip Jr. soon.

She went into the bathroom ran bath water to hide the sound of her voice, and dialed Phillip Jr. There was no answer on his cell or home phone. Then she remembered they were probably at night service. Phillip was not allowed to have his phone on in Church nor did he want to. She left him a short message to call her then she put the phone on vibrate and slipped it into her pocket. She swallowed the lump in her throat from disappointment. Just when she was about to leave the bathroom the phone vibrated. She hurried and looked at the number and almost shouted with joy. Phillip Jr. was calling her back.

It was a bittersweet conversation that ended with them setting times to meet at school. Phillip told her together they would figure out a plan for her to just stay strong. They hung up quickly. Rachel went into her bedroom, and Phillip stood in the hall of the Church thinking.

"Phillip honey, are you alright? You look lost in space."

Carol tapped Junior on the shoulder.

Phillip Jr. stared his mind on the conversation with Rachel. For a moment he forgot where he was. He blinked, smile and answered.

"Oh mom, I'm sorry, I didn't see you coming."

"Is everything alright Junior?"

"Yes, I was just thinking . . ."

"Hey Phillip," Steve called as he walked up. "Man, Church was awesome tonight, and your testimony was right on the mark. People needed to hear about your extraordinary experience in hell so they will not get caught up in witchcraft in any form the way we did huh. Thank you for doing that man, it helped me too."

Phillip gave Steve a hug. "I only did what I knew was right. Don't thank me thank God for using me. The main thing is we both found our way back with the help of Jesus. Will you listen to me, Phillip Jr. laughed, I sound like my dad, but you know it's cool. Now I know what he's been telling me."

Carol stood back beaming with pride. She knew this was only the beginning for her son. God would use him in a mighty way to help bring youth into the Kingdom of His glorious presence.

"That was an incredible testimony junior. I am so proud of you for taking a stand in Christ the way you did."

Carol kissed Phillip Jr. on his cheek. She patted Steve on the shoulder.

"I'll let you guys talk while I visit with my fellow worshipers. See you later Phillip."

She walked over to where the seniors and young ladies gathered and joined in their conversation.

All the Church members socialized in this large fellowship-dining hall. Sister Gallagher and some of the other members were busy clearing the tables, while Cam and Bernard discussed various issues with some of the young married couples.

The Pastor of the Church was in deep conversation with Phillip Sr. and other male deacons. While Pastor Webster engaged in conversation with Thomas seeing he was without his wife and looking sort of lost.

The children all joined together in another room of the Church with games, toys and Christian movies.

Joy spread throughout the Church as people testified about how God delivered them from many additions, sin and shame. They also thank Bernard and Cam for their faithfulness.

Friday night Cam and Bernard gave an inspiring class on forgiveness on marriage it was called 'Loving your mate unconditionally.' Oh how they wished one day Thomas and Danielle would take that class and get their marriage back on track. They received many thanks from the members and other visitors on how God ministered to them through this class.

Thomas wanted to stay and fellowship longer, but needed to get the children home so they could see their mother before their bedtime. He figured Danielle should be coming home right about this time and knew the children wanted to see her before they went to sleep. How he missed her and needed to see her too. He attempted earlier to contact her never getting any answers, now he was sort of concern.

Thomas said his good-byes before getting the kids into the car, helping them with their seatbelts and driving home. His mind was clearly on Danielle. He thought about how they first met, fell in love, and married, this dream wife of his, always wanting her way. Yes he knew she was spoiled, first from her dad and then from him, but it did not matter as long as she loved him.

Thomas smiled thinking of her words when he first suggested them buying furniture from the local shops in town.

"Are you crazy or what? I can't buy my furniture in this small place, not for my Victorian beautiful home. What would my friends say? Thomas look, I got some new magazines I want to show you. Look! Only the best imported furniture will be in my Victorian home."

He gave in never stop trying to please her, giving her everything she desired until it landed him in jail. Stealing he knew was wrong in any form, no matter what the reasons. He found out the hard way she didn't stand by him during this difficult time. A bitter taste formed in his mouth and Thomas swallowed it down. She didn't make him steal, no it was his fault, and he paid by losing his very prestigious job as a lawyer.

The house was dark, cold, and lonely as Thomas took the children in and got them ready for bed. There was no sign of Danielle calling. The children would not see their mother tonight. Tommy was so sleepy he didn't ask, but Sharee in her sleepy voice yawning wanted to know, "where is mommy?" Thomas hugged her while tucking her in. He had no answers for her this was a question he needed to know himself.

He checked his watch, frowning, went in their guest bedroom, changed into his warm robe and sat on the side of the bed. His eyes caught sight of her smile from a picture on the dresser. That picture was taken when they were on vacation in Hawaii two years ago. His heart skipped a beat and tears choked his throat. He took a deep breath left the room and went into the kitchen to make some coffee, anything to keep his mind from exploding.

Crying was not the answer, he needed to be strong for his children and fight for his marriage with faith. He sat down at the kitchen table leaned forward resting his elbows on his knees, forming a pyramid with his hands, his head bent down and prayed for strength.

Time slowly pasted, Thomas got up walked into their very spacious elegant, hexagon shaped living room. There dominating the opposite side of the wall over the fire place, across from the entry was a huge life size painted portrait of Danielle looking back at him from her gray, green eyes. No matter how beautiful it was this image couldn't reflect her true faultless beauty.

Her five feet nine height, her silky long legs, a body any woman would die for, and her perfect ancient goddess oval chisel face was something to behold. She truly took his breath away. Oh how his love for her ached his heart. He stood for several moments staring at her portrait painted in Rome. Without Danielle he felt his life was cold, useless, and empty. She was his reason for living next to Jesus.

Where in the world could she be? He saw from the gold antique clock on the mantel it was past midnight. They both had jobs to do in the morning. What is she thinking?

A cold callused vicious feeling crept across his mind. He heard the words loud and clear. 'She doesn't love you, and she will soon leave you. You are the biggest fool. Call her again, and really see what she is doing. Oh, but do you really what to know?' The painful words wouldn't stop just continued to taunt his soul whirling like a tornado until Thomas screamed for the voices to stop. He covered his ears praying for peace.

In Thomas weaken state, the thing ruled and slide up his body sating on his chest. Deep despair spread like venom in his heart. The tears he held all day exploded like a dam and Thomas fell to the floor beating it with his fist angry pain and frustrated.

*   *   *

All during the night Rachel tried to get some much needed rest, but sleep would not come to her tired body, only short spurts of rest.

She sank into the folds of her blanket covering her head willing her body to fall asleep. Again she awakened to negative voices nagging in her ears telling her that she would never see Phillip or his family again.

Ugly hidden shadows crept in and around her bed harboring over her head snatching her rest until she decided she might as well get up.

Rachel pushed the covers aside, stepped out of bed walked over to her opened window and looked out onto the fading twilight of morning. Time had no meaning for her. She stood there watching the stars and moon until they hid behind the early morning sun as night melted into dawn. All that was left of yesterday was dew covering the ground.

Her mixed emotions pushed in front of her brain as she thought of the conversation with Phillip yesterday. How could she live without seeing him or his family? They had made plans to meet after school as much as possible, but her mother would surely be keeping her watchful eyes out.

As the sun continued to burn away the old night she listened to the early birds chirping hunting for food God had already prepared for them. Yes; she knew God was good, and He assured her heart He would stand by her side. She just had to believe in His word and stay strong. She needed some of that strength now.

She kneeled below the windowpane and began to pray. This brought tears to her eyes as she thought about the mercies of God. Without hesitation she closed her eyes crying out to Jesus to give her strength. Rachel hadn't realized how loud her voice got she was so caught up in her need for Jesus.

Outside her bedroom door Nicky heard Rachel weeping. She quietly opened the door to Rachel's room saw her daughter brokenly on the floor. She started to rush to her side, but some strong force held her back. Part of her hated to see her daughter hurting so badly, but part of her was jealous of her daughter's newfound relationship with this God of hers.

She listened with envy. She knew she could never compete with this God and it stabbed her in the heart. She needed and wanted her daughter back. Nicky missed their closeness, their relationship and most of all their love for one another.

All at once some strange sounds begin coming out of Rachel's mouth. A new language, did she learn this at school? Nicky never heard anything like it before, so strong and rich sounding. It flowed freely from her daughter's lips like fire. Nicky backed up some, beginning to get frighten.

She watched as Rachel rocked back and forth on her knee speaking in this new language for quite some time. Nicky couldn't move her body she felt frozen. Then Rachel began saying thank you Jesus, over and over again, Nicky's heart burned, she wanted to rush in that room and shut Rachel up, but some mighty force kept her immobilize. All she could do was watch as her daughter praised a God she didn't know or care to know.

Radiant light filled Rachel's room. The Holy power in the light forced out any negative powers, causing Nicky to go sailing through the air falling against the opposite wall in the hall. She cowered in the hallway trembling in fear. Still her legs would not obey her need to run.

In the bedroom where Rachel still praised God a new sparkle radiated from her eyes. It saturated her heart with new hope. Her persistent prayers had brought not only hope, but joy beyond anything she ever experience before. This joy, happiness, and sweet peace, swept over her body and melted her into her soul.

Rachel felt this was the very presence of her mighty Savior in the Spirit. She inhaled His sweet fragrant, a fragrant like she had never known before. It filled her room saturating the air with wonder. Rachel tried to stand on her trembling legs, but they were too weak to hold her. She stared up at the ceiling as she fell back and saw the Mighty Warrior Angels of Light with eyes that sparked like diamonds smiling down at her. They came near as their wings formed a circle around her, a circle of powerful protection.

"Oh my God, how I love you Lord Jesus!" She shouted out.

Rachel body was limp and weak in awesome wonder as she laid trembling and staring at the Angels of mercy. One of the Angel's came near and touched her lightly on her lips saying.

"Oh most highly favored, your prayers were heard daughter of the Highest. You are healed from the plagues your body endured. The devil no longer has control over you. Now you must stay strong and very close to He who is true, for He desires your faithfulness. The mighty One our Master sent us to protect you from all hurt, harm and dangers. He wants you to know you are not along in this spiritual battle. Written in the book of Hebrew; 13:5, "I'll never leave you nor forsake you." And He is with you now! Keep your faith strong Rachel. This is your weapon against the enemy. You are going to need it to succeed in this spiritual warfare. Remember your faith is what moves our Master Jesus, without it you cannot please Him. You must believe that He is and He rewards them that diligently seek Him. Without faith you cannot fight the enemy and win. Remember these words "I will keep you in perfect peace whom has his mind stayed on Me, because he trust in Me." You must trust in Jesus no matter what the enemy brings against you."

The Heavenly light vanished before her eyes along with the Angels, but she based in the brilliant of that light, remembering God and the words spoken to her heart. She remained on the floor for quite some time before she became award of the natural early morning activities happening outside her window. Her room held a sweet smell that lingered long after the Angels left.

Rachel felt totally different, clean and new. She could hear Ms. Brown her neighbor calling for the old cat that drink milk every morning at her home, the newspaper man throwing papers against houses and people leaving for their jobs. Yet in her room the radiant peace remained. All fear had been washed away, and the ugly voices that followed her daily were gone. Her body washed clean. She no longer has those ugly bruises just a strength she never had before. Rachel sat up on the floor, eyes closed laughing and singing in her heart.

When Nicky could move her body she escaped, running into her bedroom.

Rachel did not see her or hear her. She got up smiling, walking around her room humming a song she learned in Church. 'How great is Thy God.'

She felt so good, she decided to make her bed, put on her robe and slippers, go into the kitchen and have some breakfast.

In the hall she paused in front of her mother's door for a few seconds hesitating should she go in or wait. Rachel wanted too share this wonder with her beloved mother. She wanted to tell her she has forgiven her of all the negative things she said. She still did not agree with her, but she now had a better understanding of those without Christ.

She could hear her mother praying to the thin air she thought was her god. Rachel understood the different and she knew Nicky's prayers were in vain.

Rachel continued to the kitchen singing under her breath, "What a friend we have in Jesus."

Angus sat at the table with a cup of coffee in one hand and Danish roll in the other. She did not see Rachel enter for her back was against the kitchen door.

"Granny, good morning how was your sleep? Granny, GRANNY!"

Angus was so deep in thought she jumped at the sound of Rachel's voice spilling a bit of her coffee on herself and dropping her Danish on the counter.

"Oh girl you almost gave me a heart attack. Don't you go sneaking up on me like that."

"I'm sorry I didn't mean to scare you. I wasn't sneaking up. No wonder you didn't hear me you forgot to put your hearing aid on again. I just came to get some breakfast before school."

"What you say? Oh yeah I did didn't I. She felt her ears shaking her head. Well I'm glad to see you have your appetite back child. Here come sit down and have some orange juice, toasted bagels, or you can have one of my favorite raisin Danish."

Rachel sat down next to her grandmother and helped herself to a glass of orange juice, a half toasted bagel added some jelly and ravenous the food.

"Slow down Rachel you don't have to be at school for another hour. You will choke to death if you inhale your food like that. How can you taste it, stuffing it down like a wolf? Chew the bagel, don't just swallow it!"

Rachel laughed wiped her mouth with her napkin, lean in kissed her granny on the cheek, got up to leave then turned around.

"You are right granny I sure not eat so fast, but I do have to get dressed. See you later."

She rushed to the bathroom washed up, brushed her teeth, combed her hair and hurriedly dressed all under twenty minutes. Grabbing her back pack she ran out the front door not noticing her mother Nicky coming out from her seclusion.

Chapter Eighteen

Agnes dressed in one of her better outfits, was perturbed as she walked on weak knees up the weather beaten front entrance, of old lady Bennett's home. Her house sat way back on a dead end street, next to an empty tall weeded lot. On the other side of this house was some tall over grown dead trees that gave the area a morbid deserted look.

The sixty five year old house stood in complete ruins with many of the bricks cracked and crumbing. It made the sidewalks very dangerous. Angus continued walking trying not to fall or stumble over some of the jagged pieces of bricks.

She frowned, cursed out loud when one of her good shoes scraped against a loose brick she didn't see causing her to almost trip over backwards. It took her a few moments before she regained her composure. She decided to continue walking on the dead grass instead of the brick walk for safety.

Agnes thought, "what in the hell am I doing here? I don't know this lady from Adam. She gets my number from a friend then calls in the middle of the night and asked me will I contact her dead husband.

She should let the dead bastard stay dead. I sure the hell can't see myself contacting my late heartless no-good for nothing husband."

The old negative bitterness awakened in Agnes's heart as it did many times. Contempt for the man she once loved so long ago took new shape. The hot pain of yester years formed tears in her gray deep set sagging eyes. She hastened them away in anger, before she reached the door of Mrs. Bennett.

Dirty, dingy, peeling, paint once yellow, hung off the house. And the torn screen door was literally hanging off its' rusted hinges. The door swung back and forth in the wind looking like it was about to fly off at any minute.

Agnes viewed this in disgusted. She wondered why anyone would live in such shambles. She rang the bell twice before she heard a high pitched squeaky voice shouting.

"I'm coming, I'm coming."

The door opened wide to an aging, white headed, old woman who looked to be in her mid or late nineties. She wore a long, dark gray, faded, ancient, high-neck dress that smelled horrible of stale musty unwashed bodies and something more Agnes didn't quite catch.

Agnes hurriedly covered her nose with both hands, staring with shock at the frenzy mess in front of her. It wasn't just the house that shocked her, this woman's eyes looked huge and disturbed behind those large overly thick magnify glasses she wore. What made it worse was the hard, crusted yellow puss in the corners of those huge eyes and the odd milky dull look in them almost sent Agnes running the other way, and she did not scare easily.

Her hair didn't help matters it looked like white thinning straw, spiked out in points. Her leather dark orange sagging skin with her twisted thin mouth and long crooked nose gave this woman a real ghastly appearance.

"What you gonna do stand here and stare all day? Come, come on in . . . I was just about to have some of my home made hot tea."

Agnes real reluctant followed her inside gagging from the stench. The place smelled like decomposed bodies, molded rotten food, and some putrefy smell Agnes did not recognize. The whole seem was so much more than Agnes wanted to handle. Her first reaction was, get the hell out of there fast. She stumbled back toward the front door trying to grab some much-needed fresh air. She quickly ducked her head out breathing in all the air her lungs could handle. The stink still burned her nose.

From the doorway Agnes shouted back,

"What do you want with me old woman? This place stinks so badly you could kill people just from entering here. Your home smells like an old graveyard full of dead animals. What are you hiding in here anyway and why did you want me?"

In a very high pitched whining voice the old woman pleaded;

"Please don't leave yet! I need you! I cannot do this alone. I can pay whatever you want. I just need my husband to come home. I got plenty of money from my Henry's savings fore he die. We always saved every dine we could. I got it right in here locked away. Come, I'll show you. We didn't need much cause this here old house is paid for. Please stay. You see, I hear some people tell me you talk to the dead and I need to talk to my Henry. I miss him something awful."

Agnes turned back still reluctant holding her nose, but the thought of all the money she could make, help her to decide to listen. She reached into her purse took out a small bottle of cologne, put a drop under her nose, closed the door slowly and walked back. They went down a hall into a dirty, greasy, gloomy dark kitchen.

Agnes sat on a chair near a block beat up wooded table. This table held trash, stale food, and dirty dishes.

Mrs. Bennett slowly put a cup of hot tea in front of Agnes and sat down at the table next to Agnes.

Agnes back, pushing her seat as far away from the woman as she could. The thought of drinking that tea turned her stomach. It not only appeared nasty, but small insects were swimming on top of it. She hurriedly pushed it aside and tried to concentrate on the money at hand.

She had to force herself to sit and listen as the old lady told her story about the death of her husband Henry.

"Anyway, one late night some months back, my Henry came to bed. He had been acting strangely all day saying his guild was taking him home, but before he left my Henry told me he was gonna love me like he done in the past. I did not know what that meant seeing we both old and we could not get our old bodies too corporate. He had a heart attack right here while he lay on top of me.

I just couldn't see them putting my Henry in the cold ground, where I would never see him again, so I had to think of something to keep him with me. I didn't report his death to the authority. His old body is still lying upstairs in our bedroom just like I left it six months ago. I try to preserve him as much as I can by putting hot ice over him. I get the local store to send me hot ice once a week by one of their youths working there. Don't worry, I don't let the boy in, I just meet him out front. When I hear you talk to the dead, I knew you were the one to bring my Henry home to me."

Agnes wanted to throw up. The women had to be mad. How could she think Henry will ever live again? She began thinking maybe his spirit is caught between two worlds and she could lead him back into his old form. Agnes had never done anything like this before, but with the right kind of money . . .

Mrs. Bennett hesitated, her lips shook and she was about to cry. She drank more of her tea, set the cup down and continued.

"Agnes I can't sleep or live without him no longer. I miss him and need him. You see this here dress I'm wearing? He bought this on our honeymoon some sixty years ago."

She tenderly smoothed down her soiled smelly dress with her twisted fingers, and gave Agnes a toothless grin.

"I will not take it off till my Henry talks to me. Please can you help me?"

For several minutes both sat in total silent, before Mrs. Bennett's bottom lip began to tremble and her tears were close behind. Her grief burst forth threatening to over take her, as some animal like sounds erupted from her throat. The horror of that sound tore through the house and bounced off the walls.

Agnes completely irritated now, rolled her eyes up toward the ceiling waiting for this woman to stop. She did not want to see or hear this woman's cries. She just wanted her to shut up! Agnes did not intend to stay a moment longer than she had to. The horrible smells in the house suffocated her. She felt like jumping up running out and never looking back. How could she hurry this woman along and get the hell out of there?

Without much thought she reached over and patted the woman on her raw boney arm, then snatched her hand back quickly as if on fire. She rubbed her hand on her sleeve briskly wanting to get the smell of this woman off her.

In a negative tone she almost shouted,

"Now, now stop it will yah, don't go getting all mushy on me. I don't like tears, so hush up! I'll see what I can do, but it will cost you plenty old woman. And before I come back you better air this place out real good, cause I won't come back here with this horrible smells the next time. Your Henry better be on more than hot ice, he better be in the bathroom with the door closed, locked, and far away from me okay? I don't need to see his stinky body to bring him back. Now hush up I say, before you wake the dead."

The bad choice of words brought laughter to the old woman and she burst out in a high shill voice that made Agnes jump to her feet and run out the door.

*   *   *

It was a very long sleepless night for Thomas. He tossed and turned most of the time trying to understand why his wife hasn't called or come home. The more he thought about it the more anger filled his heart. He knew Sharron was a party girl and Danielle who always followed her lead. They could be anywhere, doing anything, with anyone. He had to stop thinking this way. Thomas got up before five a.m. He wasn't sleeping anyway so he might as well do something besides thinking negative thoughts.

He went into the kitchen to make some black coffee and grabbed his cell phone again to see if maybe she tried to call him during the night. No. Not a single word from her. He dialed her number again still no answer just her voice mail. Thomas could kick himself for not remembering Sharron's cell number. He knew her home number, but assume she wasn't there since Danielle wasn't home yet.

He went into their bedroom and got his wife's personal phone book she kept in the closet on top of the shelf, and looked up Sharron's cell number. He dialed it leaving a message for Sharron, hoping against hope she would call back and say they were on their way back.

Crying grabbed his attention and he went into young Tommy's bedroom. There was his little son in his bed crying in his sleep. Thomas went to him gathering him in his arms. He kissed him and squeezing him close.

"Its' okay son, daddy is here, no bad dream can hurt you now. I'm here."

Tommy opened his eyes with warm tears still running down his face.

"Daddy, I'm glad you stayed with me, cause I had a bad dream."

"I'll never leave you son. Must have been some dream that had you crying cause you are my big boy. You are awake now and I'm here, you know daddy loves you."

"I love you too daddy, but I dreamed mommy not coming home. Daddy where is mommy?"

Tommy looked up in his father's eyes still lying in his arms.

"Son, she hasn't come home yet. Tommy that was a mean dream, you know mommy will come back don't you? I bet when you get home from daycare your mom will be waiting right here for you."

Thomas knew that might not be true, but surely by then she would be home. Right now the most important thing was to comfort his son's fears.

"I know Tommy what we can do, want to help daddy fix you and your sister some breakfast?"

Tommy smiled and jumped up and down on his father's lap happily.

"Can I daddy?"

"Sure can, let's get you washed up first then we can start breakfast okay?"

"Okay!"

Thomas helped Tommy make his bed, and then gave him his bath before they went into the kitchen.

They were busy all morning. He fed the kids instant oatmeal, toast and milk. Tommy stirred the oatmeal while daddy fixed toast. Thomas combed their hair, dressed both of them, and got them ready for school on time before he got ready for work. Before he left he also cleaned the kitchen, tossed their dirty clothes in the washer then rushed out the door.

Thomas was tired, sleepy and cranky all morning but he never did he allow his children see this. After the children were safe at their schools Thomas drove to the campus to teach his law class. The whole day dragged. He tried to stay focus on his classes and give his best as he usually did, but today there was nothing left of himself to give. He barked at students who were tardy, and fussed at them for not doing their homework.

His attitude mingled with their bad attitude, and no one was happy or got much accomplished. He couldn't wait for his classes to end. This had to be, the worse day he ever spent, on his job he loved.

Now back in his car still parked in the parking lot on campus, he tried both ladies cell phones again. What a surprise when Sharron answered hers.

"Well hello Thomas what do I owe this pleasure?"

"Sharron! My God I'm so glad to get you. Where in the world is my wife? Why didn't you two call? Did you have car trouble or what? Did she forget her cell, maybe left it at the hotel? I've been worried sick about her, and the kids . . ." The words rushed out over lapping one another.

"Thomas, Thomas slow down get a grip! I can't understand a word you are saying. You are talking too fast."

Thomas took a deep breath and started again a bit more slowly.

"Where is Danielle, is she with you?"

Sharron laughed, "With me? Oh my big guy, you mean to tell me she is not home yet? I can't believe my girl played the innocent child and . . ." She laughed even harder.

Sharron will you stop playing games! Tell me I want to know, where is my wife?"

Sharron could not resist. In a very sexy voice she purred.

"Oh do you. Well, my friend as a matter of fact, I haven't seen her all day or yesterday either. I haven't seen her all week end Thomas." She waited for his reaction. "Do you need Sharron to come over and comfort you big guy? Because all you need do is to say the word and I'll come running, you know that did you not?"

Thomas was beside himself with anger. He assumed she was playing some bad joke and he wasn't in the mood for jokes. He yelled,

"SHARRON, STOP YOUR SILLY GAMES AND TELL ME WHERE MY WIFE IS OR I'LL COME THROUGH THIS PHONE AND . . ."

"And what, tie me up, make me tell? She laughed again, you silly man you don't have to do that I'll tell you. She is with her lover boy. Yes, your goody two shoe wife stayed in Mexico with her boss. And don't tell me you didn't know about their little affair. Even you are not that naive."

All the air forced its' way from Thomas lungs. His chest deflated with pain and he thought he was dying. For a moment his brain couldn't focus. What did she say? Did he hear her right? When he could think more clearly, he dropped the phone and gave into the earth shaking pain that squeezed his heart in knots as it broke in pieces.

Sharron hung up the line still laughing.

*　*　*

"Honey what do you want me to say? I said I'm sorry. You tell me what I could have done different?"

Bob held Danielle close in his arms reassuring her not to worry.

"With our phones out of range, the boat not starting . . . All I can say is I'm sorry."

He sounded sincere, but deep down he was gleeful. Having more time with Danielle was pure joy. He lifted her chin and gazed into her eyes.

"Am I forgiven?"

"Yes, I know it was not your fault. Its just Thomas will be very upset with me. How am I going to explain this to my family? Not to mention my children Bob what about them?"

Danielle shook her head trying to clear it. She pulled away from Bob concern written all over her face and sadness in her gray green eyes. She wasn't happy. How could the boat just stop working and in the middle of the ocean? If it had not been for the stranger in his large yacht who happened by late on this evening she didn't know what they would have done.

A cold selfish black demon crept closer to Bob, it slider up his leg and beat on his heart. Bob opened the door and the thing crawled inside. Bob smiled,

"Don't worry babe we will think of something. Your husband I'm sure is taking care of the kids. He thinks you are with Sharron doesn't he? So call her and let her know we will be home early Tuesday morning. Have her tell your husband you spent the night again at her house."

"And what will I say the reason is?"

"You will think of something, say Sharron wasn't feeling well, and being the friend you are, you nursed her back to health."

The black, hairy troll, beckoned to Danielle from Bob's eyes. The evil was so intense she blinked and backed away. It winked at her from behind Bob's eyelids then crawled from his eyes onto his face and into his mouth. It looked out from his mouth. The hideous black eyes burned with hate left an ugly make on Bob's face for several minutes. Its' body was half ape, half wolf it turned red like blood and oozed down Bob body until both became one.

She screamed just as Bob came near her. Danielle fainted in his arms.

The deform spirit wrapped its self around Bob and Danielle laughing hideous.

*   *   *

Deep in the underworld of darken space, the demons rushed about on ancient assignments making preparations for the festival Ward was having for the witches and warlocks in just a few days. They used gullible people who engaged themselves in ritual ceremonies calling on the devil to do their evil work. They had no idea of the plans and purposes of Satan over their lives.

Some of the decomposed slave of darkness roared with unearthly glee at the destruction and despair they brought on Queen City's citizens. Not all of them were satisfied.

Destroyer roared, "How did you let that Rachel girl escape our clutches again?"

"We had her in pain and held down in despair, but she prayed to Him and you know we can't come through the blood. He whimpered, master she is too strong. Now she has mighty warriors fighting for her, and those Christians are praying against us strongly!"

"You must get her back! Without her we can't keep her mother. Must I do everything?"

"Captain we are on it."

The lower beast fell down trembling. Heckling erupted throughout hell.

"Why are you laughing we can't stop until we have every human on earth worshiping our master weather they believe or not. Dump on them, take away all hope. Use dirty movies, vulgar music, sexual parties, and satanic games, voodoo, use fear, despair, hopelessness, take away their finances, their homes, cars, family, friends, mates, do whatever it takes to get them in HELL, but get them NOW!

*　　*　　*

Late that Monday afternoon Sharee's school Principal Mrs. Grant, called Danielle's home phone, then her cell, there was no answer on either. She dialed Thomas' cell, still she got no answer, now getting concerned she phoned Carol's home needing to know where Sharee's parents could be. They were never late before.

Both of them seemed to be responsible adults, she couldn't figure out why either parent didn't pick up their daughter. Nothing like this had ever happened at this school, there must be a good reason why no one came to pick up Sharee.

She stood at the counter talking to her assistance vice principal about this.

"Why Mister Thomas and his lovely wife are on the school board, model citizens, a pillar of this community. They would never forget to get their precious daughter, not to mention that poor dear child must be devastated. Something had to have happened to delay them I'm sure."

The vice-principal agreed.

"Yes, yes I know, I'm glad we got in contact with Mrs. James. She will shed some light on this. Look! Here she comes now."

Mrs. Grant a tall lean neatly dresses, middle age lady, with dyed red short hair, hurried over to greet Carol who came running up the hall straight into the outer office.

"Mrs. James, it's so nice of you to come so quickly. As I said over the phone I cannot understand why your daughter didn't pick up Sharee today, but I'm sure there is a good excuse." She gushed.

Carol bit her bottom lip, with a weak smile replied.

"Nice to see you Principal Grant and thank you again for being so understanding of the situation, now can I please see my granddaughter I'm sure she is hungry and tired. My husband is on his way to the daycare to get my grandson and we need to get the children home. I'm sure you understand."

She rushed past Mrs. Grant went into her enter office to find Sharee busy drawing a picture at Mrs. Grant's desk. Sharee dropped the crayons and screamed.

"Grandma, grandma, she ran into Carol's arms.

"Oh honey I'm so sorry I was late, were you scare?"

"No grandma, I knew someone would come. I think daddy went to get mommy that's why he didn't come get me." She said in her child like innocent.

Carol held Sharee tightly, kissing her over and over again.

"Honey I'm so proud of you, you are so brave. Maybe your dad did go pick up Danielle. Let's go to my home okay?"

Mrs. Grant stood just inside the doorway with her arms folded and a slight frown on her face.

"I guess that ends the mystery, your son-in-law going to pick up his wife I see. Where is she by the way?"

Carol was in no mood to answer such a question. She didn't know where her daughter or her son-in-law was, and she sure wasn't about to tell that to the Principal.

"Mrs. Grant I'm sorry, but that is none of your business. As I said before I appreciate all your help and concern, I really must be going now."

Carol was about to leave when Sharee shouted,

"Wait grandma, my picture, I got to get my picture I drew."

Sharee ran over to retrieve her drawing. Up until now the vice principal, a slim younger woman in her late thirties hadn't said a word, now she spoke in her soft tone.

"No problem Mrs. James, we knew there has to be some good reason your daughter or her husband hadn't showed up for little Sharee. We always try to comprehend the situations before arriving at any conclusions."

She looked at the frown on Mrs. Grant's face and continued.

"You must understand our position as well. I hope everything is alright with . . ."

"Yes, I'm sure it is, thank you again."

Carol grabbed Sharee's hand and rushed past the two ladies out into the parking lot before any more questions could be asked. The last thing she needed was having these nosy ladies prying into her family business. Next thing, everyone in Queen City hall will have an ear full of some judgmental gossip.

She put Sharee in the back of the SUV, because she didn't have her car seat. It was in Thomas' car and she sure didn't want a ticket from the police for driving without it. She prayed silently for Phillip Sr. to have the sense to do the same.

Sharee talked nonstop about her teacher, classmates, what she did in class. She talked about her experience in the Principal's office too. Concern, confusion, and a dull headache kept Carol mostly quiet on the ride home. She did answer some silly questions her granddaughter asked from time to time, but her mind was on Danielle and Thomas. How could they be so thoughtless and leave their children? What in the world would be so important to them that they forget? Where are they now? She knew Danielle and Thomas were not careless or irresponsible people. Something had to happen to keep them away, but what?

With these unanswered questions on her mind she pulled into the drive just as Phillip Sr. was getting Tommy out from the back seat.

Phillip Sr. rushed over to open the door to the SUV.

"Honey have you heard any news?"

"Not a single word, let get the children inside so we can talk private."

Phillip carried Tommy on his shoulders as Carol unlocked the front door with Sharee at her side. She hurried and made them tuna sandwiches and poured chocolate milk into their glasses. After the children ate their meal, she sat them down in the family room, where they could watch a children's Christian movie, then she went back into the kitchen with her husband. Carol started to put some coffee on when Phillip took her by the hand, lead her to a seat at the table.

"Don't worry about coffee, right now we need to figure out where our daughter and son-in-law are. Did you call her friend Sharron?"

"Honey, I phone Sharron, her job, old friends, new friends, her cell, Thomas cell and nothing. No one at the job has seen her, and none of her other friends has talked with her in weeks. I called Sharron's home twice, no answer just her answering service. I don't know what else to do."

She rubbed her temple to keep the headache from escalating.

"Maybe we should call the police, don't you think?"

Phillip Sr. went to Carol, pulled her up and held her in his arms not saying anything for a few moments. Then he added,

"The police will not do anything until after 24 hours. That was the first thing I thought about and wanted to do when you phoned me at work."

"This is not like them Phillip, somebody must know something! Call Bernard and Cam see if . . ."

"Honey I don't want them to worry unnecessarily. Maybe the children are right they could be together . . ."

"Who are you talking about?"

Phillip Jr. rushed in and went straight to the fridge, grabbed a soda, popped the can and drink thirstily.

Phillip Sr. smiled at his son, "Just you sister, you know how she is off somewhere . . . How was your day Junior?"

"Saw Rachel, man she is something. She received the 'Baptism of the Holy Spirit,' and was speaking in tongues at school. She didn't care who heard her."

"Oh my goodness that is wonderful news." Carol walked over and gave Junior a big hug. Hearing this somehow took the sting off her.

"Yes, so that's the best news we heard all day. Now, when did this happen?"

"Well dad, she was praying to God for strength, and He gave her the best gift next to salvation. I can't wait until I receive the gift of the Holy Spirit."

"I sure wish Danielle would repent and let God use her. She does have a good heart if she would only . . ."

"I was going to ask why the kids are here. My sister has not come home yet?"

Carol and Phillip sat back down while Junior stood leaning against the counter.

"We had to pick up the children because you sister and her husband are off somewhere and forgot to get them."

"Say what? Not my sis no, she worships those kids."

He thought for a second then said,

"But you know, now that I think about it she was distracted before she left Friday."

He sat his can down went to join them at the table, pulled his chair up close, in deep thought.

"Remember mom, how she didn't want to come in and she left almost running to get where ever she was headed. I remember thinking, what was the rush?"

"You are right Junior, but that doesn't tell us where she is now."

*   *   *

For three or four hours Thomas sat in a state of numb stock. The teachers, students, and other school faculties went about their evening as usual. No one noticed the man lost within himself, who sat alone in his car deep in his own misery.

The night turned deadly cold for this time of year. The high winds kicked up and shook Thomas' car, while the coldness seeped through some small openings wrapping around his body.

Thomas shivered willing his stiff body to move. Some twisted reality sang in his heart, and bitterness brought more unwanted tears that ripped through him. The tears scalded down his face as Thomas forced his brain to obey and drive home. Instead he drove with purpose to the nearest liquor store and brought two bottles. He sat in the parking lot drinking the warm liquor trying to drown his pain. It only helped to warm his body, but not his soul.

As the night worn on and the cold beat against his car, some instinct told him drive home. Nothing seemed to make sense. His mind was in such a tight fog.

He got out the car, slammed the door, as the cold hit him in his face and chilled his hands. He pulled up his collar, ducking his head inside the suit jacket as he walked up the front door of his home, unlocked it and went inside.

He, stumbled and fell going up the stairs to the guest bedroom, moving slowly alone the wall even crawling to get to his room as best as he could.

Thomas looked and noticed a dim light somewhere down the hall this helped him make his way safely. Where the light came from he did not understand, so he followed the faint glow. As he got closer and closer, he realized it came from a door slightly ajar this was his and Danielle's bedroom. Questions formed in his mind. Did he leave the lights on?

Thomas stopped in front of that door frozen in his tracks. His ears perked up, was that water running? From the fog of his brain, slight reality began to sink in, was Danielle at home? When his body could continue moving he pushed against the door until it was fully opened. He saw her suitcase opened lying on the bed. His heart skipped a beat, along with hurt and anger.

Thomas tried to take a deep breath, but his chest hurt, and his body shook uncontrollable. With soiled clothes, unkempt hair, unshaved hard stubbles, and foul breath, he staggered with some effort to the closed bathroom door.

Rage spat on his brain, "How could she leave her family and go off with some man she hardly knew, for what some illicit immoral sex games? What in the world was she thinking that some cheap affair would solve their marriage problems?"

He tried to push back the hostility that was building up before going into the bathroom, but that was hard to do. He needed to understand her reasoning why.

The clear blue door to the shower was closed and with the water running Danielle did not hear him enter. She unusually kept her eyes closed while showering.

Thomas slumped to the bathroom floor too tired and drunk to stand, deep in displeasure waiting for Danielle to finish showering.

Ten minutes later, Danielle opened the shower door, and stepped out before she caught sight of Thomas slumped on the floor half asleep at the other end of the bathroom. When she did spot a man sitting there, she screamed before she recognized it was her husband looking like a madman from some horror movie.

"Oh my god Thomas you scared the hell out of me! Where did you come from? When did you get home? Earlier when I got home you were not here. I thought you might have spent the night over my parents or something."

He looked up at her and the look he gave made all the other words freeze on her lips.

She grabbed a towel with trembling hands hurriedly wrapping it around her nude wet body. That look in Thomas' eyes spoke volumes, made her feel guilty, and somehow soiled. With his eyes burning holes into her nude flesh she looked away.

Thomas couldn't seem to take his eyes off her. He stared at her face then her half covered body. His red eyes were wild, cold as steal. The unreal insane look frightened her even more than the inhuman evil she saw crawling from Bob's eyes. Thomas look was more dangerous, mixed with malice, and cruelty. He got up slowly and walked toward her never taking his eyes off her quibbling and frighten face.

This man who was her husband, a man she had known for years resembled a madman out to kill. He took another step closer, and she backed away shaking her head clutching the damp towel closer around her body. There was no room to back up except the wall near the toilet. Petrified she whispered, "Thom-as, you are not going to hurt me are you? Plea-se, I'm so-r-r-y I was late. I tried to call you . . . but . . ."

Thomas reached out before she could tell another one of her lies, ripped the towel from her resisting hands, threw it to the floor. With one backhand swing he slapped her so hard across the face she stumbled backwards falling against the toilet covering her bruised face screaming. Thomas had never hit her before and she knew he was beyond any control.

"SHUT UP, YOU ROTTEN SLUT, AFTER YOU HAVE BEEN GONE FOR DAYS WITH YOUR LOVER, YOU COME HOME AND LIE TO ME! YOU BETTER SHUT UP your lying mouth before I

KILL YOU! I know where and what you been doing SO DON'T LIE TO ME!"

He pointed his finger in her face daring her to say something. His voice held thunder, and it threatened to explode. She had never seen her husband this angry before. She knew he hated people who lied. She could smell the stale liquor on his foul breath, and knew she could not continue this deception. Whatever it took she had to find the words to tell her husband the truth even if it meant . . .

Danielle reached out for Thomas wanting this nightmare to end. He pushed her hand away. Brokenly she cried and tried to stand up.

"Oh my god babe, I'm sorry, I'm so sorry. I didn't mean to hurt you!"

Thomas grabbed her and shook her shouting.

"SORRY, YOU SAY I'M SORRY? LIKE THAT IS GOING TO CHANGE THINGS. SORRY DIDN'T DO THIS YOU DID! He spat out. I'll teach you sorry . . . is this what you gave him!"

Thomas pulled her by the arm dragging her from the enclose area of the toilet out in the center of the bathroom on the cold hard marble floor. He covered her body with his body, unzipped his pants, then plunged his manhood into her with such force she screamed out in terror. He kissed her brutally. It had been so long since he touched his wife, and he needed her so badly even if he had to take it by force.

Danielle screamed over and over again from pain and the savage treatment. She tried to get out from under his heavy form, but Thomas held her weak body immobilized while she thrashed about frighten beyond hope. With each brutal kiss he gave her, he called her every cursed name he could think of.

He bit her ears, her nipples, her neck and the pain raked over her soul. But it was much deeper than that. Thomas whom has always been gentle raped her like she was a common slut. The rape torn at her heart like nothing she had ever experienced before. This man whom had always been so caring in their lovemaking, hurt her beyond any dignity, yet deep down she understood his reasoning and that hurt so much more. How would she ever get over the shame of letting another man have her?

When Thomas had released himself into her he got up, stumbling out the bathroom, he went into the guest bedroom fell across the bed crying, brokenly.

Danielle still crumbled on the floor was balled in a fetal position. Great despair took over her mind and body. Hot tears fell down her face. Those tears were not for her broken heart, but because of the loving marriage she just destroyed, also for the man she reduced to this sinful shame. Time had no meaning. She didn't know how long she lay there before her brain registered the absent of her children. Did Thomas put them to bed? What if he was so anger with her he . . . What will happen to her sweet little ones, if Thomas and she spite up? Her brain tried to focus as she went inside their rooms.

The children, where were they? Danielle ran naked into Thomas' room.

She rushed over shaking him until he looked up at her confused.

"THOMAS WHERE ARE THE CHILDREN? Please tell me what you did with them! You didn't hurt them did you?" Danielle repeated over and over.

Thomas looked at her for several minutes until it dawned on him what she meant. When his brain finally caught up with her words, he jumped off the bed looking for his cell phone with Danielle on his heels. He found it on the floor of the room where his pants lay.

His hands shook as he dialed his in laws home. When Carol answered the phone he asked her alarmed, did she pick up the children? He held his breath waiting for her answer, while Danielle stood next to him in tears.

After Carol reassured him the children were safe and in bed, he gave her some story about why he didn't pick up his kids.

Soon as they disconnected from the phone, he crumbled to the floor thanking God for their safety. All anger drained from his drunken body. With a clear mind both he and Danielle broke. They hugged and cried in total relief, knowing things could have gone a lot different.

How could he be so stupid and so caught up with his own selfish needs that he would forget one of his reasons for living? He shouted this to Danielle over and over while she too cried and accepted her own guilt.

*   *   *

Throughout the night until the begging of dawn, Thomas and Danielle sat in their beautiful spacious kitchen drinking black coffee and discussing their dysfunctional, disenchanted relationship. Both admitted to his' and her own mistakes. There was a lot to discuss and understand from both sides. They knew there had to be a lot of mending, but they were willing to try again. Neither placed blame on the other.

During the midnight hours, Danielle turned her life over to Christ. Thomas repented of his sins and his negative behavior. They prayed and confessed to God and each other their weakness, asking for God to guild them and asking for strength.

Hours later, tired yet happier than they both have been in quite a while, Thomas said to his wife.

"Danielle I don't know what came over me, it was like I was possessed or something. I could only feel hate, rage, and jealousy. I felt like two different people wrapped in one body. One who loves you, and one who hates you. I couldn't seem to separate the two. When I thought I was losing you the negative one took full control and now I know that was the devil trying to force me back into the old unsaved Thomas. He wanted to destroy both of us through lust, hate and un-forgiveness. Satan is a lie and I will not ever buy into that trap again!"

"Thomas, I was the one fooled the most. I allowed the enemy to take full control when I knew it was wrong. I let lust, and desire get the better of me. I lost all focus of what was right and wrong. You know that is not the way my parents raised me, and I knew better, but I gave in. I was so caught up in having my own way . . . Thomas the only thing that really matters now is our children and being there for them. Past mistakes cannot come between that. Do you realize we could have lost them because of our own stupidity? Praise God the school didn't call the authorities instead of my mom. They could have used abandonment and taken them away from us.

She leaned forward and took his face between both her hands looking him in the eyes.

"Thomas from the bottom of my heart I'm truly sorry. It took this near tragedy for me to realize, I never loved Bob the way I love you. Whatever spell I was under babe it's dead now!"

She gazed at him with such tenderness in her eyes, this man whom earlier had raped her and slapped her face so hard it still burned and she smiled.

"Thomas, I still love you with all my heart and I'll do whatever it takes to get our marriage back on track. If this is what it took for me to know the truth, and find Jesus, then I'm willing to pay the cost. If you don't want me anymore I'll understand."

Huge tears slid down her face. She rested her tired head on the table letting the tears flow unrestrained. Thomas lovingly pulled her on his lap gathering her close in his arms. He too cried as he rocked her holding onto her for dear life. Both made promises that nothing would ever separate them again. Their conversation continued until the sun rose over the horizon.

About 8:30 a.m. Thomas called Carol, asking her to tell the children they would pick them up at lunchtime and take them to the 'Kiddy fun Center.' He again gave her a story about why they never picked the children up. Thomas knew lying wasn't right, but some of it was true, he and Danielle were working on their marriage and forgot about the time. Maybe his mother-in-law didn't quite believe him, but she had the decency not to question them.

Chapter Nineteen

Nicky drove through the hustle, bustle, streets, heading toward 'Stones and Feathers' gazing out the open window. She hasn't taken the back roads as she sometimes' did, although the trip would have been much faster. She hated the ugly feeling she got every time she went that way. This morning she just wanted to enjoy Queen City's early morning activities, she didn't care that she stopped for jay walkers, lights and heavy traffic.

She really enjoyed seeing the postmen going from house to house, and the heavy delivery trucks bringing in fresh vegetables, meats and other products to the local markets. Nicky never mention this to anyone that she also liked seeing the morning joggers and walkers leading their lapping happy dogs down trails and sidewalks. This always brought calmness to her soul and spirit. It remained her of the pooch she once had growing up her father brought. She missed her little Fluffy that strangely died just before she went off to high school.

Ward didn't like pets nor did he allow them in the house therefore Nicky couldn't get Rachel a real pet.

Although she did bring in strays from time to time hiding them in the backyard out of Ward's sight.

When Nicky arrived at Ward's place of business, she noticed the 'closed' sign posted in the window. Nicky thought,

"That's strange it is only a little pass ten, why would Ward keep the closed sign out when he normally opened at 8:30 a.m.? Maybe Ward is in the back working on something or getting things ready to open late."

She climbed out the SUV and walked over to the door unlocking it using her spare key.

"Ward?"

She called . . . The place was completely soundless. She walked to the back of the store into the hall and knocked on his office door, still not a peek. Usually when Ward wasn't in his office the door was kept locked, but today as she turned the knob, it opened, and Nicky cautiously went in.

She gazed around looking for nothing in particular, just wanting to feel closer to her husband whom had been arriving home later every night for weeks. She sat at his desk for a few moments, swirling in his big black leather chair, dreaming of the old days when they first fell in love and she would sit on his lap in a chair much like this one.

SCREECH! What was that noise? Her ears perked. Did she hear something? She stopped swirling and looked around listening. Screech! Yes, there it was again, the noise was coming from that large closet Ward used as a storage place. She got up walked over to the closed closet door and stood for a brief moment wondering if she should enter then she twist the knob. Open it thinking there had to be a small wild animal, who maybe got trapped inside there somehow.

The old heavy door squeaked, as it swung wide open. She gazed into the darken area waiting before she reached for the light switch, then turned on the dim light overhead. She thought the trapped animal would come running out scared and she had mentally prepared herself for this to happen.

'Ward must be using only a 25 watt in here. She thought, because it is still really dim.'

She walked inside the closet door. She saw some old clothes tossed about. She knew these clothes were sometime worn when Ward cleaned up around the shop. Nicky also noticed there were boxes stacked on top of one another. What caught her attention was the wooden box off by itself in the far corner of the storage half cover with a worn blanket. She wondered what Ward could be keeping in that box and why was it off by itself, half hidden from view?

For a minute she stood in the middle of that closet staring at the forbidden box, then her suspicion got the better of her. She licked her lips and seized the chance to find out what he hid in that box.

In the stillness of the close space with the door half closed, she walked over bent low, removed the blanket, and lifted the lid. She screamed too afraid to move. What she saw in the box and what she heard would haunt her for the rest of her life. The sound was like some morbid angry half human half wolf with no body.

Nicky's cry tore though the air causing her heart to stop for several seconds then beat harder and faster against her chest. She tried to swallow back the tormenting fear, but her throat was frozen in time. The grotesque horror stared back at her with the most revolting, hideous, ghastly evil smile she had ever seen.

Nicky's body would not move, her heart threaten to break through her chest. Her body sweated so badly she thought someone must have poured water on her.

She shook as paralyzing terror to over her body and mind. She tried to scream again, but this time no sound would escape her wooden lips, only a deep wheezing noise came from her chest.

A vomit taste floated into her mouth, and the taste almost chocked her. She was so nauseated and cold chills ran up her spine and neck. She tried to move still her legs wouldn't obey, only her eyes could move, but they were transfixed on the soulless bodiless horrifying image facing her from the jar. She couldn't seem to take her eyes off the ghastly-beheaded image.

Nicky was petrified from fear. With all her might she willed her body to run, but her legs would not obey her brain.

The decay inhuman thing stared back at her and smiled licking black maggots that fell from its repulsive inhuman mouth. Right at that moment another savage dark force lashed out from the deep abyss and grabbed her legs from behind. Now she found her voice, and screams ripped through the air, her legs obeyed her brain and Nicky kicked at the force, as she tumble to the floor fighting with all her might. She was able to get up and she ran out of the closet, out of the office, and out of the store. Nicky jumped in her SUV leaving Ward's front door wide opened, she did not care. What she experienced in that closet would be embedded in her brain forever.

The beheaded thing laughed a loud dry howling sound. The sockets used where eyes should have been were huge deep black holes. They seem to go on forever.

They shot out fire as they looked about the closet, searching for the human women who came into the bodiless domain of death. This empty small area irritated that horror inhuman part animal causing it to swell bigger within the close confinement.

Full of hate, vicious vengeance, and ruthless greed for souls, this thing thrives on fear and needed a host body to become all-human. Thoughts were if this woman wouldn't come to it, then it would come to the woman.

*   *   *

Carol tiptoed into the sunny honeycomb colored bedroom she used for her grandchildren whenever they stayed over night. She had decided not to take them to school today, knowing both children needed to see their parents, and besides she didn't want to explain why their parents did not come pick them up yesterday after school.

Carol peeked at her sleeping grandchildren and her heart swelled with pride. Watching them as they lay peacefully she noticed the way Tommy's bottom lip pouted in his sleep. His sweet plump baby face looked angelic. This brought tears to her eyes thinking of Danielle, Bernard and Junior when they were this age. She missed having them as small children, but watching them grow into responsible young adults made all the difference in the world.

At least Bernard, and now Phillip Junior, she wasn't so sure about Danielle yet. She still did not understand why neither Danielle nor Thomas went to pick up their children from school yesterday, nothing should have been that important to keep them away from their sweet children. Well they were home now, and serious about working on their marriage. She decided she wasn't going to make an issue out of it at least not today.

The room was small, but very cozy. The twin beds separated only by a mirror chest. This room used to be Danielle playroom when she was a child.

Her father had set up her dollhouse on one side, and her play kitchen on the other. It seemed like only yesterday when Danielle would hurry too eat breakfast on Saturdays so she could rush and play dress up. She loved having both her parents over for her tea parties.

Deep in thought, she didn't hear Sharree stir until she said,

"Grandma, is mommy home yet?"

Carol turned to the bed Sharree occupied. She smiled at her cute innocent granddaughter with long pigtails hanging off the side, laying half under her yellow blanket.

"Honey, I did not mean to awaken your beauty rest. Did you sleep well?"

Carol came and sat down on the bed and took her grandchild in her arms giving Sharree a kiss on the cheek. Sharree wiped the sleep from her eyes and returned the hug.

"I sleep alright, but I dreamed of mommy and saw a man I didn't know with her. Is she back yet, grandma?"

Carol looked closely at Sharree before she spoke, she didn't make a comment on the dream, what could she say?

"Yes, your daddy and mommy are both back and coming later to get you both. And today you and Tommy will not be going to school, because your parents have a surprise for you later. Do you want to get up and help me fix breakfast?"

"A surprise, what kind of surprise?"

"That I can't tell you, but I'm sure you will love it. Now how about we go into the kitchen and fix Tommy and granddad some breakfast."

Sharree's voice rose with excitement and she clapped her hands jumped out the bed running over to Tommy's bed shouting,

"Mommy is home, mommy is home, Tommy wake up! Mommy and daddy are taking us somewhere today, but it's a surprise! Come on Tommy wake UP!"

"Sharree not so loud, you'll wake the dead, maybe Tommy wants to sleep a little longer. Come on so you can put your clothes on and brush your teeth."

Little Tommy hearing all the commotion sat up looked around, and in his high-pitched voice piped in.

"Yippy, yippy, mommy and daddy are home? But where are they?"

Carol laughed, picked up Tommy and carried him into the bathroom with Sharree not far behind.

"Your mommy and daddy are together at your home they will be here around lunch time so for now let's get you too washed up, and fix something to eat okay?"

*   *   *

Danielle awakened from a short, but restful sleep to Thomas propped up on one elbow smiling down at her.

"How did you sleep my love?"

His familiar strong voice warmed her heart. It was like the present just melted away yesterday's dread and the sun shone bright in her heart. She thought about other times, Thomas would wake up before her, and gaze lovingly at her while propped up on one elbow just like today. What a wonderful feeling. He had that same rich deep love in his eyes. What completely surprised her was the contentment she felt laying beside him. How could that be, after months of not wanting him here she was yearning for his touch. Love is a mix emotion she still didn't understand. This kind of love could only come from God's healing grace.

She thought she loved Bob, but nothing like this feeling she had for her husband. She knew now it was only lust, and a need too feel desired, from a powerful successful man like Bob that made her call it love.

She never saw in Bob's eyes the look she now saw in Thomas'. There was such tender compassion, sweet joy hope for the future, and a pureness that can only come from someone truly in love. He loved her beyond her negative self and she now understood the difference.

"Honey, are you alright? You are so quiet, I hoped that . . ."

Danielle placed her hand gently over his mouth and smiled up at him. She touched his hard stubbles on his unsaved face, and in that single moment something wonderful happened. It brought thrilling emotions and new excitement. She wanted to taste her husband fully. His male scent moved sweetly up her nostrils as she maneuvered closer to him. Like electricity the excitement charged her heart as love and desire mingled.

Thomas felt the same consuming power of their love. He took her lovingly in his strong arms as his desire mounted to a blazing fire in his loins and heart.

This was so much more than just desire. There need for each other mounted to a fever pitch as each showed all the love in their hearts. She shivered from her need to have their union complete. Thomas too felt that deep emotion, for it had been his for so long. Oh how he loved this woman.

He bent and gently kissed her lips, soon their passion completely engulfed them and their love exploded with a power neither of them expected. They melted into each other's arms becoming one, one spirit, one body one soul. These feelings were something they never experienced before. This sweet new wonder carried them on a passion that neither of them ever wanted to end. Time had no meaning, it stood still as they filled each others desires, with ecstasy beyond anything the two ever had, nothing else mattered.

*   *   *

Ward came in from the back of the shop carrying supplies in his arms. He sat the bags on the counter top and noticed his front door standing wide opened. He quickly closed the door then looked around to see if anything was missing, saw nothing out of place. 'Who or what kind of intrusion stepped into his domain,' he wanted to know.

He went into his office and saw his closet door also standing opened. Now he was angry. Ward thought, "It must be that noisy mother-in-law, for who else would come messing around my things, and not take anything. She probably took Nicky's key without Nicky knowing."

"I'll teach that old witch not to go snooping around in my affairs." He cursed out loud checked his boxes before closing the closet door. "I know what I'll do, have her meet my little friend, yes, then she will know who is supreme!" Ward laughed out loud before he called his brother from out of town.

"Glad you are moving here little brother. I got some things lines up for us to do . . . Yes, I'm getting everything ready. I think you will be quite impressed."

*   *   *

Nicky drove without any destination she just needed to get away from the horror of that box. Now she found herself in a part of town she wasn't use too heading down a one-way street. She swallowed back frighten tears. Nicky was not ready to go home to an empty house she needed to see people.

She turned down a bumpy alley. It was full of bent trashcans with rotten spoiled food and homeless dirty cats. The mangy cats that infested this alley ran around jumping into trashcans eating the left behind smelly food, this made Nicky sick of the stomach to smell.

She held her breath as she drove through the alley almost hitting a sickly looking scraggly cat. She slammed on her brakes hard and yelled, "get out my way you scrawny beast!"

At the end of the alley she turned left down other slum area of old un-kept house with dried up dirt yards. Her eyes straight ahead she thought she saw her mother about to get into a waiting yellow cab parked in the driveway of one of the worse homes on this street. What was she doing in this awful area, or whom did she know living here?

Nicky slowed down and parked behind a huge tree waiting to see what her mother was doing in a neighborhood of this kind. When the cab drove away she slowly pulled up to the house and parked. She sat for a moment looking at the bad condition the house was in. She thought she knew all her mother's friends. After all she took her by their homes once in a while, but this home was unfamiliar.

Nicky remembered their old family doctor telling Agnes some years back, that her knees were filled with crippling arthritis and it was best for her not to adventure out alone. Her knees could give out at any time causing much pain. From then on Agnes hardly ever went anywhere without Nicky knowing where she was or who she was with. Many times the pain was so excruciating that she had to lay off them for hours. She knew Agnes hated feeling helpless, but she had to understand her legs could give out at any moment if she ventured out on her own. So why was her mother out here in some strange neighborhood?

Nicky wanted to find out who was it that lived behind that door. She got out walking on the same broken bricks Agnes walked on earlier. She ringed the bell and waited.

Mrs. Bennett opened the door squealing,

"Is that you Agnes? If it ain't, who ever you are I'm not buying nothing so you can peddle your junk else where."

Nicky quickly put her hands over her nose and backed away.

"I'm not selling anything Ms. She said standing away from the door."

"Then state your business women, I'm not getting any younger standing around here waiting for . . ."

"I just saw my mother leave here a moment ago and . . ." Nicky said nervously.

The old lady stepped in closer to Nicky's face. She adjusted her large thick glasses on her nose, squinting, looking up at Nicky more clearly.

"Oh yes I see some resemblances. Yah, she was just here. She's going to bring my Henry back to live with me. You see he died some months back and I miss him something terrible. But today your mama contacted him from the dead, and my Henry talked with me. Next week when I pay her more money she'll bring him back to life."

"You mean to tell me my mother told you, you would actually see your husband alive again."

"Yes, that's what I said."

"Look Mrs. Henry or whatever your name is, my mother can allow you to talk to him although you will not see him. She can't bring him back to life. Do you understand the different?"

"I saw him today when Agnes called his spirit back from the dead. He told me he would return soon."

Nicky thought, 'This woman is very buzzard, maybe a bit insane if she thinks she seen her husband and my mother can bring him back. This whole morning has turned out to be a very frighten and disturbing one for me. Has the whole world gone mad?'

Nicky wanted to reason with this woman, make some sense out of all this.

"Look, my mother and I both contact the here and after to bring some closure to people who are hurting by conducting a séance. I believe that is what my mother means when she said you can talk to your husband again, but by no means will he live in the flesh. That is black magic and we do not participate in such doing."

"I paid for my husband to return to me and your mama gonna do it! I don't care how she does it just as long as he comes back home soon, now I gotta pee so get out of my doorway and good day."

She stepped back into the house and slammed the door on Nicky who stood in shock, first the horror thing in the box, and now this!

*　　*　　*

Agnes sat back in the seat of the cab thinking of the past. Old bitterness, her long time companion, lay in her heart as the ugly negative memories forced their way to the front of her brain. She closed her eyes letting them take full control.

Where did it all begin? Yes, how could she forget? Some forty-five years ago when her daughter Nicky was about two years old, late one day Agnes came into the living room and found her husband bouncing their baby daughter on his lap. She informed him it was past Nicky's bedtime and to put her in bed, but Charles didn't budge. After telling him several times to no avail anger got the better of Agnes. She huffed out the living room, into their bedroom pouting, hoping that Charles would soon follow. When this didn't work, Agnes retuned wearing a long white sexy night gown and paraded in front of him, saying sweetly,

"Honey we can put Nicky to bed now, it is way past her bed time, and I got something real nice waiting for you, she winked.

Her husband informed her, this was the only time he had to spend with his daughter that she could wait a while longer. They went around and around about this and Charles put his foot down.

He continued to blow on little Nicky's tummy laughing when she giggled and wiggled trying to get out of his embrace in a loving child manner. Nicky's blue eyes were wide with excitement, as she laughed running around the room looking so sweet and innocent. Agnes watched as Charles chased her picking her up and twirling her around and around.

She stood staring, heart beating faster. The anger took her to a new level of pain. She called Nicky, abruptly telling her to come to bed now, but neither father nor daughter heard or paid any attention to her demand. Agnes, who stood in the middle of the living room practically shouting for them to stop, noticed they were not listening. They both acted like she did not matter. She ran into her bedroom taking off the gown and ripping it in pieces. She threw it on the floor, furious. Her young daughter and husband were in a world of their own, oblivious to her rage.

As the years wore on, things got much worse between husband and wife. She and Charles grew miles apart. He adored his daughter attention and seemed to despise Agnes's. Her husband spent his every free moment taking their daughter places, and buying her nice things he never would spend on Agnes. They became so close you couldn't cut one without the other one bleeding. Their closeness was beyond Agnes understanding, always leaving her out of their time and fun. One day it was too much her jealousy, and rage manifested into a hard ball of hate. It began to feel to Agnes, like Nicky was his one true love. This pain ripped out Agnes heart. She watched them day after day becoming even more inseparable.

The final insult came the day she found out her husband was dying of cancer. Nicky knew for months before Agnes even heard. When she got the news it was far too late, he had only three weeks to live. This man, her husband, died in Nicky's arms not hers. This was the year Nicky turned seventeen. Agnes knew the two of them kept this from her not to spare her, but to bring more hurt upon her. Their private secrets still to this day burn like fire in her heart. Over time Agnes discovered her husband did treat Nicky as his wife. From the time she was ten. Incest is such an ugly word, but all to true. Charles used Nicky and she never told Agnes. She found out only because she heard Nicky crying in her sleep for her lover, her dad.

Looking back she should have seen the signs, trips out of town just the two of them. Him sleeping in her room because he said she was afraid to sleep alone. Buying Nicky whatever she desired. Her never have dating in high school.

Agnes couldn't let these thoughts go they plagued her mind day in and out. Her thoughts continued, bringing her to that year he died.

Charles had gotten so thin, losing his appetite, and not getting out of bed for days. She remembered being so caught up in her own misery she just never put two and two together. When Charles died, that's when it all made sense.

The reading of his will was like a train hit her full in the face. She found out Charles left everything he owned to his darling daughter Nicky. EVERYTHING THEY worked so hard for was now Nicky's. Even his insurance policy Agnes kept going. Their house payments Agnes helped him with. Both cars bank accounts, land everything Nicky inherited it all. Agnes was left with nothing but hate!

She swore to her grave she would get even. She would make her daughter Nicky pay for all the many years of pain she suffered and encountered, because she stole her husband.

Agnes plotted for years to find the perfect plan. She didn't want to just kill her, not yet. To suffer like she did was the perfect plan. When she met Ward Steward by chance at a party, she knew this would be the perfect down fall for her daughter.

This no good, nice looking man of the world was perfect to use. He had a coldness ruthlessness manner about him, a man seeking his own power, yet he had a charming side too. This charm she knew would attract Nicky to him fast.

Nicky her daughter was simple, so sensitive so gullible, a real wimp when it came to people using her was ripe for the picking from a man like Ward. Nicky at that time was twenty-nine when she first met Ward. She had never married, always alone, feeling she might not ever have children she jumped at the chance for marriage.

Now that her dear old daddy wasn't around to protect her Agnes felt Ward would surely destroy Nicky in every way.

Agnes used every opportunity she could to hurt Nicky, daily insults, rudeness, coldness, giving her no love or attention was all part of the plan. She knew Nicky craved being loved and would do anything to have it. 'Poor baby, not from mommy dearest you won't!'

When she first intruded Ward to Nicky she assumed his dominating spirit would crush Nicky's weak spirit, and she would become a slave to his cruelness. That did happen, and then they got married. Agnes knew Ward only married Nicky for her money. She hoped he would take all her money and leave her cold and homeless. Maybe that was his original plan until Nicky became pregnant with Rachel a few months after their wedding.

Agnes was furious with this news. She never took that into consideration. Her first plan was to kill the unborn child after all she was the one tending to Nicky, but she feared Ward more than she cared to say. He wanted that child and if he ever suspected her she was the one who would be dead.

When Rachel was born, Agnes recognized the same love in Ward's eyes for his daughter Rachel, as she had seen in her deceased husband's eyes for Nicky. She knew her plan had to be alternated and fast. She had to prevent any new pregnancies. She did this by slowing spoon-feeding Nicky arsenic poisoning. If she gave it in small doses, she assumed it would burn a whole in her stomach and she never would be able to carry another pregnancy.

She put the poison in her drinks as well as her food. When Nicky complained of stomach pains, burning esophageal, vomiting of blood, visual impairment, Agnes fed her a little dimercaprol just enough to strengthen her immune system.

The poison worked killing any change of her ever having more children. The drug was toxic enough to badly weaken her fallopian tubes and almost destroy her uterus tissues.

One day Nicky found out about the poison and stopped taking it just in time before it totally destroyed her body. After she confronted her mother she was informed the poison was for someone else and had been given to her by mistake. She was warned not to mention this to Ward or he may decide to leave her if he knew she could never give him a son. But deep inside she hoped that would be the reason he would leave her.

Another part of her plan was to sleep with Ward her son-in-law. In the beginning she still has her looks, so on many occasions for the first ten years she slept with her daughter's husband, until one day Ward told her was too old, ugly and useless.

Still Ward stayed with Nicky. He loved the fact that his genes lived on after him even if it was through a daughter instead of a son. Yes, he desired a son, but when that didn't happen he gave Rachel his full attention and fulfilled all her desired.

Agnes knew Ward slept with many other women. She believed Nicky knew also though she never mentioned this to her. It felt good to keep a secret from Nicky.

Now Agnes adjusted herself in the seat of the cab thinking, 'my gullible daughter took all his infidelity, his cruelness, his evil ways, and still gave him her heart, how stupid is that. That's how Ward got 'Stone and Feathers,' from the money Nicky gladly gave him. And he made sure his name was the only one on the deed. It was a smart move on his part, a very dumb one on hers.'

With Agnes' lack of money she had to live with them. The job she once had did not pay enough money to cover all her expenses. Only a small SSI this humiliated her most, the two people she hated she needed. Lately she depended on them even more with old Art in her tired aching bones. She probably could not take care for herself anymore anyway. All her good years were gone, dried up. She blamed Nicky for this too.

At the mentioned of arthritis, he started to cause more pain in her knees and back. She rubbed them almost crying out from the intense pain.

The cab driver turned down Main Street. Agnes looked out the window wondering how everyone could look so happy walking their pets, and kids. She saw lovers holding hands and almost threw up at the sight.

It was a warm day with temperatures in the mid eighty. The sun electric as the rays wrapped around the outdoor citizens like a blanket, but Agnes sat cold, sick and restless. What did she have nothing but her hate for everyone but Rachel. Why she cared for her granddaughter she did not understand.

The caber peeked at her from the mirror above. He knew she looked miserable and thought some pleasant conversation might help.

"Beautiful day out." he smiled

Agnes glared at him with contempt in her eyes.

"What's so beautiful about it? You see the same old people doing the same old things in this same old dirty farm town. Now I ask you what's so beautiful about that! Just leave me alone and do your job or you won't get paid!" She spit out the words in a hateful tone.

"Some people," he said under his breath shaking his head.

*　　*　　*

Chapter Twenty

T he school hall was full of laughing talking teens some hung in the halls others on their way to class.

Rachel phoned Phillip earlier asking him to meet her in front of her math class after his second session. Totally excited to see him again she waited anticipating his arrival. Yesterday she spoke to him, but only for a few moments before class. Today she wanted to finish telling him about the Holy Angels of God and he knew her speaking in tongues experience.

She peeked at her watch for the forth time just as he called out her name from down the hall.

"What took you so long Junior? She happily asked. I got so much to tell you I hope it's enough time before your next class begins."

Phillip pulled her by the hand over to the lockers, and gave her a big warm hug saying, "would an extra hour help?"

"An extra hour, how?

"Well, he grinned, I'm still a bit sore from the car accident, so I got an excuse from the nurse not to take sports for two weeks, and you I'm sure you are still aching from your fall."

"Babe that's what I told you about yesterday, don't you remember? I'm healed Jesus healed me! I have no more pain."

She turned around and lifted her hands laughing, and then reached for his hand again. She explained to him in deeper details what happened the day she saw the Angels of the Lord shinning light in her room. Phillip laughed grabbed her other hand and swung her around until she begged him to stop in her playful voice.

"Phillip, I missed you so much, let's go outside for a while my next class is not until 2:00 so we can take a walk to the park if you like."

"If I like, are you nuts? Rachel you are all I been thinking of all day and I got a lot to tell you too."

The two walked hand in hand off the school grounds, down two blocks to the park. They sat on the baseball bleachers wrapped in each other's arms, engrossed in conversation. Phillip Junior stopped taking and gazed into her gray eyes, he kissed her nose then her lips still holding her tightly. Tears ran down her face.

"I miss you so much Phillip. I can't wait until I'm old enough to move out on my own. Two years seem forever. You know, nothing is the same without seeing you your family or going to your wonderful Church.

I hate having to sneak like this. I want to shout to the world what God has done for me, not hide behind . . ."

Phillip Junior lifted her chin with two fingers with his other he wiped the tears from her eyes.

"We will get through this together Rachel just have faith okay?

They sat for ten minutes just holding onto each other. The day was bright and beautiful and Phillip wanted Rachel to feel the same. He had to encourage her to stand on faith. He turned to her with love in his eyes.

Babe you got to get your mother to accept Jesus as her Lord and Savior. She seems to be the only one in your family who might believe and if she is saved I know you could . . ."

"But how, she is so into her gods, how will I ever help her to see the truth?"

"With the help of the Holy Spirit God gave you. He, the Holy Spirit will help you find a way. Just trust in God for the answers. Let's pray for God's direction, protection, and wisdom okay?"

They bowed their heads, closed their eyes, as Phillip began to pray.

"Dear Jesus . . .

"Hey you guys what's up?"

They could feel the darkness as it pressed in and around them. Phillip and Rachel opened their eyes seeing Mad Dog walk over to them.

"Haven't seen you too in days, where have you been hiding?"

He sat down next to Phillip looking across at Rachel. Cold chills ran up and down her spine.

"Hey Mad Dog. Rachel whispered."

Phillip Junior reached out and started to pat Mad Dog on his back, but the evil forces coming from Mad Dog, made him pull back quickly.

"Hey dude what's up with you." Phillip replied without much joy in his voice.

Part of him wanted to witness to this kid whom for many months had been his friend, but at this moment he wanted to be with Rachel alone. They did not have that much time, and Phillip did not want to share the precious moments they had with Mad Dog.

It wasn't just that, something bothered him about Mad Dog, an evil that he never recognized before rested on him, and Phillip wanted no part of that world. The look on his old friend's face watching him stare at Rachel also upset him.

"Nothing much . . . Saw your old man the other night Rachel. Man, he is real cool, Worm have you met him yet?"

"No I haven't and the name is Phillip, I go by my given name now."

Phillip didn't want to seem rude, but the area around them was dark. This could only be coming from Mad Dog's spirit. Being a newly born again Christian Phillip didn't know how to deal with this. There was no doubt in his mind he had changed because all the things he and Mad Dog once shared, Phillip no longer wanted any part of. It was sort of funny in a way, the things they did just a few weeks earlier, now seemed so empty and so insignificant. Phillip wanted Mad Dog to leave and never come around them again. He knew this was not being a witness to a lost soul but . . .

Mad Dog had been staring back at Phillip, trying to figure him out also. He rubbed his chin cocked his head to one side and said,

"Phillip, you say? Mad Dog grinned looking Phillip up and down with contempt. Yah man I can see why you would call yourself Phillip again, with your old fashion way of dressing, your hair dyed back black, and neatly combed, how can I put this dude, you look like some preppy school kid who sold out to the man."

"Sold out is the right word, but not to the man, I'm sold out to Jesus my Lord and friend. I'm proud to say I'm a born again believer!"

Still watchful, Phillip could not touch Mad Dog or bear to sit next to him any longer. The evil that penetrated from Mad Dog made both Rachel and Phillip want to throw up. It was all they could do not to get up and run out of there.

The evil licked the air and Phillip tasted blood in his mouth. He saw something moving from just under the skin on Mad Dog's face. This caused his face to look strangely distorted. Like some deranged inhuman invasion taking over his body crawling beneath his face.

Rachel noticed it also and it was all she could do not to scream. She began to speak in tongues under her breath holding Phillip's hand tightly.

Phillip tried to act normal, after all this was someone he knew for almost a year. He held Rachel's hand reassuring her God was stronger than this evil force. In his mind he prayed for strength and for God's protection for him and Rachel. The blood he earlier tasted disappeared from his mouth and he spoke.

"As I said, I have changed, and I'm glad of it. Jesus gave me another chance to live a righteous life, and I'm doing it with all my heart. This is something you should seriously take under consideration Mad Dog. Jesus paid the price for our sins and He is soon come. He is coming back for a Church without any stains on their garments. That means we are not to do any form of evil. The things you are still into are from Satan man, and he is out only to steal, kill and destroy you. He hates you man can't you see that? He can only bring damnation on you."

"Will he?" Mad Dog smiled coldly.

The atmosphere around them began to change. The Holy Spirit of God radiated Supreme glory in and around Phillip and Rachel as she continued to praise Him in tongues of glory. You could feel the changes as the darkness started to fade away.

Mad Dog looked over at Rachel as her voice became louder. "What are you saying Rachel? What kind of language are you using?"

Rachel didn't stop, but continue to speak in unknown tongues lead by the power of God. She closed her eyes against all evil and allowed the Holy Spirit to take full control as her volume became even louder.

"SHUT UP RACHEL, STOP IT! WHO ARE YOU TALKING TOO? I DON'T WANT TO HEAR THIS!"

Mad Dog was completely freaked, not even Wolf or the demons he seen, or even the thing in Wolf's box scared him like this did. He thought he was invincible, but something about this language terrified him.

He jumped up and quickly backed away walking as fast as he could. He almost tripped over his own feet trying to escape the power of her voice, but he couldn't stop staring at her. It was as if some mighty force greater than he drew him like a magnet, but he refuse to obey. He did not understand why, all he knew was the power in those unknown words frightened him beyond comprehension.

This power was far greater than the one he'd seen Ward use. It hit him deep inside his soul, still he refuse to yield his spirit. He allowed his heart to continue hardening. Satan held him and wouldn't let go, and the Holy Spirit of God does not force one to yield, it's a choice, he chose to stay blinded in darkness.

He began to scream out no over and over. His screams were like nothing either of them had ever heard before. He resembled an animal in great pain. He screamed covering his ears refusing to accept the truth. His body flipped around on the ground like a fish out of water.

Phillip grabbed Mad Dog by his arms trying to calm him down, but nothing could stop the horror from the demons that continued to scream out of him NO. They refused to leave Mad Dog's body, because he gave into their lies.

Rachel who had her eyes closed in the beginning opened them wide. She witnessed this frighten ordeal and stopped speaking abruptly. She saw Mad Dog fall to the ground drain and wilted. He lay there a moment before Phillip reached to help him up. Savagely Mad Dog kicked him back. He wanted no part of their repentances he just wanted to get out of there presents now.

Out of his foul mouth came these words:

"You will never get him to call on your God he gave himself to our master and he belongs to Satan forever!"

Phillip jump out of his way just before Mad Dog's foot tried to kick him in the stomach. He knew only powerful prayers could help this poor lost soul.

"Satan I rebuke you by the power of Jesus to loose him now!

They laughed "but he wants us to dwell in him."

Heavenly Father, please break this filthy stronghold that attached itself to Mad Dog and release him by Your Mighty Power, he is deceived into thinking he can't be saved but Satan is a lie. We claim his soul . . ."

Mad Dog jumped up and ran from the park as if the very demons within were chasing him.

* * *

Chapter Twenty-One

Doctor Jahner stood in front of the charts trying to figure out the bizarre case from the x-rays he had taken a few days earlier. This had him most perplex. How could three different individuals, from three different backgrounds, who never met each other have the same symptoms and receive the same kind of bites? In all three of the cases their right hand was severely swollen with an unknown red bite in the middle.

The teeth prints found on each person, he couldn't identify what kind of animal could have made them. They looked to him maybe it could be a wolf or some kind of snake, but how? There was no proof weather these marks had any poisons or infection involved yet but he had to find out.

What he did understand was the burning pain each person told him they experience. Each person explained they would rather have their hand removed than keep feeling the intense pain.

Every one of these victims came to him within days of each other. They all informed him saying they saw some evil force come out of the twenty-dollar bill just before it bit them. It happen so quickly nobody else saw it happen. In fact most believed the victims wanted free services and invented the so-called bites.

In each case the person who gave the money was at a different location in a different part of town. Authorities were called, but could not find any reasons to arrest anyone. They wrote it up as pranks because the money that was supposed to be used had no affect after the incident.

The first man came to Doctor Jahner, said he received a bite after buying oil for his car at a gas station. One of the two women had gotten bitten after asking for her money back from a ripped dress she bought a few days earlier. The last woman had gotten her bite when she took her two children to the 'Kiddy Fun Center' and received twenties from a hundred dollar bill.

All of them said it came from twenties dollar bills they gotten that seem to turn into some dark shadow just before the bite. In each case nothing else out of the ordinary happen before the bites. No misunderstandings with anyone, no arguments, no anger of any kind. The reasons was such a mystery too because, all of these people seemed to be law abiding citizens, and all of these places were local places where many citizens frequent.

"Umm . . . Excuse me Doctor Jahner I came as soon as I could."

Doctor Blank stood in the doorway waiting for Doctor Jahner to invite him in.

Doctor Jahner still with a puzzled look turned around and cleared his throat as he extended his hand.

"Oh yes do come in doctor, I was waiting for you. As I told you over the phone I have a great deal of concern over why these bites appeared out of nowhere, especially since nobody seems to believer my patients were bitten. I find it odd that the teeth marks were not sufficient enough for the police to do anything about it. What I don't know is, if there is some kind of breakout of poisons coming from money being passed around why others did not received bites? Knowing you are a specialist in animal bites I wanted you to see what you could find out about this strange situation. I don't want to start a panic over nothing, but if this is some kind of outbreak we need to stop it before it spreads further."

Doctor Blank walked over to examine the three x-rays hanging on the chart board. He adjusted his glasses to look closer. While he examined the x-rays, doctor Jahner pointed to the area on the charts.

"Doctor, look closer at this spot, don't you find this odd? As you can see nothing, that's why I need another opinion, some advice really on what to do next. I'll be quite honest. This case has me mystified. No modern medicine can explain how or why these bites appeared on these people. I did prescribe some antibiotics hoping to alleviate the pain, but without knowing the true cause well . . . I also gave them something for the swelling, but finding the prognosis is well . . . this is why I call you in."

Both men stood studying the x-rays for several minutes before either of them said a word. Doctor Blank too was also bewildered. He could not understand why the x-rays did not show anything out of the ordinary except for some swelling. He needed more information and to examine the patients before he could analyze the situation.

"Doctor Jahner when can I take a look at your patients?"

"As soon as possible I'm sure."

"Let me study their charts farther, then I'll take a look at them."

He pulled his glasses down some to see better through the bifocal part and sat down at the desk for a moment looking over each of the charts more carefully. After several moments he said . . .

"There must be something I'm missing. Doctor can I take these with me, I'll return them tomorrow. As you stated there has got be some connection with these bites, why them?"

The men continue to discuss the matter until doctor Jahner's nurse came into the room reminding him of his next appointment. Both men shook hands making dates to communicate later in the week.

*   *   *

Jenea was glad they were moving a few days earlier than planned. She couldn't wait to move in Queen City and see Mad Dog again. Her first thought was, 'daddy decided to move the date up because he broke up with his last girlfriend,' than later she was told her uncle wanted them there sooner.

Some of her old friends she would miss, but to hang out with her cousin Rachel was going to be a blast. Both girls are around the same age, and have been very close friends all their lives. They use too share all their mischievous little secrets with each other, doing things that their parents never knew. Lately things had changed. She didn't understand why Rachel had not called her these past few weeks, or answered her text messages. Could be she and her boy friend Worm, were so in love they tuned out the world. She smiled at that thought, and zipped up her last bag.

"Daddy I'm all ready." Jenea shouted from her upstairs room. She had packed all she could get into the four large suitcases, and one even larger garment bag. Yesterday was her last day to say good-bye to all her Washington friends who promised to call and text her daily.

Jenea's heart beat faster thinking of all the wonderful adventures she was about to unfold in this small town of 2,500. 'Wow this town is completely different from the big city I'm leaving. We had that many students at my old high school.'

What really excited her was the boy Mad Dog, this mysterious boy she met earlier this spring, when she visited Rachel.

Mad Dog knew how to find suspense, and that was just what she wanted. He wasn't like any of the boys she dated here in Washington DC, no this boy liked living on the edge just like she did. He told her about his new friends Sandy and Raymond, had her laughing about some of the crazy things they did together. What intrigued her most was the money Mad Dog said had power to hurt anyone he please. Now that is the kind of magic she liked.

Mad Dog also told her of the times he visited her uncle Ward. She always felt that he was a bit strange. This man enjoyed scaring young people all in fun she assumed. Although he did take being a Shaman serious and according to her father he now dibbled in other black magic. Harmless she thought. Maybe that's just his way of getting people to respect him more.

Although she admitted, my uncle can be quite the devious person if you got in his way.

"Jenea come on I want to be on the road before traffic gets too heavy, so get a move on."

"I'm coming!" She took one last look around her room thinking of all the many times her friends came over for practice, fun and games before she bounce down the stairs like the cheerleader she was. "Oh well, I can always join the cheerleader's squad in Queen City."

She smiles and told her dad to go get her bags.

*   *   *

David was at home sitting on his chase staring at the soundless TV set, drinking a glass of warm brandy. He had finished working on the case he needed for tomorrow. Now bored, his thoughts turned to Marlena and her disappointing call, informing him she was moving back to her hometown in Virginia. Reasons unknown at least she hadn't discussed them with him.

He turned up the volume on the TV, went channel surfing, saw nothing exciting and flipped it off.

With nothing better too do, he decided to call Sharron for some tender loving sexual care. Thinking of her body cause his manhood to react. He had not seen her for days and he kind of missed her enticing company. He pulled out his cell and dialed her number.

"Hello beautiful lady, want some company tonight?"

"Oh it's you David, you don't have work tonight to keep you company?"

Her voice sounded aloof distant foreign to his ears.

"It's you David? Since when did you stop looking at your caller ID? Or were you expecting someone else named David?" His tone became a bit gruff brought on by her cool manner.

"I do date other men besides you David I'm sure you know that. And no, I didn't look at my caller ID, nor was I expecting you to call."

David a bit ticked off, wondered why was she treating him so cold? He knew her well enough to know she always looked at who called her. She had to know it was him, why was she playing this silly game?

"Sharron, if you got something better to do, or if somebody is coming over, just say so, I'm not in the mood to play games tonight."

"You're not? I thought that's all you did was play game with women David. Didn't you say, love them and leave them, that is your motto, is it not?"

Her tone was controlled with an edge of resentment crawling up her spine.

David couldn't keep the growl from his voice, bearing fury he said.

"What in the hell are you talking about Sharron, you know very well where I stand. Yes I do date other women just as you do other men! I never lied to you about that! Is that what this is all about, me dating other women?"

In cool indignation, Sharron said with quite boldness.

"My darling David, you can date whom ever you please, but you don't have to lie about doing it. I saw you the other night at Sam's with that woman you call Marlena. You said you had briefs to work on, I guess it was her briefs you meant. She was hanging onto you or was it you onto her for dear life. You couldn't be pulled apart if your life depended on it. Now you call like nothing ever happened asking me for sex? That is what you what is it not Mr. David?"

David got up hitting his fist against the wall hard. He was about to bang the phone against the wall his anger became so intense. The tautness in his jaw tighten, his lips snarled, and he thundered,

"I DON'T NEED THIS FROM YOU SHARRON! I did have briefs to finish the other night! I worked my butt off until it got to a point where I needed a drink! So I went to the local bar and grill, happened to see Marlena so what? And for your information she went home alone without me, not that I didn't want her! Look if you can't handle this relationship, tell me now!"

"Relationship, Is that what you call us? My, my big boy you do need to calm down. All I'm saying is you could have been decent about it, called me told me you were going out. You are grown and can see whom ever you please.

Sharron stopped for a moment, took a deep breath before she continued. She had him where she wanted him now she needed to milk him dry.

But don't worry lover I know how to play your little game, and buy the way David, I am expecting company over tonight, he will be here any moment so I got to run. Next time you want sex, she purred, call Marlena. See yah."

The phone clicked in his ear. David was beyond just angry, something else mingled with his fury hit him hard. It was so foreign he didn't recognize it, but neither could he hide it. Jealousy, punched him right in the middle of his stomach. He never felt jealous before and he sure did not like the feeling now. Who was this guy she was seeing? She knew she belonged to him, or so he thought. This could not be love that tore at his heartstrings. No he never loved any woman. It had to be his pride. That's it! His pride was deeply crumbled. It did not make sense even to him why she got to him this way. He never allowed any women to get that close, well only Marlena for a moment, and that was because of her beauty.

David threw the cell on the carpet, sat back down trying to calm down. There was no calmness in him to be found. He had to see for himself who Sharron was seeing. He got up quickly left the house headed for her place. He would park and wait outside and see who came to call on his woman.

*   *   *

A lot of activities were going on at the hospital when doctor Jahner arrived. He could hardly wait to converse with doctor Blank and hear the results he found out from this mysterious case.

Doctor Jahner quickly unlocked the door to his office sat at his desk listening to his messages on the answering machine, there was nothing too pressing. He looked at his watch, five minutes left. He called his nurse asked her to clear his calendar for the rest of the day and not disturb him.

A knock came on the door.

"Come in, come in,"

He stood waiting for doctor Blank to come inside. He was a much shorter and slimmer man than doctor Blank who was a much older man. After a few moments of formality the two men got down to business.

"So doctor Blank, what are your findings?"

"Well, these bites are very interesting. What I know is they are not from any kind of snake known to man yet they have the same kind of venomous poison found in copperheads or cobras. The poison did not spread to any other part of their bodies, that in it's self is strange, but good to a degree. What I don't know is; how could it not spread? You say each was bitten by something coming from a twenty-dollar bill. My question is could it be that someone laced the money with poison, and could it be some kind of witchcraft? In that department I know nothing about, but I do have a sister-in-law who is a good Christian, maybe she can get her Church to pray against this. In the meantime, we need to find some answers fast, because they are not responding to any treatments.

*   *   *

Sharron was disappointed that David did not fight for her attention longer, and demand she see him. She felt the underline fire coming from him so why didn't he say he'd come over? She guessed that was completely out of David's comfort zone. She knew he only cared about himself and the best she could expect from him was some superficial pretend love. She bet he would call her later in the week acting like nothing ever happened needing some sexual attention. Yes that was David a real pig, nobody else mattered but his fulfillment satisfaction. The very thought hurt her. Her heart screamed, 'not this time he will not give her only a part of himself.' If he could not completely care about her or her feelings as she did his, she wanted no part of him. She would not be his sexual pet, his sidekick, or his part-time lover.

Nathan was so much more different than David. This man had sent her flowers two days ago, called her asking her nicely could he take her out to dinner. Sharron couldn't help but accept the date. She told him on one condition that they eat at her place. He could bring the dinner or make dinner whatever was easier for him. Nathan she knew would jump at the chance to spend some time with her. Why couldn't David be like that?

Sharron looked at the time knowing he would sound arrives. She was dressed to kill in a very erotic, sleeveless, emerald green, low cut, long grown, with gold hoops at her ears and a gold strand at her neckline. Her soft curls hung loose down her shoulders added to her sexual appeal. She glanced in the mirror adding more sugar plum gloss to her already full, luscious lips. She knew she had a perfect body, one that men fought over and women were jealous of.

The doorbell rang twice before she heard it chime interrupting her naughty thoughts. Sharron moved with grace and purpose to the door not wanting to get there to quickly. It was better if Nathan waited a moment anticipating their first real date.

She stopped in front of the door peeking out. There was sweet Nathan carrying flowers in one hand and a large bag from some nice take out in the other.

Sharron smiled opened the door, "Come in Nathan I was just about to put on some soft romantic music. Now that you are here, you can help me pick out something we both would like."

Nathan stood there for a brief instant just taking in her beauty. He had forgotten how incredible she looked. How could he be so lucky?

"Nathan I said come in, I won't bite," she gave him one of her charming smiles.

Nathan smiled back, gave her a big hug before he handed her the fresh cut flowers, and following her inside.

From the other side of the street just a house or two down sat David fuming, staring at the two of them from his car window. He waited until the couple went inside contemplating whether or not he should knock on her door. He knew this had to be some man she picked up at the local bar just to make him angry. This new suitor could not have the same connection with her he had. He had to admit he hurt her pretty bad for her to go out searching for dates and with some stranger . . .

He though 'I bet she will sleep with him tonight.' He thought of the two of them wrapped in each other's arms helped him make up his mind. 'Yes when she sees me she will send him packing.'

David exit his car walked across the street and boldly banged on the door.

After several hard knocks she and Nathan came rushing to the door. Sharron was in front of Nathan saw David first. Arms folded, face red she was furious.

"What the hell are you doing banging on my door like some crazy maniac David? What gives you the right to come over my place after I told you I was having company? Who do you think you are? Do you expect me to fall into your arms? Honey, those days are long gone!"

Nathan's face was somewhat quizzical he looked from one to the other, saying nothing. David on the other hand bit his bottom lip, drew his brows together, shot a dark ragging look at Sharron. Their eyes met and locked like fire restrained, two forces waiting for the other to bend. He wanted to say something to her, what could he say without making a bad decision worse?

David bent first, deep in his heart he didn't want to leave, but he couldn't stay either, not with another man standing in the wings. With one last pleading look David waited. When she did not bend he shook his head, turned on his heels and walked across the street, got into his car, all without another backwards glance. If she did not want him he wasn't going to beg.

Sharron completely unnerved by his reaction stared as he drove away. Part of her wanted to run after him begging him to come back, the other part was evoked by anger. How dare he walk away why didn't he demand to stay? What did he want from her blood? If he really wanted me back why didn't he fight for me? She took some fresh air into her lungs trying to calm herself down. After a moment she turned to Nathan. Sweet Nathan just stood there waiting for her next move.

"I'm sorry you had to witness that awkward scene. I had no idea he was coming over tonight. Earlier he called wanting to see me, I told him no, you were coming over, but I guess he couldn't take no for an answer."

Nathan gave her a bashful whimsical smile.

"That's alright, if I was him, I'd probably do the same thing. Sharron you are truly a beautiful, enticing bewitching woman. How can any man resist you?"

Sharron's mood changed instantly, she loved receiving compliments, especially from a

good-looking man like Nathan. She moved in closer
to Nathan put her arms around his neck pulling him
closer to her with her front door still standing wide
open, she kissed him deeply. After several minutes
he picked her up carried her inside closing the door
with his foot. They never made it to the bed, or sofa,
nor did they care about dinner, right on the floor of
the entrance way they both found release in each
others arms letting there passion explode.

*   *   *

Sandy cried out during his sleep tossing and
turning kicking the covers off, they tumbled the
floor in a heap. Cold sweat drenched his clammy
body. Images in his dream tore though his brain
causing him to wake from his own screams. He tried
to sit up, but was forced back down from hideous
dark image that held him motionless. The thing sat
on Sandy's chest like dead weight with sharp claws
around his throat choking him. Many other black
figures spud all over his room, sounds of scorn.

Sandy tried to breath. He pushed with al his might
hoping to free himself to no avail. The bloody eyes
that stared back at Sandy was ice cold, vicious, and
devious. It appeared like a lizard skin snake about
to release its' venom. Some had large frog legs, but

more than their frightful look was the smell. It was unbearable, like decaying dead bodies parts.

The anguish image bared his rotten sharp teeth biting Sandy on the neck. Huge magnets fell from the thing's mouth onto Sandy's face crawling all over his body. They crawled up his nose and embedded in his stomach through his mouth. Sandy tried to scream, but no sound could find its' way out from his lips. He so terrified his voice froze beyond his capability.

His eyes as big as saucers, could only stare back at the dark morbid force tearing through his skin. Pain ripped into his flesh sweeping over his weak sweaty body. He knew if he didn't try to get away he would surely die. Sandy fought with all his might against the evil twisting and turning calling out for it to stop as the torment continued.

Thoughts enter his mind that maybe this was a bad dream and he could force himself awake. If that were the case, why did it hurt so much? Dream or no dream he had to find a way to get out of this nightmare. Didn't he hear once 'If you resist the devil he would flee?'

He tried to think the word Jesus. With all his might he twisted his tormented body to the left, tears running down his face. That one word screamed in his brain again that word was Jesus, if he could just call out that name Jesus . . . He closed his eyes against the dark forces willing the word from his lips, Jesus . . . Black scaly hands held his mouth shut tight, but Sandy began to think the word over and over again until the word finally escaped from his frozen lips. "JESUS!"

The darkness tried to stop him, but Sandy kept saying Jesus, until it became louder and louder. God's mighty Angels of light came surrounding Sandy as the demons flew into thin air burned by the power of Jesus' name.

Sandy shook uncontrollable soaked to his skin. The pain still raked his body, but he was free at last. When he could move his arms he turned on the nightlight on the nightstand. A soft glow lit his room, and Sandy hurried out of bed and ran into his parents' bedroom.

*   *   *

Raymond had not seen his friend in days nor had he spoken to him. Sandy wasn't in school again today and Raymond was getting concerned. Maybe it was because of the rain. It stated raining two days ago continued all night and throughout the entire day. It rained so hard yesterday the school let out early. Now opened most kids were back except for Sandy.

Rain or no rain Raymond needed his sidekick. It made him feel more supreme having Sandy at his every whim. So where was he? Could his parents have taken him on one of their runs in this rain? This was not like Sandy not even to call. Whatever the reason, Raymond wanted to know.

When his last class was over he phoned Sandy. He listened to the upbeat ring tone on the line that served as his ringer. At last a tired frighten voice came over the line.

"Hello Raymond."

"Hey Sandy what's up, where have you been man?"

"I've been out of town with my folks. My dad had a short run and decided to let me tag along."

His too quiet voice disturbed Raymond.

"And you didn't call me your best friend to let me know where you were?"

Sandy closed his eyes remembering the horror. After some hesitation Sandy decided to come clean as to why he left so abruptly without a word to anyone.

"Actually Raymond, I begged my dad to take me along with them. I had to get out of this house, this town. Man I tell you, something evil is living in these parts and I don't want any part of it."

"Evil, is that all, man stop tripping just because of the last time we were all together you got chicken on me? I thought you were stronger than that Sandy. Boy, you got to master the evil not let it master you. Use it for your gain."

Sandy closed his eyes for a brief moment. He had been afraid to close them for days. Every time he did he could still see the ugly faces starting back at him from under his eyelids. He had been too terrified to sleep, only short bouts at a time, and only when he was close to his parents. He assumed because his parents had met some new Christian friends while traveling a couple of mouths ago that they mastered fear. He remembered they had called him with great excitement telling him about these born again people. At the time he could care less, now he wasn't so sure.

"Sandy, are you still there?"

"Ah, yes . . . look Raymond, you might not believe in demons or things like that, but my parents been telling me there is a devil who wants to destroy all of mankind. He is evil I know this cause I saw that evil, it came into my room the other night choking me and biting me, I thought I was going to die!"

"Sandy, man, you are tripping, come on devils? Goblins? Next you'll be telling me witches with tall black pointed hats are after you. It was probably just a bad dream."

"I wish that was it, but I still got the scares on my neck from the bites and red marks from the choking to prove it was real."

Sandy tried to relay to Raymond without reliving the terrifying events that took place that hideous night. "There were voices screaming, images moving, and excruciating pain I experienced it." No matter what he said Raymond laughed it off.

Actually Raymond was quite intrigued with the possibility of some force he could master for his personal means. Excitement raged in his heart as Sandy continued to explain. Now he understood what Mad Dog and Wolf felt. They had this powerful force and now Raymond wanted it too.

"Hey listen pal don't I always have your back? Nothing to fear, but fear itself. Look, don't go letting something like this stand in your way of fun. We are going to have a blast this Friday man, come with us."

When he did not receive the response he wanted he continue to plead.

Come on Sandy what could go wrong? If for some reason you are frightened we will leave okay? We will all be together, don't forget the girls will be there too. Guess what, I invited most of the football team and the cheerleaders to Ward's party. You know you don't want to miss that. Remember what Ward said, bring lots of pretty girls, we can have all the drinks we want, drugs, sex, what more do you want dude?"

The more Raymond talked the sillier that night seemed soon Sandy gave in and said he would be there. He didn't want to appear weak, as long as Raymond had his back . . .

*   *   *

CHAPTER TWENTY-TWO

For three whole days and nights the gusty wind and rain blew hard against the old buildings structures in Queen City causing the citizens to stay inside. The rain poured down in the streets drowning some areas with deep puddles and causing farmers some worry.

Many of the farmers had asked the people of God to pray for the rain, now they asked them to pray for it to stop. It was good to see the rain for it was needed to water their dry vegetarians so the town could continue to prosper, they just didn't want to see so much of it.

On the forth day the rain had sudden stopped.

Sometime during the early morning hours Phillip Junior awakened to a radiant Saturday California morning with the sun steaming though his windows.

He turned over yawned, stretched, opened his eyes and began to worship God thanking Him for a brand new day. After his morning prayer he hurried out of bed ran into the bathroom to brush his teeth and bathe. Even the cool tile under his feet could not disturb his peace or happiness.

For the last two weeks he devoured and emerged himself in the word of God. His faith had grown so much in a short time causing him to crave even more of Jesus. He desired to have everything God intended for him. Just to have His Holy light manifesting in his life was beyond compare. He hummed a love song to Jesus, as he got ready for the day.

The book of Romans had become one of his favorite books of the Bible and he enjoyed reading chapter 12, learning about 'presenting his body a living sacrifices' that meant Holy and pleasing unto God. This was all he wanted with his whole heart.

After his shower, he ate breakfast Carol had prepared for him, than studying the Bible learning more about the gifts of God.

Carol was just about to wash the dishes before she left for her weekly volunteer work. She did volunteer for the Church where she helped feed the homeless. Phillip surprised her by volunteering to wash dishes for her.

"Mom I can do that for you. You can go finish getting ready for Church."

"Are you sure? I have time and it won't take me long to clean the kitchen."

Phillip smiled, "Mom, go on ahead, I think I can handle a few dirty dishes and wiping down the table and stove, don't you? It is about time I help around the house."

Carol laughed as she thought back on his words not to long ago. 'I will never do dishes even if I was married and my wife was sick.' When she came back into the kitchen ten minutes later she witness Phillip sweeping the floor, all the dishes done, counter tops and table wiped clean.

"My, my you did a great job Phillip. I couldn't have done better myself. She smiled and kissed his forehead. Tell your father I'll be back no later than three or four to start dinner. He went to make sure the rain didn't hurt Mr. Bens, hardware store. Thanks again Junior."

Junior decided to take a walk after the kitchen was finished. It had been a long while since he enjoyed walking just for the sake of it.

This small town could be covered in a few miles before you reached the outskirts of town. Most of the outer areas were farmland and woods. As he walked he remembered back when he was a child around eight. He and his friends would disobey their parents, and wander into the woods looking for adventure even though they were told it was very dangerous. Looking back he could see now why his disobedience caused him great trouble.

The town's folks traded many evil stories about how the witches used these deserted areas for secret meetings deep within these woods. They told stories how they summoned up demonic spirits to do their evil biddings and sacrificed young babies to the devil. So the children were forbidden to go wandering off, but Phillip did not understand the reasoning, off he went stepping into the forbidden territory of evil. Now he could see the affects this had on him.

Over the years he became very rebellious to all authority. He lied, cheated, started smoking pot, then drinking, got involved in all kinds of illicit sex, and unknowing into witchcraft.

Finally at the tender age sixteen, the demons tricked him into believing he was supreme and nothing could hurt him. With his life in extreme shambles he allowed wickedness to manifest itself into his life. He ran from the voice of the Holy Spirit, into the mouth of death from a car he didn't see coming into the lot of the hospital. It hit and killed him. Phillip fell into the blazing pit of hell. While his parents, loved ones, and Church folks fought in the Spirit in prayer for his life, the demonic underworld fought the Angels of light for his soul. Tormented by these forces Phillip called on the only name that could save him. Through the power of prayer and the mercy of God Phillip returned to life.

Now as the sunlight shone warm on his face tears fell from his eyes. He looked up and pondered, how gracious and merciful is God's love toward them who believe and love Him. Phillip was so thankful that Jesus delivered him from a life of sin, and shame, stood on the corner weeping. His only desire, to please Jesus, and help bring more youth into the Kingdom of God! No matter what it took he was ready and willing, to fight the good fight of faith.

As he continued walking through heavy traffic pass cars, trucks, buses, he finally came to the deserted area two miles north of Main Street. The traffic here was thinner with no building you could see the bright blue open sky clear.

Wearing his protected sunglasses, Phillip gazed up toward the beautiful sky. Straight ahead he thought he saw a brilliant white light. In the center of that light appeared to be an Angel of God. He was so bright. Phillip became afraid falling on his knees covering his face shaken to his very bones. This bright light descended from the sky came closer and closer to him.

Phillip screamed out, "Whatever wrong I've done is over, I repented. Please don't let me die not again. I'm sorry!"

The Angelic being floated just above the sidewalk near him smiled. He was huge, mighty in stature with bulging shiny muscles. His skin sparked like crystal diamonds. It was like watching light within light. His face radiated and, pure liquor love dripped from his eyes as those eyes glowed with burning fire. His voice thundered off the skies, yet in the most gentleness of tone Phillip ever heard. It sounded like huge speakers turned down soft.

His love reached and saturated through Phillip's spirit, pulling him closer.

"My son, do not be afraid. Your prayers are heard in Heaven. They fall upon the ears of mercy. I have come to bless you with the gift of the Holy Spirit. You will need this. Keep on whole armor of God to fight the evil one with mighty power from on High. Even now he is planning strategies against your family and all the saints of Christ, but God who created the universe is faithful and true. He sent His Angels to protect you from all evil because of your faith. You will triumph over Satan if you stay strong in your faith and not waver."

From deep within Phillip's spirit he heard this verse.

"He causes the vapors to ascend from the ends of the earth; He makes the lighting for rain; He brings the winds out of His treasuries. He does not treat us as our sins deserve or repay us according to our iniquities. For as high as the Heavens are above the earth, so great is His love for those who fear Him."

Phillip embraced these words like a warm blanket in his heart, and he knew God had truly forgiven him. He also knew with the help of God he would triumph over all his enemies and win!

The Angel touched Phillip gently on his lips and the mighty power of God reached inside filling his mouth with glorious praises. These praises flowed from his lips first in English than in spiritual tongues of fire! Phillip worshiped God in the beauty of Holiness with his whole heart.

Time meant nothing! Phillip again fell too his knees this time in awesome wonder, worshiping God to his fullest. He didn't care who saw him, nor did he care how long he stayed on his face praising his Savior. All he knew was he would never be the same again.

*   *   *

It had been four days and still Danielle avoided answering Bob's nagging phone calls. She was glad it was Saturday. She prayed he assumed her not coming to work was because of the rain. The truth was she did not want to talk to him or ever see him again. She now ashamed of all their dirty flirtation and sexual games, the whole thing had become such an embarrassment in her spirit. How stupid could she be, to have an affair with this man risking losing her beloved family, for a fleeting moment of sinful desire? She knew not answering her phone is the cowardly way out, but she didn't care. Just the thought of him made her nauseated.

Danielle decided she would call Sharron and asked her to pick up the personal belongs she left at the office. She wouldn't tell her the real reason she decided to leave, because Sharron still saw David and she didn't want her former boss to know the truth, not just yet.

The phone rings in her ears as she waited for Sharron to pick up, finally her friend answered.

"Hello girlfriend where have you been hiding?"

"Where have I been? The phone works both ways my dear friend. Anyway the reason I'm calling is to ask a favor of you. Thomas and I have been working on our relationship and we realize it will take a while for us to completely turn our marriage around, so we decided to seek some professional help. With taking the children to school, house work, being here for Thomas, I felt I should quit my job and . . ."

Sharron half listen, still sleepy from the past nights spent with Raymond, until she heard Danielle say she decided to leave her job, stay home with Thomas, her ears perked up.

"What did you say? Wait a minute girl back up tell me again what you just said. The last time we talked you were with Mister good body down in Mexico having the time of your life. Now you'll telling me you and Thomas are back together? What did I miss?"

"It's a story I don't intend to rehash at this time. Look, all I need you to do is go pick up my belonging I left at the office that's it. Can you do that for me please?"

"You are not getting off that easy Danielle, so you better tell me what really happened. Did he hurt you? You know I never did trust that bastard."

No he didn't hurt me. Sharron, look, I realize in the past we have talked about most everything, under her breath she mumbled, a dumb mistake I made. Louder she continued, but this time I really do need you to just be a good friend and pick up my things without asking questions. Can you do that for me or not?"

Sharron frowned she knew something must have happened for Danielle to change so drastically and she was hurt Danielle wasn't going to share the info with her.

"Touchy, touchy, chill girl, why can't you go yourself, or are you ill?"

Danielle flushed. Too many questions she only wanted this to end. She did not intend to convey what happened between Thomas and her to her nosy friend. To Tell Sharron her personal business was like telling the world. Next thing David and Bob would know her real feelings about them. She took a deep breath, closed her eyes and continued wanting to hurry off the line.

"That's okay whatever I left behind can stay there. Sorry to bother you, go back to sleep."

"Now you got me really curious Danielle, but if you don't want to share your news with me, let me share mine. Are you ready for this? I broke up with Mister David. Umm saw him with that woman Marlena the night he was supposed to be working. Yah! Anyway you know the night you went to Mexico and left me. Well I got tired of playing second fiddle to his other . . ."

Before she could start cursing Danielle spoke up quickly.

"Okay, I get the picture Sharron. It's about time you recognize the truth. I told you he didn't want any kind of commitments and you know how he loves pretty faces. I know it hurts, but I'm just glad you walked away before things got worse."

"Too late for that, he's done his dirt. But no worries, I'm fine now. Got me a new suitor, name is Nathan, and he hangs onto my every word."

"Not again Sharron. Don't tell me you're falling in love with some stranger again."

"Not this time sugar, in fact never again! Let the men fall I'll just enjoy the ride for a while until I get bored."

The two ended up talking for another twenty minutes promising to see each other later the following week. They hang up without mentioning Bob's name again.

*   *   *

Bob was beside himself worrying about Danielle. He couldn't understand why she didn't answer his calls? Did her husband find out about their affair, maybe he was holding her hostage or something? Bob had to find out the reason Danielle didn't call him. He stood in his office staring out the window watching traffic pass by on Main Street hoping against hope that Danielle would drive up in one of those cars.

It was half past ten, and Bob had come in the office to finish some briefs he needed for Monday. Now done, he decided to go check on Danielle and see if she plans to come in on Monday. He headed for his car, drove the distance to her home in ten minutes. Parked out front he waited to see weather Thomas was home or not. With no action outside the home and he could not tell weather Danielle was home either. Her car could be parked in the garage.

Exiting his car he hurried to her door rang the bell four times waiting for someone to answer. He already had planned if Thomas answered, what he would say.

Danielle heard the bell. She hurried to the door expecting to see the TV repairman. She had called a local TV repair company yesterday asking to send someone to fix the children's set. They told her he would be there Saturday morning between 11:00 and noon.

Things sure had changed inside her. In the past she would just buy a new TV set and dump the old one, but now with only one income coming in she knew they had to be mindful of what they spent.

Without looking to see who was at the door, she opened it, wearing red shorts and one of Thomas's tee shirts. All though cleaning was not her thing, she had been mopping the kitchen floor. They could no longer afford cleaning services, and Danielle wanted to surprise Thomas of how she had changed.

"Oh my god, Bob, my goodness what are you doing here?"

Danielle hand went quickly to her hair out of habit smoothing it down. Than her face flushed red and she stumble over her words.

"Bob, I said, w.h . . . a . . . t do you w.a . . . n.t?"

"I wanted to see you, and see if you were alright. Why haven't you answered my calls?"

Danielle tried to think of some excuse, when none came to mind she decided just to tell the truth. She looked at him beneath the outward appearance, she saw his true self. She wondered what she ever saw in this man. Deep in his eyes were evil darts she never recognized until that last night she saw him. His twisted smile frighten her, she wanted him far away from her as he could get.

"I'm sorry Bob, but you knew I was a married woman. My husband and I are working on our marriage and we decided it's best for me to quit working so would you please leave."

Bob face turned dark and stormy, his eyes narrowed squinty with anger and his mouth pulled tight almost hiding his lips. She backed into the half opened door, getting ready too close it, when he reached out pushing the door more open rushing at her. It banged hard against the inside wall.

"Oh no you don't, Danielle I came here to get some answers and I'm not leaving until I know the truth. I don't believe you are fixing your marriage, because I know you love me. This is what he told you to say isn't it, isn't it?"

Bob grabbed Danielle arm pulling her closer to him. She put her hands on his chest pushing him back. She stood there shaken and frighten. His face looked so evil, nothing like a man in love, not even Thomas, when he was drunk the other night looked this malice. Bob had a meanness and spitefulness about him that terrified her.

Before she could react a second time he grabbed her by the arms and pushed her further inside the house her back hit the wall hard.

"What are you doing Bob? Please get out of my home and let me go! I will call the cops if you don't leave now!"

"Oh will you. We will see about that little girl. You don't use me for your pleasure than throw me away like trash."

"That's not what happened, please Bob I never wanted to hurt you."

He stared at her before he forced a wet kiss on her lips. As she twisted to free herself from his tight grip, her tee shirt rose higher exposing her ice blue bra. This only turned him on more. He forced her arms back high over her head against the wall. He was just about to tear her top off and have his way, when the door bell rang again. This time it was the TV repairman, they could see him from the still opened front door. A surprise Bob let go of Danielle breathing hard. Danielle quickly pulled her shirt down and ran to let him in, with fear swimming in her eyes.

"Please do come in, I was waiting for you."

The TV repairman smiled before he noticed her fear. This huge black man with gentle brown eyes that became stormy when he recognized that fear asked quietly.

"Are you alright Ms.?"

Danielle motioned with her eyes backwards shaking. The large man nodded his head, came inside walking toward Bob with a look that could kill. Bob saw the look, decided to leave rushing past the workman out the door. He turned back once catching

Danielle's eye with a promise of return, than walked swiftly away. When he was gone Danielle closed the door and said.

"Thank you sir, you don't know how much I appreciate you coming so quietly. He, that is the man who just left was my boss, he came by to, but he . . . I . . ."

"It's okay he's gone now. I don't think he'll be back anytime soon. Now where is that set you want me to look at?"

His smile reassured her she was fine at least for now, but she knew this wasn't the last time Bob would try to see her. The evil she recognized crawling from Bob's eyelids was the same evil she seen in Mexico. She knew it lived within him. It breathed with Bob's breath. Again Danielle wondered how she could have been so stupid and not recognized the truth. She never wanted to experience anything like that again. She thought about calling her husband than decided he had enough of Bob to last him for a lifetime. As long as she stayed far away from Bob, she would be alright.

*　　*　　*

Bob droved the few miles to old 'Sam's Bar and Grill.' He sat in an empty booth in the back where it was darker and ordered a scotch on the rocks. He didn't care that it was early in the day. He needed a drink now!

Two drinks and twenty minutes later an old Army buddy whom Bob gotten out of jail on several occasions came in headed for the bar stool. He had such a loud booming voice, not to mention an ugly scared up face, you couldn't help but notice him. He was as large as the Black TV repairman, but much meaner looking. He resembled one of the prisoners you saw in a TV movie, mean ugly and nasty.

He got the scares from his many fights, getting hit with broken beer bottles. He once got sliced across his nose to ear. He didn't play when it came to fights whatever scares he received the other fighter had much worse.

Bob glanced up when he hear his voice. He knew who it was and called him over to his booth. The two men sat for a while catching up on old war stories, odds and ends, than they exchanged some small talk before Doug said.

"Man I can't thank you enough, every since you got me off, I've been meaning to thank you more properly. You know what I mean? Whatever I can do for you just ask buddy, cause if it hadn't been for you, let just say me and prison would have a long life together."

"No problem man, what are friends for? I'm just doing my job, but come to thank of it, there is something you can do for me. You couldn't have come at a better time. I need your help to do . . . let's just say it's something right up your alley."

Both guys leaned in closer.

"Name it man, it's done."

Bob began to unravel a plan that he had pondered over the last hour in his mind. That plan was how he could force Danielle to come back to him. Now more details began to take form and shape as he remembered Doug had an old log cabin deep in the woods, a shake really. It was used as his hideout when he stole money from a large bank in San Jose. He had taken Bob there once some year's back. He paid Bob from some of the money he hid buried underground from that robbery because there was no trace on the bills. Now Bob needed to see if he still had it available.

"Man do you still have that old shack in the woods?"

"Yah man, I haven't been up there in a couple of years, but it still stands. Probably got huge cobwebs massive amounts of bugs, mice, and dirty, nothing a good cleaning, flash lights, some candles and a fire couldn't handle, if you know what I mean. Got no generator, I didn't want anyone to discover the where about of this place. You could stay there for weeks without ever seeing a soul if you bring in dry foods. Why do you need to use it?"

"Yes, what I need is for you to help me kidnap a woman. There is a woman I'm seeing, well was seeing. Her husband is deceiving her into believing they can make their relationship work out, but she is mine and that is not going to happen. Danielle belongs to me!"

Bob shook his head and gritted his teeth. He took a huge swallow of scotch sat the glass back on the table hard looking Doug in the eyes.

"Man I've never had any woman get to me the way this one has. She is in my every thought, under my skin. I see her face in my dreams every night. She makes me all twisted up inside whenever I'm with her. I can't work, I don't want to eat, and all I do is think of her. She is all I want. Can you understand what I'm saying?"

"Yeah, you do have it bad. What can I do to help you get her?"

"I need you to help me stake out her house for a few days. Find out her schedule, where she goes you know, whom she sees. We can take turns watching and exchange details. I have a picture of her right here."

Bob pulled out his wallet and showed a snap shot of Danielle.

"But we got to make it look like some random attack, nothing that can be linked back to me. I need to call her and apologize so she believes we are okay. I'll make her think I'm fine with the breakup."

"Good looker that one, what will we do with her at the shack?

"I don't want her hurt, just frightened. I want you to keep her blindfolded, make her believe you want money from her husband in exchange for her life. You know, kidnapping. When he doesn't pay because we won't contact him. She'll think he doesn't care enough. In a few days, I'll pretend to discover this place by accident, rescue her and save the day."

"What if something goes wrong with your plan?"

"We will face that situation if and when it happens. I don't foresee any problems, but if there is, well, I'm sure you will protect me. Know what I mean?"

He winked at Doug and they both laughed.

"You can count on me my friend."

"Look, her husband works days and some evenings. She told me this herself and her children are in school until mid-afternoon. She is left alone during all that time."

"You know Bob I'm thinking,' he rubbed his chin, 'it might be better to grab her outside the home. No mess, or struggles, no finger prints. She has to leave her place sometime, like shopping, friends, I can be waiting with an unmarked van . . ."

"Sounds like a good idea. Okay I'll find out when she does her shopping. Yeah, I can find out some of her plans through her friend Sharron. I can get my buddy to help in that area, he dates Sharron and I'm sure he can get her to tell him Danielle's plans."

The men concluded their devious scheming departed for a few days with promises to meet again with more details.

* * *

Danielle reached out to smooth a wisp of hair from her beloved daughter's sleeping peaceful face. She bent to kiss her soft cheek, noticing how much Sharee favored her daddy, almost the spitting image of him. She smiled thinking same light brown hair highlighted with gold streaks, same long pointed nose, wide round dark blue eyes and that crooked cute smile.

She thought how much she loved her daughter, this sweet child whom God blessed her with. She remembered when her doctor said that she might not be able to deliver without a cesarean, because her pelvis was too small. Through prayers she had this beautiful 9 lbs. child without surgery even though she suffered with bad labor pains for 30 hours. She never regretted having Sharree.

Danielle covered her daughter with the Cinderella blanket her daughter received from Carol last Christmas.

She stood and tiptoed to the door turning the light out. Very quietly she closed the door turned around saw Thomas just as he closed the door to their son Tommy's room. Their eyes met, they smiled tenderly at each other. Danielle waited for Thomas to catch up, she reached for his large hand, he took hers in his and they continue to walk down the hall to their bedroom.

In complete bliss they enter their room, than Thomas took her into his arms and held her close to his chest. He just wanted to listen to the beat of her heart. Oh how he adored this woman, his wife, his soul mate, and his reason for being her man. Her body close to him brought chills of joy running up his spine. There was nothing he wouldn't do for her.

Danielle surprising felt the same way about him. He was her big teddy bear, her life, and her soul mate why she couldn't see this sooner was beyond her thinking. She breathed on his manly skin and turned her face up for the kiss she knew he wanted.

* * *

CHAPTER TWENTY-THREE

Ward lean back in his seat with his feet propped up on his desk. His elbows rested on the arms of his chair, his hands in a pyramid and his nose resting on the tip of his fingers, meditating.

He was so proud of all his accomplishments during the last two weeks. He now had followers from all walks of life. Raymond and Mad Dog had done as they was told and brought over 100 youth to Ward's black mass. His brother gathered at least 50 people from Washington who gladly came. Among them were teaches, policemen, doctors, lawyers, business owners, and many others who liked dibbling into the cultist practice. Ward had them eating out of his hands. Everyone was fascinated with his great super natural power. They crowd him 'Sir Wolf' a name used only at gathering such as this. He wore a black cape and huge gold crown on his head his brother had brought for him.

His powers bewitched, fascinated, and terrified them at the same time. He held them spellbind within this power as he exercise control over their minds having them do as he pleased.

He used delicious foods to allure their appetites. Many kinds of drugs and all the alcohol they could drink. Sexual pleasures added the flavor to the night's entertainment.

When they were completely under his control so high on drugs and drunk on liquor, he demonstrated his greatest authority, by using the skull creature from the jar. Oh what fun that had been, seeing them frozen in mid air.

Many of the youth feared his power. Then there were some who secretly desired to possess that same power, but was afraid. All did exactly what Wolf desired.

They saw and experienced headless forms floating in thin air, black ghastly grotesque shadows creeping in and out of dark corner, touching them sexually. They heard blood-curling screams of torment all around them. There were chairs they sat in that became hideous animals grabbing them biting them and tormenting them. There were so many morbid things happening at once, foul smells were everywhere, as decay imps tormented them with brutal force.

Many of the younger set, assumed they were on some bad trip, believing what they saw couldn't be real, it had too be coming from the drugs made real by their minds. Some believed they were sleep-walking. Screams came in many tones as the terror continued.

Ward told them if they wanted it to stop to fall on their knees and beg him. He laughed 'I can stop the pain or kill you using it, it's your choice.' After some reluctant he finally stopped and all was as it had been. All knew he was a man to be feared and no one wanted to challenge him.

At midnight he had them sign their names in blood making him their king forever. They were told if any of them reviled what they saw or experienced they would be burned alive, cut in pieces, fed to the skull in the jar never to be found again.

As Ward continued thinking of that night his mouth twisted into an evil sneered. The phone rang causing him to curse loudly. He looked at the caller ID, picked up the phone and snarled.

"What the hell do you want Nicky?"

Put off by his ugly attitude Nicky almost hung the phone back up. She swallowed hard and said sweetly . . .

"Honey, I wanted to know if you were coming home for dinner tonight."

Her voice shuddered in fear as she waited for his reply. But she didn't expect him to be so brutal.

"You MISERABLE GOOD FOR NOTHING xxx-ooo, his voice dripped with rage. I TOLD YOU NEVER TO BOTHER ME WHEN I'M WORKING UNLESS I CALL YOU FOR SOMETHING! Now get that through your stupid little skull before I

CRUSH IT WITH MY BARE HANDS! You sicken me!"

Nicky couldn't hold back her cries. The tears ran rapidly down her face almost choking her words.

"What are you saying to me Ward? What did I do, I love you!"

The contempt he felt for her raged in his spirit. He hated her weakness, her gravelling, and her total lack of respect for herself.

"Did you say love, what is that? Why would I care about you? You are nothing but an old ugly hag who doesn't even try to fix herself up. Nicky, I told you, you sicken me. Now use your ears, and hear me clearly. If it wasn't for Rachel I would have left you years ago or killed you. The only thing you can do for me is my bidding. NOW get the hell off this line before I . . ."

Nicky dropped the receiver on the floor like it was fire. She fell across the bed covering her ears trying to drown out his angry voice brokenly wiped. The pain of those words hurt to the very core of her being. What hurt most was the fact he stopped loving her a long time ago, maybe he never did. That reality bothered her more than anything he said. There was no love from her husband, no love from her selfish mother, and now her daughter, Rachel maybe stopped loving her also.

Unloved by anyone tore at her heartstrings. The pitiful thoughts raced through her soul, killing every part of her spirit. She cried out her torment to her gods, but there was none to hear.

A dark demonic shadow slowly formed into a snake and slider across the floor over to Nicky. It crawled up the side of the bed and twisted itself around her body. Oppressing heaviness came swishing from the ancient sin she carried, it conjured up other supernatural demons beckoning her into them. Nauseating pain and fear caged her in as they sucked themselves into her stomach through her vagina. Like a whirlpool they ripple throughout her entire body bringing torment. Nicky fought for her sanity trying desperately to keep from giving into this deadly evil. There was nothing to hold onto, her spirit release itself into their power.

Back at the office Ward smiled at the filthy putrid head sitting in the closed jar. He closed his eyes embracing the darkness never seeing those eyes staring back at him with hate.

* * *

Late in the wee hours of the night a man who was bitten by the twenty, awaken to excruciating pain. Drenched in cold sweat he got up stumbling to the bathroom just before he threw up all over the floor and defecated on himself. Cold chills covered his entire body as he gasp for breath. He stumbled over to the sink to wash his face and notice his lips were blood red. Panic hit him and his heart began to race fast. He knew he was dying and he fell on his knee trying desperately too crawl to the phone. By sheer will power he made it to his cell and dialed 911 just as the blackness over took him never having a chance to say a word. He died on the spot from not enough oxygen getting to his blood cells.

About three miles north of the man's home, one of the two ladies bitten from the toxic money experience the same fate, although she never made it to the phone. She was an older lady who died alone in her bed gasping for air as her body shut down and her nosebleed running into her mouth. She choked on her own blood as it spilled from her nose and mouth.

On the far side of town Mrs. Brown awaken to labored wheezing. Her husband lay next to her sound asleep. She tried to catch her breath as blood gushed from her lips and horrifying pain choked back her cries. She could fill her body shutting down and for a spit second her mind thought of her two children left behind without a mother. Not much time to think before her bowels let go at the same time she threw up all over her still sleeping husband.

She died in a pool of blood, diarrhea, and vomit mingled together, laying next to her sleeping husband, who continued to snore.

Each of these victims had received a twenty-dollar bill through black magic sent out from Ward meant to kill them. These were ex-customer who no longer dealt with Ward they left with anger in their hearts toward him.

The man had been angry at Ward for cheating him out of two dollars for a product Ward no longer had on sale, but the sales tag wasn't removed. He swore he would get even with Ward. Ward got to him first.

The older woman didn't like the way she was disrespected because she returned a gift card someone bought for her at Ward's store she didn't want. She told him his store would be cursed. He cursed her instead.

The younger lady brought back something one of her children bought by mistake, said she couldn't understand why anyone would want to do their shopping at his place who sold demonic gifts to children. She told him she would make sure all her friends stayed far away form his place and she would pray against him. He prayed against her with her life.

*　*　*

The same nightly pain and fear that plagued Nicky for weeks came at her again between twilight sleep and wake. In the darkness of that spiritual realm, the demons lashed out at her viciously as other witches and warlocks used her body as they pleased.

She tried to completely awaken from unrest sleep, but the negative spirits taunted her mind with images of the eerie head in the jar coming after her soul, as they did nightly.

Nicky's body wrenched back and forth soaked in sweat as she tried to open her eyes. With much effort she finally was able to open her eyes. She completely startled stared into the soul of fear as her eyes caught sight of her reflection in thin air. Her own face came before her like an ugly vision. Her features twisted, distorted, and deformed she closed her eyes too keep from seeing the horrible image wincing.

When that didn't help she kicked the blankets off her weary, depressed, tired frame.

Nicky knew she needed more sleep, but how could she sleep when horrible images appeared to her nightly. She was afraid to close her eyes again. She seemed to be afraid all the time now. She never experienced this kind of stark fear before, not like this. That horror in the jar haunted her day and night. Ward's attitude frightened her constantly. The thought of her loveless mother even brought terrifying fear to her spirit. No peace could be found no matter where she went.

Nicky, lost in her own hellish nightmare with no one to help, lay crying softly eyes wide opened wondering if her daughter Rachel was sleeping. She needed Rachel so badly. How she missed their formal closeness, their time spent together has been so special. She remembered the times they would wake up go into the kitchen for warm milk and cake, talk for hours, sometimes until the sun rose up high over the horizon laughing about everything and nothing, just having mother and daughter fun.

Now her daughter presumably lay in her room down the hall feeling distant from this family. How did it get this way? Nicky understood the emotion her daughter must be feeling because it became her everyday existence, but Rachel didn't seem to have the fear Nicky had.

Loneliness pressed down on Nicky's spirit, joining fear, as the black doom threatened to over take her mind. It wasn't just her family she feared, something very evil now lived in her body and she didn't know how to get rid of it. She could feel it crawling inside her stomach and her vagina with excruciating pain and the foul raging fumes blew over her body every time she tried to sleep. She could feel it raping her body nightly like a savage beast out of control. On top of all that she had horror nightmares of the repulsive face in the bottle she witness in Ward's closet. How would she rid herself of this terror?

Agonizing over what it was and how did it get into Ward's hands tore at her fragile brain. Could that evil have manifested inside her body? Is that why she had these feelings of killing herself daily? The very thought tormented her. 'Why has my husband hid a hideous head of demonic evil in his office closet? What is his plans' for it?

Many times she saw the eyes of that thing following her around even in the day light she could not rid herself of the face.

A shape pain hit her in the pit of her stomach again and ripped down her side. Nicky cried out covering her mouth not to awaken her daughter in the next room.

In the past Nicky never minded sleeping in the dark. Now she hated the darkness and she kept a nightlight on at all times, but still the darkness came.

Tonight the eerie glow turned to dark shadows creeping across her bed and body. She closed her eyes against the gloomy sight. Where was Ward? Why did he hate her so? What happened to the love they once shared? What was to become of her? These were the questions that pressed in on her mind.

Loneliness grabbed hold of her heart and squeezed it tight Nicky felt the pain coil around her chest. She took her fist and beat her chest, trying to stop her heartache. Large tears kept flowing down her face into her mouth. They wet the pillow as she watched shadows crept closer in the semi darkness of her room.

* * *

Just two doors down the hall Agnes sat in her old wooden padded rocker staring out the window into the night. She too could not sleep for different reason.

The night bled dampness under the windowpane and she pulled the quilted blanket up higher around her shoulders. She embraced the deep-rooted bitterness in her spirit not letting go although she longed for some peace in her mind.

There was a time when she almost felt that peace. When Nicky was first born she loved holding such a small sweet infant up close to her heart. Having a newborn child who needed her and would love her no matter what was beyond her understanding. She had forgotten how it felt to love and be loved. Those times long ago forever forgotten, lost in the bitterness of her life that same daughter she now hated.

Something about night drew her into like a magnet, as she continued sitting allowing her mind to go back, bringing old memories to the surface. Her heart soon turned ice cold when those memories caught up to the day her husband refused to put Nicky down to bed. Agnes lips twisted in a snare as the negative thoughts took hold of her heart and wouldn't let go.

Arthritis sat smiling and waiting at the far end of the room, for the right time to in-flick her with crippling pain. The evil laughed and raced up her legs, arms, and back. Agnes bit her tongue to keep from screaming out as the pain ripped through her old body.

All her praying to her goddess, her homemade potions did nothing to stop this old pain that sits on her like a rock. There were times when she prayed to her goddess and things seem to change, but that didn't always happen. She thought maybe they were angry with her. She cried out again, over and over telling the air how sorry she was, begging for forgiveness if she did anything not pleasing, but nothing changed.

"Oh-h-h-h this is so go-o-d, the old lady is weak. I like seeing her weak and frail. She looks so helpless. Look at her curled in a tight ball like a trapped animal praying to her goddess for help. Just a dried up old woman; useless to our needs, so why do we want her around? Pain, coil yourself tighter around her frail body!"

The hideous pig faced, black troll, stumbled jerky over and sat on Agnes limp lap. He struck her hard with more shape pain piecing her spine. The crippling pain shot up her legs and back from the inside out causing her to double over almost falling to the floor hurting so badly. She could hardly sat back before another intense pain came, worse then the one she had before twisting its sharpness around her old body. Agnes held onto the chair for dear life, her fingers turning white as snow, she bit her lip still praying for relief.

The demon of pain, slid closer on its belly pounding her on the head with brutal force. This demon was deprave destroyer, he brought every sickness know to man. The face was so hideous not even pig face like looking at him. He dripped with crudeness said.

"Yes, I'll do just that. As you say she is no more useful to us, why not kill her now?"

"Hold on you two, we need her one more time!"

Out from the abyss came Rage, he slapped Agnes face so hard she fell to the floor this time crying out. The carpet muffled her voice, as she fell face first.

"We need her to think she is casting one more spells on Bennett's dead corpse husband, so we can embody his body. That old lady Bennett will be so pleased to have him back she will not recognize the change in him."

All three rolled with laughter. The howling could be heard in Agnes and Nicky's ears.

*   *   *

It was way past midnight as Rachel wrestled restless on her bed until she decided to get up. Rachel wasn't sleepy anyway she decided to go to the kitchen for a glass of warm milk.

It had been too long of a day not seeing Phillip although she had spoken to him over the phone. He told her he wouldn't be at the library today, because of doing some work with his dad. She missed being with his family and having her Church friends close. Nothing could take the place of going to Church where she could learn so much about her Lord.

She crept out of bed quietly not to awaken anyone, put on her robe, walked down the hall into the semi darken kitchen. She decided not to turn on the light for there was ample light from the lace curtains hanging at the large window as the moon shone brightly.

For the last two weeks Rachel had moved around the house feeling lonely, set apart from her family. She missed spending time with her mom on these late night warm milk adventures. She missed her mom so much. If only she could get her mother to understand the realization of having Jesus in her life, how things would change for her and their relationship. Rachel knew Nicky never had any real peace. Having the answer did not help if she couldn't get her mother to listen to the truth. She had tried communicating with Nicky on several occasions to no avail. It was like something held her back from understanding and accepting the truth.

On many mornings Rachel got up early and left for school before her family came down for breakfast. When she came home from her classes she went straight to her room where she stayed until dinner. Most times she did not come home until much later, going to the library to study and secretly seeing Phillip Jr. This being the only other time she got to see him except at school.

Her grandmother Agnes had questioned her on many occasions as to why she wasn't home much anymore. Rachel gave a lame excuse about how she has so much homework to do and studying for test kept her busy. There was no way she could confide in this heartless grandmother about her salvation. That would be the dreaded day her family would send her away to some distant witch family member to live and study wicker, until she was twenty one, if her dad didn't kill her first.

After her warm drink she opened the back door and stepped out onto the patio for some much-needed fresh air, leaving the door a jar. Her home wreaked from filthy demon spirits manifesting throughout the house. She could always smell them. She felt them every time she got home swarming allover, except her room. That was the only safe place in the house where they could not come through the blood of Christ. Her room stayed covered by the blood of Jesus. She kept her Bible opened to Psalm 91, and prayer was constantly going forth for her safety.

The cool night air blew across her face as she sat on the wooden two-seated swing on the left side of the patio. Her face turned gazing out at the stars in deep thought.

"Hey Rachel, what are you doing up so late, don't you have school tomorrow?"

Rachel jumped, hearing the deep voice of her father. She turned around facing him standing in the doorway. She hadn't heard him come up. Ward's huge frame almost completely covered the space of the opened door. He stepped out and in two long strides was beside her.

She jumped again involuntarily when she saw her father come closer to her. Rachel's hand flew to her chest and she heard her labored breathing as fear came upon her.

"Oh d-a-d . . . you startled me, I didn't hear you coming. I just wanted some milk to help me sleep.

W-h-at about you, why are you up, it's past four isn't it?"

Rachel could not take her eyes off his dark knowing eyes. She was drawn to them as she saw evil staring at her out of the middle of his iris so intense she covered her face and turned away. Ward continued to stare wondering what was different about his daughter. A thought came to mind and Ward rejected it. He did not want to think his baby girl no longer was a part of his spirit . . .

He rubbed his mouth with the back of his hand still pondering if the demons were telling him the truth. He decided to question her choosing his words wisely.

"Rachel, what have you been up to lately? I haven't seen you hardly, got any new friends that's keeping you from your family?"

Rachel turned suddenly back surprised at his question, her heart in her throat. She knew what that look meant, 'you better not lie to me.' It was as if he could see into her very soul. She knew she had to be careful of her answer or he would know the truth she hid. Rachel tried to come up with some clever words to distract her dad. She laughed got up walked over to the flowerbed with her back to him.

"Oh daddy, you are so silly, who would be new in Queen City? I just been busy with classes, you know test, homework . . ."

Ward had quietly come up behind her he put his hand on her shoulder and tuned her around to face him. Rachel body began to shake.

"Rachel you were never a good liar. Now tell me the truth, who have you been seeing?"

Her heart raced, her palms became sweaty as she looked at him trembling inside trying to find the right words to say. Although it was cool outside big beads of sweat formed on her forehead. She looked down at her hands willing herself to think of something quick, anything but the truth of her salvation.

"Dad-d-y, I don't know what you are talking about. I do have friends at school you don't know, but new . . . ?"

"Ward, Rachel, I thought I heard voices out here. What are you too talking about? Rachel why are you up so early on a school day?"

Nicky had come in the kitchen for warm milk too. She saw the door opened noticed Ward hovering over Rachel like a tiger about to pounce on its prey. A mother's instinct told her Rachel needed help now. Not knowing for what reason, she like a mother hen came outside to protect her child.

Ward turned around frowned when he saw her. At the same moment Rachel hurried over to her mother breathing hard.

"Mom, just the person I want to see. I have a question about my party dress for the school dance next week. You promised me a month ago we would go shopping together and buy a new one. Is that date still on?"

Rachel did not really want a new dress nor did she want to go to the party. She said the first thing that popped in her mind. It threw Ward off seeing Nicky in her old blue long gown she worn for years. All the negative emotions he felt about her came to the surface. She looked old, worn out, dumpy and loveless. He couldn't stand the sight of her. He walked swiftly into the house, grabbed his blankets from the hall closet heading for the den where he intended to sleep without another word to either of them.

Rachel hugged her mother for several minutes' eyes closed just feeling her mother's love. Nicky was so taken back tears steamed down her face. This was the first time since her daughter became a Christian that they embraced this way. It was her fault because Rachel wanted to embrace her many times before, but Nicky had been afraid of her own daughter.

"Honey, do you want to go for a drive? I need to escape these four walls for a moment and I sure could use the company."

Rachel gladly agreed she too needed to escape this morbid atmosphere, if only for a little while.

Nicky hurried and got her kegs and purse. Neither stopped to dress, just got in the SUV in their robes, drove through the quiet streets laughing and taking just like old times. Rachel decided this was the perfect time to explain her faith in Jesus. She had prayed for days for another chance like this.

"Mom, I know you told me never to bring this subject up again, but in light of what's been happening I can't help but try to convince you about the truth of what witchcraft really is."

Nicky started to protest shaking her head giving Rachel the 'I'm not listening look.'

"Please hear me out before you say anything mom. You know I love you, but you need to learn the truth, and if you are not totally convince when I'm done then I guess that's that."

Nicky thought about all the times she missed her daughter and how lonely she had been. This helped her to make the decision to listen.

"Okay Rachel, I'll listen to what you have to say, but I ready don't think it will change my mind."

Nicky pulled over found a parking space in a small neighborhood park not to far from their home, shut off the engine, sat back, and folded her arms. She decided she would listen with half an ear, and that was only because it gave her more time along with her daughter.

"I'm all ears."

Rachel closed her eyes praying to God silently saying.

"Dear Heaven Father, I believe my mother can be a powerful for your Kingdom. Please Father, give me the words to say that will touch my mother's heart and turn her around for Your glory! Anoint my words as I glorify your name in Jesus mighty name Amen!"

"I'm waiting Rachel, time is not standing still, you have classes in a few hours and I'm tired."

Rachel smiled reached over and hugged her mother. While in her arms she began by saying.

"I love you mom with all my heart, but as much as I love you, Jesus loves you more. He loves you so completely that He gave His life so that you may have Eternal life in Him! All your life I know you have longed for this kind of love given unconditionally. You know I love you, but do you know that my love could not be complete until I found Jesus? You see mom I didn't know what real love was until my Master showed me. Now I have peace in my heart like never before. I have joy everyday deep down in my spirit!

I became whole only when I met Jesus. I believed everything we did was good because we never tried to hurt anyone only help. But I did not understand what good was until I met the only one who is good, and that is the Almighty God. Through Jesus' word I found out we were all born in sin through Adam."

"You see Adam the first man, brought sin into the world. He, and Eve disobeyed God's commandment, as a result sin was manifested. Through disobedience came sickness, shame, all matter of sin and death upon all mankind. I can't say it just the way it's in my heart, but I know in the Bible in the book of Romans, I think in chapter 5, verse, 12 talks about this."

Nicky thought, 'if he is such a loving God why can't he heal my pain?' She shifted in her seat from side to side trying to get more comfortable. The foreign demonic objects living in her stomach kicked her hard, bringing sharp cramps wanting to discourage her from listening any farther. Nicky bit her bottom lip to keep from screaming out. Rachel noticed her mother's frown, assumed she did not want to continue listening and hurried to get to the point.

"Mom, just hold on a bit longer okay, I'm getting there."

Nicky sadly nodded her head and decided she was going to listen after all even if it killed her. She needed this peace her daughter talked about so badly.

"Jesus came to destroy the works of the devil and to set mankind free from the power of wickedness. He is the only way back to our Heavenly Father. No matter what you have done, Jesus is here to set you free."

All of a sudden the pain ripped through Nicky like white lighting she bent over screaming.

"What about this thing living in my body? Can your God take away this horrible pain! I CAN'T STAND THIS ANY LONGER, I NEED HELP NOW!"

At that moment something sounding like an ugly growl roared from Nicky's lips. She began to thrash about in her seat, jerking her head back and forth. A deep manly growling voice roared from her lips saying,

"YOU CANNOT HAVE HER, SHE IS MINE! The voice was so loud and hateful it brought fear into Rachel until she heard the voice of the Holy Spirit say to her 'Do not to back down, rebuke the foul spirit!'

Strength came into Rachel as she spoke these words.

"YOU FOUL UNCLEAN AFFLICTING SPIRIT, I COMMAND YOU BY THE POWER OF THE LIVING GOD TO LOOSE YOUR HOLD OFF MY MOTHER NICKY NOW! BY THE POWER AND AUTHORITY OF JESUS CHRIST GIVEN UNTO ME, I FARTHER COMMAND YOU TO FLEE HER NOW IN JESUS MIGHT NAME! YOU CANNOT HAVE HER SOUL, THE BLOOD OF JESUS IS

AGAINST YOU, AND YOU MUST LEAVE NOW! YOU ARE NOT WANTED SHE DOESN'T WANT YOU IN HER LIFE SO LEAVE NOW IN JESUS MIGHTY NAME!"

The voices spoke in a more sinister tone, "Oh she does want us to stay and you cannot make us go, this is our home."

Nicky still trashed about the seat with the nastiest look on her face Rachel ever seen. Her mouth twisted and her whole face greatly distorted made her appear like a horror movie come to life, right before Rachel's eyes. Rachel did not know if the demons living within her mother was going to attack her or not. She had never faced anything like this before and didn't quite know how to handle this. She spoke out aloud.

"Jesus, please HELP ME. TELL ME what do I do?"

Deep within Rachel's spirit peace rested and the Holy Spirit gave her the words to say.

"Satan, you are a liar! She told you to leave. She doesn't want you now leave in the name of JESUS!

Rachel grabbed her mother by her arms and gave her a shaking.

"Mother denounce this evil tell them you don't want them to stay, than call on Jesus mighty name. He will give you the strength and save you, please mother, do it now!"

Nicky looked at Rachel with the demons still inside. Part of her wanted to kill her and part of her wanted to run away from her so her daughter could be safe. As Rachel kept crying out for her to resist the evil inside Nicky shut her eyes tight against the forces that wanted to hurt her daughter Rachel. She knew if she did not call on Jesus soon the negative forces inside her would kill her daughter. With all her might she screamed,

"GET OUT OF ME YOU FOUL SPIRITS. I DENOUNCE YOU BY THE BLOOD OF RACHEL'S GOD JESUS TO LEAVE ME ALONG! I RESIST YOU NOW BY THAT SAME BLOOD! JESUS, PLEASE HELP ME! PLEASE, COME INTO MY HEART NOW WITH YOUR POWER TO HEAL, SET ME FREE FROM THESE UGLY SPIRITS! I REPENT TO YOU OF ALL MY SINS, I REPENT OF ALL MY SINS! COME INTO MY HEART JESUS!"

The deceiver had a deadly hold around her throat choking her. When they knew she meant it they threw her backwards with might force before a loud cry sounding like wild animals raged from her body, as the Angels of light and the spirit of Truth lit the SUV making room for Jesus entry. The might King of Glory came to rest in the heart of Nicky.

All demonic forces were cast back to the abyss in trembling fear. The pain left Nicky's stomach instantly.

Nicky could hardly believe the wonderful peace that melted her heart and came to rest within her.

Rachel noticed the glow on her mother's face where the demon had been just moments ago.

Tears ran down both faces as they hugged each other wrapped tightly laughing with joy. They stayed that way for a long time just laughing and crying happily together.

The night's silver white stars gave over to the early morning dawn, and the sky cast orange, yellow and red across the horizon. Finally Nicky stopped laughing and said.

"Honey, why didn't you tell me soon about how wonderful Jesus is?"

"I tried, but at the time you were not ready." Rachel laughed again.

"I know you did sweet heart, I guess you were right at the time I wasn't ready. I never understood Him until now."

A frown crossed Nicky's face, as she thought about how they would live under the same roof with Ward and Agnes. The same thought crossed Rachel's mind too.

"Rachel, we cannot go back to that house now. We need to move out, how I don't know, where I don't know, all I do know is if Ward or mother found out about this we are both dead. Your father and grandmother are very evil people honey. They would stop at nothing to destroy us. They would think of us as their enemy."

"I was thinking the same thing mom. The way dad looked at me earlier tonight was so terrifying. I never knew he was so evil until I looked into the eyes of Satan himself."

"Listen, maybe we can tell them we decided to take a trip just the two of us. Ward could care less where I go and we could tell him you passed all your classes so you don't have to attend school the rest of the school year."

Nicky held Rachel back so she could see into her eyes. Rachel shook her head slowly.

"Mom, I know we have to think of something, but lying is not the answer. It is a sin. Look I got friends who are mighty Christian and I know with their help we can come up with a much better plan."

Nicky searched her daughter's eyes looking for hope. A thought came to her mind that had been a secret for years and she knew this was the time to share it.

"When your grandfather died he left me with all he owned, money in the bank, the house, stocks, and bonds. Most I gave to Ward to start the store, but I did keep back some nobody knew about. I was saving it for you when you started college after you graduated. It is in a bank in San Jose. Ward and I went there for our honeymoon it seems so long ago, that's when I deposited it. Ward at the time had no idea how much money I had neither did your grandmother. I bet with interest we could live on it for many months maybe even a few years until we get jobs. I haven't checked to see how much is still there for years."

"Mom, that's wonderful, but I don't want to leave Phillip and his family. Mom, just wait until you meet them, I know Mr. James will give us some good advice."

"Who is Mr. James Rachel?"

"He is Phillip's father. A real wonderful person, full of love like the whole Church is. We can tell dad we decided to stay over night in a motel since it was so late and later today we can go meet the James' family okay?"

Nicky wasn't so sure of the plan, but she did recognize they needed help if they were to escape this madness safely.

"Okay Rachel, I'll meet them, I sure hope you are right honey. I'm afraid of what could happen to us if your plan doesn't work out."

Rachel whispered a prayer asking God to protect them from all evil. She too wasn't completely sure what they were up against. All she knew was she had to trust her God and His mighty warrior Angels.

*   *   *

Chapter Twenty-Four

"What can you tell me from their autopsy reports? Yes, I know poisons generally have certain primary effects with secondary symptoms. You say their bodies were absent of cytochrome oxidase, and no oxygen could get to the blood cells. So what you are you telling me is corrosion, or something similar, caused the deterioration of blood cells . . . yes, that could cause the destruction of the human tissue usually by mere contact, but other people had to come in contact with this too. So how? . . . Yes, I know the symptoms match, but how could they . . . Okay Dave, yes . . . Thanks again. Say hello to your wife and family . . . Good day."

Doctor Jahner placed the phone in the cradle, sitting back in deep thought. A few minutes pass before Doctor Jahner picked up his phone. Dialing doctor Blake's number and after a few rings . . .

"Hello"

"Doctor Black, I just got off the phone getting the autopsy report from those cases of poisoning. You were right someone is putting poison on money and causing the blood cells to explode. It could very well be witchcraft."

Doctor Blake shook his head at the thought of someone out there killing people with money laced with deadly poison.

"As a killer of blood cells, it prevents the absorption of oxygen throughout the body causing the cells to explode. Burning pain is usually the initial symptom followed by vomiting, uncontrollable diarrhea, bloodstain feces, and/or systemic bleeding. This caused their death."

"So when they put their hands in their mouths, thereby swallowing the poison. Yes, I see now how that could have killed them."

"What I don't understand is why and who would commit such a gruesome crime, and right here in Queen City? We all heard the stories of sacred meetings and sacrifices being done in the woods for years, but I thought they were old wise tails. I've lived here all my life and never seen anything like this. What are the police saying?"

"From what I heard they are calling it a random prank. They aren't saying too much about it, too soon I guess."

The two doctors conversed more, both coming up with wild reasons until they decided prayer had to be the only way to stop this evil.

*   *   *

Raymond, Mad Dog, Sandy, and their three dates sat in his SUV at the Queen's Park drinking cold beer and listening to the latest rap song from Raymond's CD collection. They were discussing all the possibilities they would have in their new apartment. He and Mad Dog were in the process of sharing an apartment that Raymond's parents owned. His mom had told him he could have a roommate as long as that person was a responsible tenant. So he chose Mad Dog, because Sandy was too young and he knew Sandy's parents wouldn't approve of him living on his own. Deep down Sandy was glad, because he still had nightmares and wanted to stay closer to his family.

The previous tenants were a young couple who had moved suddenly out of town last week, because of the mysterious death of the wife's sister. That sister had been one of the victims poisoned by the money. The dead woman's widower and their two young children also moved right after the funeral. None of the family wanted to hang around wondering if they would be next.

The teens all skipped school for the afternoon with lame excuses given to their teachers who did not seem to care anyway, as long as the students passed their classes.

Two of the girls were from Twin Oaks High, who was friends with Jenae, Rachel's cousin. They became friends when she moved to Twin Oaks City over three weeks ago. The three young girls quickly became best friends. Jenae introduced them to the boys who asked them to skip class today.

Jenae and her father found their house on the web weeks earlier and decided to move to Twin Oaks, because there were no vacancies available in Queen City.

Twin Oaks City was just twenty miles south of Queen City and was very similar except it had a larger population of about 4,500 people.

"Hey dude, got some smokes?"

Raymond reached into his brief case pulled out some homemade thin cigarettes, lit up a couple and passed them around. Everyone took long drags inhaling the drug into their lungs. Each boy took a girl and got ready for some sexual pleasure. Mad Dog had fifteen-year old Jenae in the back seat practically inhaling her. She didn't care. At fifteen she thought she was in love.

Raymond picked the taller girl because he was taller than Sandy and he liked blonds. Sandy did not care who he got. All three girls were fine to him. His date a slim cute brunette cuddled up closer. She smiled at him ready for some fun and action.

Out of the blue her cute face became horrifyingly distorted, like some inhuman animal. Her eyes dripped blood, from the corner her mouth crawled slimy green and brown heads of bodiless huge bugs. Their hideous faces rolled down the young girls face onto her breast licking them like ice cream, and then melting within her skin.

Sandy screamed, jumping back as quickly as he could, falling into Mad Dog and his date. They were in the back seat making out. Mad Dog pushed Sandy back, angrily.

"What's up with you dude, are you crazy? Get back on your side, and keep it down."

Sandy turned just in time to see a hideous dark creature drooling under Mad Dog skin. His own image began to vibrate then melt like wax, as he caught a glimpse of his refection from the over-head mirror from the front of the SUV. All at once ugly black creatures with holes in the place of eyes embedded under Mad Dog's skin and he started laughing at Sandy. He closed his eyes trying to block out the wild images. He tried to clear his vision and clogged mind, hoping it was only the smokes.

With his eyes closed, he witnessed the most terrifying sight ever. Black hideous demons of all kind swam before his face. Sandy screamed again opening his eyes to the face of death beckoning him to join them. Black hooded people with evil eyes grabbed at him to join them from the spiritual world. Everyone in the SUV had disappeared as these grotesque haunt figures came to life. They reached for him, pulling him down in the seat. Sandy blacked out from total fright.

*   *   *

It was Wednesday night and the members of the 'Shepherd's Way In Church' were filing in ready for the meeting. Everyone greeted each other lovingly as they made their way to their seats.

Normally they had Bible study on Wednesday, but this night was different. You could feel it in the atmosphere; something unusual was about to take place. The members did not know what to expect after the call each received, asking them to pray for the meeting.

The service started out with praise and worship songs, then prayer lead by Sister Gallagher. Pastor Blake stood up, took out his handkerchief wiped the sweat from his brow, cleared his throat and began speaking to his congregation.

"My fellow saints, it has come to my attention of a serious matter concerning witchcraft being used against some people through money in the form of twenty-dollar bills. This money has been laced with some sort of deadly poison. It has taken three people's lives already and we don't know how many others may be affected."

You could hear the congregation intake of breaths and whispering. Pastor Blake held up his hand for silence. Everyone glued their eyes on him waiting for more details.

"Some of you may know I am a good friend with the coroner here in Queen City. We have been friends for quite a while. Normally he and I do not share our personal matters, for it is privilege information, but under these unusual circumstances he wanted the Church prayers. We need to pray for the safety of others who could be next in line against this demonic curse.

As I understand this, they coat the bills with some sort of poison, when the person comes in contact with the money they experience a burning pain and it begins to kill, or dries up their blood cells. This causes their bodies to shut down completely and their body functions explode. Now I cannot say I understand the doctor's terminology, but I do understand the strategy of Satan.

I am calling for a three day fast and shut-in, here at the Church starting this Friday morning at six until midnight Sunday. All who can come out and pray with us please do. For others, I want you to fast at home and pray during these three days. We must fight together against this diabolical evil force. I like to see a show of hands as to how many can come down to the Church for the shut-in."

Most everyone raised their hands, including the James' family. Only three people who had to work Friday morning said they could join the Church later that evening.

Pastor Blake continued to encourage the believer as they bowed together in faith falling on their knees crying out to God for help.

*　　*　　*

Nicky never experienced a better night sleep than she did the night after her new conversion. Peaceful sweet dreams had her mind in a relaxed mood. She awoke to the sun streaming through the windowpane, casting brilliant colors across her walls from the glass flower vase sitting in the window.

She stretched her arms over her head smiling for the first time in many years thinking about yesterday when she and Rachel came in well after ten, finding Agnes sitting on the sofa watching her favorite soap opera. The look she gave them was dirty.

Agnes had never liked being bothered while her shows were on so when Rachel leaned over and gave her a kiss on the cheek she abruptly pushed her away, frowning.

Ward left earlier for work, both Nicky and Rachel could not have been happier. Neither wanted to face him until they came up with a good solid plan.

Mother and daughter spent the rest of their afternoon in Rachel's room laughing, talking, and sharing jokes. Then they decided to prepare dinner for the family until they got the call from one of Ward's ladies, saying he was staying over her house and would not be home tonight. Ward did this on occasions to irritate Nicky. He liked messing with her mind. Calls like this in the past would have hurt, but now it was the best news Nicky could receive. This helped her have the best good night sleep she's had in a long time.

Now lying in bed she thought about how she would get her money from the bank Friday. She decided to wait until Agnes and Ward were out. Fridays were Agnes' day with her friends and hairdresser. Most of those times Agnes stayed long past dinner and her friends would drive her home late. In the past Nicky hated taking her mother cause, it left her lonely. She did not have any close friends of her own.

A forceful knock at the door brought her mind back to the present. She knew whom it was banging on the door. Who else could it be but her mother? She took a deep breath, got out of bed, slipped on her robe, slippers and went to the door and unlocked it.

"Why you lock that darn door Nicky? Who are you trying to keep out?"

"No one mother, what is it that it couldn't wait until I got up?"

Agnes gazed at her daughter for some time before she said in a suspicious tone.

"What are you and Rachel up too? And don't give me that crap about mother and daughter bonding, cause I see the stupid looks on both your faces. Yesterday when you both came in, I could tell something ain't right with the two of you, and if you don't tell me now, I'm gonna find out just what it is anyway."

Nicky covered her mouth to keep from laughing. Having the same look as her daughter was a compliment she embraced. Feeling good and certainly not thinking, she went to hug her heartless mother who pushed her back hard. A mean scowl appeared on Agnes already distasteful face.

"Mother, why are you so serious, mean, and so disapproving of everything I do? I can never please you can I? Look, why don't I fix you a nice breakfast and take you to get your hair done today instead of tomorrow? Maybe the two of us could have lunch later at the café Di, I could use an outing and so can you mother. Would you enjoy that with me mother?"

Agnes thought for sure the woman standing in front of her was from out of space maybe some alien from another planet had embodied her daughter's body while she slept. The only time Nicky ever asked her out for any meals were birthdays and that was rare. 'And it sure ain't my birthday.' No something was surely different about Nicky and she did not like it.

She moved back away from Nicky shaking her head no. As quickly as her old wobbling legs could move, she went into her room slamming the door shouting through it.

"I will never have lunch with you girl! If you really want to be of some use I suggest you take me over to that Bennett woman's house now! I need to continue some unfinished business. On second thought maybe you can help me. Come with me over to this woman's house so we can bring her Henry back from the dead. That's what you can do for me. Help me with calling his dead spirit back into his body!"

The smile quickly vanished from Nicky's face and shock took the place. Every part of Nicky's spirit recoiled against such evil practices that only yesterday would not have been so devastating. Now she hated to think about the deception her mother perceived as truth. How can she persuade her mother into doing right without telling her the real truth? If she knew about Rachel's and her conversion what would Agnes do? The real question is what would happen if she decided to tell Ward?

"NICKY answer me! I said I want you to go help me . . ."

"I know what you said mother and I'm sorry I can't."

Nicky walked over to Agnes' closed bedroom door and spoke as sweetly as she could.

"Mother, as you know I got shopping to do. I want have time to accompany you. Why would you disturb an old man from his sleep like that anyway? You know in the past, we only helped bring some closure to the families hurting, by allowing them to say their final good-byes."

Agnes opened the door pointing a bony finger at Nicky snarling,

"This old lady is paying me enough to choke a horse. I don't care a hoot about his darn sleep, or if he's in la-la land I want THAT MONEY! You are trying my patience girl. Now I have asked you nicely to bring me over to her house and stay with me until it's done, all you need to say is yes, do you hear me missy!"

Nicky turned her back from her mother something she never done in her whole life. She needed some strength and the words to tell her mother how she felt about this whole mess. She remembered Rachel telling her prayer is always the answer, and asked

Jesus to please give her the words she needed to say. Peace, entered her spirit and in a quiet tone she answered.

"No mother, I will not subject myself to your greed and evil. All my life I've put up with your selfish cruel ways. I've gone along with everything you felt was right just to have your approval . . . that never happened, but not anymore."

Nicky turned back to face the shock written on her mother's face. She stood there looking small, helpless, defeated and something more scared. The look almost stopped Nicky from saying what was in her heart, but she knew she must tell her. After a moment of pause she continued.

"I don't want to hurt you mother, even when you have hurt me so many times, but there is something I have wanted to say to you for a such a long time now. It is burning in my heart to tell you Mother that your own miserable misery has made your pathways evil. This caused bitterness to grow in your heart, and this bitterness you feel has eaten up any love you might have had for Rachel, yourself, or me. You practice so much deceit believing riches will make you happy! Nothing can give you happiness if you don't change from your wicked ways. You have become a prisoner in your own twisted reality running from love when it was right in your face.

Why mother have you not cared enough about me to ever say I love you?"

Nicky was close to tears waiting for some answer. Agnes seemed to shrink before her eyes. The evil would not let go of her mind. Agnes held onto the negative thoughts of old. She turned away saying . . .

"I'll catch a cab. I don't need you or this crap! Where there is a will, there is a way. Now get away from my door, I don't need you."

Nicky could not help but cry. Agnes blunt behavior was all too real. The tears fell down her face as her heart hurt for the loss love she would never have from her mother. The words tumbled out from her mouth.

"Your soul will forever rot in hell if you don't listen now mother!"

Nicky ran to her room slamming the door behind her. The dam broke and she shed the tears that broke her heart.

* * *

Chapter Twenty-Five

When Sandy opened his tired eyes, he still lay in the back seat of Raymond's SUV. The guys sat laughing and talking about how silly Sandy looked when he opened his eyes and saw them. Mad Dog told him he have a bad reaction to the pot and was screaming for help before he blacked out.

Sandy reviled his hallucinations seeing hideous faces drooling under their skins. The guys did not take Sandy seriously. To them he was always frightened of something. Seeing haunts was no different.

The guys informed Sandy they had taken the girls home, and they were taking him home also.

On the ride to Sandy's both boys joked and laughed about nothing much, only Sandy sat scared frighten for within. Somehow he knew what he saw was real and this was no laughing matter.

*   *   *

It was Sharron's birthday. She never liked to celebrate birthdays. It reminded her of old age, turning the big thirty that certainly was no fun. She wanted to think of herself as forever twenty-one.

Danielle had forgiven Sharron as always of her little arrogant flirtatious attitude after all they were best friends. They had been best friends every since they were in junior high. 'Anyway what are best friends for?' Danielle said to Sharron, when she called to wish her a happy B-day.

"Honey you do look good for thirty if I do say so myself. I'm thirty-two with two children and I'm not complaining even though at times . . . Look girl, why don't I take you to see that movie you wanted to see last week. You know the one in 3D, 'Zombies in the night' It is still playing, we can call it ladies night out. We can have dinner at the café Di, one of your favorite eating establishments. We'll have a great evening just the two of us. It will be like old time. Come on girl live a little, it's Friday. I'll pick you up around six, no buts."

Both ladies laughed, Sharron finally agreed, they decided to eat first than see the movie.

It was a wonderful, but sweltering day. The girls decided to spend more time in the coolness of the restaurant, waiting for the weather to cool down. They thought it might be fun to leave Danielle's car parked in the lot of the restaurant across from Queen's park, they would walk down the three blocks to the movie east off Main Street. They would later walk back to Danielle's car hopefully in the coolness of the night like they done countless times in the past.

Their dinner was superb and the champagne flowed freely, at least for Sharron. Danielle only drank two glasses. She promised Thomas she wouldn't drink and drive. That was one of the main reasons for walking to the movie. Thomas only agreed because it was Sharron's birthday. He still did not like his wife hanging around with Sharron, a loose single woman of the world of whom he did not trust.

The air condition was refreshing and neither girl wanted to go out in the sweltering heat, so they ended up staying at the café way passed their original time, so late the placed was about to closed.

Danielle called the theater to find out the last showing of the movie. It started at ten-twenty, just enough time to walk the three blocks east of Queen's park, buy tickets maybe get drinks and sweet refreshments since they did not have dessert.

She called Thomas so he would not worry about her coming home later than plan. She informed him what time the movie would be over and about what time she should be home.

Hardly anyone was in the movie theater at that time of showing. In this small town most citizens were home around eleven at night even on Friday except for Sam's club.

There were only two young couples in their twenties, four laughing older women who giggled the entire time, and three male teens, Mad Dog, Raymond, and Sandy.

That movie was everything they heard and seen from the trailer, fast action, scary, and with it being in 3D very haunting. When the movie ended Danielle and Sharron went to freshen up before walking to the car.

Stepping outside into the hazy night was a bit of shock. A deep dense fog had rolled in off the horizon so thick and heavy the women could hardly see two feet in front of them. There were no stars in the skies to be seen. When and where did this fog come from was a mystery. The weatherman had not predicted fog said it would be clear.

"Wow Danielle, look what we have to endue because YOU wanted to celebrate my B-day."

"Don't blame me I was not the one throwing down drinks one after anther until the placed closed on us. We could have gone to the movies earlier and been home by now but no-o-o you wanted to . . ."

"Okay, can it! It's just this dew is messing up my hair . . . Let's just hurry to the car before my hair becomes completely limp . . . Girl, where did we park your car?"

"Three blocks away, remember we left the car parked at the Café Di, because at the time we thought walking would be cooler, besides drinking and driving does not go together. Here I got a scarf take it. I'm not using it."

Danielle pulled out her blue scarf from her gnocchi bag, gave it to Sharron who tied it around her head half covering her face.

"You got that short natural curly hair and this weather won't hurt yours like it does mine. Thanks Danielle.

Vanishing trails etched against the black sky. The girls had trouble seeing where they were headed. Sharron's foot slipped on the uneven pavement. She almost fell. Danielle caught her just in the nick of time before she tumbled face first to the ground. She swore angry at herself for being so clumsy.

"My goodness Sharron, are you alright? It is so dark and wet out not a star in the sky and the lights must be out in this area because there are no streetlights on either. Must be a power shortage or something you think?"

"Am I alright? How can I see in this dam dark fog? I hope we are going in the right direction Danielle cause . . ."

"It's the right way Sharron, just keep holding unto my arm so we both can support each other."

They walked for a minute before Sharron mentioned the movie.

"That flick was something else. I have never seen a more gruesome, scary movie in a long while. I almost peed in my pants. Especially when that zombie came creeping up behind that poor girl cutting her in pieces and eating her flesh . . . oh god her blood went everywhere, I thought it landed in my lap! Why would anyone make a movie like that?"

"It's what sells my friend. Don't talk about it anymore not while we are out in this dark mess. 3D movies are always so real. I would rather be at home, dry, with my family, having Thomas hold me close."

"Stop it, you're making me sick. Besides it wasn't that bad . . ."

The fog continued to thicken as moister fell. There was not a single person on the streets besides them walking briskly arms locked together, shoulders hunched, trying to stay dry. They listened to the clicking of their heels on the sidewalk.

About twenty five yards from their destination they turned left toward Queen's park, where earlier the trees kept them cool, now those same trees looked morbid against the night skies. They had to pass this dark park before they quickly headed toward Danielle's car just across the other side.

Both girls heard it at the same time. Some scraping sound in the near distant. This scraping noise made them stop spooked in their tracks. They listened with hearts racing faster. After a minute when they did not hear any other sound, they perceived toward the parking lot, holding onto each other even tighter.

Just twenty steps away the predator shrank back waiting in the huge low branches of a tree, teeth clenched under his black hood that covered his face. Crouched down behind that large oak, he anticipated how long it would take them to reach him. He watched as they approached under the covering of the fog and very dim lighting. Some streetlights were out in this area tonight.

With his old black van parked on the grass out of view, how perfect was this. It was late and no one around in the deep dense fog. He laughed to himself at his own cleverness to choose this night.

He watched the two come near the area he invaded just before the park ended and just a few feet away from the Café Di. He waited for the right moment for them to pass him. His upper lip and hands were sweating. Like lighting he jumped out and grabbed both ladies from behind, one arm around their small waist and the other a knife at Danielle's slim throat.

"If you make a sound I'll kill you right here, right now. Just move with me over to that van and maybe you won't get hurt."

"Oh my god, who-o-o-o are you? If you want cash we don't have much, but you can . . ."

"I said not a sound." He hissed into Sharron's ear.

He forced them both over to the van and pushed Sharron in first. The head blue scarf slid down falling to the ground, before her she fell on the hard floor in the back of the van. Her attacker did not notice it falling off.

There were no seats inside nor could she see anything for he had covered the windows with some dark substance. Next come Danielle's stiff body tumbling to the floor of the van. He quickly got in behind them, tied their hands and feet together with duct tape than placed black hoods over their heads.

The women were taped back to back, tightly huddled on their sides. This was the first time Sharron was totally speechless. She trembled slightly willing herself not to give into her fear.

Tears made their way down Danielle's face, as she thought about her family. Would she ever see them again? She was beyond terrorized she was still in shook. Just as she and Thomas were putting their marriage back on the right track this happens? If only they had not gone to that last showing. If only she had listened when Sharron didn't want to celebrate her B-day anyway.

She knew it was too late for regrets. Would she die right here in this stuffy old van going who knows where? Worse would he rape them before he killed them? She had to know their fate even if that meant she died first.

"Please tell me what is it you desire? If it is money take everything we got, but please don't kill us, I have two small children at home."

"I said SHUT UP!"

He reached over and hit her hard across her shoulder with the back of his hand. Danielle held her cry of pain for fear of more. He seemed to enjoy hitting her and she did not want to upset him further.

When he finished tying them he got in the front seat of the van, and drove about twenty-five miles north before he stopped. Both girls tried to imagine where they might be headed. They knew their area well enough and assumed the bumpy ride meant a back woods road. There were only a few dirt roads that led deep into the woods. Danielle hoped he did not take them into the deserted witches area.

He sat for a moment in the van smiling gratified. He enjoyed hitting that woman. He really hoped the other one said something smart giving him an excuse to slap her also. Oh how he would love to beat both of them. Tear their clothes off, see them bleed, naked and begging. He smiled at the thought. Who knows . . .

*   *   *

That Friday evening the guys got together after school and decided to see a movie. It took some doing talking Sandy into going to see that horror 3D flick about zombies. Raymond always had a way of convincing him to follow, and against his better judgment Sandy went along with them. They stayed through three showing until they saw the last movie of the night. When they went outside saw it was a nasty night they booked carrying Sandy home first.

Now later after seeing that movie, Sandy walked to the door of his empty house, spooked to his bones. He just wanted the night to end peacefully. How did he allow Raymond again to talk him into doing something he didn't want to do, and in 3D? What was he thinking? He knew he was coming home alone. They had their apartment together, but neither asked him to stay over. Sandy's parents were still out of town. He knew they would not be home for another two days.

Sandy stood in the entrance way cautiously. He started to turn on the lights and found they were out. He tried again, but the light was either burned out or . . . new fear grabbed hold squeezing his heart as he looked up seeing something moving quickly past him. He tripped over something running through the living room at a high speed, was it a large rat? He tried another light with no success. Frantically, Sandy searched for some candles or matches in a drawer his mother kept them in. He couldn't find any.

In every area of the darken rooms he seemed to see dead zombies creeping through the walls, coming from the floors, moving out through the doors. Sandy forgot about the matches, he ran to his room falling into the half closed door. He quickly got up feeling his way with his hands to his bedroom. There were no matches to light the two candles his mother always kept in his room. He did not even own a lighter, nor did he carry matches around in his pockets. Whenever he needed a smoke, Raymond always supplied the lighter.

In the stillness of his room Sandy could hear voices speaking in low moaning murmurs. When he turned toward the noises it was as if he stepped into another dimension. The voices were not human. From the corner of some eerie dark space, he could see things changing all around him. Sandy soon found himself in front of a huge blue red fire, with gigantic ten feet hideous creatures swarming everywhere. They snarled at him and curled their long black claws in a 'come closer to me' way.

Sandy totally petrified turned to run. His feet were glued down and he fell to the ground on his face trying to escape. There was no place safe. Large hairy-blooded hands grabbed him by his feet turning him upside down, dangling him in the air before slamming him on the ground than dragging him over toward the open fire.

Out of the fire came a crackling sound like none he never heard and a hideous demonic head of a dragon appeared. His voice was so loud and deep. Sandy covered his ears, his face crying out in total torment. His fear could not describe. The horror of the face he saw would be lasting.

Two huge horns stood on each side of its head. The evilest deep-set black eyes stared back at him. Blood oozed out from every part of Sandy as he watched the long fangs from its mouth breathing yellow red fire. The fire blazed from all parts of the dragon's nose, mouth, and eyes licking at Sandy tormented limp body. He smelled his own flesh burning.

Pain and fear saturated his soul. He wished for death, but death did not come. Sandy prayed 'just let me die' over and over again. Than the thought came to him maybe he was already dead. How horrible to die and not be aware. He must have died when got to his bedroom, maybe from a heart attack. His mind screamed at back at him WHY?

Something inside would not let him give completely up. A small sense of strength deep within his soul cried out to fight and not give in. Then he remembered his newly born again parents, telling him prayer changes things, that Jesus is the only answer. Even in this place of torment he called on Jesus.

The hideous angry monsters pulled him into the fire with brute force, and the waiting dragon opened his mouth wide to receive Sandy's weak trembling body, mind, and soul.

The fire around continued to lick his body, bringing such fierce pain that every part of his body turned into black charcoal, but still he felt the pain.

The dragon laughed with all the demonic forces joining him at Sandy. Sandy knew if he was dead they could not be so angry with him calling on Jesus. He cried out to Jesus even more with all his heart. Where his strength came from Sandy never knew, all he knew was every time he called on the name of Jesus more strength came.

"JESUS PLEASE HELP ME LIVE, I DON'T WANT TO DIE IN THIS PLACE OF TORMENT. I'M SO SORRY, PLEAS HELP ME, I NEED YOU JESUS!"

The tormenter continued to vex Sandy sorely. His own flesh smelled of burning rotten meat falling off his bones than reappearing to fall off again. This seemed to go on for hours his fleshed burning and burning. The move he burned the louder his cry became. How that could happen was beyond Sandy thinking.

"JE-S-US, PLEASE . . . SA-VE ME . . . FROM THIS TOR-MENT! I'LL . . . DO ANYTHING YOU

ASK PLEASE LORD DON'T LET ME DIE HERE,
I'LL SERVE YOU, HONOR YOU AND LIVE FOR
YOU ONLY PLEASE HELP ME!

With the pain so intense and his fear so complete,
Sandy wondered why he still could scream. He
could see his burning body turn black, as if he was
in a never-ending movie. Blacken charcoal flesh
fell from other dead bones inside the inferno. His
screams tore through the underground of doom and
than there was no more.

In the spirit world mighty warrior Angels of light
came racing to rescue Sandy from the burning pit of
hell. They fought the dragon and soulless creatures
and won the battle for Sandy's life!

Sandy was gently placed on his bed, back in his
own smooth flesh, peacefully asleep, now dreamed
of beautiful blue waves riding down the stream and
tall green grass swaying in the sweet breeze and the
warm sun shining on his face, the nightmare was
over for now . . .

*   *   *

Thomas looked at the time again, yes well past
midnight. Where could she be? She said right after
the last showing she'll be home. That was almost
an hour ago. He went to the door and looked out on
the night, mighty nasty looking. Maybe they had

car trouble. If so why didn't she call him? He dialed her cell again getting only her voice mail. He called Sharron's cell and it went to voicemail also. Thomas worried, knowing she was a new Christian, still he believed she would never betray him; not this time. No something must have happened to cause her to be this late.

He pasted back and forth from the living room into the den and back to the front door peeking out the window. If it were not so late, he would call Carol asking her to watch the children while he went to look for her.

Thomas' mind went to every scenario possible trying to figure out what might have happened. Soon he threw all caution to the wind. They could be stranded somewhere . . . hurt, in trouble . . . Whatever happened he knew he had to find his wife.

Decision made, Thomas raced into the children's bedroom grabbed his son wrapping him in a blanket. He laid his still sleeping son on the sofa while he got his daughter up. She half asleep yawned.

"Daddy, why did you wake me? I'm still sleepy."

"Sorry sweetheart daddy needs to find mommy. I know it's late, but you can sleep in the SUV okay?"

"Okay daddy." Sharree fell back asleep waiting on the sofa for Thomas to dress, warm the SUV and get them securely inside.

He first drove to the movie theater. The lot completely empty only dim lights lit the area. As the fog subsided he parked, got out stood next to the SUV looking for some clue as to where she might be. He got back in drove closer to the building hoping to find something, anything that might shed some light on this perplexing mystery.

After twenty minutes of driving around the theater, he drove to the closed restaurant Danielle and Sharron had eaten dinner earlier. There in the lot sat Danielle's Mercedes. Thomas suddenly has a premonition that his wife was indeed in deep trouble. His heart panicked as he raced over to her car burning rubber. He parked, got out searching frantically for his wife inside the car. He thought she could have passed out or . . . when he did not find any signs of a struggle inside or out, Thomas knew he had to call the police.

On the second ring he heard a professional women's voice answer. Thomas hurriedly told her the scenario hoping they would start on the case immediately.

"Sir, slow down, it has not been twenty four hours. All you know she and her friend might have met up with other friends and could be heading home at this moment. Look there is nothing that can be done tonight. I suggest you take it easy, wait and see if she returns. If by this time tomorrow she has not come back you can file a missing person's report.

*   *   *

The old run down shake leaned slightly sideways, barely standing on its' rotten foundation. The smell of molded wood, dead skunks, decade animal body waste, and some putrid invasion she could not identify hung in the air.

Huge diseased rats also inhabited these premises, completing the morbid atmosphere, with thick cobwebs covering the few pieces of furniture in this horrific shack.

This place has a crude kitchen off to the side, with an old fireplace to the right center. A single twin sagging mattress lay on an iron cot in front of the fireplace, and there is an old run down faded blue sofa in the middle of this room. To finish the gruesome deco is a brown ragged card table with three scratched up, half broken mixed matched chairs.

Big dust balls blew around the room so thick and heavy the girls had to hold their breaths. Still they sneezed and choked on cloud of debris.

The dark mask predator had cut the tape from their feet and disconnected them from each other enabling them some freedom. With their hands still taped behind them and hoods covering their faces, he pushed Danielle in the door of the cabin with Sharron following. His huge rough hands bruised their delicate skin and Danielle bit her tongue to keep from crying out.

Low whimpering moans escaped through Sharron's lips, as he threw her on the damp sofa first, before Danielle vigorously came crashing down on her back, she also kicked Sharron's leg trying to get off her. Poor Sharron got the wind knocked out of her. She cried out in pain.

"Hey you two sit still and be quiet!" he barked as he coiled the duct tape back tightly around their ankles. The girls still in masks, tried to simmer down. They did not have to see the condition the place they were in to know it was grotesque. The women knew by the thick dusk and smells this place had not been occupied in a quite some time.

After their feet were bounded together, he took off the masks allowing them to see for the first time the condition of their prison. Both women blinked against the bright flashlight he held up to their faces. All they could see of him was the hood he wore with two holes used for him to see out of. His hateful eyes stared back at them. His body blended into the darkness of the room.

"Sit tight if you know what's good for you. I will be right back."

His voice held deadly malice. Neither girl wanted to experience his wrath so they huddled on their sides each facing the opposite way, trying not to inhale too much of the foul fumes.

He turned off the flashlight turning the room back into complete darkness while he walked outside for some supplies he brought with him. They could hear him wresting around in the van bring in objects sitting them on the card table. How he could see in the darken room without light was beyond them. Maybe he had hawk eyes.

Ten long minutes later he lit four thick candles, he sat two on the card table and the other two near the fireplace on the floor. The light cast creepy shadows across the ceiling bring the terror closer.

What a shock to both ladies to finally see the enclosed inhabitation of this space they were slaves to. From out of nowhere a big huge rat ran from the old ashes of the fireplace over toward the sofa. Danielle saw it first and screamed, involuntary trying to put her legs up higher on the sofa wetting her pants at the same time. The warm liquid mingled with the already dampen sofa causing Danielle to suck in her breath nauseated swallowing back vomit.

Sharron who screamed because Danielle did searched the room looking for a bathroom she too needed to empty her bladder badly.

The man in the hood rushed over and backhanded Danielle hard across the face, than he slapped Sharron on her head.

"What did I tell you too huh!"

"I'm so-r-ry, I s-aw a big r-at. He ran somewhere under this sofa."

The man rolled his head, threw his shoulders back like a warrior ready for battle. Both ladies froze staring at him intensely, fear gripping them. Was he going to strike them again?

"You better be glad I didn't feed you to him. Is that what you what?"

Seeing them completely frighten, feet balled up on the sofa shivering, and noticing one wet her pants, gave him a bit of sympathy toward them.

"Look, if you do as I say you might live. Do I make myself clear? Meanwhile, I got some sleep to get and I don't want either of you moving or saying a word or you will wish you were already dead. So sit tight until I say move, do you hear me?"

Both ladies nodded their heads. The man walked over, sat at the table searching in his backpack for cigarettes. Sharron held her pee for as long as she could take it without saying a word. She had to ask where the darn bathroom was located before she too used the sofa like her friend. With his back to the women, he inhaled his smoke while making the bed using a sleeping bag to cover it. Sharron whispered.

"Sir, please, I do not want to disturb you from your work, but I can't hold it any longer. Can I please go to the bathroom before I burst?'

He turned with a smirk, pointed toward the back of the shack.

"You have a choice. You can repeat what your friend did. Go to the outhouse located in back, but I don't recommend it seeing it has no roof and only a hole in the ground, as I'm sure animals use. Or you can do as I did and pee out front next to the house."

"What! Pee out in the open, are you crazy! I mean . . ."

He smiled enjoying the look on her face. In a mild voice he continued.

"I said you have a choice. Who is there to see you? We are miles away from any civilization. Come on now, you are a big girl. I'll go with you."

The very thought of this man watching her urinate was insane, but to hold it a moment longer . . .

"Please just untie me, I can't go until I'm free from this darn tape."

The man stuffed out his cigarette on the table, came over and released Sharron's from her prison hold. He grabbed her by the upper arm with her hands still tied behind her back pulling her forward roughly. She fell against the inside door stomping the same toe she hurt earlier. He jerked her back by the hair, opened the door with the other hand pushed her out in the opening. Half ripping off her dress, he tore down her panties, forcing her to squat, all within a minute.

Sharron cried out in pain as she stumbled in the darkness tripping over her own feet. She was far beyond humiliation all she wanted was to escape this horror. She had to find a way to get out of this mess. Maybe there was a way she could trick him into letting them go. Maybe she could use her sex appeal, her charm, her body whatever it took she didn't care as long as she escaped. It was her birthday for goodness' sake. She should not be here! These thoughts rambled around her brain.

"Please I'll get pee all over my shoes and I don't have tissue paper."

"Look lady you are trying me! If you want to pee, you better do it now, cause this is the last time you will come out tonight!"

The meanness in his tone was enough for Sharron to obey. She quickly relieved herself. It felt so good to let go she almost forgot about him. Almost that is, he grabbed her arm and hooted her up dragging her back into the shack. He retied her together with Danielle, who softly wept into the dampness of the sour smelling sofa.

"You ladies better lay here and keep quiet. You don't want to get on my bad side now do you! And ladies don't even think about escaping. If the wild animals don't eat you alive, I will. These woods are so thick it will take a lifetime to find your dead bones. Do I make myself clear?"

*   *   *

CHAPTER TWENTY-SIX

About nine o'clock Saturday morning, Ward sat on the loveseat in his home pondering over some paperwork. Business looked good, from his standpoint even with the economy the way it was his business did well. He left his brother in charge of the store today, for some much needed personal time. With his family gone for the entire afternoon, he could sit back without any interruptions just the way he liked.

Wrapping up his business he thought about the video he prerecorded during his last 'sacrificial atonement of souls' given to Satan over two weeks ago. The DVD, recorded without the knowledge of his guests. He had it hid behind a picture in his office.

Ward got up retrieving the DVD. This was the first time Ward would see the reactions and surprise on their faces from the video. Ward enjoyed the feeling he got when scaring his gullible weak guests. Nothing made him feel more supreme and in complete control, as when people both feared and respected him. What a high!

Now smiling at the frighten looks his guests experienced, he smiled devious. Ward wished he had invited Katrina over to watch this with him she too enjoyed seeing people hurt. After his niece moved to town, Katrina his niece become fast friends. Now they seem inseparable. He did not know yet if that was favorable or not.

Thinking of the girls caused Ward's mind to reflect on the things that had been bothering him lately, his daughter and wife. Come to think of it, both have been acting strangely. For the past two weeks, both would come home from being someplace heads bent whispering in soft low voices. They were inseparable all of a sudden. Yes, they always been close, but now it's a different kind of closeness.

Funny, Nicky did not seem to care if he stayed out later, or even if he had other women. That was a real surprise. She, a clingy woman, always needy, what has happened to change that? The more he thought about it, his daughter Rachel most times avoided him altogether. Even his mother-in-law kept out of their way. Why? What were they doing that he was not aware of?

With his pride deflated, anger step in place. Nothing went on in his domain without his total knowledge and approval! He would get to the bottom of this and they better have their stories straight.

Ward glanced toward the video again, seeing Sandy so frighten his mind became intrigued. He watches as Sandy wrested to free himself from one of his demonic chairs in the shape of a lion's body. That chair came alive as demonic forces used it to move about the room. The iron hold bounded Sandy in. Tormenting claws harder than nails bit into his flesh. His blood splattered on the chair. No matter how hard Sandy tried to get loose, the chair would not release him. Ward heard blood-curling screams bouncing off air like echoes in a canyon.

Ward closed his eyes and breathed in Sandy's fear. This toxic power born out of hell motivated him. The more frighten Sandy or anyone became the more Ward literally inhaled their feelings. He loved the power it gave him and he couldn't get enough. These demons infested throughout the darken room, casting haunting shadows on the walls licking their fear made Ward laugh as he continue watching. They lurked in every corners of the room waiting . . . Oh how this intrigued Ward.

Oh what a grotesque sight to experience the bottomless pit tormenting his gullible guest. How un-sorry he felt for these sorrowful weak spirits. Fear, Torment, Defeat, were tools used to strengthen Satan hold over despicable, deceivable souls who allow wickedness to embrace them. Ward enjoyed every bit of the sinister vision.

He broke out in malice laugher, emerging from within. Abruptly he ceased as his eyes caught sight of a photo of Rachel on his desk. The photo brought his focus back to why Nicky and Rachel were so happy? Again anger stepped in his heart taking over his mind.

Ward turned off the DVD went into the kitchen to make himself a pot of black coffee. While drinking his coffee, his pondered over reasons why Nicky smiled more, and came up with nothing. Whatever the cause he did not like it, and he was determines to find some answers soon.

When he emptied the coffee pot he went into their bedroom where Nicky occupied herself alone, searching in her closet finding nothing at the moment. He rambled in her dresser drawers tossing things around the room searching for some hidden clue. There hid under her nightclothes, a thick red book with the word Bible written on it. His became so intense with rage he grabbed the book threw it against the wall snarling. He ran and pick up the Bible, ripping out the pages trying to tear the leather in two with his bare teeth. He realized that was not going to work not before he almost pulled his teeth out trying. He grabbed scissor cutting the leather in pieces.

Like a mad man he rushed over to the phone on the nightstand, almost jerking it from the wall socket, dialing Nicky on her cell very impatiently.

"Hello . . . Ward . . . is there anything I can bring you home from the store?"

"You can bring your fat rats behind home right now! I got something to show you!"

"What is wrong now Ward? I got shopping to finish, clothes to pick up at the cleaners . . ."

Ward stopped listening he wanted to jump through the phone choke her neck right than and right now! But common sense told him screaming was not going to get her back home. Lately, Nicky did not reacted negative to his control, so he decided to try his charm con act. That usually worked on her mind.

"Look Nicky, wife of mine, I'm sorry I was so rude. What I'm trying to say is I need you to come home. Can you do that for your husband Nicky?"

Something in his voice unnerved her, a forewarning of some kind. Ward's voice sounded calm, but with negative undertones, plus he had not talked nice to her in a long while. His voice, seem to speak volumes of caution to her spirit, warning her not to return home.

"Nicky my sweet did you hear me?'

"Yes Ward, I heard you . . . I told Rachel . . . I would pick her up right after the library today . . . She still has to study for her test . . . Rachel's expecting me to come get her in two hours . . . I can come as soon as I'm done okay?"

"What about lunch? Is Rachel coming home for lunch?"

"I do not expect her. She might have other plans, but I can pick up something for you Ward, what would you like?

"I would like to see my family eat lunch today."

Nicky so caught off guard could not think fast enough. Ward wanting her with him for lunch as a family she must be dreaming. This was something she prayed for so long. Was God finally answering her prayer?

"I could stop by that Chinese place off West Berry and bring lunch, if that's okay."

"My dear wife how very thoughtful of you, yes do bring Chinese food for lunch. Why don't you bring Rachel home too, she can study later after lunch. We haven't had a family meal together in quite a while now have we?"

The smoothness in his voice was so controlled, it sounded to her ears like he really cared and wanted her again. Was this the same man who a few weeks ago told her he did not love her, wanted nothing to do with their marriage. This the same man who has not been home on time for any meals in months?

Pure happiness saturated her soul blowing warm bubbles in her heart. She wanted so badly to believe Ward still loved her. She immediately smiled, ignoring the warning negative signs churning in the pit of her stomach. She assumed it was joy. Without prayer her heart responded.

"Ward what a wonderful idea! I'll go get mother from the hairdressers, stop at the Chinese's place, than pick up Rachel. I should be home no later than one okay?"

"One it is my dear, one it is.'

After they hung up Nicky sailed on blissful hope of love, but Ward rode on revengeful hate motivating him to kill.

* * *

"Look Mr. Richards let us do our jobs okay? This town is too small for anyone to get lost in. You say you were having marital problems and this is not the first time she left town without telling you? Maybe she just needed to get away for a day or two."

Thomas sat across from Officer Smith, a slim man with a rounded stomach in his late fifty and a thick mustache that almost cover his thin top lip. The officer scribbled a few notes on his notepad. Than glared at Thomas waiting for his response.

Thomas sat up close to the officer desk shaking his head no. He had to convince this lawman that he and his wife had a solid relationship now, that the past was just that the past.

"Officer Smith listen my wife and I made some mistakes in our relationship as we already conversed, but now we have a solid foundation in our marriage. She would never leave her car parked in a deserted lot. Look, I don't know what happened to them after the movie was over, but I know my wife was coming home. She called me . . ."

"She called at what time?"

"It was right before 10 p.m. As I already told you, they were going to see that zombie movie. The last showing was at ten-twenty. The movie lasted for two hours. I stayed up waiting for her. Remember the fog was so heavy last night anything could have happened. I called her on her cell about one ten. Her voice mail came up, I left a message for her to call she never did. I tried Sharron's number also neither answered."

Thomas rubbed his head imagining the worse. Tears rolled down his face at the images in his mind. If he had to tear down every house in Queen City with his bare hands, he would find his wife.

"Alright Mr. Richards, we got enough for now. We will ask some questions and see what we come up with. In the meantime try not to worry, maybe we will get lucky and she'll contact you."

"Thank you officer, please call me if you get any information."

The officer stool and reached out his hand to shake Thomas hand.

"Don't worry we will call you when we have some news."

*   *   *

Sandy lay under the blankets with his head cover up. He did not allow himself to think about last night's fear. Still very frighten and tired, he wanted only to sleep.

He did not hear the door to his room open until he heard his dad's deep voice talking to his mom. He jumped further under the covers shaking.

"Sandy, what is wrong with you today? Didn't you hear us calling you? We come home and you act like you seen a ghost. You knew we were coming home a day early, we told you that yesterday. Why aren't you up and dressed? You're not on any kind of drugs are you?"

Sandy pulled back the blanket just a bit to see them. He was happy to see his family yet still afraid to get up from the bed. Peeking out from under the covers shaking uncontrollable he said.

"I'm sorry dad . . . no I'm not on drugs . . . I'm tried, but didn't get much sleep last night I guess."

His mother came over and sat on the bed next to him. She noticed the fear trapped in his eyes. Her concern for him brought tears to own her eyes.

"Sandy, what is it? You can tell us anything son. You know we love you."

She reached over and kissed his forehead. His dad pulled a chair up to the bed. His keen insight knew his decision to move was the right thing to do for his family. Sandy, his only son left alone here while he and his wife drove the eighteen-wheeler out of town, week after week this was going to stop. He wanted his whole family with him always. That was why he decided to move closer to his runs.

"Sandy, your mother and I are here for you. Now tell us, what is the matter? Come on you we are your parents, you can trust us."

They waited until Sandy sat up licking his dry lips. He looked off in a distance before he focused his attention on them.

"Dad, do you believe in demons?"

"Son, I know they exist if that is what you mean, why?"

"Cause lately, I'm been seeing them everywhere. It's like they are in my head and I can't get them out."

"Honey why didn't you tell us this over the phone yesterday we would have come home sooner."

Sandy took his mother's hand and placed her palm against his face loving.

He kissed her hand while large tears fell.

"I was scared I guess."

"How long have this been going on Sandy?"

Sandy turned toward his father's strong frame and answered him in his cracked voice.

"Over a month now, it all started when my friend Raymond and I met this guy named Mad Dog. Well we knew him from school, but anyway. He took us . . ."

"Mad what? Who are you referring to Sandy? Is that his real name?"

"Mad Dog, is his nickname, or the name he likes to be called. Anyway he took us to meet this man who believes in black magic . . ."

Sandy told his parents every detail he remembered concerning Ward, Mad Dog and the drug parties Ward had. It felt so good to release this burden from off his shoulders. When all was said, he fell in his mother's arms crying sadly. She held him until his tears subsided. His father got the Bible he purchase three weeks ago and found the verse he wanted to read.

"Sandy I truly am sorry I didn't see this coming. I knew Raymond was a spoiled rich kid, getting everything he wanted, but I did not know he hung around with a bad bunch like this kid Mad Dog or this man Ward.

Raymond never had to work for anything. Sometimes that kind of wealth causes young people to miss out on the mercies and goodness of God because they think they don't need him. They believe they have everything and depend on themselves. Most rich kids are bored and try to find ways to occupy their minds by using drugs, girls, drinking, and yes, even witchcraft. It's sad, but they get into witchcraft as a way of fun, not realizing that Satan is no toy. He is out to steal, kill and destroy all mankind."

"Sandy Jesus came so that you may have life that that more abundantly. He came to destroy the works of the devil! You can have freedom in Him only when you trust in Him with faith."

"Sin is a weapon the enemy uses to trap people into doing his will. With Jesus He gives you have power over the enemy."

"The Bible says in Galatians chapter five verse sixty. ***This I say, walk in the Spirit and you shall not fulfill the lust of the flesh.***"

"Sandy we want you to go with us to Church Sunday. We decided to move out of Queen City to a place where all of us can be together and you will not have to be along anymore."

The tears that Sandy cried earlier were nothing compared to the tears of relief he now shed.

"Sweetheart those boys are doing witchcraft and that man Ward is using them for his own selfish pleasures. I believe he is a warlock, a tool of the devil. I feel sorry for Raymond's parents. I bet they have no idea what he sees or what he does when he is not around them. I don't want you to see those people ever again Sandy. Do you hear me? Okay son?"

Sandy had mixed feeling about this decision. On one hand he liked being Raymond's friend, because he never had many all his life. Raymond was so popular with many of the kids at his school. Now that they were moving out of town, he guessed that wouldn't make any difference.

"Sandy, I said I don't want you hanging around with either of those boys again."

"Yep, mom, I get it."

Sandy got up went into the bathroom feeling relieved for the first time in a long time. After he did his business he came back into the room to find his parents in each other arms and his mom crying softly.

Sandy rushed over and put his slim arms around his dad and mom.

"Mom don't cry, I'm sorry I should have been stronger, you always taught me to think for myself and not let anybody . . ."

"It's okay son, we are not judging you. We all make mistakes. It's what we do about our failures that count."

"Dad, I want the peace you and mom have. How can I have that peace?"

"The only way to have true peace is through Jesus Christ. Do you want to accept Him into your life Sandy? We would never make you do anything you don't feel lead to do, you know that don't you?"

"Yes dad, I do, but I need to feel peace. I can't sleep at night, I have so many bad dreams I'm afraid to close my eyes."

"Than say the sinner's prayer with me Sandy, Jesus will take away your fears if you ask Him."

Sandy bent his head in total submission. He repented what his father said with an opened heart and faith.

"Dear Heaven Father, I come to you a sinner. I believe you are the Son of the living God. I repent of all my sins and ask you into my life as Lord and Savior. Father, give me your peace, love, understanding and mercy. My life has been filled with things you are not pleased with. Please forgive me of all my sins including witchcraft, drinking, drugs and whatever I've done that is not right in your sight, I accept you Jesus as my Lord and Savior now . . ."

He finished the prayer with refreshing tears of joy. This time they were tears of real happiness as a release came over his soul. Laughter lit his heart! Joy melted his spirit! He jumped up screaming over and over again.

"I'M SAVED, I'M SAVED, I'M SAVED!

*   *   *

CHAPTER TWENTY-SEVEN

Deep in the blackness of the underworld the darkness plots on how to defeat mankind and bring him to total destruction. The head sergeant wrath threw commands at the lesser imps.

"We are losing souls daily. Continue to entice them using dirty movies, scary movies, sexual parties, yes and a lot of satanic games, these tools always brings in the most souls for our master Satan."

"Whatever you say me lord. These things are essential to their destruction."

The head commander walked back and forth with his huge arms behind his hairy back. He snorted curses at them roaring.

"Just keep them distracted daily! Use every kind of nonsense there is that will keep them bound in chains! Bring fear of losing their homes, their jobs, their cars, their family, and their finances! These are some of the best tool we have. They always work! We need total control of their minds! Do you inferior monkeys hear me?"

The demons flew back against the darkness too afraid to speak. This only made him angrier. He flew on broken wings over to them huddled in the blackness shaking.

"I said I want them down here in hell! If we got to stay in this place forever because He doomed us here, than we need to fight back using His prize passion those Christian!"

"Make them weak destroy them set them on fire with all kinds of temptations!"

"Master those mighty Christians are so strong. They don't fall for our tricks or temptations. How can we get them to succumb to our evil if they have Him on their side?"

"FIND A WAY!"

All the underground feared the mighty Christian who prayed daily with faith in Jesus having on the whole armor of God.

The head demonic one knew because even though he hated to say it, he too fears them. Those prayers of faith are a might weapon used, always blocking their spears bring fear to the underground!

"We can get the weak Christian who give in too our plan. We can make them do whatever we please. But the mighty ones . . ."

"Keep using overeating that will bring sickness, like diabetes, heart attacks, obesity. If we use enough pain in their bodies they will think He doesn't care!"

"What about their minds, weaken their minds? That seems to work for centuries!"

"Master our most successful tools for the mind has always been fear of the future, doubt and confusion, we can't go wrong using them, can we?"

The raw humor of using the words 'go wrong' has them roaring with laughter. They slider, twisted, rolled and fell into each other. Bickering erupted throughout the underground as they fought each other for the master's attention.

"Shut up you filthy scum bags, I got better things to do laugh at nothing! This is no joke! If we are to succeed we better produce new souls quick. He said He is coming back for His Church! We don't have much time so get your ROTEN BUTTS UP and find me some WEAK believers! If you disobey your heads will be on the chopping board DO YOU HEAR ME? I SAID GO!"

Horror of what would happen to them held them in check than each deformed, inhuman demon raced out into the opening seeking weak human souls.

*   *   *

Phillip and Rachel walked hand in hand up the steps of the library smiling at each. Nicky had dropped Rachel off at Cam's home this morning before she got the call from Ward asking them to come home. Phillip spent the night over his brother, Bernard's home after attending a youth group Cam and Bernard was head of the night before. They were helping Phillip to be prepared for taking over the group soon.

Now Phillip and Rachel were to go to the library to study meeting Nicky later for Bible study.

For several days things were almost perfect in Rachel's life. After she and her mother mended their relation with Nicky giving her heart to Jesus, Nicky met Phillip and his family, going to Church every night praying at the altar and studying the Bible with them daily. The best news was Nicky accepting Christ and giving up witchcraft something she practiced all her life. Now she traded witchcraft for learning about the love and mercies of God. Yes a change had truly come over her mother Nicky, what could be better.

Rachel's phone began ringing. She grabbed her cell from her jean pocket flipped it opened, saw it was her mother silently mouth the word 'mother' to Phillip, and hit the talk button.

"Hi mom, Phillip brought me to the library. When we finish studying, we will head back to his house for Church service tonight. You can meet us there when you . . ."

"Honey great news! Your dad has asked us to join him later for lunch. Can you believe this, he wants you and I to have a meal together with him like a normal family!"

A nasty vile feeling churned in the pit of her stomach. She swallowed back vomit threatening to choke her. Rachel felt like she was suffocating. Her breath became short and quick. She dropped the phone grabbing a fist full of Phillip's tee shirt falling against him. Phillip held her close so she would not fall.

"My God Rachel what is wrong? Did something happen to your mom?"

Concern for the girl he loved caused him to sit her down on his lap of the steps. Both forgot about the cell phone as Rachel's eyes filled with tears. Nicky kept yelling Rachel's name to no avail.

When Rachel could talk she shook slightly trying to calm herself.

"Phillip . . . my . . . mom . . ."

"Take it easy Rachel, whatever has happened we will deal with it together okay. I promise with God's help we can over come any obstacles that we face."

Phillip began to pray.

"Father God, You know everything even before it happens. I'm asking you to release your peace within my Rachel. Take away her fear and set her free from worry. There is nothing to hard for you Lord, we trust you completely, in Jesus mighty name Amen!'

Rachel smiled sadly resting in his arms. "My father wants us to come home for lunch. That was my mother, calling to say we are going home for lunch today. Phillip my dad has not eaten a meal with us in like forever. My dad doesn't do family meals anymore. I feel he is tricking mom into coming home so he can . . . I don't know, but I feel it won't be for anything good . . ."

Phillip held Rachel away from him so he could look into her eyes. He did not believe a person could change for the better. He had, but did Ward change? His thoughts were 'maybe he had a change of heart toward Nicky and wanted to make up with her.' His mom and dad had such a wonderful marriage and his brother Bernard did to with Cam, even Danielle did with Thomas now. Marriages are supposed to be happy.'

Phillip I know what you are thinking, but not my dad. He is such an evil man, and he doesn't want to change. I feel in my spirit he is up to something bad and I don't want mom to get hurt! I'm talking about real physical pain!"

"Do you really believe your dad would hurt your mom?"

Her look convinced him she was right.

"Okay Rachel if you believe that I understand, and I'll do whatever you say. Where is your mom now?"

"Oh no Phillip, I forgot about her, she is still on the line!'

Rachel searched around frantically for her cell phone. She spotted it on the grass next to the steps and hurried to retrieve it.

"Hello mom, are you still there?"

"Yes Rachel, what happened, I kept calling your name and got no response."

"Sorry I forgot you were still on the phone. Mom, please listen to me don't go home tonight! Do you hear me? We both know who dad is, and he has not changed. He is up to no good. You know, maybe he somehow found out about us going to Church. One of his many dark friends could have seen us getting out of the car at the Church, or maybe . . . This is a small town nothing is safe around here you know that! We can't take anything for granted mom."

Rachel held the phone tightly against her ear hoping she would not lose her mother's attention. Her words tumbled out quickly with an edge of panic while Phillip continued to pray for the safety of Nicky.

"Honey, I know how your father can get, after all I've been married to him for over twenty years. Listen to me Rachel he has never asked me to come home not even in our early years together. I do believe he wants us with him today. I have prayed for this for a long time, now it is finally happening."

"Mom, no don't go! Remember mom you prayed to the wrong god. That was before your salvation.

It's a lie . . . dad has not changed. You know the evil he can do. You saw that in his office closet that thing with no body!"

She heard the determination in her mother's voice by her intake of breath. She knew nothing she said had made a different. Her mother could be stubborn when she wanted to be, but Rachel had to keep trying.

"I'm picking up some Chinese food. I told Ward you would join us Rachel. I think we should honor your father's wishes. I love him Rachel, and maybe he realizes he loves me too. I would like you to join us as a family . . . are you coming or not?"

Hot tears fell from Rachel's eyes. Just moments ago she was so happy and now this. She had to go with her mother. If she went with her maybe she would be there to protect her. Rachel sat thinking about the slight possibility she could be wrong.

Maybe she wasn't thinking straight and he would be in a good mood . . . Who knows?

"Mom I can't let you face dad alone. I'm coming with you. I'll get Phillip to drop me off by the time you get there. I'm still not sure if this is the right thing to do, but . . ."

Phillip's phone rang three times before either of them heard it. He recognized his mother's number.

"Yah, mom what's up? What . . . when . . . last night? Does anyone know where they might be? I'm on my way home just let me drop off Rachel okay?"

"Phillip what is it?"

A blank look appeared across his face, placed by confusion. He spoke in a quiet tone.

"My sister's been missing since last night. It was her best friend Sharron's birthday and they went out to celebrate, but never came home. Nobody knows where they are and my family is worried. Look Rachel I got to go home, my mom needs me. She said to tell you, we could continue Bible study at another more convenient time. I don't want to leave you like this."

"Phillip it's okay. I'm a big girl and your family needs you, I understand. Go home. I can wait here and have mom pick me up."

"Rachel, are you sure? You better call her now to make sure."

Rachel pushed redial and a moment later her mother was back on the line. She explained what happened, asking that she pick her up from the library.

Nicky spoke to Phillip reassuring him as much as possible that God was in control. All promised to meet tomorrow at Phillip parents' home. Rachel told him she would call later to check on the status of Danielle's situation. They hugged kissed, said their good-buys. Phillip drove off still perplex about where his sister might be, while Rachel waited for her mother.

*　　*　　*

Thomas did not intend to sit around waiting for the investigation officer to give him some information while his wife could be laying somewhere hurt in a ditch. He had to find her himself. Somebody knew what happened to Danielle and Sharron. He would search this town tearing it up side down until he found her! He could not allow his mind to think the unthinkable. No she had to be somewhere alive, and he would find out where.

He called his in-laws as soon as he came back from the police station informing them of the circumstances. Phillip and Carol called all the leaders of their Church asking them to pray for their safe return.

Phillip called Thomas back offering to drive, knowing Thomas was in no condition. He was running on zero sleep, besides Phillip wanted to come along and help.

Phillip asked Carol to wait by the phone just in case someone called about ransom, or if the police had any kind of information. Neither Thomas, nor Phillip had much money, but whatever the attackers wanted they knew somehow they would try to pay it.

Both men knew Danielle had to be in some kind of trouble when she abandoned her car. She loved that car and would never just leave it parked in a vacant lot.

Logic told them she had to have been kidnapped, although the police didn't think so, but Thomas being a lawyer used his instinct for crime. What else could it be?

Now he appeared like an insane person sitting next to Phillip. His hair uncombed, wet and sweaty, with hard scratchy stubbles lining his face, and still wearing the same clothes he slept in the night before. His eyes were so red, swollen from the sleepless night, and his face flushed, puffy, with his head bent down he looked like a madman ready to strike.

Long strands of damp hair touched his nose as he shook his head trying to get his hair out of his face. Out of the blue came a big wet sneeze; saliva flew from his mouth onto Phillip's face. Phillip frown grabbed a handkerchief out of his breast pocket cleaning the spit off without turning to face Thomas. He needed to keep his eyes glued to the streets just in case he noticed something out of the ordinary.

"Man, I'm sorry! I did not see that coming."

"Don't worry about it, we got more important things . . . Here it is, I think we should go in ask for the people working on the night shaft last night, see if they remember anything unusual. Maybe someone saw something that will give us a clue as to what might have happened. Could have seen a stranger watching the girls . . . or leaving at the same time . . . Someone could have followed the girls to the movies and waited . . . I know this is all speculation, who knows what ready happened."

Thomas kept his head down. He to embarrassed from sneezing on Phillip just nodded his head yes.

Phillip glanced in his direction for a second before continuing.

"Look man, don't worry about me, I'm fine. A little spit never hurt anyone."

"I am sorry buddy. Forgive me for being so rude. My mind is only on Danielle and finding her."

'No problem, I know you are trying to stay positive and so am I."

He hit the steering wheel with his fist, holding back angry tears.

"Just the thought of my little girl out there somewhere needing . . . I'll kill the bastard, who hurts my daughter!"

Thomas reached over and patted him on the shoulder feeling the same way Phillip felt. He had to hold it together for the sake of his children and his wife Danielle. He looked out the window and saw a parking space near the front entrance of the restaurant. He pointed to the vacant spot.

"Pull over into that empty spot Phillip."

Phillip drove the short distance parking near the front. They got out walking briskly up the walk and the two steps. A young hostess greeted them just inside the door. She wiggled her nose when she saw Thomas in his rankled clothes and up-kept condition. He stood in front of Phillip looking above her head into the crowd being seated.

"Can I help you with anything? Do you want carry out sir?

Her eyes never left his face thinking, 'surely this man doesn't plan to have breakfast here looking like this. He may frighten our other customers . . .'

Phillip noticed the look and hurriedly asked. "Is the owner or manager in please? We like to speak with him if you don't mind."

Her eyes rolled over to Phillip, and she smiled.

Sure, the owner is the manager. I'll get him right away."

"Thank you Miss."

She walked to the back and through a door. A few minutes later, she came back with a heavyset man in his late forties. He smiles broadly at both men.

"What can I do for you today?"

"My wife and her friend were in your restaurant last night having a birthday celebration. I know you will remember seeing them, because they stayed until the place closed. They were two very attractive women drinking a lot of champagne. We need to find them."

The manger stood back pondering, his hand rubbing his chin. A huge grin lit up his pleasant face.

"Yes, I do recall. The staff brought them a small cake, lit with a candle and song happy birthday to the one named Sharron! They said they were headed for the movies to continue celebrating. Is everything alright?'

"We don't know yet. They never returned home last night and nobody seems to know their whereabouts. One of the ladies missing is my daughter and the other is his wife. Her name is Danielle. They were supposed to come in after the last showing of the movie, but they never showed up. We were wondering if maybe someone here might have noticed . . ."

"I'm sorry sir, but we run a nice place here. No riff-raff goes on. I, and a few of my staff worked the late shift last night. Both ladies you are referring to left alone when we closed at ten. It was very foggy out, so maybe they had car trouble, layover at a motel, slept late, and forgetting about the time. They did drink quite a lot of champagne."

"No car trouble, my wife's car was still parked in the lot of this restaurant last night when I went looking for her. I had it towed back home early this morning. The cops are investigating their whereabouts as we speak."

Phillip reached in his pocket and drew out two business cards, gave one to the manager and the other to the hostess.

"Look if either of you remember anything you think might be important, please don't hesitate to call me. I know the cops will be asking you some questions later, but I need to know everything you tell them. She's my daughter, and her two children are waiting for their mommy to come home. The sooner we get to the bottom of this the better."

The manager took one card putting it in his breast pocket. He kept staring at Thomas until some recognition came to his mind. He did not want to appear rude, but he thought he knew Thomas from somewhere. A spark came into his blue eyes as he remembered where he had seen him.

Three months ago his son wanted to drop per-law. He was having trouble keeping up in his classes, and trying to work. Thomas had encouraged him to stay in law even helped him with his studies. Now his son was doing well in school, thanks to Thomas for mentoring him.

"Now I know where I've seen you! Mr. Daniels, it's me, Charles' father. You encouraged my son to stay in per-law a few months ago, and he is doing quite well, thanks to you. If there is anything I can do to repay you sir, just ask."

Thomas smiled thinly. All he wanted was to see Danielle home safe and sound.

"Yes, I know Charles. He is a very bright young man. He just needed a push in the right direction and

I'm glad I could give him that. As my father-in-law stated, if you or your staff have any information that will help solve this mystery please don't hesitate to call us."

He nodded his head as they shook hands, said their good-buys. Thomas and Phillip left headed for the movie theater.

*   *   *

Detective Blackman head of the investigation team, assigned to the case of the two missing women, sat at his desk going over the notes one of his officer handed him while eating a chocolate donut.

He earlier sent one of his agents out to the theater to talk to the employees on duty last night. He sent another one to the restaurant to find supporting evidence of possible kidnapping.

After questioning Thomas earlier, he told the detectives maybe his wife and Sharron had been kidnapped or maybe some other more deadly fate awaited them. They were to leave no stones uncovered.

Blackman was going to check out Sharron's neighborhood as well. He needed to talk to Thomas again. Maybe he knew something he wasn't telling.

If there was a kidnapping, so far there wasn't any evidence to substantiate that.

Detective Blackman had his own suspicion as to what might have happened.

No one was exempt not even Thomas. He found most times when there were missing spouses involved you need only look at their mate. It is usually someone close, someone who knows the victim. What he needed was now was motive. He's seen it happen many times before, husbands reporting their wives missing after they killed them. 'Yes, he thought could be a jealous triangle. Husband thinking his wife is still having an affair, or money problems.' Whatever the case may be, he was sure he would get to the bottom.

He finished his messy donut licked his fingers, grabbed a bottle of water and drowned it dry. That had been his breakfast. He arrived to work this morning around 5:30 a.m., not wanting to wake his wife. Donuts and black coffee were always plentiful around here.

He looked over the notes again, he figured someone is this small town had to have seen or heard something. People didn't just disappear. People in this small community loved to talk. Most knew each other. Someone may have seen them being taken if that's what really happened.

This case was no different than the many cases he solved when he was head of vice in Miami.

He had lived here only two years after his father died and left him the house. His dad bought the house right after he retired. Blackman's dad always wanted to live in a small farming community. This was the perfect spot.

He had moved here eight years ago until a heart attack took his life. Detective Blackman only ended up staying because the crime rate was so low. His wife and kids loved the old farmhouse and fresh air, so he transferred here, now this.

It kind of excited him in a way. For the last two years nothing pressing or exciting happened until now. He smiled to himself thinking of the other case involving the poison money killing three people, just a week ago. Now two prominent women missing, what if they were somehow related?

"This town is beginning to make more sense after all, no crimes my foot." He wrapped up his paper work ready for action.

* * *

CHAPTER TWENTY-EIGHT

C arol and her two grandchildren sat in the family room watching one of their kiddy shows on TV. Although Carol looked at the screen her heart was far from it. She just needed to keep her mind occupied. The very thought of foul play, sicken her stomach.

The children's favorite show ended and they were ready for some outdoors play. Tommy got up from the floor and claimed on Carol's lap. His big blue-gray eyes looked up into her face with his wide cute smile asked.

"Can we go outside and play now grandmama?"

Carol smiled back and kissed his chubby cheeks. She gave him a big squeeze and tickled him in the stomach. He giggled and squirmed to get down out of her arms. Sharree ran over and joined them in the battle of the ticklish tummies. Carol grabbed her in her other arm and for three minutes nothing else mattered but the fun they were having.

The TV news broadcasted their feature story of the day. Betty Pullman, the local newscaster came on the set. Carol held the children close and braced herself waiting to hear, if any, information they might have found out about Danielle. The earlier call from her husband did not give her much to go on, and she hoped by now someone had seen or heard something new.

Now the news broadcasted only bits and pieces concerning the case. Nothing she did not already know.

"Local authorities launched an all out investigation for two missing women, last seen leaving the movies around twelve thirty last night . . . police suspects foul play, but have no details at this time . . . the events surrounding the case are baffling . . . after finding their abandoned car left in the parking lot of the theater . . . their names have not yet been released . . . We will give you more updated information as this case progresses . . . I'm Betty Pullman coming to you live from WXTV Channel seven . . ."

Tommy squirmed his way out of Carol's lap. He wanted to play outside now. Having no idea this was about his mother he and Sharree hurried to the back door heading out. Sharree grabbed her younger brother's hand taking the big sister's approach.

"See ya later grandmama." they both shouted in unison.

Carol, so deep in thought did not notice them gone. She sat back folded her arms across her chest running her fingers up and down them thinking of her first-born daughter.

Her eyes cloud over threaten the dam she held in all day. She broke down pouring out her tears, for ten minutes she cried brokenly rubbing her arms up and down as she rocked back and forth until she was dry.

The TV showed a commercial about a mother and daughter that reminded Carol of herself and Danielle years ago. She sat in a daze, gone back in time with sweet memories of things gone by.

Finally her mind came back as noises from the backyard brought her back to reality. Her ears picked up her two loving children playing in the back yard. Some stability and responsibility found the way back into her spirit. She turned off the set, went into the kitchen to prepare mid-morning snacks for her loving grandchildren.

*   *   *

On this beautiful sun shining morning deep within the woods, Mother Nature took care of her business watering the wild flower from her early morning dew. The birds flew from treetop to treetop chirping their songs in the sweet morning breezes, as squirrels scampered about the damp ground hiding food from their predators. The larger animals pray upon the smaller ones, all seeking food for the day like every other morning.

Yet on this day hidden in secret, lay two very frighten women, Danielle, and Sharron. They awaited their faith hoping against hope this would all go away like a bad dream.

All night Danielle dozed in and out of fretful sleep. Her back hurt so bad she couldn't have slept much if she wanted too. Not only from the smell in the room stinky, but the sofa was nauseating. Springs in that couch pressed into her spine. Pain ran down her hips and legs. She tried to maneuver her body and lay on her other side to be more comfortable, but with Sharron's feet still connected to her feet it was very difficult.

Early morning rays shone through the cracks in the walls, bright sunshine outside and dark bleakness inside, she knew she was not in Kansas.

Danielle raised her head ever so slightly to peek at the man who lay snoring on the cot in the far corner of the room. She wiggled her legs back and forth to awaken Sharron who lay up against the back of the sofa in a ball at the opposite end. Good thing both women were slim built or they couldn't have fit on this cramped old sofa.

Sharron squint her tired red eyes. A huge headache accomplished her slightest movements. The drinks from last night were threatening to come up. She swallowed back vile that force its' way into her mouth. Her tongue was thick dry and tasted horrible. Something kept kicking at her feet. She couldn't see for a moment than her eyes adjusted to the room, terror caught in her throat as she remembered where she was.

Danielle again slightly moved her feet to get Sharron attention, trying not to awaken the sleeping giant.

"Sharron, she whispered, you awake? It's me Danielle."

A moan escaped her dry lips. She licked them before she tried to speak.

"Yes, how can anyone sleep balled up in a knot half the night in a horrific environment like this?" She said in a low dull tone.

"I know, I didn't sleep hardly myself and I got to pee again. What do you think he's planning to do with us?"

"That I don't know, but we got to come up with a plan of escape, cause I can't stand being trapped like animals."

"Sharron you are good at plans and getting men to do what you want, can you think of something?"

Sharron closed her eyes against the full-blown headache. As she thought, a plan began to formulate in her dull mind. The more she focused on the plan the better it sounded. If she could just get him believing she desired him maybe she could get him to . . .

"Danielle, I got some sleeping pills and drugs in my bag. If I can get him to untie me I could put them into his drink, he will be knocked out in no time. I could untie you and we will be out of here."

"Where is out of here leading?"

"Stop worrying and play along with me okay? I know what I'm doing."

"If we ever do get out of here, I'll find my way home. This town is too small for me not to make it out. I grew up knowing these woods like the back of my hand."

"That a girl, now listen I'm going to get him to untie me, watch and learn little girl."

Sharron began to sing a sexy song of a lovers making love. {'I just want to love you all night long . . .' She has a pretty decent voice and her rich smooth tone carried into his sleep putting him in a sexual mood. He opened his eyes to her taunting voice. The words to the song caused his body to react and he got up quickly from the cot with the black mask still covering his head.

"What are you yapping about over there woman? Can't you see I'm trying to sleep?"

Sharron answered seductive in a Marilyn Monroe voice. "Honey, I sure could use some cool water. My mouth is so-o-o-o dry. Can I please have something to drink?"

He walked over looking at them. Then shook his head and walked over to his backpack got a bottle of water from his bag and tossed the bottle at her. Sharron got angry, but she knew if they were to get out of this alive she had to play the game his way, or at least make him think she was.

"Sweetie, how can I drink it without being untied? I won't bite, please allow me that much pride."

He responded to the plea in her voice and was moved by her honesty, walking back over he untied her hands. She reached out and rubbed his arm batting her lashes.

"Thank you kind gentleman, now if you be so kind as to loosen my feet so I can sit up and enjoy this refreshment I will ever be grateful."

"You do take liberties don't you?" His voice held amusement.

"I'm not usually so bold, but after being tied up all night it feels so good to just sit for a moment, I'm sure you understand."

Her Marilyn voice continued to impress him. He rubbed his manhood looking to see if she was paying attention. He wanted her badly. Even with her long hair toss and messy, her make-up half gone and smeared, her face flushed and puffy, her eyes red, she still was a beautiful sight to behold.

He reached down, untied Danielle's hands and feet keeping his eyes on Sharron. Not because he did not trust her, but he liked the way she handled herself.

"Tell you what, come sit with me. I'll get your friend a bottle of water too. Both of you can relax for a while. There is nowhere you can go anyway."

He grabbed Sharron by the arm jerking her up and pulling her over to the bed. The very thought of sleeping with this bad breath sickened her. She had to think fast!

"Wait lover! I gotta get my tampons out of my purse before I bleed all over myself. Old mother nature visited me during the night."

He shook his head to clear it. Part of him wanted to continue fondling her, and the other part despised the bloody bath. Never being married he assumed she was flooded already.

He got up went to his backpack near the fireplace, and retrieved her large bag from inside. Before he gave it to her, he searched it and took her cell phone then gave her the bag.

"Here, and hurry back inside or else I'll take my frustration out on your friend here!"

Danielle held on for as long as she could. She felt her bladder about to burst and she did not want to urinate on herself again.

"Please sir, can I go with her? I got to pee so badly. It will only take a minute. As you said, where would we go?"

He took a deep breath cleared his throat shook his head slowly, before saying yes.

"Remember ladies I can run a lot faster than you and I got my trusted friend with me. You would not want me to mess up your pretty faces with this do you?"

He waved the gun that he carried in his jacket in their faces for a moment before he stepped back so they could go outside.

Sharron couldn't believe their luck. She gave Danielle a glance before hurrying to the door. Danielle slightly nodded following close behind almost running into Sharron, who quickly removed the locks off the door.

They stepped outside in the freshness of the morning. At least it smelled better than that rag, tag, hole in the wall cabin they been stuffed in all night.

It felt so good to get some needed air in their tight lungs. Both stood for a moment just breathing in the outdoors air. Although they smelled damp musty dirt, distant skunk odors, and animal defecation, but it was heaven compared to inside that closed up shack.

Danielle bent to relieve herself while Sharron thought about running away leaving Danielle to her own defenses. It was a passing idea that faded as quickly as it came. She couldn't leave her best friend alone with this madman. So she stayed outside only long enough to take five tablets from the inner zipper of her bag. Three strong sleeping tablets, and two opium tablets she used when she couldn't get to sleep from a bad headache. She was told by her doctor to only take two sleeping pills at a time. 'These three pills would have you sleeping in under an hour, adding the two others well, we'll see,' she said softly. How she planned to give them to him was another problem she hadn't thought of.

She opened the door of the cabin putting on a fake smile, stole a look behind at Danielle winking, before she switched over to the dark masked man.

He looked up nodded when they came through the door. He had a bottle of beer in his hand drinking it thirstily.

'Oh my goodness what luck' she thought. 'If I can get him away from his beer just for a moment maybe . . .' She sat on the bed next to him still smiling more sincere.

Danielle walked back over to her private prison on the faded blue sofa sat down and drank her water. She knew they would need fluids in their bodies and this might be the last time they received any.

Every part of her fibber hated the thought of sitting on that nasty thing. Repulsed by what she saw, she closed her eyes against it praying. 'Dear Jesus, please help us to find a way out of this despicable place. I miss my husband and children so much. I'm so sorry for disobeying you with Bob. Lord I repent . . . Oh God, I love Thomas so much. I never realized how much until I almost lost him. Now I'll give anything to see his face again.' Tears caught in her throat, she held them back knowing they would not help her.

"You know what I was thinking big guy? How about I give you a back rub after you finish that beer? You look like you could use one after sleeping on this old cot all night." Sharron patted the cot with disfavor in her face. She crossed her legs so she could not touch the bed with her body anymore than she had too.

"Am I right about you not sleeping well last night? I just wanted to show you how grateful we are for you kindness. After I'm done, you can retie me if you so desire."

He held the beer in mid air from his face looking at her from head to toe. He still wore the hooded mask over his head. He wanted to take it off, but thought better of it. 'Boy, he thought, I could surely use a back rub. I'm tired, hungry, and horny these are not good things to be feeling.'

Needless to say he was not in a good mood. All he wanted was for Bob to hurry and get these silly women so he could get paid, and get the hell out of there. Bob told him he would come around 2:30 p.m. That was hours from now.

He grabbed the back of his neck and gave it a slight massage. He stretched out backwards and lay on his back for a moment. These women were starting to get to him, why he did not understand. Maybe it was his need for sex. He knew he better not think of raping Bob's girl, or he would get a bullet in his head and that Sharron girl was bleeding. He sure did not intend to have her.

This brought him back to memories of his two younger sisters who endured heavy monthly bouts of real bad bleeding with heavy clots, smelly bodies, evil moods, and bad cramps. No he couldn't see himself having Sharron in her condition. Surely he would get another chance before this was over. He would wait until then.

"You said back rub? Well I could use a good back rubbing from a pretty little thing like you. How about joining me in a drink first?" He held his beer up like a toast and nodded his head.

"Why yes, don't mind if I do."

He grabbed another beer from his back pack opened it with his teeth and handed it to her. Sharron sat her water bottle down, took a swallow of the warm beer almost choking on it. He patted her hard on the back.

"What wrong with you woman can't you hold your liquor?" He said with a smirk.

"I'm fine, just went down the wrong way." She bit her lip to hold back her anger. "Hey I got something that will help us both feel better. It was a birthday gift from one of my friends. She pulled out the pills from her bra and handed them to him as he sat up.

"What is this?" He looked at the strange pills suspiciously.

"It's just some drugs to get you high. As I said it's a gift and who better to share it with than you."

He looked at her open hand with the five pills resting in the palm of it, and grabbed all five. He stuffed them into his mouth and drawn a huge swallow of beer.

"Why were you holding back on me? Now I see that's why you wanted those tampons so you could get high on these huh. I bet you had yourself a good time outside . . ." He yawned wide. "Well little girl, I want the rest of your birthday gift so give it up."

Sharron knew it wouldn't take long for the pills to take effect if she could get him to relax.

"Honey that was all there was. I never got to take mine. You grabbed them all. Now for that back rub."

She got on her knees on the cot behind him and began to massage his back. He closed his eyes giving into the wonderful feeling from the rub and drugs.

"Sweets why don't you just lay back and let Sharron take care of you." She whispered seductively in his ear.

He closed his eyes and gave into the drowsiness.

Five minutes later he fell in a dead sleep. Like a huge lug he fell on top of her backwards covering her whole body. Her legs bent under her she could not budge him. She struggled under his heavy weight trying to get out from under him. This man who was almost three times her size, she knew she needed help to get him off.

"Danielle, come help me please! Her voice sounded muffled and distance. I'm trapped under this big lug get him off of me quickly, I can't breathe!"

All this time Danielle had been in deep prayer. She did not pay any attention to what was happening on the other side of the room. Now her ears perked up from the panic in Sharron's voice. She raced over to the huge man, with all her strength and pushed him off of Sharron.

Sharron fell off the cot to the floor as his body covered the rest of the bed.

Both women laughed and clapped their hands happily jumping up and down. Then it dawn on them he might awaken soon. They quickly gathered their belongings from his backpack and ran out the log cabin without any sense of direction.

*   *   *

Ward waited anxiously for his wife and daughter to come walking through the door. He did not have a clear plan as to what he would do once they arrived, but he knew it would involved his secret weapon hiding in the jar he went to get earlier.

He wanted them both of them to feel unleashed terror like neither experienced before. Then they had to understand he was the master of his home and they would pay for their disobedience to him! His rage mounted to boiling as he waited.

Ward thought he could lock them in the upstairs bedroom closet it was located in the inner part of the house. They could bang and bang on the door for days without anyone hearing them, if they lasted that long. He added to his sinister plan, no food or water.

One problem crossed his mind, Angus, what to do about her? Should he include her in his plot or kill her first? He knew she cared about Rachel, her only granddaughter. That is if she had a heart to care, something he never was sure of.

Ward needed to play this game by ear, before he made his final decisions. He did not need any other problems arising from his perfect solution to torment them than cut them up in pieces, stuffing them in his huge brown duffel bag.

He checked his watch 11:27 not very long to wait. He sat back in his overly stuffed chair, legs crossed hands in a pyramid resting them on the arms of his chair. His chin rested on the tips of his fingers.

Blazing pits of fire sparked within his eyes. Deep folds creased between his brows. Ward's mouth tighten; in a thin line, causing him to appear even more demonic. Demons wrapped themselves around his neck, back and legs and more demons rested on his lap waiting for the two born again Christians to return home.

Laughter eroded from the hideous inhuman, soulless, devils echoing from deep within Ward's heart.

*　*　*

CHAPTER TWENTY-NINE

In the mysterious quietness of Mrs. Bennett's old home laid her dead husband's corpse. It was cold, hard drained of blood and decomposed. The demons drained the blood from his body when he died months ago. Now his soulless form sat on the bed waiting for the old woman.

Hideous trolls came from deep within the underground crawling over and in the stiff remains of Henry's form, while his real soul screamed in hell, trapped in the forever eternal blackness.

The soulless skeletal frame sat there smiling waiting for just the right moment.

Mrs. Bennett had risen early made herself some hot tea sat in her scummy kitchen praying to her god for Henry's soon return. Poor woman never did have a relationship with the living God, it never would have occurred to her the demons used her husbands' body lying to her who believe he would return.

The prince of darkness laughed a low grumble that thunder in hell. He, who cause weak people to be so gullible, stupid, and fearful, these people who believed in a lesser power not knowing the truth, he wanted to drag them all to hell by their teeth. He knew where he was headed it was his fate to burn in everlasting fire.

It did not matter if the wayward ones thought they followed him he hated them just the same. If they did not have the great Master of life, in their hearts they were his. His hate saturated throughout this house and soon the old lady would know she too belonged to him.

Her house suddenly became pitch black, as if all the lights in the world shut off. A low moan erupted from the underground and this house shook viciously. Mrs. Bennett thought surely it must be an earthquake. She hurried under the table for protection as her heart beat faster and her breath gave out. She close to death prayed to her god without results. She ran on weak legs up the stairs to her bedroom as soon as she saw Henry looking like something from another world she screamed, falling to the floor, peeing on herself. This was not her Henry, not that evil looking creature staring at her.

He came close to her laughing and reached down grabbing her leg. She tried to kick him off, before she died laying in her own pee with her dress of her youth hanging off her boney body.

The trembling stopped abruptly and the house became as it was; a dim lit dirty kitchen with one dangling light hanging from the ceiling. The old lady is finally with her Henry BURNING IN ETERNAL HELL!

Heckling demons laughed as they tormented her lost soul in the bed of death!

*   *   *

"Mom, as I said over the phone please don't go home. I cannot explain to you, but I know something will happen to both of us if we go home! Dad is up to something evil, I can feel it and I fear for our lives."

"Honey that's preposterous, your dad would never hurt you, and I willing to believe, he won't hurt me either!"

She turned to Rachel who sat next to her in the front seat of the SUV stopping at a red light.

"Listen, sweetheart, when I talked with your dad earlier he was in a better mood than I've seen him, in a long time. I do believe what I learned in your Church remember the pastor saying something like, 'all things working together for good to those who are called according to His purpose.' Did not you tell me we are all called who believe in Jesus?"

"Yes, but that only applies to those that belong to Christ, not those who practice in witchcraft like dad. Mother you know dad dibbles in black magic! We always hid our faces not willing to accept what we saw happen, but mom we can no longer hide behind a lie! Dad is a warlock, or sorcerer, of the worse kind. He truly enjoys hurting people. Over the years he has set people up for failure! Look at how he's hurt you all these years, and all you've ever done was love him."

"To be a loving wife, to my husband is my job Rachel. I can't be like your granny. You have no idea how bad she treated dad. She ran him off and he turned to me. I know now that is not right, but at the time I accepted his affections as his lover, all because my mother did not have a heart!"

Nicky pressed her foot on the accelerator heading south, for two minutes she drove in silence focusing on the road. Rachel sat trying to think of a way to change her mind when Nicky turned back to her.

"Rachel is it not in the Bible about a wife being submissive to her husband? No, don't say anything let me finish. All Ward wants is for his family to have a meal with him, that's not unreasonable. We are going home to give him that okay?"

She reached out her free hand squeezing he daughter's hand reassuring her. She gave Rachel a thin smile as she watched her from the corner of her eyes still on her way home.

"Honey I'm glad you are coming with me. It's going to be alright, you'll see."

Rachel knew nothing would stop her from going home and it sicken her to her stomach. Tears fells from her eyes rolling down her cheeks. She wiped them away before her mother could see them with the back of her hand. She felt trapped in a web like a spider. She felt in her spirit this was a bad mistake, but how could she convey this to her mother? She had to make one last attempt before they reached home. She held her mother's hand still extended toward her.

"Mother please do me a favor, will you stay close by me and be watchful? If for any reason, dad gets crazy, we can help each other to get out of there. Please do me that favor. If you feel ANYTHING out of the ordinary we are out of there okay?"

Nicky patted her hand back. "Deal, now let's think positive."

She continued down the street just three blocks from their home when all at once Rachel screamed. Rachel's stomach knotted up and she tasted vile. Sick to her stomach she knew she would throw up.

"OH . . . MY . . . GOD . . . mother please STOP!"

"My goodness Rachel what in the world is wrong with you?"

Nicky watched as her daughter heave holding her stomach with one hand and trying to open the window with the other. Nicky quickly pulled over to the side of the curb as Rachel opened the door. She threw up all over the floor and the door of the SUV.

Nicky quickly grabbed wet wipes she kept in the glove compartment, and handed them to Rachel.

Rachel leaned her head out the side choking still vomiting with labor breathing. Nicky got out came around to the side of the vehicle helped Rachel out, and held her in her arms tightly. It did not matter the about the vomit or smell all she knew her baby needed her now. When the heaving stopped both cried in each other's arm for quite a while. People pass by looking at this strange sight, but not a soul asked if they needed help. People in this town like to come to their own conclusions.

"Rachel you really are afraid to go home I can see it in those eyes. Honey, I don't know what to do your dad is expecting us home right now. We are only moments away, but in light of what just happened, I'm not so sure if we should . . ."

Rachel could hardly catch her breath to speak. She held her mother by the forearms standing back crying out.

"Mom, can . . . can we . . . please stay in a . . . h-o-t-e-l tonight? We can tell dad I wasn't feeling well and needed to rest. I don't know, but please help me think of something. I just can't go home and you must not either! We can call Mr. James, Phillip's dad he'll know what to do."

Her voice thick she could hardly talk. Her eyes pleaded with her mother as tears continued steaming down her face. Nicky's love for her daughter brought concern to her heart and she yield to her feeling. There was nothing she wouldn't sacrifice for her Rachel, if going home brought such a negative reaction to her maybe they shouldn't go, at least not now.

What in the world would she tell her husband, rang loud in her ears! She thought about it again and made up her mind Rachel meant more than the world to her, Ward would have to wait.

"Alright honey, we will do it your way. I've got some money on me, and more in the bank if needed. We can find a place in town, but there are not many to choose from. You know your dad can be stubborn, if he has a mind to do so he will find us."

"Mom we don't want dad to find us! How much money do you have?"

"We are only staying overnight child. What did you think we were doing, running away?" She stared at Rachel perplexed.

"Mom dad can't find out where we are; do you understand? He is dangerous!" The words agonizingly tore from her throat.

The look Rachel gave Nicky scared her more than her crying words did. Her eyes big as saucers looked frighten beyond compare. Rachel bit hard on her lips until they bleed. She did not notice them bleeding until Nicky reached out to wipe them with a tissue.

"Okay Rachel, we will go someplace where Ward will not suspect. But we got to tell him something or he will call the police and you know he's friends with all the authority here in Queen City."

"Then call him and tell him the truth. Let's just be honest with him and see what happens. You believe he has changed this will surely tell if that's true. I believe he will be very adamant about us coming home tonight or else. Only make that call after we find a hotel far away from Queen City!

BOOK THREE: 2014 "CONFLICTING SPIRITS UNMASKED TRUTH" The saga continues . . .

Find out what happens when born again mother and daughter dare to stand for truth against the enemy.

When a small town is faced with much evil evasion, how do they fight the unknown?